Praise for Marta Perry and her novels

"Opens with a great scene that doesn't disappoint. The characters are delightful and endearing."
—*Romantic Times BOOKreviews* on *Hunter's Bride*

"Marta Perry knows how to write romance and *A Mother's Wish* is another fine example of her talent."
—*Romantic Times BOOKreviews*

"In Marta Perry's *Unlikely Hero*, emotionally charged characters and situations will leave readers entranced. The realistic portrayal of someone caught in abuse will resonate long after the last page is turned."
—*Romantic Times BOOKreviews*

"Marta Perry's *Hero Dad* shows the power of God and family to overcome trials. Detailed characterization brings the story to life."
—*Romantic Times BOOKreviews*

MARTA PERRY
Hunter's Bride
&
A Mother's Wish

Steeple
Hill®

Published by Steeple Hill Books™

STEEPLE HILL BOOKS

Steeple
Hill®

ISBN-13: 978-0-373-65121-4
ISBN-10:   0-373-65121-X

HUNTER'S BRIDE AND A MOTHER'S WISH

HUNTER'S BRIDE
Copyright © 2002 by Martha Johnson

A MOTHER'S WISH
Copyright © 2002 by Martha Johnson

www.SteepleHill.com

Printed in U.S.A.

CONTENTS

Books by Marta Perry

Love Inspired

A Father's Promise
Since You've Been Gone
*Desperately Seeking Dad
*The Doctor Next Door
*Father Most Blessed
A Father's Place
Hunter's Bride
A Mother's Wish
A Time To Forgive
Promise Forever
Always in Her Heart
The Doctor's Christmas

True Devotion
Hero in Her Heart
†Unlikely Hero
†Hero Dad
†Her Only Hero
†Hearts Afire
†Restless Hearts
†A Soldier's Heart
†Mission: Motherhood

*Hometown Heroes
†The Flanagans

Love Inspired Suspense

In the Enemy's Sights
Land's End
Tangled Memories
Season of Secrets
‡Hide in Plain Sight

‡A Christmas to Die For
‡Buried Sins
Final Justice

‡The Three Sisters Inn

MARTA PERRY

has written everything from Sunday school curriculum to travel articles to magazine stories in more than twenty years of writing, but she feels she's found her writing home in the stories she writes for Love Inspired.

Marta lives in rural Pennsylvania, but she and her husband spend part of each year at their second home in South Carolina. When she's not writing, she's probably visiting her children and her six beautiful grandchildren.

Marta loves hearing from readers, and she'll write back with a signed bookmark or her brochure of Pennsylvania Dutch recipes. Write to her c/o Steeple Hill Books, 233 Broadway, Suite 1001, New York, NY 10279, e-mail her at marta@martaperry.com, or visit her on the Web at www.martaperry.com.

HUNTER'S BRIDE

For I know the plans I have for you, says the Lord.
Plans to prosper you and not to harm you.
Plans to give you hope and a future.
—*Jeremiah* 29:11

This story is dedicated with much love
to my daughter Lorie, my son-in-law Axel,
and especially to my grandson, Bjoern Jacob.

And, as always, to Brian.

Chapter One

Chloe Caldwell was in trouble—deep, deep trouble. She tried to stand up straight against the intense, ice-blue stare of her boss, Luke Hunter. He wore the look some of his business rivals had compared to being pierced by a laser. She began to understand the feeling.

Southern women have skin like magnolia blossoms and spines like steel. Gran's voice echoed in her mind. *Have you lost yourself up north among them Yankees, Chloe Elizabeth?*

Maybe she had. She took a strained breath and met Luke's gaze. "I don't know what you mean."

He arched his black eyebrows. "It's a simple question, Chloe." He held up a sheet of off-white note-paper covered with spidery handwriting. "Why does your grandmother think you and I are a couple?"

Possibly, if she closed her eyes, she'd open them to

find this was all a dream—no, a nightmare. *Oh, Gran,* she thought despairingly, *whatever possessed you to write to him?* Luke must have picked up the mail when she'd been out of the office for a few minutes. If she'd seen it— But she hadn't.

Luke was waiting for an answer, and no one had ever accused Luke Hunter of an abundance of patience. She had to say something.

"I can't imagine." *Liar,* the voice of her conscience whispered. "May I see the letter?"

She held out her hand, trying to find enough of that steel Gran insisted she had so that her fingers wouldn't tremble and give her away. Luke held the paper just out of her reach for a moment, like a cat toying with a mouse, and then surrendered it. He leaned back against the polished oak desk that the Dalton Resorts considered appropriate for a rising executive. He should have looked relaxed. He didn't.

She shot a hopeful glance toward the telephone. It rang all day long. Why not now? But the phone remained stubbornly silent. Beyond the desk, large windows looked out on a gray March day in Chicago, an even grayer Lake Michigan. No sudden tornado swept down to rip the sheet from her hand.

She forced her attention to Gran's letter. She'd barely begun to decipher the old-fashioned handwriting, when Luke moved restlessly, drawing her gaze inevitably back to him.

She'd long ago realized that Luke Hunter was a study in contradictions. Night-black hair and eyebrows that were another slash of black contrasted with incredibly deep blue eyes. The strong bones of cheek and jaw reflected his fierce tenacity, but the impression was tempered by the unexpected widow's peak on his forehead and the cleft in his chin.

It didn't take one of Gran's homegrown country philosophies to tell her what to think of Luke. A man with a face like that had secrets to hide. He wore the smooth, polished exterior that announced a rising young executive, but underneath was something darker, something that ran against the grain. She'd been his good right arm for nearly six years and had never seen more than a hint of it, but she knew it was there.

She took a breath. "I'm sorry that you received this." The paper fluttered in her grasp. "I don't know why Gran decided to send you an invitation to her eightieth birthday party next Sunday."

"Oh, she says why." Luke leaned forward, invading her space. "She thinks I'm your 'beau.'" His tone put quotes around a word she'd never expected to hear from him. "Why does she think that?"

"My grandmother is an elderly lady." She would try to convey the image of someone frail and confused, while sending a fervent mental apology to her peppery

Gran. No one who knew Naomi Caldwell would dare to call her frail or confused.

"She sounds pretty coherent to me." He plucked the letter back from her, and she had to fight to keep from snatching it. "If she thinks that, it must be because someone gave her that idea."

Please, Lord.

She stopped the prayer before it could become any more self-serving than it already was. Obviously no heavenly intervention was going to excuse her from the results of her own folly.

"I'm afraid I must have." She picked her way through the words carefully, as if she were back on the island, picking her way through the marsh grasses. "I think it happened when you gave me those symphony tickets. When I told her about it, she misunderstood. She assumed we went together."

"And you didn't correct her?"

She felt color warm her cheeks. "I thought…" *Well, that sentence was going nowhere. Try again.* "My grandmother worries about me. You have to realize she's never been farther from home than Savannah. Chicago is another world to her. Once she thought I was dating someone safe, she stopped worrying so much."

His eyebrows lifted. "Am I safe, Chloe?"

She'd stepped in a bog without seeing it. "I mean, someone she'd heard of. Naturally, I've often spoken of my boss." Probably more than she should have. "I didn't tell her any lies. I just…didn't clear things up." It was time to get out of this situation with what remaining dignity she had. "I'm sorry you were bothered with this. Naturally, I'll tell her you won't be coming to Caldwell Cove."

Luke looked again at the letter, with some sharpening of attention she didn't understand.

"That's in South Carolina, isn't it?"

She nodded. "It's on Caldwell Island, just off the coast."

"Caldwell Cove, Caldwell Island. Sounds as if you belong there, Chloe."

The faint trace of mockery in his voice made her stiffen. "I belong *here* now."

"Still, to have a whole island named after you must mean something."

"It only means that my ancestors were the first settlers. They gave their name to the village and to the island. It doesn't mean every descendant stays put." *She* hadn't.

She held out her hand, hoping he'd give her that embarrassing missive so she could destroy it. "Again, I'm sorry."

But he turned away, dropping the letter onto his desk. He glanced back at her, amusement in his eyes. "I'm not. It's been an interesting break in the routine."

"Speaking of which—" She looked at her watch. "You have a meeting with Mr. Dalton at eleven."

"No." The amusement disappeared from his face. "He was in early and he talked with me then."

It went without saying that Luke had been in early. She sometimes wondered when he slept. "I see. Are there any meeting notes I should take care of?"

"None." His voice contained an edge. "Just get me the Branson file, that's all."

He moved effortlessly back to Dalton Resorts business, obviously dismissing her and her small problems from his mind. She could escape. She'd reached the door when his voice stopped her.

"Chloe."

"Yes?" She turned back reluctantly.

"Too bad I won't be seeing Caldwell Cove. It might have been fun at that."

Fun? She tried to imagine Luke Hunter, urban to the soles of his handmade Italian shoes, in Caldwell Cove. No, she didn't think that would have been fun for anyone, least of all her. She gave him a meaningless smile and scurried out the door.

Once safely behind her desk, she took a deep breath, trying to quell the flood of embarrassment. *It's your own fault,* the voice of her conscience said sternly, sounding remarkably like her grandmother. *You set this in motion with your fairy tales.*

Fairy tales, that's all they'd been—innocent fairy tales. Letting Gran believe she and Luke Hunter were a couple had let her believe it, too, for a time. She shied away from that thought.

She should have realized that sooner or later this would backfire. She pressed her fingers to her temples, trying to erase the pounding that had begun there. She'd known he'd never give up until he had the whole story. That tenacity of Luke's had played a major role in his success at Dalton Resorts.

She'd seen that quality when she first met him, when she came to Chicago six years ago. His office had been the size of a broom closet then, and she'd been the greenest member of the secretarial pool, homesick for the island and trying to find her way through the maze of corporate politics.

She'd learned fast, though probably not as fast as he had. She'd discovered that she had to get rid of her soft Southern drawl if she didn't want to be made fun of. She'd found that there were as many alligators in the corporate structure as she'd ever seen in the lagoons on the island. And she'd realized that if you wanted to survive, you attached yourself to a rising star.

That star had been Luke Hunter, with his newly minted MBA and his fierce, aggressive intelligence. They'd come up together, working long hours, until they'd become a team, almost able to read each other's thoughts. She'd identified herself with his interests, and she'd never regretted that move. Until, possibly, today, when her two worlds had collided.

She looked at the framed family photo on her desk, and warmth slipped through her. The Caldwell kin, everyone from Gran to little Sammy, aunts, uncles, brothers, cousins, even second cousins twice removed, had gathered on the dock for that picture. It was a wonder the weathered wooden structure hadn't collapsed. She could still smell the salt tang in the air, feel the hot sun on her shoulders and the warm boards beneath her bare feet, hear the soft Southern voices teasing.

She'd told Luke she belonged here now, but she wasn't sure that was true. She'd made friends, found a church home, learned her way around, but she'd never developed that sophisticated urban manner her friends wore so easily. Maybe the truth was, she was trapped between her two worlds, and she wasn't sure which one claimed her.

But Luke Hunter didn't need to know that. Any more than he needed to know the real reason she'd let Gran believe she was dating him. Not for Gran's sake, but for her own.

You've got a crush on that corporate shark. She could still hear the incredulity in her friend Marsha's voice when she'd let her secret slip. *Girl, are you crazy? That man could eat you alive.*

Chloe hadn't been able to explain, but she hadn't been able to deny it, either. Marsha hadn't seen the side of the man that Luke sometimes showed her.

Chloe traced the family photo with one finger. When the call had come two years earlier about her father's accident, it had been Luke who'd taken control in that nightmare moment. She'd been almost too stunned to function at the thought of her strong, vibrant father, the rock they all depended upon, lying still and white in a hospital bed.

Luke had arranged her flight home, he'd driven her to the airport, then he'd stayed with her until the Flight was called. He'd even watered the plants on her desk while she was gone. He'd never questioned her need to stay on the island until Daddy was on his feet again.

No, Marsha didn't understand that. All the same, she'd been right. Chloe Caldwell did indeed have one giant-size crush on her boss.

Luke spun his chair around to stare out at the city. His city. Having a window big enough to look at it meant he was on the verge of success.

Or failure. The brief skirmish with Chloe had diverted his attention from the problem at hand, but now that situation drove back at him like a semi barreling down the interstate. Chloe had innocently mentioned the meeting with Dalton. She couldn't have known just what kind of bomb Leonard Dalton had set ticking this morning.

A vice-presidency was in the offing, and the CEO had laid it out very clearly. Luke could prove he was ready by finding the ideal location for the next Dalton Resort and negotiating a favorable deal. If not—

Luke's hand formed a fist. Opportunity didn't knock all that often. He intended to answer the first time. He'd come too far, and he wasn't going to be denied the reward for all his effort.

His mind took a reluctant sidelong glance at just how far he'd come. He didn't let himself look often, because that was looking into a black hole of poverty, ugliness, rejection—a hole that might suck you back in if you looked too long.

He forced the image away by sheer willpower. No one in his current life knew about his past, and no one would. He'd be the next vice-president, because he wouldn't accept anything else. And Chloe, quite without meaning to, might have given him the key.

Amusement filtered through him. That must have been the first time he'd seen Chloe Caldwell—quiet, composed, efficient Chloe—embarrassed by something.

Well, however embarrassing Chloe had found the exposure of her little fib, he'd have to thank her for it, because the mention of Caldwell Island, South

Carolina, had rung a bell in his memory. He spun back to the computer and flicked through the past several years of site survey reports.

There it was. The area surrounding Caldwell Island had appeared on a list of possible sites for a new Dalton Resort three years ago. Dalton hadn't established a new resort at that time, and this report had quietly vanished. He might be the only one in the company who remembered Caldwell Island.

He skimmed through the report quickly, his excitement mounting. Something—the little vibration he'd learned to trust—told him this was worth pursuing.

He leaned back, smiling. One of the hardest things about looking over a possible site was keeping the locals from learning what you were doing and thus sending prices soaring. Chloe, with her sweet little deception and the frail old grandmother she wouldn't want to disappoint, had just given him the perfect way to check out Caldwell Island for himself.

Chloe hadn't had enough time to forget her humiliation when the buzzer summoned her, insistent as an angry mosquito. Snatching a pad, she marched toward Luke's office. All right, there was to be no reprieve. She'd go in there and show Luke that they were back to business, as if the morning's fiasco had never happened.

"Chloe." He looked up from a file on his desk. "I was thinking about that letter from your grandmother."

All right, she wouldn't be able to pretend it hadn't happened. *Steel, Chloe Elizabeth.*

"Please forget about it. I'll take care of it." She raised the pad. "Was there something else you wanted?"

"I can't forget about it." He leaned back in the padded executive chair. Beyond him, gray rain slashed against the window, as relentless as he was. "I keep picturing your frail old grandmother being disappointed on her birthday."

Wouldn't he be surprised by the real Gran, one of a long line of strong Caldwell women who'd wrestle a gator if necessary to keep her family safe. "Gran will be fine." She tried to put a little of that strength into her voice. "After all, the rest of her kin will be there."

The word slipped out before she could censor it. Northerners didn't call people "kin." She'd been thinking too much about Gran today.

"But not her favorite granddaughter." He smiled. "I'm sure you are the favorite, aren't you?"

Warning bells began to ring. When Luke turned on the charm, he wanted something. "That's probably my sister, Miranda. After all, she's produced a great-grandchild."

Luke swung forward in his chair, his feet landing on the carpet. "In any event, she'd be disappointed. I just can't let that happen."

She stared at him blankly, not sure where he was going with this. "I don't…"

"Besides, what is it to us? One short weekend out of our lives to make an elderly lady happy."

Panic rocketed through her. He couldn't be saying what she thought he was.

"You can't be talking about going." Her voice rose in spite of herself.

He stood, planting both hands on the desktop and leaning toward her. "That would solve everything, wouldn't it?"

"No!"

"Why not?"

Her mind worked frantically. "We can't pretend to be dating in front of my whole family."

"Again, why not?" His words shot toward her, compelling agreement.

Her throat closed on the difficulty of telling him all the reasons. As usual, standing up to Luke Hunter was about as possible for her as flying to the moon. "We just can't, that's all."

"Nonsense. Of course we can." He swept past her objections, and with fascinated horror she saw him launching into the deal mode that no one ever managed to stop. "In fact, I've already done it."

"Done what?" Her thoughts twisted and turned, trying to find a path out of this impossible situation.

"I called and talked with your father." There might have been something a little malicious in his smile. "He was delighted that we're coming. I'll fly down with you on Friday. We'll come back Sunday night after the birthday party."

"But I can't. *We* can't."

"Of course you can. All you have to do is reschedule my Friday meetings and pack, and we'll make your grandmother happy. Aren't you pleased, Chloe?"

Pleased? She could only stare at him, the horrible truth rolling inexorably toward her. Thanks to her weakness for storytelling and her total inability to stand up to Luke Hunter, she was condemned to spend the weekend pretending to her family that he cared for her.

She might have dreamed, in her weaker moments, of going back to Caldwell Cove with Luke on her arm. But this wasn't a dream. It was a nightmare, and yet it was only too real.

Chapter Two

"We're almost there." Chloe leaned forward in the passenger seat next to Luke, sounding as eager as a ten-year-old on a vacation.

"How can you tell? It all looks the same to me." Luke pressed his hands against the steering wheel of the rental car and stretched. The trip to Caldwell Island from the airport in Savannah was less than an hour, but the narrow, two-lane roads wove through apparently endless miles of tall pines alternating with dense, dark undergrowth. It might have made sense for Chloe to drive, since she knew the road, but he hated letting someone else drive him.

He was also starting to have serious doubts about this whole expedition. Nothing he'd seen so far would lead him to consider this area for a Dalton Resort. It looked more like Tobacco Road.

Chloe flashed him a smile. "Just a little farther, and you'll see the bridge."

He'd see it. Then he'd see this precious island of hers. He'd be able to tell in half an hour, probably, if Caldwell Island was worth further investigation. If not, what he'd want to do was take the first plane back to Chicago.

But he couldn't. Like it or not, he'd committed to this weekend, to pretending he and Chloe weren't just boss and secretary, but something more. A faint apprehension trickled along his nerves. Chloe, with her honey-colored hair and her golden-brown eyes, was appealing, but certainly not his type. He went for sophisticated, not girl-next-door. Pulling this off could be tricky.

"There!" Chloe's exclamation was filled with satisfaction as they emerged abruptly from yet another stand of pine trees.

He blinked. Ahead of them, lush grass stretched on either side of the road, golden in the sunshine. It might have been a meadow, but the grass grew in water, not earth. In the distance a cluster of palmettos stood dark against the sky, like an island. Sunlight glinted from deeper streams, turning the scene into a bewildering world between earth and sea. His apprehension deepened. Everything about this was alien to him.

Chloe hit the button, and her window whirred down, letting in a flood of warm air that mixed salt, sea and musky vegetation. "Smell that." She inhaled deeply. "That's what tells me I've come home." She hung out the window, letting her hair tangle in the breeze.

"Doesn't smell like home to me. Not unless it includes exhaust fumes, sidewalk vendors and pigeons."

"Sorry. Would you settle for a great white heron?" She pointed, and he saw an elegant white bird lift its long neck and stare at them.

This was a different Chloe, he realized. One who knew everything here, one who was in her element. Just as he was out of his. The thought made him vaguely uneasy.

The road swept up onto a white bridge, shimmering in the sunshine. Tall pylons marched beside the bridge, feet in the water, carrying power lines.

"We're crossing the inland waterway," Chloe said, pressing her palms against the dash as if to force the car to move faster. "And there's Caldwell Island."

The car crested the hump in the middle of the bridge, and Chloe's island lay ahead of them. His breath caught in spite of himself. The surrounding marsh grass made the island shimmer with gold, and it stretched along the horizon like an early explorer's dream of riches.

"Golden isles," Chloe said softly, as if she read his thought. "That's an old name for the sea islands. The Golden Isles."

The channel merged with marshes, then the marshes merged with the gentle rise of land, as if the island raised itself only reluctantly from the sea. A village drifted along the curve of shore facing the bridge, looking like something out of the last century, or maybe the century before that. A church steeple bisected it neatly.

The island was beautiful. It was desirable. And unless there was something unexpected out of his sight, it was also completely uncommercialized. Excitement stirred in him.

"What's the ante-bellum mansion? A hotel?"

She glanced toward the far end of the village, then shook her head, smiling. "That's my uncle Jefferson's house. Uncle Jeff's family is the rich branch of the clan. There aren't any hotels on Caldwell Island, just the inn my parents own and a few guest houses."

He didn't want to raise her suspicions, but he risked another comment. "You're not going to tell me vacationers haven't discovered this place."

She seemed too preoccupied to notice, staring out as if cherishing every landmark. "There have always been summer visitors, but they're people who've owned their homes here for generations." She pointed. "Turn left off the bridge. Town's only three streets deep, so you can't get lost. We'll go straight to the inn. They'll be waiting."

He followed her directions, wondering a little at the sureness in her voice. *They'll be waiting.*

He passed a small grocery, a bait shop and then what

seemed to be a boatyard with the Caldwell name emblazoned on its sign. Before he could ask if her family owned it, Chloe spoke again.

"There it is. That's The Dolphin."

The inn sat on their right, facing the waterway, spreading out gracefully under the surrounding trees. The core of the building looked only one room deep, but succeeding generations must have added one wing after another as their families, or their ambitions, grew. Gray shingles blended with the gray-green of the lace-draped live oaks, and rocking chairs dotted a wrap-around porch.

"Those are our boats." She pointed to a covey of boats at the dock on their left. "Everyone's in. I told you they'd be waiting for us."

Apparently here they counted boats, instead of cars, to tell them who was where. He drove into a shell-covered driveway and pulled to a stop, discovering a knot of apprehension in his gut.

Ridiculous. He dismissed it quickly. Chloe's family had no reason to suspect him of anything, and their opinions didn't matter to him in the least. Simple country people, that's all they were.

Simple, maybe. But had Chloe warned him there were so many of them? He stepped out of the car into what seemed to be a mob of Caldwells, all talking at once. Chloe was right—they'd been waiting. An unidentifiable breed of half-grown dog bounced around the crowd, its barks adding to the general chaos.

He looked to Chloe for help, but a woman who must be her mother was enveloping her in an enormous hug. A younger woman, with Chloe's heart-shaped face but auburn hair and green eyes, wrapped her arms around both of them. All three seemed to be talking and crying at once.

"Don't suppose we'll get any sense out of those three for a time."

The rangy, sun-bronzed man who held out a large hand was probably about Luke's age. Big—that was his first thought. Luke stood six foot, and this guy had a couple of inches on him at least. The hand that grasped his had power behind it. One of the brothers?

"Guess I'd best do the introductions, since our Chloe's forgotten her manners," he continued. "I'm Daniel. This is David."

Luke blinked. There were two of them. "Chloe didn't mention her brothers were twins." He shook hands with the other giant, trying to assess the differences between them.

There weren't many. Both men were big, both sun-brown, both lean and muscular. They had identical brown eyes and identical sun-bleached hair. David wore a pair of wire-rimmed glasses, apparently the only way Luke would ever tell them apart.

"She wouldn't." Daniel seemed to do the talking for the pair of them. "She always said it wasn't fair there were two of us to gang up on her." He reached out a long arm to pull over a gangly teenager. "This one's Theo. He's the baby."

The boy reddened under his tan, shooting his brother a resentful look before offering his hand to Luke. "Nice to meet you, sir."

"Luke, please."

His effort at friendliness just made the boy's flush deepen. "Yes, sir."

"That's Miranda's boy, Sammy, trying to make his mutt pipe down." Daniel gestured toward a boy of six or so, wrestling with the dog over a stick. "And this is our daddy, Clayton Caldwell."

Luke turned, and his smile stiffened on his face. There could be no doubt of the assessment in the sharp hazel eyes that met his gaze. He was abruptly aware of intelligence, shrewdness, questioning.

"Luke. Welcome to Caldwell Cove." Chloe's father was fully as tall as his twin sons, his grip just as firm. But despite the words of welcome, the quick friendliness Luke had sensed in Daniel and his brothers was missing here. Clayton Caldwell looked at him as if he'd been measured and had come up wanting. "We've been waiting to meet Chloe's…friend."

Everything in Luke snapped to attention. Chloe's

father, at least, couldn't be classified as "simple country folk." He wasn't accepting Chloe's supposed boyfriend at face value.

So this little charade might not be the piece of cake he'd been telling himself. The thought only made his competitive juices start to flow. When the challenges were the greatest, he played his best game.

Chloe had finally broken free of her mother and sister, and he reached out to grasp her hand and draw her close against his side. For an instant she resisted, and he gave her a challenging smile. *This was your invention, Chloe, remember? Now you've got to take the consequences.*

She leaned against him, perhaps a little self-consciously.

Luke smiled at her father. "We're happy to be here. Aren't we, sweetheart?" He tightened his grasp into a hug, faintly surprised by how warm and sweet Chloe felt against him.

"Yes." Her voice sounded a bit breathless. "Happy."

"Well, so tell me all about him."

Chloe had started for the dining room with a large bowl of potato salad, when Miranda caught her by the waist and spun her into the pantry. She went with a sense of resignation. She couldn't have hoped to avoid Miranda's third degree much longer. They'd always shared everything.

Miranda's green eyes glowed with curiosity. "You've been awful closemouthed, sugar. Come on, 'fess up. Are you serious about him?"

The question twanged inside her, reverberating like a plucked string. She tried to shut the feeling away. She didn't want to lie to her sister. Probably she couldn't if she tried. Miranda knew her too well.

"Serious?" She tried to smile. "I don't know if *serious* is the right word. It's complicated. He is my boss, after all."

Miranda eyed her sternly. "Complicated. That means you do care about him, but you don't know if it's going to work, right?"

"How did you get so smart, little sis?" She tried to turn their perpetual rivalry over the eleven months between them to her advantage, hoping to distract Miranda.

Miranda shook her head, but not before Chloe had seen the quick sorrow in her eyes.

"I didn't get smart quick enough, remember?"

"Oh, honey, I'm sorry." Chloe plunked the bowl onto the linoleum-topped counter and put her arms around her sister. "I shouldn't have said that." She'd wanted to distract Miranda, not remind her of the man she'd loved and the marriage that had ended almost before it started.

"It's okay." Miranda's strong arms held her close for a moment. "I'm okay. Really." She answered the doubt she must have seen in Chloe's eyes. "I'm happy. After all, I have Sammy and the family."

But not the only man she'd ever love. The thought lay there between them, unexpressed.

"I just want you to be happy." Miranda squeezed her. "You be happy, sugar, okay?"

"I'll try." Chloe swallowed the lump in her throat. People said that Caldwell women were destined to love only one man. If true, that didn't bode well for either Miranda or her.

She tried to reject the thought. She didn't *love* Luke. She admired him. She admired his intelligence, his tenacity, his ambition. She'd been touched by his kindness to her, by the unexpected, intangible longing she sometimes surprised in his eyes, as if he yearned for something he couldn't have. But that wasn't love.

The thought lingered at the back of her mind all through dinner. She watched as Luke turned to answer some question Theo had asked. The chandelier's light put shadows under his cheekbones, showing the strong bone structure of his face, the determined jaw, the quick lift at the corner of his mouth when something amused him.

It also showed a certain tension in the way his hand gripped the fork. That sent a ripple of unease through her. Was he just nervous about this charade he'd embarked on? Or was something else going on—something she didn't know about?

As soon as the meal ended Luke gravitated to her

side. Her heart gave a rebellious little flutter as she looked up at him. "Get enough to eat?"

"I don't know how your family stays so thin if they eat like that every night." Luke patted his flat stomach. "One more of those buttermilk biscuits, and you'd have to roll me away from the table."

"They don't sit in an office all day."

He grinned, and the unexpectedly relaxed expression fluttered her heart once more. "Touché. I'll have to remember that." He glanced around the large room. "But the inn doesn't seem to have any guests right now."

"This is Gran's birthday weekend. They don't take reservations this weekend, so the whole family can celebrate."

"They turn away paying customers?" He seemed to imagine an entire row of Dalton Resorts executives, all frowning at such folly.

"They put Gran first, that's all." The defensiveness in her tone surprised her. "The Dolphin Inn isn't a Dalton Resort."

"Obviously not." His lifted eyebrow spoke volumes. "Anyway, this isn't a busy time. We don't start getting a lot of guests until Easter weekend." It had never occurred to her to wonder why the inn wasn't more successful than it was. *We make enough to get by,* Daddy always said. She shouldn't have to defend her family's values, but that seemed to be what she was doing.

"I can understand why, if you close down for a birthday party."

She came perilously close to losing her temper with him. "If you—"

"Gran's here," Miranda called from the porch.

Every other thought flew from Chloe's mind, and she raced out the door. Gran marched up the shell path. Chloe met her halfway, to be wrapped in arms still as strong as ever. Gran's familiar lily-of-the-valley scent enveloped her.

"Gran, it's so good to see you." She pressed her cheek against her grandmother's.

Gran held her back a little, putting her palms on Chloe's cheeks. Her gaze was every bit as laser-like, in its way, as Luke's.

"'Bout time you were getting home, child. Where's this young man of yours?"

"I'm right here—"

She spun at the sound of Luke's voice, smooth as cream, behind her. He held out his hand to Gran.

"I'm Luke Hunter, Mrs. Caldwell."

Gran focused on him. Every one of Chloe's nerve endings stood at attention. How had she ever thought she'd get away with this? Why had she let Luke maneuver her into it? Gran's wise old eyes saw everything. They'd see through this.

But Luke seemed to be standing up well to that fierce inspection. After a moment, he asked, "Will I do?"

"Guess it'll take a bit of time to decide that." Gran looked him up and down. "You look a little fitter than I figured, for a city fellow."

"So do you. I expected someone a lot more frail."

He shot a challenging glance toward Chloe, and she felt herself shrivel. If he told Gran what she'd said, she'd never live it down.

"Chloe must be fibbing about the number of candles on your cake."

Gran gave a little snort that might have been a chuckle, and then nodded shortly. "Might as well call me 'Gran.' Everyone else does." She took Luke's arm. "Let's go set on the porch a spell."

Chloe, following them, discovered she could breathe again. But she couldn't fool herself that happy state would last for long. She should never have let Luke talk her into this. She just should have told them all the truth and found some way to live with the disappointment in their eyes.

Gran settled in her favorite rocker. The others filtered out of the house to receive Gran's kiss and find a place to sit. Nothing they had to do was so pressing that they couldn't enjoy the warm spring evening.

Chloe perched on the rail, and little Sammy hopped up to lean against her. Gran motioned Luke to the seat next to hers, and Chloe felt as if she were waiting for disaster to strike. Surely, sooner or later, Luke would falter, and someone would realize he was playing a part.

But Luke seemed content to lean back in his rocker, his gaze moving from one member of her family to another, letting them do the talking. What did he think of them? It shouldn't matter to her, but it did. And what did they think of him?

She took a breath, inhaling the sweet scent of the azalea bushes around the porch. It mingled with the salty scent of the water. *Home.* If she'd been plopped here blindfolded, she'd know in an instant where she was, just by the smell.

She glanced around at the familiar faces, and love welled in her heart. She wanted to tell them the truth. She didn't want to hurt Gran. She didn't want them to be disappointed in her.

Please, God. She wasn't sure what to say. *Please. I don't want to hurt them. Please just let me get away without hurting them.*

She probably should be praying for the courage to tell the truth and be done with it, but somehow she couldn't. In a long line of brave Caldwell women, she must be the one exception.

Sammy wiggled against her. "Gran, tell the Chloe story, please?"

Her breath caught. That was one story she'd rather

Luke didn't hear, especially now. "Sammy, you must have heard that story a hundred times, at least."

He grinned up at her. Sammy's heart-shaped face came straight from Miranda, but those dark eyes of his were just like his father's, and just as apt to break hearts.

"But I love that story, Aunt Chloe. Don't you?"

"'Course she does," Gran said. "She's that Chloe's namesake, isn't she?" She glanced around.

Daniel groaned. "Have a heart, Gran. Sammy might just have heard it a hundred times, but I've heard it a thousand."

"Won't hurt you to listen again," she said tartly. "You might learn something." She turned her chair so that it faced Luke's. "Chloe's beau ought to hear it, anyway."

Chloe sent a helpless glance toward Luke.
He leaned forward, smiling at her grandmother. "I'd love to."

"Well, it's this way." Gran half closed her eyes, as if she saw the story unrolling in her mind. "Years and years ago, before there was a Caldwell Cove, a girl lived here on the island. Her name was Chloe. A wild creature, she was. Folks said she talked to the gulls and swam with the dolphins."

Sammy slid off the railing and went to lean against Gran's knee. "Wasn't she afraid?"

"Not she. She wasn't afraid of anything."

Completely unlike the modern-day Chloe. The

thought inserted itself in Chloe's mind and clung like a barnacle.

"One night there was a storm. Not an ordinary storm, no. This was the mother and father of all storms. It swept ships from their courses and snapped the tallest pines like matchsticks. In that storm a boat capsized, throwing its crew into the sea. Only one sailor made it through the night, clinging to a piece of wreckage, all alone."

Gran's voice had taken on the singsong tone of the island storyteller. As often as they'd all heard the story, still everyone leaned forward, listening as intently as if it were the first time.

"What happened to him?" Sammy's voice was hushed.

"He was played out. Poor man could see the island ahead of him, glistening like gold in the dawn light, but he knew he'd never make it. He gasped a last prayer. Then, before he could sink, creatures appeared next to him in the waves, holding him up. Chloe and her dolphins. They saved him. They pulled and pushed him through the surf until he staggered up onto the sand and collapsed, exhausted. But alive."

As often as Gran told the story, it never altered by an iota. She told it the way her mother had told it to her, and her mother before that.

Sammy leaned close. "Tell what happened to them, Gran."

Gran stroked his cheek. "You know that part of the story— He opened his eyes, took one look at her and knew he'd love her forever. He was the first Caldwell on the island, and he married her and started a family, and we've been here ever since."

"And the dolphin."

"He carved for her a dolphin out of a piece of cypress washed up by the storm. They put it in the little wedding chapel, and folks said every couple who married under the gaze of the dolphin would have a blessed union. And so they have."

Chloe's throat was so tight she couldn't possibly speak. It was plain silly, to be so moved by an old story that probably didn't have much truth left in it. But she was. They all were, even Luke. She could read it in his intent gaze.

"Is the dolphin still there? I'd like to see it."

Luke must be aware of the strained quality of the silence that met his question. Here was the ending to the story no one wanted to tell.

"Chloe's dolphin is gone," Gran said softly. "Stolen one night by someone—no one knows who." Her wrinkled hand cupped Sammy's cheek. "But the story still lives."

Chloe's father stood, the chair rocking behind him. With a muttered excuse, he walked inside, favoring his bad leg as he did when he was tired.

His departure was a signal. David stood, stretched

and held out his hand to Sammy. "Come on, guy. Time you were in bed."

"But—"

He swept Sammy along, stilling his protest. "Best get some sleep. I need you to help me take Chloe and Luke dolphin watching tomorrow, okay?"

Gran smiled. "Seems to me Chloe and Luke could stand a bit of time away from family." Her hands fluttered in a shooing motion. "Go on, now. Take your gal out for a walk in the moonlight."

Fortunately, it had gotten dark enough that no one would be able to see her flush. "Gran, we don't need to take a walk."

But Luke had already risen and was holding out his hand to her. "Come on, Chloe. Do what your grandmother says."

Apparently she didn't have a choice. She stood, evading his hand, and started down the three steps to the walk. But by the time she reached the bottom, his hand had closed over hers. It was warm and firm, and the pressure of his fingers told her that if she tried to pull away, he wouldn't let her.

Shells crunched underfoot, then boards echoed as they walked onto the dock. Moonlight traced a silvery sheen on the water. The mainland was a dark shadow on the horizon, pierced by pinpoints of light. They came to a stop at the end of the dock and leaned on the railing.

Chloe cleared her throat. This was amazingly hard. "I'm sorry about that. Gran has certain expectations about what she'd call 'courting couples.' I should have warned you."

He turned toward her. She couldn't be sure of his expression in the soft darkness, but she thought he was amused.

"It doesn't matter, Chloe. She's right, this is a beautiful moonlit night. I don't mind taking a walk with you to fulfill her expectations."

It was the kind of phrase he'd use in reference to a business deal, and the language didn't mesh with the gentle murmur of waves against the dock and the cry of a night heron. He didn't fit here, and maybe she didn't, either, any longer. The thought made her shiver.

"You're cold."

Luke ran his hands down her arms, warming them, sending a thousand conflicting messages along her skin and straight to her heart.

"We should go in." But she didn't want to. She wanted to stay here with him.

"That would disappoint your gran." His voice teased. "I'm sure she'd expect me to warm you up in a more old-fashioned way."

Before she could guess his intent, he'd leaned forward. His lips touched hers.

The dock seemed suspended in space, and she put

her hand on Luke's shoulder to steady herself. This was crazy. She hadn't bargained on this. The shape of his mouth felt firm against hers.

Crazy. This whole charade was crazy, but at this moment she never wanted it to end. Tenderness and longing swept through her in equal measure with despair.

Chapter Three

Luke frowned at his laptop the next morning. Chloe's face kept appearing on the computer screen, overlaying the words—soft and vulnerable, with the moonlight turning her skin to ivory.

He was trying to get down his impressions of the Caldwell Island area in a preliminary report. He'd settled in one of the rockers on the porch after breakfast, letting the herd of Caldwells scatter to whatever occupied them. He had to work, not think about Chloe.

That kiss last night had been a mistake. He'd begun by teasing her, but he'd let himself be carried away by the charade. The next moment he was kissing her, and he'd known in an instant he shouldn't have. You didn't get involved with people who worked for you. Chloe was too valuable to him as an employee to risk ruining that.

He had to concentrate on the job he'd come here to

do. That was his ticket to success. His initial impressions of the island were favorable, but plenty remained to be determined. He'd focus on collecting the data he needed, not on how unexpectedly beautiful Chloe had looked in the moonlight.

"Hey."

He glanced up, startled to find Chloe next to him, and snapped the laptop shut. He'd have to tell her what he had in mind at some point, but not yet. Chloe, in denim shorts and a T-shirt, looked ready for anything but business.

"Hey, yourself." He'd already noticed that everyone he met here used that word as a greeting.

She glanced pointedly at the laptop. "Are you ready to go? We have a date with David and Sammy to go dolphin watching, remember?"

Dolphin watching, as in…taking a boat out. The huge breakfast Chloe's mother had forced on him turned to lead in his stomach. Or maybe it was the grits, gluing everything together. "Why don't you go without me? I have some work I'd like to get done."

"Work?" She frowned at the computer. "I thought you were taking the weekend off. What are you working on?"

He didn't intend to answer that question. "Just keeping up with some reports. I don't care much for boats."

Being on the water gives me the shakes. No, he

wouldn't admit that to her. He didn't like admitting it to himself. His childhood hadn't included a place like this, and there hadn't been swimming pools in the back alleys that had been his playground.

"Come on." She held out her hand. "The *Spyhop* runs as smooth as silk. Besides, it's the best way to see the whole area."

That was the only argument that would get him on a boat. She was offering him the chance to see just what he needed to, in an unobtrusive way. And he couldn't keep refusing without having Chloe guess that what he really felt was something a lot stronger than reluctance.

"Okay. I'll put the computer away and be right with you."

Fifteen minutes later he stood on the dock with Chloe, wishing he'd stuck to his refusal. "Kind of small, isn't it?"

"The *Spyhop?* She's a twenty-six-foot catamaran. You should see the crowd they fit on her later in the summer, when the visitors are here. I'm sorry she's riding so low, but the channel's tidal. It's not hard to get into the boat."

Chloe stepped from the dock down to a bench seat in the boat, then to the deck, balancing as lightly as if on a stairway instead of a rocking deck. She looked up at him.

"Need a hand?"

Aware of David and Sammy watching from the boat's cockpit, he shook his head, grasped the post to which the boat was tied and clambered down. Okay, he could do this. Nobody needed to know that his stomach was tied in more knots than the mooring line. With luck, they wouldn't find any dolphins, making the trip short and uneventful.

David turned the ignition, and the motor roared to life. He waved at Chloe. "Cast off, will you, sugar?" He grinned. "Or don't you remember how?"

Chloe stuck out her tongue at him, then climbed nimbly over the boat's railing to perch on the narrow space at the back and lean across to untie the ropes. Luke had to clench his fists to keep from grabbing her. Chloe had probably done this all her life. She wouldn't thank him for making a big deal of it.

Then the boat started to move, and he clutched the seat and concentrated on not making a fool of himself. Chloe dropped onto the bench next to him and gave him an enquiring look. More to distract himself than because he cared, he nodded to the cockpit.

"I thought Daniel was the one who ran the tours."

"They both do, but David's the real expert on the dolphins. His degree is in oceanography, and he's officially in charge of the dolphin watch for this region."

"Degree?" He couldn't help the surprise in his voice. "But I thought—" What had he thought? That they were a bunch of uneducated hicks?

The amusement in Chloe's gaze said she knew just how surprised he was.

"David knows his stuff, but he doesn't really like doing the narrative for a boatload of tourists. Daniel does that." She smiled. "You know how it is in a big family. We each have our roles."

"I was an only child." At least, he guessed he'd been. Nobody had stayed around long enough to tell him. "Tell me about it."

"Well, Daniel's the oldest, so he always thinks he has to be the boss—"

She wrinkled her nose, something he'd never seen her do in the office. It intrigued him.

"David's the quiet twin. Miranda is the beautiful one. And Theo, whether he likes it or not, is always going to be the baby."

He found himself wanting to say that she was just as beautiful as Miranda, and quickly censored that. "And what about Chloe? What is she?"

He thought a faint flush touched her cheeks, but it might have been the sun. "Oh, I guess I've always been the tomboy. Having two older brothers does that to you."

He nodded toward Sammy and spoke under the rumble of the motor. "Where does Sammy fit in?"

She stiffened, as if he implied something with the question.

"Miranda was married briefly when she was eighteen. It didn't work out."

Her tone told him further questions weren't welcome. "Sammy seems to have plenty of family looking out for him." He recognized, with surprise, a twinge of jealousy. He hadn't had a father, either, but no one had stepped up to take on responsibility, at least not until he met Reverend Tom and his Fresh Start Mission.

"Yes." The tension in Chloe relaxed. "What with the twins, my father, my uncle, the cousins—he probably has more male role models than most kids."

"Lucky boy," he said, and meant it. The tempo of the motor changed suddenly, and he grasped the seat. "Is something wrong?"

Chloe looked surprised, then shook her head. "We're just going around the end of the island, into Dolphin Sound. There are a few of the summer houses I told you about, and that's the yacht club." She pointed to a covey of glistening white boats, lined up neatly along a dock. "Summer sailors," she said, as if dismissing them.

Waves slapped against the hull, and a fine spray of water blew in his face. He nearly ducked, but saw Chloe lift her face, smiling.

"Now you can see it." She leaned forward, sweeping her arm in a broad gesture. "This is Dolphin Sound, between Caldwell Island and the out-islands. Beyond is the ocean."

Luke drew in a breath. He might not be much of a

sailor, but he knew what would draw vacationers to a resort area. Sunlight sparkled on the sound and reflected from the white wings of seagulls. Small islands shimmered on the horizon like Bali Hai, with empty golden beaches and drifts of palmettos.

"It's beautiful."

"Cat Island, Bayard Island. Angel Isle." Her voice softened as she gestured to the most distant of the three. "My favorite."

Sammy scampered back to them, moving nimbly as the boat danced through the water. He touched Chloe's arm, then pointed. "Look, Aunt Chloe. They're here."

He followed the direction of the boy's hand, seeing only the gentle swell of the waves. "I don't—"

A silver crescent broke through the surface of the water, not more than twenty feet from them, describing a glittering arc as the dolphin plunged back beneath the waves. Before he'd caught his breath he saw another, then another.

"Chloe, get the camera," David shouted. "The whole pod is here."

Chloe yanked a camera from its case and knelt on the bench seat, snapping as one glistening shape after another wheeled before them. David throttled back, and the boat slowed to a stop, rocking gently.

"Oh, you beauties," Chloe breathed, leaning out perilously far.

He couldn't help himself—he had to grab the loop on her denim shorts. "Be careful, or you'll be swimming with them, like your namesake."

She glanced back at him, face alight with laughter. "Can't do that. It's against the law to swim with wild dolphins now, much as I'd like to."

David left the wheel to grab a clipboard and jot down notes, murmuring as he did so. "One of the best sightings I've had lately. You two brought us luck."

"Look, Uncle David, that's Onion for sure." Sammy bounced next to Chloe on the seat. "It is, I know it!"

"Got it in one, Sammy. You're a good dolphin watcher." David reached out to tousle the boy's dark hair. "Your name will go in the log."

"You're really keeping track of them?" Luke glanced at David's notes, which certainly seemed to be some sort of official report. "Is this your job?"

"Job?" His glasses shielded David's brown eyes, but Luke couldn't miss the passion in them. "Not in the sense of being paid for it, that's for sure. We're part of the dolphin watch that runs all the way up the coast."

One of the dolphins balanced on its tail, looking at Luke with enquiring eyes and that perpetual dolphin smile. Luke stared back. "I'd think there would be money in this one way or another."

David shrugged, not seeming to care. "We make a bit on the dolphin cruises. That's enough."

Enough? Luke opened his mouth to argue, then closed it again. It wasn't his business to talk David into seeing what he had here. If he tried, he'd only emphasize the difference in their values. That would make staying any longer more difficult.

And he had to stay. He'd seen enough today to convince him of that. This place was the perfect site for the next Dalton Resort hotel, and setting that in motion would take more than a brief weekend that was already half over. His mind ticked away with all he had to do. Chloe could—

"She's always been able to do that," David said softly.

Luke turned. Chloe leaned over the railing, reaching out toward the dolphin, and the creature lifted from the water as if saying something to her. The curve of her body matched the curve of the dolphin, and the sunlight made both of them glow with a kind of harmony that startled and disturbed him.

It was as if the Chloe he knew back in the office had transmuted into a different being here, one as alive and natural and free as that first Chloe. He didn't know how he felt about that—but he did know it was going to make their relationship different in ways he couldn't even imagine.

"Chloe Elizabeth, I hear you brought a young man home for your family to meet." Her father's second cousin, Phoebe, squinted across the crowded dining room at Luke. "'Bout time you were settling down. When is the wedding? Not June, I hope. That's nowhere near enough time for your momma to get ready."

Chloe nearly choked on a mouthful of shrimp toast. Was that what everyone was thinking? "We're not ready to set a date yet," she murmured.

Cousin Phoebe gave her a sharp glance. "That's not what your gran says. She's already planning the wedding quilt for you. Asked me to look out some fabric for her, so I said I would. You'd best decide on colors soon, heah?"

The shrimp turned to ashes in Chloe's mouth. Could this get any worse? If she denied it further than she already had, Cousin Phoebe would be rushing off to Gran with the story. Perhaps she could distract her.

"Cousin Phoebe, is that Aunt June's daughter over there?"

The sight of another relative she could interrogate always appealed to Phoebe. She veered off, replaced immediately by Gran herself.

"Gran, are you enjoying your party?" Chloe hugged her, feeling a rush of love at the soft, papery cheek next to hers. And feeling, too, a rush of guilt. She shouldn't be letting Gran and everyone else believe a relationship existed between her and Luke.

Gran patted her cheek. "It's a good party, Chloe girl.

But the best part is that you're here, and you've finally brought a nice young man home with you." Gran's eyes twinkled. "Even if I did have to invite him myself."

The "nice young man" seemed to be the topic of the day with her elderly relatives. Chloe glanced across the room. Luke stood by the window, deep in conversation with her cousin Matt. Matt, a television news reporter who'd come all the way from Egypt for Gran's birthday, ought to be able to talk about something Luke would understand. She recognized a similarity in them and wondered if Luke would see it—they were both driven, intense, competitive.

"I think he's having a good time." She couldn't actually bring herself to say she was glad Gran had gotten her into this fix. In fact, the truth pressed against her lips, wanting to burst out. If she told Gran all of it, Gran would understand, wouldn't she? Or would she look at Chloe with disbelief that her granddaughter had behaved this way?

Gran held Chloe's hand, her gaze fixed on Luke, too. "Maybe one of my grandchildren will finally find a lasting love. I'd started thinking the dolphin ruined that for all of you."

Chloe blinked. "What are you talking about?"

A faint flush mounted Gran's cheeks. "'Spose you'll think it nonsense."

"You know I'd never think that. But what do you mean? What dolphin?"

"Chloe's dolphin, child. What else?" Gran's eyes brightened with tears. "That dolphin carving disappeared from the church, and no Caldwell has been married under it since. It's not right."

"Gran, you're not superstitious, are you?" She'd known Gran mourned the loss of the dolphin that was part of the family heritage, but hadn't imagined it meant more than that to her. "You don't really believe that old story!"

Gran looked at her sternly. "Chloe Elizabeth, there are more true things in stories than you can explain. I'm not saying folks can't have happy marriages even though the dolphin's not there anymore. Look at your daddy and momma—they're as much in love as ever. But it seems to me God's plan got messed up when that dolphin disappeared, and we need to see him back where he belongs."

Gran had always had a strong streak of the romantic in her, but Chloe hadn't expected this. She didn't know what to say.

"Don't worry about it, Gran. We'll all find the right someone to love, eventually." It was the most comforting thing she could think of, though none of the grandchildren had managed a happy ending yet.

"It's not just that." The lines in Gran's face deepened as she looked from Chloe's father, on one side of the room, to his brother, as far away as he could get and still be in the same room.

The breach between her daddy and Uncle Jefferson had existed long before Chloe was born, an established fact all her life. Everybody on the island knew that Uncle Jeff called Daddy a straitlaced prig and a failure, and that Daddy felt his brother's ambition had killed off his honor. They kept up a semblance of civility for Gran's sake, but their feud obviously still hurt her.

"I'm sorry," she said softly.

"Not much we can do about them, I'm afraid. But as for you young ones—seems to me you've found someone to love, dolphin or no, haven't you."

"I don't know. It's not…not really serious between us—not yet, anyway."

Gran's wise old eyes studied Chloe. "Don't think you can fool me, Chloe Elizabeth."

Her heart stopped. "What do you mean?"

"I mean, I can see how well the two of you fit together. You care about him, don't you?"

She couldn't lie about it with Gran looking at her. "Maybe so. But that doesn't mean it's going to be a lifetime love or anything."

Gran patted her hand. "You just keep in mind that verse I gave you on the day you were baptized. God has plans for you, plans to give you hope and a future. You trust in that, you hear?"

She blinked back tears, thinking of the needlepoint

sampler Gran had made—the one that went everywhere with her. "I'll try."

"Besides, now that Luke's here, maybe we can help things along."

Panic ripped through her. "Don't you dare do any matchmaking. If things are meant to happen between us, they will."

"No harm in helping it along. I want to see another Caldwell bride before I'm too old to enjoy it."

"Gran—"

"Are you ladies having a private conversation, or can anyone join in?"

Chloe's breath caught at the sound of Luke's voice. She'd been so intent that she hadn't noticed him cross the room to them. She looked up, trying to smile, hoping Gran hadn't heard that betraying little gasp. Hoping even more that Luke hadn't heard it. There were no two ways about it—the sooner they got back to Chicago and their normal lives, the better for everyone.

"Always glad to have a good-looking man to talk to." Gran fluttered her eyelashes at him outrageously. "Especially one that I haven't known since he was in diapers."

"Gran," Chloe murmured. *Just a few more hours, and we'll be on a plane. I'll forget this weekend ever happened.*

Luke's baritone chuckle was like a feather, tickling her skin. "If you want someone to flirt with, Mrs. Caldwell, I'm your man."

"Thought I told you to call me 'Gran'. Everyone else does. How are you liking Caldwell Cove, now that you've been here a spell?"

"Beautiful," he said promptly. "Now I know why Chloe is always talking about this place." He put his arm around Chloe's waist, and she tried not to pull away. "It's the most peaceful spot I've seen in years."

"Well, then, you ought to stay a bit longer." Naturally Gran would pounce on that. "Spring's a perfect time for a vacation. Why don't you two stay on?"

Chloe waited confidently for Luke's excuses—they had to get back to the office, he had other plans, anything. They didn't come.

"You know, that might not be such a bad idea." He squeezed Chloe. "What do you think, Chloe? How about if we take a few vacation days and stay for a while?"

If the rag rug at her feet had jumped up and bitten her, she couldn't have been more shocked. "Are you…?" *Crazy* was what she wanted to say, but she bit back the word. "I don't think you've thought this through. We have work waiting for us at the office." She flashed him a look that should have singed, but he just smiled.

"Work will always wait." He turned to her grandmother. "Don't you agree, Gran?"

Before Gran could answer, Chloe took a step away,

her fingers biting into his arm. "Let's go out on the porch, *dear.*" She added the endearment through clenched teeth. "I need to talk with you."

Fuming, she tugged him through the crowd, emerging at last onto the porch and a quiet corner. She swung to face him, anger overcoming the deference she usually felt toward him. "What on earth was that all about? Why did you let my grandmother think we might stay longer?"

"Because we're going to." His smile was the one he wore when he crossed swords with a business opponent. "You should know I wouldn't kid about something like that."

The porch floor rocked under her feet like the *Spyhop* in a storm. "I don't understand. We're leaving in a little over an hour. We have tickets for tonight."

"We can change those easily enough."

"Probably, but why should we?" Her head began to throb. "This charade was meant to last a brief weekend, remember?"

"Relax, Chloe." He leaned against the porch railing, but his face was anything but relaxed. "I'm talking business, not romance."

From the house she could hear the cheerful buzz of voices, of people having a good time and forgetting everything else in their celebration. But here, the sagging old porch had taken on the air of a corporate office.

"What do you mean? What business?"

His gaze seemed to grasp her. "Hotel business. I'm looking into siting the next Dalton Resort hotel here, on or near Caldwell Island."

"Here?" She could only gape at him. "I don't understand." Then she did, and it hit her like a blow. "That's why you wanted to come here with me, isn't it. You wanted to check it out."

You didn't come to help me. Disappointment filled her heart. She'd thought he had done this out of misguided kindness, out of that urge he had to direct everything, because he cared about her. He hadn't. He'd done it to advance his career.

He shrugged. "You needed to be bailed out with your family. I needed a good excuse for being here, so I could see if the area was suitable. It is. Now we have to stay until I can decide on a specific site and put the acquisition in motion." His gaze sharpened. "What's the matter? I thought you'd be jumping with joy at the idea of bringing a little prosperity to the old hometown."

"It means change," she said slowly, trying to sort out her feelings.

"Of course, it means change. Jobs, for one thing. You're not going to tell me this area couldn't use a nice fat payroll."

"I suppose it could." No more lean times when the fish didn't run. No need for young people to leave home to make a living. He was right, she should be happy.

In the room behind them, someone, probably her father, had begun playing the fiddle. "Lorena," one of her grandmother's favorites. The haunting air stirred misty echoes of a past that wasn't forgotten here. It was an odd counterpoint to the discussion they were having. "I'd like to tell my father about this."

"Absolutely not." His voice snapped, and her gaze jerked up to his.

He glanced beyond her, toward the door, then clasped her arm and drew her to the end of the porch. He stopped there, his back to the house, his arm around her. Anyone looking out would think they were seeing a romantic tryst.

"Sorry." His voice lowered. "It's not that I don't trust your family, but you know what it will be like if word gets out as to why I'm here. Every landowner in three counties will be trying to con me into paying top dollar for a piece of worthless swamp. We can't risk it."

His arm was warm and strong around her waist. That warmth crept through her, weakening her will to resist. *We,* he'd said. They were a team, like always. "But…you can't mean to continue this charade even longer." She hoped she didn't sound as horrified as she felt.

"Why not?" He hugged her a little closer, and his breath touched her cheek. "We've been doing a good job so far. There's no reason for anyone to guess we're not involved."

"I don't want to tell any more lies to my family." She tried to pull free, but he held her firmly.

"You don't have to lie. We just let things go on the way they are." His voice was low, persuasive. "Think about how happy they're going to be with the results, if everything goes the way I think it will. Good times come to Caldwell Island, everyone's happy, we go back to Chicago. In a month or so, you can tell your family we decided to date other people. It's going to be fine."

No, it wasn't going to be fine, not at all. If she did this, she'd have to spend another week, maybe longer, pretending to be in love with Luke. At this precise moment, with the revelation of his motives still stinging, she didn't even like him very much. But she was getting entirely too used to the feel of his arm around her.

No matter how this worked out, one thing was crystal clear. Chloe Caldwell was in deeper trouble than she'd ever imagined.

Chapter Four

Luke shifted his weight restlessly, waiting for Chloe's response. He could feel her tension against his arm. It was as if everything in her resisted him. He wanted her cooperation—needed it, in fact. Didn't she understand that?

It was probably the first time he'd seen his competent assistant show anger toward him, and it startled and fascinated him. He'd always found Chloe a bit too controlled. Apparently when it came to her family, she could be passionate.

He bit back the urge to demand. He wasn't at corporate headquarters now. This was Chloe's turf, not his, and she was a different person here.

"Well, Chloe?" He tried to keep his voice gentle, as if he really wanted her input on the decision. It was tough to do, when the vice-presidency shimmered as close as the blossom from a trailing vine that brushed Chloe's hair and perfumed the air.

"I wish there were some other way of doing this." Her face tilted toward his, troubled.

He tamped down annoyance. "There isn't. And this is your future, too. Wouldn't you like to be secretary to a vice-president? You'll move along with me. I can't do without my right arm."

It was an argument that would have swayed him, but it didn't seem to have much effect on Chloe. If anything, the resistance strengthened in her.

"I don't like the idea of fooling my family."

He bit back the reminder that she was the one who'd started it. "This isn't going to hurt them."

"How can you say that? How would you feel if it were your family?"

Her question hit him right between the eyes. *My family, Chloe? What family? The father I never knew or the mother who walked away when I was six? Or maybe you mean the string of foster families who didn't want to keep me.*

He took a breath, locking those questions behind the closed door in his mind. He didn't let them out because they made him think too much of where he'd been instead of where he was going. He wouldn't let Chloe and her old-fashioned family make him start remembering.

"If it were my family," he said evenly, "I'd think about how much they'd benefit in the long run. They will, you know. There'll be more business for all of them once a resort hotel comes in. You know that as well as I do."

She nodded slowly, her face still troubled. "I suppose I—"

"Hey, cousin."

Chloe turned, her face lighting with pleasure. She pulled away from him to hug the man who approached, abandoning their conversation in an instant. "Matt. I haven't had a chance to talk with you yet. How are you?"

Luke leaned back against the porch rail, searching for patience, as Chloe and her cousin caught up with each other. This one was Matthew Caldwell—Chloe's grandmother had introduced them earlier.

Chloe turned back to him, her arm still around Matt's waist. There was no stiffness in her as she leaned against her cousin. Apparently her guardedness was only for Luke.

"I'm sorry, Luke, I'm forgetting my manners—"
The turn of phrase was an echo of her family's speech. Chloe's cultivated urban tones were dropping away, and she probably didn't even realize it.

"You've met my cousin, Matt Caldwell, haven't you?"

Luke nodded. Matt had the strength and height that

marked all the Caldwell men, but his dark eyes looked as if they'd seen too much, and there was a somber cut to his mouth when he wasn't actively smiling at Chloe.

"We already talked about Matt's reports from the Middle East. A tough spot to be in right now."

Matt nodded. "And Gran's told me all about your new beau, Chloe Elizabeth."

Most of it imaginary, unfortunately. The thought startled him. Unfortunate that he wasn't Chloe's beau? No, of course it wasn't. Chloe was the last woman in the world he'd become involved with, for more reasons than he could count.

"So how long are you staying home this time?" Chloe's tone was teasing. "Long enough to satisfy Gran?"

Matt shook his head. "I have to head back right away. And you should know nothing short of settling down in Caldwell Cove for life would satisfy Gran."

"Good idea. Maybe if you were here, Gran would stop teasing me to come back. You could become the publisher of the *Caldwell Cove Gazette.*"

"You know, some day I might just do that. But not today." Matt tugged gently at a lock of Chloe's hair. "How soon are the two of you leaving?"

Luke caught a sudden, almost anguished look from Chloe. Then she smiled, and he thought he must have imagined it.

"We're going to hang around for a while," she said

as easily as if they hadn't just been arguing about it. "Luke's decided to take some vacation time."

"That'll make the family happy. Well, I'd better get back to the second cousins. I haven't given Phoebe a chance to interrogate me yet." Matt held out his hand to Luke, hugged Chloe again and turned away.

The screen door banged behind Matt, and Chloe turned to Luke, straightening as if she faced something unpleasant.

"I guess that means we're staying." He watched her, wondering what she was really thinking.

"I guess it does." She shrugged. "I don't seem to have much choice, do I."

"You always have a choice, Chloe. I think you've made the right one." He reached out to brush a strand of hair from her face. His fingers touched her cheek, and the warmth and softness of her skin seemed to radiate up his arm.

He had a choice, too. If he were smart, he'd choose not to touch her again, not to take too much pleasure out of playing the role of her boyfriend. He suddenly realized the smart choice might be a difficult one to make where Chloe was concerned, and that surprised and disturbed him.

"Chloe, love, don't forget to water these in." Chloe's mother put a flat of marigolds into the trunk of the car the next morning.

"I'll take care of it." Chloe hovered, impatiently holding the trunk lid, ready to snap it down. She wanted to get moving before Luke came out and volunteered to go with her.

But Sallie Caldwell lingered, her strong, capable hands brushing the flowers and releasing their spicy aroma. "Have you talked to Theo since you've been home?"

The question caught Chloe off guard. "Well, of course I've talked…" She frowned. Theo had been elusive yesterday. "I guess not much. Why? Is something wrong?"

Her mother looked up, and the sunlight gilded her cheeks and brought out the warmth and welcome in her golden-brown eyes. Chloe felt a fervent hope that she'd be as lovely when she reached that age. Her mother never seemed to age, even after five children.

"I don't know." She shook her head. "Theo's always been such an open child. All of a sudden he seems to be keeping secrets. Something's troubling the boy, and I don't know what."

"Adolescence, maybe." She remembered how she'd been at sixteen—full of dreams and impatient to get on with grown-up life.

"Maybe it is just that. But he might confide in you. Will you see what you can find out?"

"I'll try."

Her mother's smile broke through. "Well, I know

you'll give him good advice, whatever it is." She touched Chloe's cheek lightly. "It's good to have you home."

Her mother was talking to her like another adult, instead of a daughter. It felt odd but gratifying.

"I'll try to catch him alone and see what's up." She shifted her hand on the trunk lid. "I probably ought to get going. Gran will be waiting."

Nodding, her mother stepped away, and Chloe closed the trunk. She jingled the keys in her hand. "I'll see you later."

"Where are you going?"

Chloe jumped at Luke's voice, the keys slipping through her fingers. He made a lunge and caught them, tossing them lightly in the air and catching them again. He lifted his eyebrows as if to repeat the question.

She'd thought he was safely lingering over his coffee and one of her mother's famous sticky buns. Looked as if she'd been wrong. "I'm taking my grandmother to the cemetery." She hoped her tone was final enough that he'd get the message. She didn't want company.

He opened the car door, smiling. "Fine. Let's go."

"I really don't need any help." She could feel her mother's gaze on her as she reached for the keys. "I thought you had some work you wanted to do."

His fingers closed around the keys. "Nothing that's more important than this." He gestured to the car as if inviting her into a coach. "I'd love to see your grandmother again."

"Well, of course Luke wants to go with you." Her mother beamed at the man she no doubt envisioned as a future son-in-law.

She was outmaneuvered, and she could hardly make a fuss in front of her mother. "Fine." She got into the car, trying not to flounce. "I'm ready."

Luke closed her door, said goodbye to her mother and slid behind the wheel. She inhaled the scent of his aftershave as he leaned forward to put the key in the ignition, and she clasped her hands in her lap. This was going to be a long morning, after a longer night.

She'd tossed and turned for most of it, trying not to wake Miranda, who'd slept serenely in the other twin bed in the room they'd shared most of their lives. She hadn't been able to erase the memory of those moments on the porch. She'd continued to feel Luke's strong shoulder as he pulled her against him, continued to hear his voice as he called her his "right arm."

Right arm. Not what a woman wanted to hear, but it was an accurate description of how he felt about her—and she'd better remember it.

"Directions?" Luke stopped at Caldwell Cove's single traffic light and looked at enquiringly.

"Sorry." She felt her cheeks grow warm and was glad he couldn't read her thoughts. "Just go straight along the water. See the church steeple? Gran's house is next to the church."

"Tell me something, Chloe."

"What?"

"Why didn't you want me to come with you this morning?"

So much for her belief that he couldn't read her thoughts. She seemed to be transparent where Luke was concerned. "I just…it's hard to keep up this charade with Gran. I've never kept secrets from her."

"Never?"

She glanced at him, sure he was mocking her, but found only curiosity in his eyes. "Well, hardly ever. A lot of times it's easier to talk to a grandparent than a parent about things. You know how it is."

"No." He bit off the word, then shrugged. "I don't remember my grandparents."

"I'm sorry. I can't imagine life without Gran. She's a strong woman. One of a long line." She seemed to see all those Caldwell women, looking disapprovingly at the current bearer of the name. Maybe, if she'd been able to be alone with Gran today, she could have told her the truth.

"This house?"

When she nodded, Luke pulled to a stop by the gate in the white picket fence. She got out quickly before he could come around to open the door, then joined him on the walk. "Gran has a green thumb, as you can see." She pushed the gate open, and they walked up a brick path between the lush growth of rosebushes. "Hers is one of the oldest houses on the island."

The white-frame cottage was like Gran—strong, functional, enduring. Before they reached the black door, Gran opened it, seeming to accept Luke's presence as routine. She handed him a galvanized bucket filled with seedlings.

"Mind you put that someplace shady. I don't want those petunias wilting before we get them in the ground."

"Yes, ma'am." Luke smiled and held out his arm, as if he spent every day escorting an elderly woman wearing a chintz dress and a battered man's straw hat. "We'll take good care of them. And of you."

Chloe fell in behind as they started down the walk, foreboding growing. Luke being charming was something to behold, and her grandmother, flirting outrageously from under the brim of the straw hat, was even worse.

Please, Lord, just let me get through this morning. The verse Gran had given her popped into her mind and wouldn't be dislodged. If God did have plans for her future, she suspected those plans didn't include Luke Hunter.

"And that's Chloe's great-great-great-aunt Isabelle." Gran pointed to the worn headstone. "She kept her family fed and safe right through the war, and that was no small thing."

Chloe wondered if Luke realized Gran was talking about the War between the States, and then she decided it didn't matter. He was being polite and acting interested in Gran's litany of family graves, and that was the important thing.

"Your family's been here a long time." There was a note in Luke's voice that she didn't recognize, and she wondered what it meant.

"Back to the first settlers," Gran said with satisfaction. "Caldwells belong here."

Chloe stirred restlessly. "Some of us have found lives elsewhere, Gran. Maybe we don't belong here any longer." *Did she?* That thought had been in her head too often since she'd been back.

Gran patted her hand. "You belong, all right. Your roots run too deep here to forget, even if you do run off to outlandish places."

"Matt will be safe." She knew her grandmother was thinking of Matt's early morning flight. "We'll hear from him again soon."

Gran nodded, then fanned herself with her hat. "Chloe Elizabeth, I'm going to set a spell on the bench. You finish, all right?"

"We'll take care of it, Gran. You relax."

"Are you sure she's all right?" Luke frowned, watching

as Gran tottered off to settle on the wrought-iron bench under a live oak. "Maybe we should take her home."

"She's not tired." Chloe knew her gran too well to be fooled. "She's matchmaking. Giving us a chance to be alone."

She waited for a sarcastic response, but it didn't come.

Instead Luke gestured toward the gray stones, tilting across the long grass. "You do this often?"

"What?"

"Come here, plant flowers. Read off the names."

He obviously didn't understand the Southern attitude toward cemeteries, and she wasn't sure she could explain it in a way that would make sense to him.

"Gran would say it's a shame to the living if the family graves aren't taken care of properly. I've been doing this since I was a little girl. We all have. It feels natural to me." She touched a worn stone, and it was cool beneath her fingers. "This was the first Chloe."

Luke knelt, frowning at the faded words. "What's that beneath the dates? I can't make it out."

"Her Bible verse. 'May God grant you His mighty and glorious strength.' All of us have our own verses." She shrugged, a little embarrassed. "It's a family tradition—a scripture promise to live by. Gran gave each of us a verse on our baptism, just as her grandmother did."

He stood, and he was very close to her. "What's your verse, Chloe?"

She looked up at him, wanting to turn the question away with a light comment. His blue eyes seemed to darken, staring into hers with such intensity that she couldn't escape, and he took both her hands in his. Her breath caught in her throat.

"It's from Jeremiah." She forced the words out, trying to sound natural. "'For I know the plans I have for you,' says the Lord. 'Plans to prosper you and not to harm you. Plans to give you hope and a future.'"

"Hope and a future," he repeated softly. "That's a nice promise, Chloe Elizabeth."

The lump in her throat was too big to swallow, and she could only nod. It had been a mistake to bring Luke Hunter here. She should have known that it would be. Things had changed between them. They'd never be the same again.

But they'd also never be the way she sometimes wished they would be. Somehow, she had to accept that.

He had to stop letting these people affect him so much. Luke drove toward the inn after dropping off Chloe's grandmother, trying to dismiss the feelings that had crept over him in the cemetery. Trying to tell himself the whole thing was maudlin, or quaint, or silly.

It didn't seem to work. He glanced sideways at Chloe. She wasn't really that different here than she was in Chicago, was she? Maybe not outwardly, but inwardly… He felt as if he'd opened an ordinary-looking package and discovered something rich and mysterious.

He couldn't erase the sense that she'd introduced him to a new world, a world where family meant something other than a collection of strangers held together by law. Those moments in the cemetery had moved him in a way he'd never experienced, and he didn't know what to do with those feelings.

He'd like to categorize this whole visit as an expedition into the sticks. It could be an amusing story—something to entertain his acquaintances at the next cocktail party or gallery opening. He tried to picture himself talking about Chloe's family and their quaint customs. He knew instinctively that he never would.

Okay, he'd accept that. But he'd also accept the fact that none of this fit into his real life—not Chloe, not her family. He didn't understand them, and they'd certainly never understand what he came from. He had to get things back to business, and he definitely had to trample the insidious longing to share more of himself with Chloe.

"Looks as if your father's just coming in." He drew up opposite the dock and watched Chloe's father jockey his boat into position.

Chloe was out of the car before he could go around and open her door. "Come on. We'll give him a hand."

She jogged onto the dock, and he followed reluctantly. The water was higher than it had been the last time—meaning the tide was coming in, he supposed. Waves slapped against the wooden boards, making them vibrate uneasily beneath his feet. The salt air assaulted his nostrils, and the expanse of sky made him feel vulnerable and exposed.

He didn't have to like it here. He just had to look at it through a businessman's eyes, so he could make the right deal.

"Hey, Daddy." Chloe grasped one of the dock supports and leaned out to take the line her father held, then made it fast. "Any luck this morning?"

"Nothing running." Clayton Caldwell cut the engine. "If we depended on my fishing to put food on the table, our bellies would be bumping our backbones—"

He glanced at Luke, and Luke read reserve in those clear eyes. Clayton hadn't decided what to make of him yet.

"Hop down and secure that aft line, Luke."

The small boat bounced, bumping against the dock, and Luke's stomach bounced with it. Hop down? He didn't think so. But saying no would declare him either a rotten guest or a wimp, and he didn't like either of those alternatives. Steeling himself, he took a step forward.

Chloe nipped in front of him and stepped nimbly down into the boat. "I'll get it, Daddy." She grabbed the line and looped it around the upright. "Have to show you I haven't forgotten how."

"I didn't think that, Chloe-girl." Clayton stepped easily up to the dock, then leaned down and pulled Chloe up next to him.

The man must be close to sixty, but his muscles seemed as hard as those of any bodybuilder. Clayton's level gaze rested on him, and Luke discovered he felt smaller under that calm stare. He didn't like it.

Chloe hugged her father, pressing her face against the older man's white T-shirt. "You've been saying the same thing about the fishing ever since I can remember. We haven't gone hungry yet."

Her father squeezed her, then released her. "Must be about lunchtime. You two coming?"

"We'll be along in a minute." Chloe leaned against the railing as if the dock's movement was as common as the ascent of an elevator. She waited until her father was halfway up the crushed shell walk, then turned to him.

"Are you all right?"

"Of course I'm all right." He didn't sound authoritative, just irritable. But he didn't care for the way Chloe looked at him—as if he needed her pity. "Let's go."

Chloe caught his arm, and her fingers were cool on sun-warmed skin. "You're afraid of the water, aren't you?"

"What makes you say that?" He gave her a look designed to prevent any further questions.

She smiled. "Well, it might be the way you gripped the seat when we were out with David and Sammy. Or the way you turned white when my daddy asked you to hop down on the boat. Don't you know how to swim?"

"Everyone knows how to swim." He'd forced himself to learn in college, when he'd realized that ability was taken for granted by his classmates. "I've just never liked it, that's all. Let's go up to lunch."

Her fingers tightened. "I'm sorry. This is a bad place to be if you're afraid of the water."

"I'm not afraid," he snapped. It was none of Chloe's business, anyway. What right did she have to push him? Maybe she'd be the one telling stories about this trip to amuse her friends—how the big corporate executive was afraid of a little water.

She shrugged. "It's nothing to be ashamed of. I just thought since you're here, maybe you'd like to try and get over it."

He forced himself to look at her. He didn't see amusement in her eyes, just concern, maybe friendship. He grimaced. "Have you been taking psychology lessons in your spare time, Chloe?"

Her smile sparkled like sunlight on the waves. "No. But as long as we have to stay for a week…"

She let that sentence trail off, but the challenge in her gaze reminded him that he was pushing her to do something she didn't want to do. It dared him to do the same.

"All right." He pushed away from the dock railing. "I guess you have a deal. Now can we go?"

She nodded demurely. "Of course." She led the way off the dock.

He should feel better once he was back on solid ground, following Chloe toward the porch. He should, but he didn't. Oh, it wasn't the business of getting over his fear. He could suck it up and pretend, if he had to.

What bothered him was considerably more personal. It was the realization that he'd just shown Chloe a piece of himself. It was a piece he always kept hidden, along with anything else that might make him vulnerable. He wasn't sure how Chloe had come far enough into his inner life to see it. Or how he'd ever get her out again.

Chapter Five

"Are you ready?" Chloe stood knee-deep in the shallows of the sound, steadying the kayak with her hand. The afternoon sun was hot on her shoulders. Later in the summer the water would reach the temperature of a warm bath, but now it felt pleasantly cool. They'd spent the past two days ostensibly sight-seeing while Luke looked at possible hotel sites, but she'd finally gotten him to make good on his promise.

She watched Luke's face as he looked from her to the softly rocking two-person craft. He'd obviously clamped down hard on his feelings. This was the face he wore when he met a challenge in the business arena—impassive, determined, aggressive. If he felt any fear, he certainly didn't intend to show it to her.

"You're sure you know how to operate one of these

things?" Luke raised straight black brows and prodded the kayak.

"Daniel and David had me out in one before I went to kindergarten." She braced it with both hands. "Climb in and get the feel of it. We'll stay where we can stand up, I promise."

And where no one would see them. She didn't say that out loud, but she knew it was in his thoughts. Luke would never want anyone to see him doing something he didn't do well. But she also knew that if he once started something, he wouldn't quit until he had mastered it.

He grasped the side of the kayak. "Okay, Chloe. I'm going to trust you. But if you dunk me, I'll take it out of your salary." He climbed in gingerly, and she handed him a paddle.

"That might be worth it." Before he could react, she pulled herself easily onto the seat behind him.

Freed from the restraint of her grasp, the small craft curtseyed in the gentle swell. Luke grabbed the side, and she pretended not to notice.

"I'll paddle first." She dipped the paddle into the water, sending them forward. "When you feel comfortable, join in."

She stroked evenly and watched the tension in his shoulders. For a few minutes he didn't move. Then, slowly, he began to relax. He released his grip on the side and turned his head to glance back at her paddle.

She saw him in profile—mouth set, eyes alert, finding his way in unfamiliar territory.

"I pull on the same side as you?" He dipped his paddle into the water.

"That's right, just not too deep. Don't worry about the rhythm. I'll match my stroke to yours."

The instant he started paddling, the kayak picked up speed. They skimmed across the water. His stroke, uncertain at first, settled into a rhythm, even though his hands grasped so hard that his knuckles were white.

"Not bad," he said. "Not bad at all."

"Just remember that you control the kayak. It responds to your movements. If you lean over too far, we'll both be in the drink."

He turned toward her enough that she could see his lips twitch. "As you said, it might be worth it."

She let him set the pace, her strokes compensating for his inexpert ones. Gradually his movements became smoother, and the grasp he had on the paddle eased. She could see the moment at which he began to enjoy it, and something that had been tight inside her eased.

She lifted her face to the breeze, pleasure flooding her. She'd told herself it was only fair that Luke do something he found difficult, given the situation he'd pushed her into. But she knew that wasn't the real reason she'd wanted to do this.

This was the world she loved. Maybe she didn't

belong here any longer, in spite of what Gran said, but she did love it. Especially on a day like this, with sunlight sparkling on the water and the gentle murmur of waves kissing the shore. She watched droplets fall from the paddle, crystal in the light. She wanted Luke to love it, too.

No, not love it. That was too much to ask. But she didn't want to imagine him going back to Chicago and amusing his friends with stories of his stay here. She wanted him to appreciate her place and her people, no matter how alien they were to him.

She stopped paddling, reaching forward to touch his arm. His warm skin made her fingers tingle, and she tried to ignore the sensation. "Look."

He rested the paddle on his knees and followed the direction she pointed. She heard his breath catch as the dolphins broke the surface of the water.

"They look a lot bigger from this angle."

"We're at their level now." She smiled, watching the flashes of silver as the dolphins wheeled through the waves. "Sometimes they'll come right up to the kayak, as if they want to play."

"I think I'd just as soon watch them from a distance." Luke glanced back at her. "I'm sure you'd rather play with them."

"They're old friends." As she said the words, she realized how much she'd missed this. "They come back to the sound every year. Maybe…" She stopped, not sure she wanted to say it. It sounded foolish.

"Maybe what?"

She shrugged. "Sometimes I think they're the descendants of Chloe's dolphins."

He turned toward her, expression skeptical. "Isn't that a little fanciful?"

"I know it's not likely." She hated sounding defensive. Why shouldn't she believe that if she wanted to? "But the same pod does come back year after year. They belong here just as much as we do."

"Maybe you're right—"

His voice had softened, as if he realized it was important to her. As if he cared that it was important to her.

"But it looks as if they're done showing off for us today."

She nodded, watching the silver arcs disappear toward open ocean. "They're probably heading farther out to feed. And I don't suppose you want to go out after them…."

"I'll have to get a lot better before I want to chase down dolphins in this thing." Luke picked up his paddle. "But I'm willing to practice."

"Okay." She dipped into the water. "Let's head for the buoy. You'll be able to see that tract of land near the yacht club from there."

He nodded, adjusting his movement to hers, and

in a second they were paddling in unison. Luke's stroke picked up speed, sending the kayak flying across the water.

"Are we racing?" she asked, meeting his speed.

He turned his head again to smile at her, and this time the pure enjoyment in his face set her nerves vibrating.

"Too bad we don't have anyone to race."

"Don't you mean anyone to beat?" she asked.

He shrugged. "That's the same thing, isn't it?"

Maybe to him, it was. His question resonated, disturbing her pleasure in the moment. Luke excelled in competition, and she'd gotten used to that over the past few years. It seemed natural back in their business world. Here his competitiveness struck a jarring note, reminding her of the differences between them.

"There's the yacht club—" She pointed. "Uncle Jeff owns the land that adjoins it."

Luke shaded his eyes. "Is it up for sale?"

"I'd guess anything Uncle Jeff owns is up for sale, if the price is right." She heard the censure in her words and regretted it. "Sorry. I shouldn't have said that."

"Why?"

Luke sent a puzzled look over his shoulder, and she realized he hadn't even reacted to the family problem that weighed on her. This was business. And theirs was a business relationship, nothing more.

"Never mind. Let's take a break." She shifted her

weight, turning the craft toward shore. "We'd best put some more sunscreen on before we get burned."

They rode the waves to shore, then dragged the kayak onto the sand. Chloe dropped to the beach towel she'd spread out and dug in her bag for the bottle of sunscreen. She tossed it to Luke.

"So, what did you think?" She nodded toward the kayak. "Think you could get to like kayaking?"

"Not bad." Luke rubbed lotion vigorously on his neck and shoulders. "Not bad at all." He held out the bottle to her. "Thanks, Chloe. I'm glad you pushed me into it, even if you were just trying to pay me back."

She smoothed the lotion along her legs, watching the movement of her hand so she didn't have to look at him. "I can't imagine what you're talking about."

He grinned. "Chloe Elizabeth, your grandmother would be ashamed of you, telling such a big fib."

The tension she had been feeling slipped away in the warmth of his smile. She leaned back on her elbows, lifting her face to the sun, and closed her eyes. Couldn't she just enjoy the moment and forget about why they were here together?

"Tell me something, Chloe."

She opened her eyes. "What?"

Frown lines laced between Luke's brows. "Your father and his brother—what's going on there?"

No, it looked as if she couldn't just enjoy the

moment. It was her own fault for mentioning Uncle Jeff. She might try telling Luke another one of her fairy tales, but she didn't think he'd believe it. She could tell him it wasn't his business—but she was the one who'd brought him here. Or she could tell him the truth and let him make of it whatever he wanted.

"My father and Uncle Jefferson don't speak to each other unless it's absolutely necessary." She hadn't realized how odd that sounded until she said it aloud to him. "I guess that seems strange to you." She sent him a defiant look.

He leaned on his elbow, the movement bringing him close enough that she felt the energy radiating from his skin.

"I'd say it was strange, yes. How long has this been going on?"

"Since I can remember." She swallowed, knowing that answer wasn't all of it. "Since they were teenagers."

He whistled softly. "That's a long time to live in the same small community with your brother and not speak. What happened?"

"They quarreled," she said shortly. She felt his gaze on her and knew she had to say the rest of it. "No one knows exactly why, but people guess over a girl. They seemed to go in opposite directions after that. My grandfather divided the family property between them.

Daddy took the inn and Angel Isle. Uncle Jeff got the boatyard, the cannery and the real estate. He…well, my daddy would say he wheeled and dealed so much he forgot who he was. Forgot what it meant to live with honor." She shrugged. "And Uncle Jeff thinks my daddy is old-fashioned, self-righteous…" She stopped. What was Luke thinking?

"Must be hard on your grandmother."

He had hit on the sorest point. "Yes, it is. I wish I knew how to make it better, but I don't." She hated that helplessness.

He put his hand over hers. "I guess your family isn't so perfect, after all."

She sat up, yanking her hand away. "I never claimed it was." Her resentment spurted. "I suppose yours is."

"My family?" His mouth narrowed to a thin line. "No, Chloe, my family's not perfect, either. Not by a long shot."

A barrier had suddenly appeared between them. She couldn't see it but she knew it was there. All the sunlight seemed to have gone from the day.

Secrets. She'd always known Luke had secrets to hide—always guessed it had something to do with his family.

But he wasn't going to tell her, that much was clear. The illusion of friendship between them was just that—an illusion.

* * *

This was getting to be a habit. Luke sat on the porch late that afternoon, frowning at the computer screen. Once again, Chloe's face intervened, hurt evident in her eyes.

He hadn't meant to cause her pain with his questions earlier about her father. He'd just been curious, trying to figure out what made the sprawling Caldwell clan tick. But he should have realized he was prodding at a tender spot.

He glanced out at the water, absently watching a white sailboat curve across to the mainland. He hadn't imagined it would cause Chloe pain to talk about it. He had no basis for comparison when it came to families, happy or otherwise.

All the more reason he shouldn't get further entangled with Chloe and her family. He should let them get on with their work, while he got on with his.

He looked around, exasperated. The Caldwells were doing a fine job of that. Daniel and David had taken a few guests out on a dolphin cruise. Miranda had whisked out of the kitchen a few minutes earlier, deposited a pitcher of iced lemonade and a plate of molasses cookies at his elbow and disappeared again.

As for Chloe…he had to smile. Chloe was busy setting up a Web site for the inn. Her parents' reluctance had been almost comical, but she'd finally gotten through to them. It looked as if Chloe had absorbed a bit about marketing from Dalton Resorts.

He was the only one not getting on with his work. He wanted— He wasn't sure what he wanted, and that was an odd feeling.

Erasing the pain he'd seen in Chloe's eyes might restore his balance. Then they could go back to their usual businesslike relationship, with no more delving beneath the surface to discover unexpected facets of each other. That would be far safer.

Two figures sauntered down the lane. The smaller one stooped to pick up a shell, then skimmed it out across the water. Sammy and Theo, obviously home from school. They turned, saw him, and seemed to hesitate, as if his presence disturbed their usual routine.

The yellow pup raced around the house, throwing himself at Sammy in an exuberant greeting. The boy dropped his knapsack and tussled with the puppy, then boy and dog raced toward him, with Theo following at a more sedate pace.

"Hey." Sammy's gaze fell on the plate of cookies. "Molasses. Bet my momma made those. She always makes them for guests." He was obviously too polite to ask for one, but his eyes spoke for him.

"You're right about that." Luke slid the plate toward the boy. "I'm plenty full, but I don't want to hurt your mother's feelings by not eating these. You could do me a favor by taking some."

Sammy nodded solemnly. "I guess that would be

okay." He took a handful of cookies, then smiled. "Thank you, sir." Clutching the cookies, he whistled to the dog and then charged inside, the wooden screen door banging behind him.

Theo mounted the porch steps and leaned against the rail. "Sammy always acts like he hasn't had a cookie in a week, but I happen to know Miranda put three in his lunch bag."

Luke tried to picture a childhood in this place, where someone put homemade cookies in your lunch bag and you came home to the same welcome every day. He was watching it, but he couldn't quite believe in it. People didn't live like this anymore, did they?

Apparently the Caldwells did.

He expected Theo to hurry off, as Sammy had, but instead he lingered. Something self-conscious in the boy's manner made Luke look more closely at Chloe's little brother.

Theo had the height of his brothers, but his weight hadn't caught up yet. He had the sun-bleached hair, too, falling on his forehead, and his father's hazel eyes. But where the older man's gaze was confident and unhurried, Theo had the eyes of a dreamer. A certain vulnerable something about his mouth reminded Luke of Chloe.

The silence stretched uncomfortably long between them. "So, how's school?" A stupid thing to say, probably, but he didn't seem to have any common ground with the boy.

Theo shrugged. "Okay, I guess, sir. Pretty boring, most of the time."

"I remember that." He'd usually found ways of livening things up that probably would never occur to Theo, and Chloe certainly wouldn't thank him for bringing them up. "What do you do after school? Any sports?"

"Not this time of year." The boy shifted uneasily against the railing. "Actually, I was thinking about getting an after-school job."

Luke was faintly surprised at that. "I thought they kept you pretty busy around here." Certainly the rest of the Caldwells seemed occupied with the family business.

"Guess they do." A flush touched the boy's high cheekbones. "A person wants to do something without his family once in a while. Didn't you?"

He hadn't had a choice in the matter. "I guess so. What's this 'something' you have in mind?"

Theo looked at his scuffed sneakers. "There's a job down at the yacht club. They're pretty busy just now with lots of colleges having spring break. I could work there."

Luke pictured the glistening white boats he'd seen moored at the yacht club, imagining the kind of people who owned them. "Sounds like a smart idea to me. That's the kind of place where you meet people who count."

"People who count for what?" Chloe asked.

He hadn't heard Chloe come out, but she stood a couple of feet from him. She was close enough that he could feel the anger, close enough to see the sparks. Obviously he'd made a tactical error.

"Theo and I were just talking." He heard the apologetic note in his own voice and wondered where it had come from. He didn't owe Chloe an apology for taking an interest in her kid brother, did he?

Theo slid away from the rail. "Guess I'd best see if Miranda needs any help." He vanished into the inn, leaving Luke to face the accusation in Chloe's eyes.

"You were encouraging him to take a job at the yacht club." She shot the words at him.

He closed the laptop and leaned back in the rocker, meeting her gaze with his own challenge. "I'm not sure *encouraging* is the right word. We were talking about it. Don't you want me to talk to your brother, Chloe?"

"You implied that the yacht club people were important for him to know."

He stood, setting the chair rocking behind him, and put the laptop on the table. It looked incongruous next to the lemonade and molasses cookies, reminding him that he didn't belong here.

"I told him what I thought." He frowned at her. "Unless being back here has softened your brain, you know how important it is to know the right people."

She flushed, the color painting cheeks that were already glowing with sunlight. "That's what it's like in the outside world."

"What if Theo wants to live in the 'outside world'? *You* did. Are you saying he can't make the choices you made?"

She took a step toward him, her hands curling into fists.

"Theo is too young to make choices like that. And you certainly don't have the right to advise him."

"He came to me, Chloe. And you brought me here."

"Do you think I've forgotten that?" She glanced toward the inn, then lowered her voice. "This deception was your idea, not mine. You decided on it for business reasons, not because you wanted to do me a favor."

"Maybe that's true." He wasn't going to let her get away with shifting all the responsibility onto him. "But you're the one who created the situation in the first place, remember?"

"I know." She stood very straight, fists clenched. "But that doesn't mean it's all right for you to interfere with my family. I don't want you giving Theo advice. I don't want his values to be—"

"Contaminated by mine?" Whatever fascination he'd felt in seeing Chloe stand up to him disappeared in a wave of anger. "There's nothing wrong with my values. They're realistic in the world out there—" He jerked his head toward the mainland.

"Caldwell Cove is different."

"Don't kid yourself, Chloe. This place may seem like Shangri-La, but sooner or later it will get dragged into the twenty-first century. Isn't that what you're trying to do with your Web site? Your brother might need the kind of values that lead to success."

"I don't want Theo influenced by you." Chloe threw the words at him. "If you can't accept that, then maybe you'd better leave right now."

Chapter Six

Horror at what she'd just said flooded Chloe. Was being back on the island causing her to take leave of her senses? She couldn't talk to her boss that way.

Apparently Luke felt the same. His face tightened, and his ice-blue eyes chilled her to the bone. "Is that really what you want, Chloe?" His voice was deceptively soft, but she'd heard that deadly calm before, directed at other people. Her job hung in the balance.

"I'm sorry." The words came out in a rush. "I shouldn't have said that."

But it was true. The thought came out of nowhere. She tried to reject it but she couldn't. She didn't want Theo absorbing the values that seemed so natural to Luke.

Please, Lord. The prayer also seemed to come from nowhere. *I don't know what to do here. I don't know what I want, and I certainly don't know what's best.*

"You have a right to say what you believe." He shifted his weight so that he stood an inch closer to her. He was close enough that she could feel the iron control he held over his anger. "Is that what you believe, Chloe?"

"I don't…" She stopped, took a breath, started again. "I can't mix business and family together. Maybe that's one of the reasons I like working in Chicago. Having you here, letting my people believe we're involved—it's just too hard."

She expected a withering response. Instead she felt his ire seeping away as he considered what she'd said.

"All right." He nodded, still frowning. "I guess I can understand your feelings. The question is, what are we going to do about it?"

He actually seemed to be trying to understand. Maybe he'd been as surprised by their quarrel as she had. She could breathe again.

"If we told my parents the truth…"

"No."

His sharp response told her *that,* at least, hadn't changed. He tried to manage a smile, but it didn't have much humor in it.

"That's the one thing we can't do. I have too much of my time and reputation invested in this location now. If I don't come up with a proposal, I can kiss the vice-presidency goodbye."

The way his face hardened on the last words told her he wouldn't do that. It meant too much to him—maybe more than anything else in his life, certainly more than her old-fashioned values.

"All right."

She took a deep breath, trying to find an alternative they both could live with. She'd like to feel that the two of them were on the same team. She'd always felt that—until now.

"I guess I can understand that. But I'm not going to lie to anyone. And I don't want you to give Theo any more advice." Her mother's worries about the boy flitted through her mind. She'd said she would help, but this certainly wasn't what she'd intended.

"Agreed." He clasped her hand as if they'd just sealed a deal, and his fingers were strong around hers. Their warmth swept inexorably up her arm, headed straight for her heart.

She stepped back, breaking the connection. "All right, then." She reached behind her for the door, needing to escape. "We'll leave it at that."

"Just one thing—"

Luke's voice stopped her. She turned reluctantly to look at him.

"Maybe you ought to give a little thought to what you're saying to your brother, Chloe."

She looked at him blankly. "I don't know what you mean."

"You don't want him taking on my values. But your life is an example more potent than whatever I might say to him. Isn't it?"

Chloe tried to find an answer to that question throughout another mostly sleepless night. She couldn't remember when she'd felt so torn—between Luke and her family, between the past and the future. She'd made a promise to Luke, and she'd always been taught that a promise had to be honored. Taught by her daddy, to whom honor was everything.

The future, that was what worried her the most. She turned over, trying to keep the bed from creaking in protest, and stared at the ceiling. Would Daddy say that if he knew what promise she was keeping? Moonlight filtered through the curtains, sending designs across the ceiling as the branches of the live oak swayed. When she was a child, she'd imagined whole stories taking place in those moving shadows—filled with castles and dragons and knights on horseback.

Miranda's even breathing from the other bed was oddly soothing. Miranda had made her choices, and as difficult as they'd been, she never seemed to doubt the road she was on. Chloe envied that certainty.

Where was this adventure going to end? She couldn't picture it, couldn't believe that things could ever go back the way they'd been between her and Luke, between her and her family.

Maybe that was bound to happen sometime. She could hardly expect to find happiness while working for Luke—not when that meant holding her feelings secret in her heart. As for her family—her relationship with them had changed, and she hadn't even realized it. She'd looked for her career off the island, thinking that was the only way to be her own person. She'd been tired of being just one of the crowd of Caldwells.

Now—she thought of her mother, talking to her about Theo as if she were a friend. Of the pleasure she'd found in being useful here. Of the way her experiences with Dalton Resorts had begun to translate to ideas for running the inn. Things changed, whether she wanted them to or not.

She turned again, and her restless gaze fell on the framed sampler with the words of her Bible verse embroidered on it, which was propped on her bedside table. She couldn't leave it behind in Chicago, so it had come with her.

As the words reverberated in her mind, she felt her tension begin to seep away. *Hope and a future.* She might not be able to see how God's plans were going to work out, but knowing they existed should be comfort enough. Her body relaxed, her eyelids drifting closed.

* * *

She'd meant what she said to Luke about not telling her family any lies. But as Chloe watched her father talk with Luke over coffee in the breakfast room the next morning, she wondered if she'd gone far enough. Maybe she should have specified that Luke not tell any lies, either.

"Excuse me, miss, could I have another pot of tea? This one isn't hot enough."

Chloe managed a smile for the elderly guest whose tea water was never hot enough. She didn't mind being pressed into service at breakfast—she'd done it since she was old enough to carry a tray. She *did* mind not being able to hear what Luke and her father were talking about.

Why? The question nagged at her while she brought a fresh pot of tea for table four, replenished the dish of homemade strawberry jam at table six and whisked a nearly empty breakfast casserole dish from the buffet table. Why did it bother her to see her father with Luke?

Maybe it was her fear that the two of them could never see eye-to-eye on anything. Clayton Caldwell lived by a few simple rules—rules he'd taught his sons and daughters from the day they were born. *Trust the Lord, and He will guide your ways…. Tell the truth, even if it's painful…. A man's word is his bond, and without it he has nothing.*

Her father wouldn't understand the kind of business

world Luke operated in, though he'd probably equate it
with Uncle Jeff. Luke would never understand her
father. He'd mistake her father's sense of honor for
naïveté, just as her father would mistake Luke's sense
of competition for dishonesty. No, it would be far better
if she could keep the two of them apart until this game
had ended.

Carrying the carafe of coffee, she approached their
table with a sense of determination. "Daddy, would you
like a thermos of coffee to take with you?"

"I'm not going just yet, Chloe-girl." He held out his
mug, his sharp eyes inspecting her. "Fact is, I'm not
going fishing at all today. Your momma's been pester-
ing me to take a picnic lunch, go over to Angel Isle,
check out the cottage. I'm thinking we'll do that today."

Well, at least that would get him out of Luke's
company for a while. "Sounds like a nice idea. Don't
worry about anything here. I'll keep an eye on the desk."

Luke smiled and held out his mug for a refill.
"Actually, your father invited us to go with them to
the island."

Only long years of practice kept her from dribbling
coffee onto the blue-checked tablecloth. "Don't you
have some work you want to do?"

Luke was probably longing for her to give him an
excuse to get out of it, she assured herself. He probably
had no desire to go out on the boat again.

"Not at all," he assured her blandly. "Sounds like a great idea."

She set her lips into what she hoped resembled a smile. "Fine. I'll just go help my mother get things ready."

Trying to avoid her father's gaze, she whisked herself off to the kitchen. Daddy knew his children only too well. He'd always been harder to fool than her mother— not that she'd spent a lot of time trying to fool either of them, even as a child. But she'd seen the twins try, and fail, too many times. This cozy little trip together was not a good idea.

And what had given Daddy the idea? He didn't take the morning off just to— The thought struck her with a certainty she couldn't deny.

Gran and her matchmaking.

She pressed her palms to overheated cheeks. She could just imagine the conversation.

All Chloe's young man needs is a little push to propose, Gran would say. *It's up to us to see he gets it. Chloe will be the next Caldwell bride.*

Now what was she going to do about that?

She still didn't have an answer an hour later, when she stood on the dock handing a picnic basket to Luke. He'd already been on the boat with her father when she'd come down. What had they been talking about? She tried to think of one single thing they had in common, and couldn't. Except, possibly, her.

She gave Luke a sharp look as she accepted the hand he held out, and climbed onto the *Spyhop*. "Are you sure you want to do this?" She spoke under the noise of the motor. "Daddy would understand if we begged off."

Luke looked at her questioningly. "Don't you trust me around your father, Chloe?"

She definitely should have laid down the law to Luke about her father, as she had about Theo. "It's not that." Since she didn't believe herself, she felt quite sure he didn't believe her, either. "I just thought this wouldn't be much fun for you. The water might be rougher out on the sound today."

"Then, I'll have to depend on you to keep me safe, won't I?"

His low voice teased her, and she felt a little ripple of…what? Longing for a relationship with him in which teasing spoke of affection? That was a danger-ous way to think.

Luke turned away to help her mother on board, drawing her gaze. Had he borrowed the jeans and T-shirt from one of her brothers? It certainly wasn't his usual garb. Before this trip, she'd have said he wouldn't look at ease in anything but a business suit. But he seemed perfectly at ease now, with the T-shirt stretching across broad shoulders and looking even whiter against his tanned arms.

She shouldn't be noticing that, she told herself

firmly, bending to stow the hamper in the locker and taking the jug of sweet tea her mother handed her. She should imagine Luke right back into one of his expensive suits. Maybe then she'd be able to get through this trip.

She started forward, but her mother caught her arm.

"I'll go up front with your daddy, honey." She nudged her toward Luke, smiling. "You sit back here and keep Luke company."

Matchmaking, she thought despairingly. *Oh, Gran.*

Before she could come up with a really good reason to sit forward, her father was asking Luke to cast off the lines. When she made a move to do it, Luke edged past her and leaned across to the dock.

"I've got it." He nodded toward the seat. "You sit down and be a lady of leisure this trip."

He must have watched her handle the lines the last time, because he did it perfectly, with not the slightest hesitation to show how much he disliked leaning out over the water. He even coiled the lines the way she had.

"Very nice," she murmured, when he sat down next to her. "You must have been taking lessons."

"Somebody talked me into it." He smiled, then draped his arm casually across her shoulders. "Don't forget, you have to hold on to me if I get nervous."

"Aren't you afraid I'll push you in, instead?" She wouldn't turn her head to look at him. His face was too close to hers, and she was already too aware of the weight of his arm against her.

He squeezed her shoulders. "Not a chance," he said softly in her ear. "I trust you, Chloe. You'd never let me down."

She tried not to respond to that, tried not to think that he meant anything by it. He trusted her as his assistant—that was all.

The *Spyhop* rounded the curve of the island, passing the yacht club dock. The sound stretched in front of them, waves glistening in the sunlight. A laughing gull, squawking, flew overhead, probably hoping they'd give him something for his lunch. On the horizon the islands beckoned, lush and mysterious.

She felt Luke's movement as he inhaled deeply, tilting his head back as if to take it all in.

"Beautiful," he murmured.

He turned toward her, so that she felt his breath against her cheek.

"It's really beautiful, Chloe. Thank you for bringing me here."

He hugged her, his cheek warm against hers as if they really were the couple her family believed them to be.

Chloe smelled like sunshine. Funny that he'd never noticed that before. Luke held her protectively, feeling her slim figure sway against him as her father sent the boat in a wide arc toward the island. He was enjoying this, maybe a little too much.

Enjoyment had been the last thing on his mind when her father had invited them to go along today. It had been on the tip of his tongue to say no, but Clayton Caldwell's shrewd gaze had suggested he wouldn't buy an easy excuse. And then Luke had thought of Chloe and the concerns she'd brought up the day before.

He'd been angry at first over her attitude toward his talk with her brother. After all, he hadn't approached Theo. Theo had come to him.

But he couldn't help being impressed by how much she cared about her family. Her passionate defense of them was outside his experience, and he didn't really understand it. The only thing he had to compare was his friendship with Reverend Tom and the debt he owed to the man who'd taken him off the streets and given him a future.

Well, he was determined to try his best to fit in here, for Chloe's sake. This trip gave him an excuse to look over the area and make Chloe's parents happy. Unfortunately, Chloe didn't seem to be reacting quite the way he'd hoped. She sat stiffly within the circle of his arm, as if she'd pull away at the first excuse.

He squeezed her shoulder. "Come on, Chloe." He spoke softly under the noise of the motor. "Lighten up. You're not on your way to the guillotine."

That startled her into meeting his eyes. "I'm not acting as if I am."

"Sure you are." He moved his hand, brushing her hair. It flowed like silk over his fingers. "I know you don't like the pretense, but can't we at least be friends?"

Her mouth tightened, and her eyes were very bright. "Friends, or boss and assistant?"

"Friends," he said firmly.

"Maybe being friends isn't such a good idea. When we go back to Chicago…" She stopped, and her gaze eluded his. "Well, it might cause problems."

That unsettled him. He hadn't really considered what their relationship was going to be like when they went back to the city, back to their relative positions in the company. He'd only thought about that corner office, with the vice-president title on the door.

"Don't be ridiculous." It came out more sharply than he intended. "We've always worked well together, and we always will. Nothing will change between us."

"Maybe," she said softly, looking away. "Maybe you're right."

Annoyance shot through him. All right, he hadn't thought through that part of it very well. So he couldn't go back to looking at Chloe as if she were nothing more than an efficient assistant. That wasn't necessarily a bad thing, but Chloe looked as if it were the end of the world.

He opened his mouth to tell her so, but the motor suddenly throttled back and their privacy vanished. Chloe slid to the edge of the seat, putting several inches between them.

"There it is—Angel Isle." She pointed.

"Looks pretty good, doesn't it, Chloe-girl?" Her father swung the boat toward a dock, cutting the motor so that they drifted in.

"Looks great to me." Chloe scrambled to fasten the lines. "Not a thing has changed."

"Well, that's how we like it." Her mother bustled back, pulling out the picnic hamper.

Luke got to his feet slowly. He should help her, but for the moment he could only stare at the scene spread out in front of him.

The dock anchored one edge of a wide, shallow curve of shoreline. Palmettos and moss-draped live oaks fringed a pristine, untouched sandy beach. Waves rolled in gently, rippling onto the sand like a woman shaking a tablecloth. It was as isolated and exotic as a castaway's island.

Chloe had already scurried up onto the dock, and she held out her hand to him. Whatever reservation he'd sensed in her a moment ago was gone now. Her eyes sparkled with eagerness, almost golden in the sunlight.

"Hurry up. I want to see the cottage."

He climbed out and followed her off the dock and onto the shell-strewn path, leaving her parents behind on the boat. He could already see the house, although he wouldn't call it a cottage. The building was long and low and nearly as large as the inn. Gray-shingled, with a screened porch running the length of it, it fit into the setting as if it had grown there.

"Pretty big for a cottage, isn't it?" He caught up with Chloe and took her hand.

She looked startled but she didn't pull away. "I guess. I mean, the family has always called it that. Years ago, they used to summer here. That was in the days when everyone went to the outer islands in the hot weather. But that got too difficult once they opened the inn. Now we use it for shorter visits, family reunions, that sort of thing."

He tried to visualize Angel Isle as he'd seen it from the water. It had looked virtually deserted. "Are there any other houses?"

"Others?" She went up the porch steps. "No. Just ours."

He hardly wanted to look at the idea that was forming in his mind, for fear he'd see some flaw in it.

"I suppose all this is some sort of nature preserve or something, then?" That might explain why no one else had built here.

"No, of course not."

Chloe had already hurried across the porch. Standing on tiptoe, she pulled a key from a hook at the top of the door frame, then unlocked the door. She swung it open, and he had a quick glimpse of a spacious room dominated by a massive brick fireplace.

He was more interested in answers to his questions than he was in the Caldwell cottage. "Then, why hasn't anyone else built on Angel Isle?"

"Because it belongs to us. My daddy, I mean. I thought I explained that. Grandpa split things between Daddy and Uncle Jeff." Her face clouded. "Uncle Jeff thought Daddy a fool for taking Angel Isle, when the other property was so valuable."

That must be a piece of the feud between the brothers. "So all this belongs to your father."

She nodded, then went quickly across the room and began throwing open curtains and unhooking shutters. "You want to give me a hand?"

He followed her, mind busy, excitement building as he helped her tug on a recalcitrant shutter. He'd have to find out exactly how much land there was, but there should be some way of working a deal with her father. Because he'd just found the perfect place for the next Dalton Resort hotel.

He looked at Chloe, intent on the shutter. Did she really not know what he was thinking? He wanted to shout it to her, wanted her to share his excitement, wanted to feel her encouraging him to another success.

But that was Chloe back in their other world. Here—

here he didn't know how Chloe would react if he told her. Would she be excited and happy?

For an instant he felt resentment. He wanted his old Chloe back, the faithful right hand who always anticipated his needs and backed him no matter what.

"There!" The shutter popped open and sunlight streamed into the room. It lit Chloe's skin, tangled in her hair, made her eyes shine. "Isn't that better?"

"Better," he echoed. Would it be better if he had his old Chloe back? Maybe so, but he wouldn't trade this Chloe for an instant.

Chapter Seven

What did this mean? Chloe tried not to stare at the expression on Luke's face, but she couldn't help it. He looked as if he were seeing something for the first time.

"Chloe." He said her name softly, holding out one hand toward her, palm up. Something seemed to stir in the shaft of sunlight from the window, as if the very air between them would speak.

Her breath caught. She took a step toward him, and the movement was as slow as wading through the surf. In an instant they would touch—

"How's everything look?" Her father's voice shattered the silence.

Chloe's face flooded with heat as she turned toward the door. Luke turned, too, moving away from her quickly. Was he relieved they'd been interrupted? Or maybe she'd just imagined the whole thing.

"Let me take that for you." Luke reached for the thermos her mother carried. "Can I bring anything else from the boat?"

"Not a thing." Her mother set the thermos on the table. "We're just fine." She exchanged a knowing look with Chloe's father. "You young people go on out and enjoy the day. We'll take care of things here."

"No. I mean, we'll help you." Chloe couldn't be sure, but she thought Luke's expression echoed her words.

"Nonsense." Her mother shooed them with her hands, for all the world like Gran. "Luke hasn't even seen Angel Isle yet. You show him around, honey. We'll straighten up in here, then we'll have lunch when you all get back."

They didn't seem to have much choice. Chloe headed for the door, hearing Luke's footsteps behind her. He probably regretted he'd gotten out of bed that morning.

She didn't look at him as she took the path back to the shore, but she could feel his presence as surely as if they touched. She didn't say anything. What could she say that wouldn't make this more awkward?

When they reached the stand of sea oats that marked the dunes, she heard him chuckle. The sound was a bit strained, but at least it meant he wasn't angry about her parents' machinations.

"Subtle, aren't they?" he said.

"Sorry about that." She tried for a lightness she didn't feel. "I'm afraid my grandmother recruited them to do a little matchmaking."

"I thought as much." He strode beside her on the hard-packed sand of the beach. "Don't worry about it, Chloe. If we can cope with a corporate near-takeover, we can cope with a little family matchmaking."

Her tension eased at his words, reminding her of the difficult days three years ago when Dalton Resorts's future hung in the balance. They'd all worked around the clock until the danger was over. Luke had put things back on a business basis, and that was clearly what he wanted. The moment when they'd stood looking at each other in a shaft of sunlight might never have been.

"Of course we can." That was best, she assured herself. "We're a team." That was what he'd always said, and she'd taken comfort in the sense that they were on the same side.

"Always. You're my right hand, remember?"

She nodded, matching her step to his long stride. She had to stop imagining anything was changing. She ought to be happy. That meant they'd be able to go back to normal, once this whole thing was over.

She took a deep breath, inhaling fresh salt air. She wasn't sure she knew what "normal" was any longer, or if it was something she wanted or could even live with.

Maybe she'd better concentrate on introducing this place that she loved to Luke. If he could appreciate it the way she did, that would be enough for the day.

They rounded the heel of the tiny island, and the sea breeze lifted her hair and cooled her cheeks. "Now you see why they're called the out-islands." She pointed to the horizon. "There's nothing beyond them but ocean."

Luke shielded his eyes with one hand. "It's so clear I feel as if I can see all the way to Europe—"
He turned, glancing back at the island, and she heard his quick intake of breath.

"What on earth is that?"

"Strange, isn't it." Chloe walked to the nearest uprooted pine, its trunk washed free of bark, its roots a tangled mass of bleached tendrils. She rested her hand on the massive trunk that had been scoured clean by the waves. "The power of the sea."

Luke stroked the smooth wood. "Do all these trees wash up here?" He looked down the beach, where tree after felled tree formed a bizarre landscape of twisted roots and gnarled limbs.

"Not washed up," she corrected. "They grew here, until the tide started coming in farther and knocked them down. None of the outer islands are stable on the seaward side—that's why the buildings face the sound. The ocean's taking a bite out of Angel Isle."

Luke put both palms on the trunk and hoisted

himself. He reached down, smiling an invitation. She felt herself smile in response as he took her hand in a firm clasp, lifting her up to sit next to him.

She settled on the smooth surface, trying to ignore the warmth that radiated from Luke, trying not to look at how the sun glinted on his bare arms.

"It's beautiful," he said quietly, leaning back on his hands. "Weird, but beautiful, like another world."

She'd better concentrate on the scenery, too. "That's what I've always thought. Another world." She tilted her head back, letting the breeze ruffle her hair. A pair of brown pelicans swooped low over the water, and she envied their view. "Or maybe a little piece of heaven."

"I guess you could look at it that way."

His response was noncommittal, the careful answer he'd give a business colleague if the subject of religion came up. Suddenly she wanted to push him—she wanted more.

"I've always felt closer to God here than anywhere else." She didn't bother trying to edit her words or shield her beliefs from him. "And I've always thought God must love it, too, or He wouldn't have made it so beautiful."

For a moment she thought he'd ignore her. Then he frowned.

"That sounds like something an old friend of mine would say."

"An old friend?" Was she actually about to see into his private life?

"Reverend Tom—"

He was looking out at the pelicans, but she didn't think he saw them.

"A good friend."

"Was he your minister when you were a child?" He wouldn't answer; she knew that. He never talked about his childhood.

"You could say that, I guess." His mouth tightened to a thin, unrevealing line.

"You don't look as if the thought makes you very happy."

He shot her a look that gave nothing away. "It just reminded me that I haven't been in touch with him in a long time. That's all."

"Maybe you should be."

His face tensed, and she knew she'd gone too far.

"We don't fit into each other's lives anymore."

He said it as if that ended the matter. The friend was another secret Luke didn't intend to share. If they were in the office, she wouldn't have pushed this far. But they weren't in the office.

"Would he like this place?"

Luke shrugged. "He wouldn't appreciate the potential."

For a moment she could only stare at him. "What do you mean?"

His gesture took in the strange shapes of the drowned forest. "This. Hasn't it occurred to you what a commercial draw this could be? With the right kind of promotion, people would pay to visit this."

Disappointment was an acrid taste in Chloe's mouth. A commercial draw—that was all he could see. Maybe she'd been wrong about the depths she thought he hid. Maybe he was nothing more than the surface persona— the success-driven businessman who didn't care about anything but profit.

The thought shouldn't hurt her heart as much as it did.

"Look out!"

Luke took a quick step back, holding the kitchen door for Miranda the next morning as she darted through with a steaming pot of coffee. She flashed him a smile.

"Go on back. Chloe's in there."

He wasn't actually looking for Chloe, but there didn't seem any point in trying to tell Miranda that. He'd come down this morning with the single aim of talking to Clayton Caldwell about Angel Isle.

He helped himself to coffee from the sideboard while he scanned the dining room. The large oval table where they'd sat for dinner the first night was pressed into service as a breakfast buffet. Smaller tables for guests clustered around it and overflowed into the hall and onto the porch.

Only a few guests had come down this early. Chloe's father was usually one of the earliest people down, but the chair where he always sat was empty.

Luke frowned. After their return from Angel Isle, he'd spent the rest of the day learning everything on the public record about Angel Isle. Now he was keyed up and ready to roll, but his instincts told him to proceed cautiously.

Anyone could see that money was tight for this branch of the Caldwell clan. The inn couldn't be bringing in much, and Clayton Caldwell had a lot of people depending on him. He should be glad to sell part of Angel Isle for the price Dalton Resorts would be willing to pay.

But would he? Luke frowned, swirling the coffee with his spoon. He seemed to hear again Chloe's soft voice, her Southern accent more pronounced the longer they stayed here, talking about how much the place meant to her. He was used to dealing with people who had their eyes on the bottom line. Chloe's clan was something different, and he couldn't judge how they'd react to his proposal.

He'd handled difficult negotiations before. The key was simply to find the right approach. He'd sound out Chloe's father cautiously, and when he hit on the thing that would make the man sit up and take notice, he'd know it.

He set down his cup. Where was Clayton? Maybe Chloe knew. He headed for the kitchen.

The swinging door opened on a scene of controlled chaos. Sammy was taking silverware from the dishwasher, clattering it onto a tray, while Miranda cut fruit into a bowl, interrupting herself to stir something on the stove. Chloe slid a steaming casserole from the oven. All of them were talking at once, and the teakettle whistled noisily above the din.

Retreat seemed the obvious course, but that wouldn't tell him where Chloe's father was. "Chloe?"

She looked up, cheeks red from the oven's heat. "Hand me that pot holder, will you, please? I'm about to burn myself on this."

He snatched the pot holder she indicated from its hook and slid it under the hot dish, helping her negotiate the course to the scrubbed pine table.

"Ouch." Chloe snatched her fingers away, blowing on them. "Thanks." She flashed him a smile.

"Anytime. Where…"

But Chloe had already turned to her sister. "Why does Mom keep these worn-out pot holders? It's not as if she doesn't have plenty of them. Gran makes them faster than anyone can use them."

Miranda filled a pot with coffee. "You know Mom. She hates to throw anything away."

"Chloe…" He tried again.

Before he could frame the question, Miranda had put a coffeepot in his hand. "You wouldn't mind taking that to the dining room, would you, Luke? Our mother is taking one of the cousins to a doctor's appointment in Savannah, and we're a bit shorthanded."

He caught Chloe's horrified look. Obviously it never would have occurred to her to ask him to help. But that was because Chloe knew he was more accustomed to giving orders than taking them.

"Sure, no problem." He started for the door with the coffee. "I've always wanted to be a waiter."

Miranda's green eyes sparkled with amusement. "Busboy. You're just a busboy. You have to work your way up to waiter."

He smiled back at her and pushed through the swinging door. This busboy would take the coffee in once. Then he'd find out where Clayton Caldwell was and make his escape.

When he returned to the kitchen, Chloe had taken over the fruit bowl, and Miranda and Sammy had disappeared.

"Did your crew desert you?" He set an empty coffeepot in the sink.

Chloe sliced a kiwifruit with quick, even strokes, the colorful slices falling into a pattern across the top of the bowl. "Miranda had to get Sammy ready for school. I told her I could finish."

He reached for the steaming teakettle, and she gave him a startled look.

"What are you doing?"

He shrugged. "There's an elderly woman at the table by the window who says her tea water isn't hot enough. Guess I'd better take her a refill, or I might get demoted. What comes below busboy?"

"You don't need to do that."

Chloe picked up the glass fruit bowl, and he could tell she was trying to hide embarrassment.

"I'm sorry—I mean, Miranda shouldn't have assumed you'd want to help."

"What's the matter? Don't you think I can?"

Her color heightened. "It's not what you're used to."

"Believe me, Chloe, nothing about this place is what I'm used to." He had an unexpected stab of longing. If he'd had a childhood with this kind of family… "That doesn't mean I can't pitch in and help."

"Are you sure?" Her forehead wrinkled with doubt.

He should be looking for Clayton. Funny that all of a sudden helping Chloe seemed to supercede that.

"I'm sure," he said firmly. "You take the fruit. I'll get the tea water."

He followed Chloe into the dining room, watching as she deftly tidied the buffet table. She moved from table to table, smiling as she played the gracious hostess in her jeans and a red-checked apron. She'd undoubtedly forgotten about the dab of flour on her cheek. She was adorable.

"You're the fiancé from the big city, aren't you? Chloe's beau." It was the woman who'd asked for fresh tea water, and she held out her cup expectantly.

"We're not—" He stopped. He couldn't begin to explain his relationship with Chloe to himself, so he certainly couldn't to anyone else. "Yes, ma'am." He poured the tea water. "I'm Chloe's beau."

Chloe heard that. He could tell by the way she carefully avoided looking at him as she brushed by. That avoidance annoyed him, and for a moment he wondered at himself. It was nothing, he argued mentally. He was playing a role; that was all.

He caught up with Chloe at the kitchen door, aware of a number of pairs of eyes on them. *Might as well give them something to look at,* he decided with a flicker of rebellion. As the door swung, he dropped a kiss on Chloe's cheek. Her skin smelled like peaches. He didn't want to pull away.

She stepped back, startled and wary, once they were alone in the kitchen.

"What was that for?"

"We had an audience." He nodded toward the dining room. "I was just giving them what they expected."

Chloe's golden eyes darkened. "Don't bother."

She clattered a tray onto the counter, and he had the sense that she counted to ten. But when she turned back to him, she was smiling.

"I'll be fine now. I don't need any more help."

It shouldn't bother him to be dismissed that way. After all, he hadn't wanted to help in the first place. They'd drafted him.

"Fine. Do you know where your father is?"

"Out back, with Theo." She frowned. "Why?"

"Just something I wanted to ask him." He started for the back door. He'd taken enough detours for one morning. It was time he got on with business.

Before he reached the door, it swung open. Theo charged through, barreling past Luke as if he didn't see him. The door slammed hard enough to rattle the glasses.

"Theo—" Chloe didn't get the rest of her sentence out before Theo's trajectory carried him on through the swinging door and out of the kitchen.

She looked at Luke. "What's going on with that boy?"

He would have said it looked like Theo had been having words with someone, but before he could, the door opened again. Chloe's father stalked in, limping a little, his face like a storm at sea. He looked past Luke, zeroing in on Chloe.

"Chloe, do you know anything about this notion of Theo's about working at the yacht club?"

Chloe wiped her hands on a tea towel, probably buying time. "He mentioned something about it the other day."

"You know how I feel about that. You should—" He stopped abruptly, seeming to realize he was about to say something he didn't want to say in front of Luke. "Don't know what's got into him," he muttered, and slammed back out the door.

In the silence that followed, Luke raised an eyebrow. "What was that all about?"

"Nothing," Chloe muttered, turning away from him.

He caught her wrists. "Come on, Chloe, give. What's going on between Theo and your father? Why is he so upset about the yacht club job?"

"My father just doesn't like the yacht club crowd." Her gaze clouded. "I don't really know all the reasons. He's had some bad experiences with people like that."

People like that. Wealthy people, socially prominent people. The kind of people who frequented a Dalton Resort hotel. This could be a complication.

Luke studied Chloe's averted face. She'd said she didn't know all the reasons. And it certainly didn't look as if she wanted to confide any to him.

"Seems kind of hard on Theo," he commented, wondering if that would draw her out.

That brought her troubled gaze up to meet his. "I know. I wish I'd gotten Theo to talk to me about it. Mom asked me to try and find out what was bothering him, and I didn't. I haven't been a very good big sister to him."

"Chloe, it's not your fault." His instinctive desire to

comfort her surprised him. He lifted his hand to brush the flour from her cheek. "You've only been here a few days. Let's face it, we've been pretty busy dealing with your family's matchmaking."

She smiled, her smooth skin moving against his fingers. He cupped her cheek with his palm, a wave of tenderness sweeping over him at the warm, silken feel of it. Chloe's eyes widened, and he had the sense that neither of them had taken a breath in too long.

He took a cautious step back, drawing his hand away. Convincing Chloe's father to sell him the land on Angel Isle would be difficult. Convincing himself that there could be anything between him and Chloe would be insane.

He knew what he wanted his life to be like. He'd known since he was a cold, dirty kid, standing on the outside and looking at people who had it all. He'd known he was going to be one of them someday.

Sweet little Chloe Caldwell didn't fit into that world. He knew that. So why did it leave such a bad taste in his mouth?

Chapter Eight

"What are your plans for my life, Lord?"

Chloe didn't realize she'd asked the question aloud until she heard the words echoing in the otherwise silent chapel. She glanced around. No one was there to hear her wrestle with the question that had occupied her since those moments with Luke in the kitchen that morning.

She'd forgotten, during her years in Chicago, just how difficult it was to get two minutes alone to think when her family was around. She'd also forgotten how close to God she felt in the chapel, where generations of faith permeated the very air. Her church in Chicago had dynamic preaching, wonderful music, active programming. But somehow she'd never felt quite as attuned to the Lord there as she did here in a simple wooden chapel.

She leaned forward in the pew, pressing her palms against her eyes as if she could iron away the image of Luke's face. One moment he'd been touching her, caressing her cheek, his gaze filled with what she'd thought was caring. The next moment he'd moved away, face shuttered, closing her out. She felt as if the prize had been within her grasp and she'd stumbled, losing it.

What happened, Lord? Her feelings for Luke must have been written all over her face. He must have seen.

Maybe that was the answer. He'd seen, and he'd backed away. He didn't want to be involved with her.

She took a deep breath and leaned back, her hands dropping to her lap. If that was what he felt, she'd live with it. After all, that was what she'd been doing all these years. Only since they'd come to the island, since they'd embarked on this ridiculous venture, had she begun to hope for more.

The afternoon sun slanted through the old stained-glass windows, tinting her skin with rose and green where the light fell on her. She let her gaze move from window to window, drawing comfort from each—Jesus with the blind beggar, Jesus with the children, the Good Shepherd, and her own favorite, Jesus walking on the water. The glass waves reminded her of the sound, whipped by the wind. She took a deep breath, feeling the peace she'd longed for begin to seep into her.

Then she looked at the thing she'd been avoiding since she walked into the chapel—the empty shelf behind the pulpit where Chloe's dolphin had once stood. Strange, that the bare space seemed so wrong to her. She'd never even seen the dolphin. It had disappeared before she was born, but still she felt its loss.

Poor Gran. The chance of recovering it was about as slim as the chance that Chloe would find a happy ending with Luke.

She got up slowly, not sure she'd found an answer but comforted nonetheless. It was time she got back to the inn. Her Web site had gone up that morning, and she wanted to see if there'd been any response. And she had some advertising ideas she wanted to talk to her mother about. As long as she was here, she may as well put her resort expertise to good use.

She was pulling the church door closed behind her, when she heard his step on the walk, recognizing it as surely as if she saw him. She took a steadying breath and turned.

"Luke. What are you doing here?"

He gestured toward the rental car that was pulled up to the curb, and she realized he wore chinos with a short-sleeve dress shirt, his uniform on the rare casual day at the office.

"I'm going to Beaufort to take care of a few things. Do you want to go with me?"

Spend the next few hours alone with him, when her feelings were rubbed raw? She didn't think so. "I'm not dressed for that."

He shook his head impatiently. "You look fine. Come with me. I want to talk to you."

His tone was the one he used at corporate headquarters, the one that carried the assumption of obedience. She wavered. If she went along, she could point out some other hotel site possibilities she'd been thinking about.

Then she saw her grandmother hurrying toward them from her house. "Gran?" She took a few steps to meet her. "Is something wrong?"

Gran grasped both her hands. "You're needed at home, Chloe Elizabeth. Theo has run off."

"Run off?" Business was banished from her mind. "Why?" Well, she knew the answer to that question, didn't she—the quarrel with Daddy. "What makes you think he's run away?"

"He wasn't in school today. Sammy came home without him. Some of his things are gone, and his boat is missing. Your mama's worried half to death. I think you'd best get looking for him."

Chloe turned to Luke. "Did you know about this?"

His face tightened as if she'd accused him of something. "I heard some of it. Your father didn't seem upset. He said Theo was old enough to look out for himself, and he'd come home when he was ready." Luke shifted impatiently. "I have to get on the road."

Her gaze shifted from Luke to her grandmother. They each looked back with the calm assurance that she'd do what they wanted, which was impossible.

She realized suddenly that she was seeing with the clarity she'd sought in the quiet chapel. Being back on the island brought things into focus. She was caught between wanting Luke's approval and wanting her family's respect. She certainly wasn't going to have both, and if the truth came out about their charade, she'd probably end up with neither.

But in this situation, at least, her choice was clear.

"I'll take the *Spyhop* out and look for him, Gran." She kissed her grandmother's soft cheek. "Don't you worry about a thing. I'll find him."

She didn't look at Luke, because she didn't want to see the irritation she knew would be written on his face.

Why on earth was he doing this? Luke cast off the line, then grabbed the rail of the *Spyhop* and slid into the seat nearest Chloe, as she eased the boat away from the dock. He should be on his way to Beaufort right now to fax documents to the legal department, not setting off on a wild-goose chase.

"Are you sure you know how to do this?" Chloe looked small and vulnerable behind the wheel.

She flashed him a smile. "I've been doing it since I was big enough to hold the tiller." She jerked her head toward the locker. "You might want to get a couple of slickers out, though. Those clouds look like they're working up to some rain."

He made his way cautiously to the locker. He'd had it all figured out. He'd take Chloe along on the trip to the county seat, he'd tell her what he was doing and he'd parcel out some of the work to her. It would be exactly as if they were back in the office. That would get the situation back to normal between them. It would eliminate the possibility of any more moments like the one when he'd cupped her cheek in his hand and wanted to hold her forever.

Instead of taking the rational course, he'd given in to the expectation in her grandmother's face. Of course, Chloe's beau would go along with her to find Theo. Gran couldn't imagine anything else.

So he'd found himself agreeing, and he still didn't quite know why that was. He didn't ordinarily have trouble saying no in response to other people's expectations. Gran Caldwell would be a force to reckon with in the business world, if she decided to embark on a career.

He found two yellow slickers, pulled them out and moved cautiously back to Chloe. "These okay?" He had to shout over the roar of the motor.

"Fine." Chloe grabbed one of the slickers and struggled to put it on while holding the wheel. It flapped in the stiff breeze.

"Let me." He caught the sleeve, holding it while Chloe shoved her arm into it, then pulling it into place. He practically had his arms around her. He gritted his teeth. So much for that resolution.

"Thanks."

She turned the wheel expertly, sending them in a wide arc around the end of the island. Again he felt that sense of surprise at her competence.

Or did he mean admiration? He'd never pictured Chloe like this, but she was completely at home driving the speeding boat, the wind ruffling her hair and making her cheeks glow.

"Do you know where he's gone?" He braced himself with a hand on the rail as they made the turn toward the sound.

She nodded, frowning. "I think so. I hope so. Where we all tend to go when we're in trouble. Angel Isle."

"If that's the case, why are we going after him? Why not just let him come home on his own?"

He still didn't quite get this. When he was Theo's age, he'd already been virtually on his own for years. Nobody would have come looking for him if he disappeared, unless a foster parent decided to report him to the cops.

"Because my grandmother's worried. And my mother."

"And because you think you let Theo down."

Chloe frowned across the sound. "I guess."

He followed the direction of her gaze and frowned, too. No sunlight on sparkling waves today. Sullen gray water greeted him, and the wind whipped up whitecaps. A hazy mist hung between them and the islands. He pulled the slicker on.

"I suppose it won't do any good to tell you you're not responsible for him."

She shook her head. "He's my brother."

That obviously ended it, as far as Chloe was concerned. She accelerated, sending the boat rocketing across the waves, and his stomach lurched as each wave hit. Maybe the cold spray in his face would help keep him from getting sick. He held on and hoped.

An eternity later, Chloe eased back on the throttle. Luke peered toward the dock on Angel Isle. "I don't see his boat."

"Doesn't mean he's not here." Chloe pulled the *Spyhop* into position at the dock. "He might have beached his boat along the south end. That's what I did, when I ran away."

"You?" He swung the rope around the post, faintly surprised at how familiar the movement felt already. "I can't imagine you running away, Chloe."

She turned off the ignition. "I was about twelve. It's a terrible age—not quite anything. I thought Daniel and

David had been picking on me, nobody was sympathetic, I was lost in the crowd—you know, usual twelve-year-old angst."

"So you ran away to the island." Chloe would never understand the reasons *he'd* had for running away. They'd had nothing to do with teasing big brothers. His stomach tightened. They'd been ugly reasons, some of them.

"I even packed a lunch." She climbed up to the dock. "I wonder if Theo thought of that." Her mouth tightened, as if she pictured Theo lost, cold, hungry.

He climbed up beside her. "What happened? Did you get tired of it and go home?" Maybe talking about that childhood adventure would keep her from obsessing about Theo.

"Not exactly." She stopped, pushing the hood of her slicker back as she looked up at him. "I told you I always felt close to God here. This was a good place to communicate with Him. By the time I'd tried to listen to what He wanted, I knew I had to go home."

She didn't seem to expect any comment to that. She just turned and walked quickly toward the cottage.

He followed, trying unsuccessfully not to think about her words. Had he ever had that kind of reliance on God's wishes, even when he was with Reverend Tom? He didn't think so. He'd always, even at the worst of times, known what he wanted for his life. He hadn't questioned those goals.

He didn't intend to start now.

Halfway to the cottage, the rain that had been threatening arrived. Chloe jerked her hood up and bent into the wind. "Come on. Hurry."

He jogged after her, clutching the hood that the wind tried to rip from his head. This was no spring shower. The rain didn't come down in drops, it came in waves, as if someone were emptying buckets of it. The wind tore across the island, shrieking in his ears. It bent palmettos and whipped Spanish moss into a wild dance.

They pounded up the steps, and Chloe wrestled with the knob. In an instant they were inside. He slammed the door and could hardly believe the sudden silence with the storm locked outside.

"Nasty." He looked at the rain, pounding against the windows as if it wanted to break in.

Chloe shrugged out of her slicker. "Typical. It won't last too long, but we're stuck here until it eases up." She took a couple of steps into the room. "Theo? Theo, are you here?"

Nothing answered her but the clatter of rain and the howl of wind.

Luke hung their wet slickers on the pegs by the door. He looked around the large room so that he wouldn't look at Chloe, standing there with her hair tumbling in her face and a lost look in her eyes.

"This is nice," he said. He might have said home-like, except that he'd never known a home like this. He'd seen it the last time they came to the island, but he'd been so preoccupied with his idea that he'd barely noticed the surroundings.

A brick fireplace dominated one wall, and hooked rugs brightened the wide, weathered floorboards. Worn, overstuffed chairs and a couch seemed to invite him to sit. The bookcases under the windows overflowed with everything from children's books to a fat old encyclopedia.

"Yes, it is." Chloe's reply sounded absent.

She obviously still worried about her brother, and he was suddenly ashamed. He knew why he wanted to distract her. Not because it would make her feel better, but because it would make him feel better. He didn't want to deal with her emotions.

He crossed to her, reaching out to take both her hands in his. "Chloe, it'll be all right."

Her eyes were bright with unshed tears. "I just want to find him."

"I know." His fingers moved to caress her hands almost without his conscious intent. The pulse in her wrist beat against his skin. He wanted to tell her Theo would be fine, but he couldn't say anything. All he could do was look at her and long to hold her in his arms.

Chloe looked on this place as a sanctuary, but it was

dangerous to him. It made him too aware of how he'd closed himself off to God. Of how he'd tried to close himself off to Chloe. Neither of those efforts was working.

Chloe's heart pounded somewhere in her throat, so that she couldn't speak if she wanted to. Not that she did. She just wanted to stand there with Luke's hands enclosing hers and watch the play of emotions in the deep blue of his eyes.

Luke released her hands as carefully as if they were made of glass. He took a step back and cleared his throat.

"Chilly in here. You mind if I start a fire?"

So that was it. She tried to swallow her disappointment. "I'll do it."

But he was already halfway to the fireplace. "I might be a city slicker, Chloe, but I know how to light a fire."

That left her nothing to do but try to forget what he'd made her feel. Or, more to the point, keep him from knowing what she felt.

Her throat tightened. She'd thought she could be content with the status quo, but that didn't work any longer. She knew now what she should have faced a long time ago. If he couldn't care for her, she couldn't go on working for him. She'd be better off making a clean break as soon as possible and getting on with her life.

The future Gran insisted God had for her might well be here. Maybe she'd had to go away to get the experience that would make her valuable to the family.

Flames licked upward from the crumpled paper Luke had lit, quickly catching the dry pine needles from the basket on the hearth. The chill that had permeated the large room retreated.

She cleared her throat. "Would you like coffee? I can put some on."

"No." He nodded toward the couch. "Come and sit down, and stop worrying. Your father's right. Theo's old enough to take care of himself."

She moved reluctantly to sit, curling into the corner of the worn couch and pulling one of Gran's needlepoint pillows into her lap. Hugging it was vaguely comforting, like hugging Gran.

"I guess he is. But he'll always be the baby as far as I'm concerned. I'll always feel responsible."

Luke put a piece of split wood in the fireplace with as much concentration as he'd give to an annual report. The glow from the fire lit his profile, touching the frowning dark brows, highlighting his high cheekbones and determined jaw.

"I wouldn't know about that. I didn't have any brothers or sisters."

Before she could respond, he stood, shrugging as if shaking off the thought. For an instant she imagined he meant to come and sit next to her. Then he propped his elbow on the mantel, leaning against it and looking down into the flames.

"That must have been different, growing up an only child." She tried to imagine it. "Believe me, there were plenty of times when I could have done without the horde of Caldwell kids. Counting my cousins, there were seven of us, and that often seemed a few too many."

"Why? I thought your family was picture perfect, Chloe Elizabeth."

She couldn't tell whether that was mockery in his voice or not, and she hugged the pillow a little tighter. "I guess I felt lost in the crowd. People would say, 'Now, which one are you?' as if I didn't have any identity of my own."

Some emotion she couldn't interpret seemed to darken his eyes. "That's nonsense." His voice roughened. "They all love you, Chloe. Even I can see that."

Tears stung, and she blinked rapidly. "I've let them down. I should have done something about Theo, and I didn't." She bit her lip, trying to keep the tears from spilling over. "This is my fault."

"No, it's not." Luke shoved himself away from the mantel as if it took an effort. Two strides brought him across the hooked rug to stand in front of her. His body blocked out the light from the fire. "It's not your fault."

She shook her head, feeling the tears hot on her cheeks. "You don't understand."

"I understand that you're a good person," he said. "I understand that you're beating yourself up over something that's not your fault."

"It is my fault." She dashed away the tears impatiently. "Theo looked up to me the same way I looked up to the twins. I had a responsibility."

"That's who you are, isn't it, Chloe."

He sounded almost angry, as if she'd given the wrong answer to a question.

"Like it or not, you're a Caldwell. Everything you are is tied up with family."

"What's wrong with that?" Her own anger flared.

"Nothing. Everything."

Before she could guess what he was about, he grasped her hands and drew her upright. Gran's pillow tumbled to the floor.

"You're Chloe Elizabeth Caldwell." His voice had gentled, and his hands were warm and strong on her wrists. "I'm just figuring out who that is, after all this time."

She looked up at him and her breath caught. He was too close—his gaze on her face was too steady. If she let herself look into the depths of his eyes, she'd get lost and never find her way out. But she couldn't stop.

His hand lifted, very slowly, and he touched her cheek the way he had that morning. But this time he didn't pull away. She swayed toward him, as if caught in the tide.

His touch moved across her cheek gently, but it left heat in its wake. His fingers slid into her hair, tangling there. And then his lips found hers.

She couldn't move, couldn't think. She didn't need to think.

She slid her arms around him, feeling the warmth of his skin through the smooth cotton of his shirt. His arms were strong and protective, and he held her as if he'd never let go.

"Chloe." He breathed her name against her lips, then kissed her again.

This was the moment she'd dreamed about for years. The words pressed against her lips, demanding to be spoken. She couldn't fool herself any longer about her feelings. She loved him. She had to tell him she loved him—

The door crashed open, sending a flood of wind and water into the room.

Chapter Nine

Luke suddenly stood a foot away from her, and Chloe wasn't quite sure how that had happened. She was cold, either from the blast of wet air or the fact that she was no longer held in his embrace.

Theo halted on the doorstep, eyes wide, hair dripping. Then he started to leave.

Chloe's heart clenched at the thought of losing him again. She flew across the room, reaching him before he could pull the door shut. "No, Theo." She grabbed his arm, and his sweatshirt was soaked. "Get in here. Aren't you wet enough already?"

She didn't intend to sound scolding, but the response seemed natural, as if her mother's voice echoed in her head.

"Sorry." She hugged him quickly, and he felt stiff and

cold in her arms. "I'm just so relieved to see you. You scared us half to death. Where have you been?"

Theo shrugged out of her hug, but he let her pull him into the room. "Around. Can't a man be by himself in this family for a minute or two without everybody getting involved?"

She laughed a little shakily. "Funny. I was just saying the same thing myself. Sometimes you get overwhelmed with Caldwells, don't you."

She longed to hold him, but contented herself with brushing the wet hair out of his eyes.

He jerked away from her hand. "It's not the same. You're not the baby."

Be careful. Somehow she had to get through to him, convince him to go home. But she was weighted down by the sense of having failed him already.

She heard Luke's step behind her, and his hand brushed hers with a kind of wordless sympathy. "Why don't you get rid of those wet clothes. None of us will be going anywhere until the weather improves."

Theo seemed to look at that suggestion from every angle, his eyes wary. Then he nodded and yanked off the wet sweatshirt, letting it drop to the floor. A shiver ran through him. He seemed so young and vulnerable, standing there in his T-shirt and jeans.

"Theo—"

Theo shot her a glare that stopped her words. Theo

wasn't the sweet little baby she'd rocked or the cuddly toddler who'd snuggled close to her for a story. He'd turned into a gangly teenager, hovering on the line between boyhood and manhood. She longed to help him, longed to erase the disappointment hiding behind the bravado in his eyes, but she feared that she couldn't.

She had to try. "We were worried about you. Everyone was. That's natural, isn't it?"

She sensed Luke standing next to her, and it took an effort not to look at him. This wasn't his concern. This was Caldwell family business.

"I'm not a little kid anymore." Theo stalked across to the fireplace and kicked at the fire, sending a shower of sparks upward. "I don't need people telling me what to do. I can decide that for myself. You did."

She battled to keep her voice level. "I was a little older than you."

"You left." He threw the words at her. "You made your life somewhere else, where nobody tells you what to do. So don't you tell me."

Pain unfurled, closing her throat. She wanted to say something. But what could she tell him? He'd already decided she didn't have the right. "Theo…"

Luke's hands closed on her shoulders. "Chloe." His voice was low. "Didn't you say something about coffee?"

She knew her pain was written in her eyes. "I don't have time for that now."

"Yes, you do." His grasp tightened, insisting on her attention. "Go on, now. Make us some coffee. We'll all feel better when we have something hot inside us."

Leave me alone with him. She could hear the words he didn't speak. *Let me try.*

When did she start hearing the things he didn't say aloud? She wanted to argue, but he couldn't do any worse than she seemed to be doing.

"All right. I'll have it ready in a few minutes." She tried sending him an unspoken message of her own. *Be careful. Be gentle with him.*

He nodded as if he understood, and squeezed her shoulders reassuringly. "Go ahead. We'll be fine."

Theo stood at the fireplace, his thin figure outlined against its glow. His weight hadn't caught up to his height yet, and the vulnerable curve of his neck made her heart ache. She blinked back the tears that stung her eyes and headed for the kitchen.

Once safely out of Theo's sight, she didn't have to hide her anguish. She closed the door, then leaned back against it. *Oh, Lord, what am I going to do?*

Was she pleading for answers about Theo? Or answers about Luke? She didn't seem to know. She pressed her hands against her cheeks. They still felt hot, as if Luke's kisses had left a permanent mark.

No. She pushed herself away from the door, reaching for the coffeepot. She couldn't think about Luke, about what his kisses meant, not now. If she started, she'd be overwhelmed, and right now she had to concentrate on Theo's problems. She'd already failed him once, and she couldn't do it again.

She put heavy white mugs on a battered tin tray, then stood holding it for a moment, sending up another prayer. *Please, Lord. Give me the words.*

Rain spattered against the kitchen window, reminding her of the tears she was determined not to shed. Theo was her brother. The responsibility was hers. She didn't expect any help from Luke.

She took a deep breath and started to push the door open. Then she heard Luke's voice and froze.

"…just don't think running away is the answer."

"You wouldn't say that if you knew anything about it." Theo sounded as stubborn as their father. "Guess you probably never had to run away in your life."

"Never?"

Luke's echo had an odd sound—one that would have warned her off in an instant. She held her breath. Should she go in? Or was it better to let whatever was happening between them run its course?

"I ran away more times than I can count—"
Luke's voice had gone flat, and she had the impression he forced the words out.

"And I didn't have a place like this to run to, I can tell you."

"But I thought—"

"You thought I was born with a silver spoon in my mouth. Thought there was nothing in my life to run away from. Wrong on both counts."

She couldn't see him from where she stood with the door half open between them, and she wanted to. She wanted to know why he'd said things to Theo that he hadn't said to her in six years.

"Tell me this, Theo." Luke's voice had firmed. "Did running away make the problem disappear?"

"Guess not." Theo's response was a sulky mumble.

"Most times it doesn't. Here's something I learned the hard way. A man doesn't run away. A man stays and faces trouble, no matter what it is. Running away— that's kid stuff."

Chloe clutched the tray, waiting for Theo to flare up at him or to run out the door. He did neither. She counted the seconds until she heard his long intake of breath.

"Guess maybe it's time I went home and talked to my daddy about this."

She pushed the door a little farther. She could see Luke's grave expression as he put his hand on Theo's shoulder.

"I think that would be a good idea," he said.

Chloe blinked rapidly as she tried to swallow the lump in her throat. Luke had done what she hadn't been able to do. He'd shown an insight she'd never have believed possible from him.

In fact, she still didn't believe it—not from the Luke Hunter she knew back at corporate headquarters. This was a different Luke Hunter. Maybe, given the man he'd shown her since they'd been on the island, she could even believe his kisses meant something.

She pushed the door the rest of the way open and carried the tray to the coffee table. "Coffee is ready now. Anyone want some?"

Theo stood, squaring his shoulders. "It's starting to clear some." He nodded toward the windows. "We ought to be getting home."

"Maybe so," she said, trying not to let emotion show in her tone.

She looked beyond her brother to Luke, knowing that everything in her heart must be clear in her eyes. He met her gaze with a look of perfect understanding.

Her breath stopped. They knew each other. They looked into the depths of each other's souls, and they understood each other. Whatever relationship they'd had in the past, it was transformed now beyond all recognition. There was no going back.

"There's my daddy."

Luke could hear the tension in Theo's voice as they

approached the dock in front of the inn. He put a steadying hand on the boy's shoulder.

Chloe pulled back on the throttle, and the boat bounced over the waves. The setting sun touched her hair with gold as it painted the horizon in shades of crimson and orange.

"Red sky at night, sailor's delight." She nodded toward the sky. "Looks like it will be a good day tomorrow."

She was as tense as her little brother, he decided. She just hid it a little better. All three of them watched her father's spare figure climb to the dock from the small boat and stand waiting.

Theo shot Luke an anguished look. "You…you're not going anyplace now, are you?"

Actually, he'd been planning to do a quick disappearing act. The Caldwell family problems were none of his business, and he certainly couldn't pose as an authority on what families were supposed to be.

But Theo seemed to need him, and Chloe was looking at him with perfect confidence that he wouldn't desert them. So he guessed he was staying.

Chloe eased the boat into position, then tossed a line to her father. He wrapped it without a word. There was a moment of awkward stillness. Then Luke pushed the boy gently toward the dock. They might as well get this over with.

The kid's tension was riding him now. He knew what several foster fathers had done to him for running away.

He couldn't begin to guess how Chloe's father would react, but the next few minutes were bound to be painful.

Clayton Caldwell stood for an instant, his strong face impassive, looking at his son. Then he reached out and swept the boy into his arms. Theo went with a choked sob and clung to him as if holding to a rock in a storm.

Luke's throat went ridiculously dry. He cleared it, then held out his hand to Chloe. "Maybe we should go up to the house."

An errant tear sparkled on her cheek, and Chloe brushed it away, nodding.

But as they climbed out onto the dock, Chloe's father put out a hand. "No. Stay." He looked from them to Theo. "I've got some explaining to do. You two went after your brother. I expect you've got a right to hear what I have to say."

"Daddy…" Chloe began to protest, but at her father's look she fell silent.

Clayton held his son at arm's length, hands on the boy's shoulders. "I was wrong, son. I shouldn't have told you no without explaining the whole thing. Reckon I've got a good reason to feel like I do about that yacht club crowd, but you've got a right to know why."

Luke felt Chloe shift uneasily. He reached out to put his arm around her waist, drawing her close to his side.

She looked startled for an instant, then leaned against him. He shouldn't hold her, he told himself, but Chloe probably needed a little support about now. It was the least he could do. The evening breeze fluttered her hair against his cheek.

Clayton leaned against a post, his bad leg extended stiffly, and stared down at the worn planks beneath his feet. "I was just about your age, boy, the summer it started. Lines between islanders and summer people were even stricter then. They didn't associate with us, and we stayed clear of them except for working. I figured that was okay, until I met Emily."

"Emily?" Chloe sounded startled, maybe even confused. Apparently she'd never heard this story before, either.

"Emily Brandeis." The lines in Clayton's face deepened. "Wealthy folks, here for the summer. Kind of people who wouldn't talk to islanders, 'cept to give an order. But Emily was different." His expression softened suddenly, giving the impression of a much younger man.

"First love," Chloe said gently.

He nodded. "Guess so. I was crazy about her, and her about me, I thought. Trouble was, my brother liked her, too."

Could this possibly be the cause of the rift between the brothers? Luke would have expected a quarrel over a summer love to heal long ago, but clearly Clayton had more to say.

"We fought about it. Seems like we fought about everything that summer. Maybe I was getting tired of pulling Jefferson out of trouble all the time. Anyway, we had to keep it a secret, seeing Emily, or there'd have been trouble." He took a deep breath.

Luke felt Chloe tense. Did she suspect what was coming? He sensed the hurt radiating from her, and he tightened his arm around her, feeling a ridiculous need to protect her from pain.

"Emily was…" He paused, mouth softening a little. "She was different from anyone I'd ever known, or Jeff had known, for that matter. Seemed like she had everything, but she loved it here, loved the island, especially loved Chloe's dolphin in the chapel. Said she'd like to take it home with her, to remind her of that summer."

"You didn't." Chloe's voice rang with absolute certainty.

"No, sugar, I didn't take the dolphin. I wouldn't." His jaw hardened. "There was a party one night, toward the end of summer, out on Angel Isle. Emily went with me. Jeff was there a while, then gone, but I didn't miss him. I had Emily. Then Emily's daddy showed up with some of his friends."

"What happened?" Theo's face was white. Maybe he knew the answer, too.

"Pushed me around pretty good. I fell." He patted his leg. "That's how I got this stiff leg. Broke in a couple of places, and it never did heal right." He shrugged. "I never saw Emily again. And the next day the dolphin was missing."

Chloe sounded shocked. "I never knew that was when you hurt your leg. But Uncle Jefferson wouldn't have taken the dolphin, would he?"

Her father looked tired. "I didn't want to think so, either, but the dolphin was gone. And I know it was Jefferson who told her father about Emily and me. He'd do anything to get on the good side of those people. Anything." He touched his leg again. "Never, ever said he was sorry."

Chloe slipped out of his grasp, going to put a comforting hand on her father's arm. "Did you ever talk to him about it?"

Clayton shoved himself away from the post. "I spent my life covering up for things Jeff did, even taking the blame when I had to. I was the older one—I figured it was my job. But that night was the last straw. Jefferson picked his life for himself. He'd say he's got it all—the business, the big house. What I think doesn't matter to him."

"But, Daddy—"

"Leave it, Chloe-girl." He shook his head. "Point is, nothing good has ever come to this family from that yacht club crowd. Look at your sister. If Miranda hadn't been working there, she never would have run off and married the wrong man." He focused on Theo. "But it's your decision, boy. If you figure you're old enough to work there, then you must be old enough to handle it. I leave it up to you."

Theo seemed to grow an inch or two. "Thank you, Daddy."

"Guess we'd best go tell your mother and Gran you're all right." Clayton put his hand on his son's shoulder, and together they started up toward the house.

Luke stood with Chloe, watching them go, and his throat hurt with longing. Longing for—what? He'd never known a father. How could he feel homesick for something he'd never had?

He tried to shake off the feeling. "Looks like they're going to be all right."

"Yes." Chloe's voice was soft, and she leaned against him without prompting. "Thank you, Luke."

He shouldn't be enjoying this so much. "For what? I didn't do anything."

"You made Theo see, when I couldn't. You helped me bring him home—"

Her hair brushed his cheek as she tilted her head to look up at him. Something so intense that it frightened him shone in her eyes.

"You talked to him from your heart."

"Most people would deny I even have one."

Her smile trembled on the edge of tears. "Most people would be wrong. Most people haven't seen the Luke Hunter I've seen since we've been here on the island."

It came to him then. He cared about her. He cared about Chloe Caldwell, with a longing that twisted his heart.

He'd told himself that she couldn't ever be right for him. That she couldn't be the woman he needed by his side to get where he wanted to go.

Now he looked at the truth, and it didn't give him any comfort. The truth was, he wasn't the right man for her. He knew without asking what kind of man Chloe Caldwell needed—a man who'd put faith and family before anything else.

He couldn't be that man. He never would be, and it hurt.

"Are you sure you don't mind picking up Miranda?" Chloe glanced at him from the passenger side of the rental car the next day, her expression a little wary.

"Of course not." He heard the edge in his voice and wanted to bite his tongue. No wonder Chloe looked wary. He been acting like a bear with a sore paw all day. He had to put some distance between Chloe and himself. Those moments when he'd held her, kissed her—that had been a mistake. He knew that, even if she didn't.

He'd intended this trip to the county seat to be the moment he told her about Angel Isle and enlisted her help. It was past time. He couldn't keep pretending to be interested in all the other sites she pointed out, when he'd already given Dalton his enthusiastic endorsement of Angel Isle.

But somehow the moment had never seemed right, and the words remained unsaid. Maybe the truth was that he doubted his ability to get Chloe on his side over this.

She still looked at him doubtfully.

"It's fine." He forced some warmth into his tone as he turned onto the main street of Beaufort. "Just give me directions."

"Down another block or two, on the right." She frowned. "Sorry the traffic is so bad. Beaufort's a visitor magnet this time of year."

"I can see why." Quaint shops and restaurants lined the waterfront; boats moved up and down the channel. Farther down the street he could see a row of graceful antebellum mansions, lawns abloom with azaleas. "What's the name of the place we're looking for?"

"Sonlight Center. Son with an *O*. It's a mission, really. Miranda volunteers there one day a week."

"What kind of mission?" Something tightened inside him.

"Youth-oriented." Chloe leaned forward, looking for the sign. "They run after-school programs. And in the summer they bring city kids out here, give them a taste of low-country life." She turned toward him, silky hair swinging across her cheek, eyes serious. "You wouldn't believe the kind of lives some of those kids come from."

Wouldn't I, Chloe? Tension skittered along his nerves. *Wouldn't I?*

Luckily Chloe spotted the place before he had to answer. "There. There's a parking space right in front."

He pulled to the curb.

When he didn't turn off the engine, she raised her eyebrows.

"Don't you want to come in with me?"

No, he didn't. But he probably couldn't avoid it. He switched off the ignition with a sense of fatality. He was about to be reminded of things he'd rather forget.

And it was every bit as bad as he had thought it would be. No quick escape. Miranda insisted on showing them everything, from the cramped offices to the after-school tutoring sessions to the gym.

Sneakers squeaked on the polished floor, shouts echoed from the ceiling. A gang of boys elbowed one another for the ball. It bounced toward him, and he grabbed it automatically, then fed it back to the lean, gray-haired man whose whistle tangled with the cross around his neck.

"Thanks." He gave them a friendly wave, then charged down the court.

"That's Pastor Mike." Affection filled Miranda's

voice. "He still thinks he's young enough to keep up with the boys."

Like the Rev. An emotion he didn't want to identify pooled in Luke's stomach. Guilt, was that what it was?

He kept the smile pinned to his face through sheer willpower. He'd been one of those kids once—edgy, angry, taking his aggression out on the basketball court instead of the street, because one man had cared enough to try to reach him.

He took a breath, trying to still the tumult inside him. He wasn't that boy now. He hadn't been for a long time.

Coming here had been a mistake. Coming to Chloe's island had been a mistake. The place and the people confused him. They reminded him of the past he wanted to forget, and at the same time made him long for a future he could never have.

Chapter Ten

"All right, Chloe Elizabeth." Miranda turned from the dishwasher where she was stacking the breakfast dishes the next morning. "Out with it. What's going on between you and your sweetheart?"

Chloe tried to keep her face impassive as she put down the coffeepot she'd just carried in from the dining room. "Nothing's going on. What do you mean?"

"Don't tell me that, sugar, 'cause I don't believe it." Miranda leaned back against the counter. "You haven't been gone long enough to learn how to fool me. I can tell something's wrong. Something's been wrong."

"Nothing's wrong." *Nothing except that when we were on Angel Isle looking for Theo, he kissed me as I'd never been kissed before. He made me feel as if he could love me. And then he turned it all off as if it had never been.*

But she couldn't say any of that to Miranda, no matter how much she might long to confide in her sister. "Your imagination's working overtime."

Miranda looked at her steadily. "I don't think so. That night you brought Theo home, you walked in here looking...transformed." Her voice softened on the word, her face suddenly misty, as if remembering. "But yesterday Luke went off to Savannah by himself, and you've been moping around like all the sunshine went out of your life."

Transformed. The word echoed in her heart. Maybe she had been, for a short time, but it hadn't lasted. Luke had put a wall between them. And she couldn't even count on leaving in a few days, as she'd expected. He'd said the proposal for Dalton wasn't ready yet, and insisted they stay longer. Her family was too happy to have them home to probe her reasons.

"Miranda..." She wanted to say something that would put her sister off the track, but she couldn't, not when Miranda looked at her with truth and expectation in her green eyes. "I can't talk about it, okay? We just have to work it out ourselves." *Or not.*

Miranda's expression dissolved into sympathy, and she gave Chloe a quick hug. "Oh, honey, I'm sorry I poked my nose in. But if you want to talk, you know I'm here."

"I know." Chloe hugged her back, eyes filling with tears. She'd like nothing better than to confide in her sister, but the promise she hadn't wanted to make held her fast. "I will."

"Well." Miranda wiped her eyes with the back of her hand. "Enough of this foolishness. We've got to get the food packed up to take over to Gran's, or Mom will regret leaving us in charge of it."

"Right. I just hope she's keeping Gran from doing too much. If anyone can, it's Mom."

She busied herself putting ice in the cooler, relieved that the noise she was making meant she didn't have to talk.

The situation with Luke was too difficult to discuss. His withdrawal could mean only one thing—that he regretted what had happened between them.

She'd told herself that a hundred times over, but it still cut her heart into pieces. She frowned at the blueberry pies she was loading into the pie carrier. She didn't have a choice in the matter. Luke had made his decision clear without saying a word. Now all she could do was try to stay as detached as he did.

If she could. She took a deep breath. She had to. And that would make it much easier to tell him. Another little sliver of her heart seemed to break off. Like it or not, her mind was made up. Her days as Luke Hunter's right hand were numbered. She wasn't going back to Chicago with him.

"The way you're frowning, sugar, anyone would think you hated blueberry pies."

Miranda's teasing drawl roused her, and she managed a smile.

"Just wondering if these will be enough. Putting the new roof on Gran's house is going to be hungry work."

"I've been hiding a chocolate cake in the pantry," Miranda said. "Is Luke going along today?"

Chloe's heart clenched. Luke had to have heard the rest of the family talking about the big workday to put the roof on, but he'd surely make an excuse.

"I think he has some work to do today."

The words had barely left her mouth when she heard a clatter of feet in the hallway, announcing her brothers' arrival. "Don't get out of here without carrying something," she called, only too aware of her brothers' propensity for getting out of anything they'd think of as "women's work."

"Come on, Chloe." Daniel pushed the door open. "We've got the tools to take. Can't you manage that?"

"You're going to eat, aren't you?" A glimpse of Luke over her brother's shoulder made her words tart. "You can help tote."

Luke eased into the kitchen behind her brothers. "I'll be glad to carry the pies. That should give me first chance at them."

"You…" Chloe looked up at him, and the rest of her question seemed to shrivel in the need just to see him, to store up enough memories to last her when he was gone.

"Luke's coming to help." Daniel pounded Luke's shoulder in a friendly blow that should have staggered him.

Luke just smiled, apparently used to her brothers by this time. "I can't miss the chance to repay your grandmother for her hospitality. I'm glad to help."

Miranda began loading them up with things to carry. In the inevitable bustle as they started out the door, Chloe caught Luke's arm.

His skin was warm under her fingers, and she snatched them away before she could give in to the longing to hold on to him.

"You don't have to do this," she said in an undertone. "I'm sure you have work to do."

"No." His intent gaze stilled her protest. "There's nothing I'd rather do than this, Chloe. Are you ready?"

She had no choice but to follow him out the door, wondering how she'd possibly manage to keep her resolution to stay detached, when just a look from him was enough to put her fractured heart back together again.

By the time they reached Gran's, the rest of the clan had assembled. Her cousin Adam was already putting a ladder against the side of the house, while her mother and Gran set jugs of ice water and sweet tea on the picnic table. Her father and David conferred over a stack of shingles, while Uncle Jefferson hefted a toolbox from his truck.

Everyone had something to do. Even Sammy had been assigned to take water, nails, whatever was needed to the workers. Everyone had a part, she told herself, except Luke. He didn't belong here.

Did she? The thought popped into her mind so suddenly that it sent a wave of panic through her, making her feel the way she had when she'd been ten and caught in a riptide. Daddy had pulled her out that time, but he couldn't help now. She had to work this one out for herself.

"Are they talking?" Luke's baritone, soft in her ear, made her jump, then sent a tendril of warmth curling through her.

Stop it, she ordered, not sure whether she was talking to herself or Luke. She followed the direction of Luke's nod and saw that the group around the shingles had been joined by Uncle Jefferson.

"I don't know. I wish…" She let that die, because there was no point in confiding in Luke—not anymore.

"I know."

His voice was so soft it couldn't have reached any of the others, so close his breath stirred across her cheek. He enclosed her hand in his and squeezed it gently.

"I know what you wish, Chloe."

"You really don't have to stay, you know," she said in desperation. "You won't want to work up on the roof."

"I won't?" He lifted an eyebrow. "Why not, Chloe? Do you think I'm afraid of heights, just because I'm afraid of the water? That's kind of insulting, isn't it?"

"I didn't mean that. You know I didn't." Maybe if she pretended she was snapping at one of her brothers, this would go easier. "But I'm sure you've never done work like this before. It's hard." Well, that sounded even more insulting. Maybe she should just keep quiet.

"And hot, and dirty. Especially ripping off the old shingles to get down to something solid."

Her surprise had to show in her face. "You do know something about it."

He shrugged, picking up a pair of work gloves from the picnic table. "I worked construction one summer. There's nothing here I haven't seen before—"

He stopped, looking at her with something in his eyes she couldn't interpret.

"Except maybe you, Chloe."

He walked swiftly to the ladder, and a moment later was deep in conversation with her cousin.

She took a deep breath, hoping nothing was showing on her face to be noted and dissected by these people who knew her so well. What had he meant? Why had he even come today? It just made things more difficult.

She lifted the heavy picnic hamper. She had to stop thinking about him, about the possibility of a future that wasn't going to be. But each time she made a decision, Luke did something or said something to change it, leaving her caught once again on the painful edge between resignation and hope.

"Bring that hamper over here, Chloe Elizabeth." Gran called to her from the kitchen doorway. "Let me see if anything needs to go in the icebox."

Her grandmother had a refrigerator, but it would always be an "icebox" to her.

"The cold things are in the cooler, Gran." Chloe obediently took the hamper into the kitchen. At least there she wouldn't have to see Luke. Maybe she could stop thinking about him.

"What's this I hear about your young man?" Cousin Phoebe lifted the hamper lid to peek into each bowl.

Chloe suppressed a sigh. "I don't know, Cousin Phoebe. What did you hear?"

Phoebe's nose twitched. "Elvira Thompson's girl saw him in Savannah yesterday. Wouldn't you like to know what he was doing?"

"He had some work to do there." Work he hadn't asked her to share.

"Not unless he's working in a jewelry store," Phoebe announced triumphantly. She leaned on a chair back, waiting for the exclamations sure to follow.

No one disappointed her. Gran, Miranda, Chloe's mother—all pressed around her. Chloe's heart sank.

Whatever innocent purpose had taken Luke there was sure to be twisted out of all recognition.

"A jewelry store." Gran savored the words. "She didn't happen to see what he bought, did she?"

Phoebe shook her head with an expression of regret. "She couldn't get close enough for that, but it was a small box. She saw him put it into his pocket." Phoebe paused. "A ring-size box. Looks like our Chloe's going to get herself engaged."

He had to stop doing that. Luke climbed the ladder Chloe's cousin held for him, only a fraction of his attention on the rungs. He had to stop letting things slip where Chloe was concerned.

How much had he shown Chloe in the past week that he hadn't shown anyone else in the past fifteen years? He didn't want to count.

From the day he'd started college, he'd set out to reinvent himself. Reverend Tom and his foundation had given him the means to do that, and he'd gone about it with iron determination. He would turn himself into one of them—one of those favored few who took achievement and power for granted. And a big piece of his plan had involved keeping where he'd come from a secret.

That had never been a problem, until now. The persona he'd adopted had become a second skin. Until Chloe and her family started peeling it away.

It had to stop. A momentary panic washed over him. No one back in Chicago knew the truth about his background. What if they found out?

"You okay?" Chloe's cousin balanced next to him on the roof edge.

"Fine." Luke took the crowbar the other man held out. Adam, he reminded himself. This was the Caldwell who ran the shipyard. Tall, like all the Caldwell men, but with dark brown hair and a pair of steady gray eyes. "Let's get this done."

He shoved the pry bar under a stretch of fraying shingles. They came up with a satisfying rip. He'd concentrate on what he was doing. He wouldn't think about Chloe, because if he did he'd have to look at the future, and for the first time in fifteen years he wasn't perfectly certain what it held.

The morning fell into a rhythm that gradually displaced the turmoil in his mind. Chloe had been right about one thing—this was the most physical work he'd done in a long time. Playing handball at the club might keep him in shape for the life he normally led, but it didn't strain the muscles like this.

He and Adam worked side by side along the stretch of roof, with David and Daniel working a few feet above them. The steady, repetitive movements were oddly soothing, as soothing as the soft Southern voices teasing each other with the ease of long familiarity.

"Is that all you boys have gotten done?" Chloe's voice came from the top of the ladder.

"Fine talk from someone's who's been down there lolling in the shade, drinking lemonade," Daniel teased.

Chloe pulled the brim of a baseball cap down over her forehead. Her hair, more gold than brown after her days in the sun, curled around it. "Hey, it's a dirty job, but somebody has to do it. You can go down and listen to Cousin Phoebe's gallbladder story, if you want."

Daniel shuddered. "No, thanks. You'd best get back down there, Chloe-girl."

"Are you kidding? I'm here to give you slowpokes a hand. Daddy wants all the old shingles off before we stop for lunch."

"You taking Theo's place?" Adam asked, wiping his forehead with the back of his arm, then putting his cap back on.

If Theo's absence while working at the yacht club bothered Chloe, she didn't show it.

"I'm faster than Theo is." She clambered across the roof as easily as she hopped onto the boat. "Give me that pry bar. I'll loosen while you throw the shingles down."

Smiling, Adam held the bar out of her reach. "You'd best help your beau, sugar. After all, the two of you should get used to working together."

For an instant Chloe's face seemed to freeze, as if

time had stopped. Luke shoved the pry bar under an edge of shingles.

"Here, Chloe. I'll pry them up, and you toss them over the side. Let's see if we can beat your brothers to the end of the row."

That set David and Daniel off, and under the cover of their ribbing he studied Chloe's face. It didn't tell him anything, and he'd thought he could interpret her every expression. She frowned at the shingles as she pulled them free and tossed them over the side. She didn't meet his gaze.

Maybe she was as confused as he was about what was happening between them. Maybe she sensed, as he did, that they could never go back to the way they'd been before.

Probably that didn't matter to Chloe, he told himself. After all, she had roots. She had a place where she belonged, where her people went back for generations. Four generations of Caldwells worked together at that very moment, putting a new roof on a house that had stood on this same spot for two hundred years or so. His carefully created facade seemed a flimsy, Cracker Jack box thing in comparison.

Sink your roots deep in the Word. Reverend Tom's voice came from nowhere, echoing in his mind. *That's where you belong, son.*

The Rev had called all of them "son." All of the

ragtag gang of losers he'd taken off the streets had been "son" to him. It hadn't meant anything personal.

He seemed to see again Clayton Caldwell and Theo, walking toward the welcoming lights of the big old house, the man's hand on the boy's shoulder. A shiver ran along his skin in spite of the heat. That was what he'd always wanted. What he'd never had. He hadn't realized how much he missed it until he came here.

"All right." Adam reached the end of the row. "We did it." He gave Luke a friendly buffet on the shoulder. "Good job, Luke. Time for a lunch break."

It was a simple gesture, nothing to make a fuss about. But suddenly he felt accepted. As if he, too, could belong here.

Nonsense. He dropped the pry bar carefully down to the grass beneath. He didn't have any need to belong here, nor any longing to. He belonged back in Chicago, in the world he'd created for himself.

He started down the ladder, trying not to be aware of Chloe, following him down. This was her fault, bringing him here, making him question things he'd taken for granted for years.

His feet touched the ground and he reached up automatically to help Chloe. She hopped down the last few rungs, and his arms closed around her.

He heard the quick intake of her breath, felt the soft, warm, aliveness of her fill his arms, and all his certainty slipped away. Just the touch of her, the memory of her gentleness and loyalty, and his careful plans to keep things normal between them slipped crazily out of his control.

Chapter Eleven

"Chloe Elizabeth." Gran grabbed Chloe with one hand and Luke with the other. "I want you and Luke to do something for me before you go home."

Chloe was instantly wary. Anything Gran wanted them to do had *matchmaking* written all over it, and the situation between her and Luke was difficult enough already.

But Luke bent toward Gran attentively. "What is it, Gran? Anything for you."

Gran dimpled up at him. "Well, now, it's just so simple it won't take any time at all. And I'm sure you're wanting to have another look at the chapel, anyway, since…"

"Gran, we really need to get home and shower. Roofing's a dirty job." If Gran had finished that sentence, it would undoubtedly have had something to do with a wedding that wasn't going to take place.

"Now, Chloe, I need the flowers taken into the chapel for services tomorrow. You can surely stay long enough to do that."

"Of course we can." Luke patted her hand. "And I'd love to see the chapel more closely."

Her family's need to matchmake had passed the humorous point. And as for those engagement rumors— Chloe didn't even want to think about that. She suppressed a sigh. Gran was just being Gran. It wasn't her fault that Chloe was so uncertain right now about what Luke felt.

"Okay, what do you want us to take?"

"Thank you, sugar. It's too bad the azaleas are about through, but my early lilac is blooming its heart out. And there are a few tulips left that will look nice with them. I'll just get the bucket and clippers for you."

Chloe had to smile at the expression on Luke's face when her grandmother bustled off. "You didn't anticipate picking and arranging flowers, did you?"

His face relaxed in a disarming grin. "I have a lot of talents, Chloe, but flower arranging isn't among them. You'll have to do that part."

"Seems to me you're the one who jumped into this. Maybe it's time you acquired a new skill." Chloe went to take the bucket and clippers from her grandmother. She'd give her next Christmas bonus to see Luke Hunter doing flower arrangements.

Then she sobered. If she followed through with her

decision not to go back to Chicago, she wouldn't be there for the Christmas bonus. If she was lucky, she might get an anonymous printed card from Luke.

"Here's the lilac," she announced unnecessarily, as Gran went back into the house, closing the door firmly as if to remind them that they were alone.

Chloe handed Luke the clippers. "Why don't you cut a few of those flowering branches from the top, and I'll get the tulips."

"Come on, Chloe." He snipped a heavily laden branch of the old-fashioned white lilacs that were the envy of every gardener on the island. "This is a small thing to do to make your grandmother happy."

She'd heard that rationale before, and look where it had landed her. She cringed away from telling him about Cousin Phoebe's little bombshell. Maybe he'd never have to know. "You won't say that when the twins have used up all the hot water with their showers."

When they'd filled the bucket, she led the way into the chapel. Luke braced his hand against the weathered wood of the door to hold it open for her. "Isn't the chapel ever locked?"

"Not during the day. It is locked at night, since…"

"Since the dolphin disappeared," he finished for her.

She nodded, walking toward the heavy brass vases that stood on either side of the pulpit. "That's when folks realized crime could strike even here. You can fill those with water from the bucket, if you're sure you don't want to do the arranging part."

Luke smiled, shaking his head. He put the flowers on the paper she spread out, then poured water carefully into the vases. "How long ago was the chapel built? It looks as if it's been here forever."

"Just about." Chloe put a branch of lilac into the vase, trying to defeat its natural tendency to flop over. "The sanctuary was built first, back in the late 1700s, and the church school rooms added later. In those days, the islands had a kind of circuit-rider preacher, though he went by boat, not horseback. That's why they called it St. Andrew's Chapel, rather than church. And St. Andrew, because he was a fisherman."

"The islands were pretty isolated in those days, I guess." Luke walked slowly from one stained-glass window to another.

"Not only then. The bridge to the mainland wasn't built until the 1960s. Before that, folks had to be self-sufficient here."

He turned to look at her. "They still are, aren't they?"

His steady gaze made her uncomfortable. "I guess." Was she self-sufficient? Or had she lost that when she left the island? Maybe she'd never really had it. Maybe she needed to come back to find it.

"Where was the dolphin?"

She indicated the shelf reluctantly.

Luke touched the empty bracket, as if it would give him an image of the dolphin. "All this time," he murmured.

"My father didn't have anything to do with it," she said instantly.

"No." His frowning gaze met hers. "I'm sure he didn't, Chloe. But he's been keeping quiet about it. And you can't say it hasn't hurt him, at least, even if no one else was hurt."

That was more people wisdom than she'd expected from Luke, and it stilled her snappish response. "I suppose so," she said slowly. "I'm afraid the first Chloe isn't too happy with her descendants, if she knows."

He came to stand next to her, looking at the flower arrangements. The red tulips stood sentinel among the flowing white lilacs. "Nice job." He frowned. "If any part of your grandmother's story was true, that Chloe was a remarkable woman."

"Strong women." The words felt bitter in her mouth. "The Caldwells are known for strong women. Gran, my mother, Miranda—they're all good examples."

"And Chloe?"

Her gaze slid away from his. "I'm afraid the strain ran a little thin when it got to me. I can't live up to all of that." She shrugged, not knowing why she was saying this to him, but finding it impossible to keep the words back. "I guess that's really why I left the island in the first place. I needed to find someplace to belong where no one expected that much of me."

She stopped, horrified at herself. Why on earth had she said that to Luke? Exposing her emotions to him was just too dangerous. Luke probably didn't know it, but he had the power to wound her with nothing more than a look. And she'd just made him a present of her most carefully guarded secret.

Luke discovered he was holding his breath, and he let it out slowly. Chloe had opened her heart to him in a way he'd never expected, probably never experienced. She'd let him see into her soul, and he couldn't kid himself that she did that easily.

He faced a choice, and the silence grew between them as his mind veered from one to the other. His natural tendency was to say something neutral, something polite, something that by its very nature denied the importance of what Chloe had done. That would preserve the boss-secretary relationship between them.

Or he could answer her as honestly as she had spoken. That was dangerous. That would open some part of him to her, exposing vulnerabilities he didn't care to admit.

But it was too late, wasn't it? They could never go back to the way things had been before. They could only go forward.

He took her hand. It was small in his, but square and capable. "You're underestimating yourself, Chloe." He couldn't stop at that. He had to find the words that would take the hurt from those golden-brown eyes. "And leaving didn't work, anyway, did it? As long as you had to stay away to prove your independence, you weren't really independent."

She frowned as if assessing his words. Her lashes swept down, veiling her eyes.

"So coming back showed me for a fraud, is that it?"

"No!" He tightened his grip. That was the last thing he wanted her to feel. "Coming back showed you that you never needed to go away at all. I didn't know who you were back in Chicago, do you understand that? It was only after we came here, after I saw you on your island, that I understood the real Chloe."

She focused on the flowers, as if she wasn't ready to meet his eyes. "I've always thought I should be more like Miranda and my mother—strong, serene, a calm center no matter what's happening around them."

"There are different kinds of strength, Chloe Elizabeth." He touched her stubborn chin, lifting it so he could see her eyes. "Your mother and sister are admirable women, but I suspect you take after your grandmother, instead. Feisty, loyal, determined. You can't tell me that's not something to be proud of."

A flood of color brightened her cheeks. "If I believed that, I couldn't ask for anything better."

"Believe it." Warning bells were going off in his

mind but he suppressed them ruthlessly. "You're a special person, Chloe. Never forget that. I won't."

"Thank you." The words were whispered.

The moment seemed to stretch out infinitely. He could smell the sweetness of the lilacs, see dust motes floating in the shaft of colored light from the stained-glass windows, count every freckle on Chloe's sun-kissed skin. The silent chapel was caught in time, as if it could as easily be a hundred years ago, or tomorrow.

Chloe moved finally, breaking the spell. "We...we'd better go. My mother will wonder what happened to us."

He followed her up the aisle, pondering just what *had* happened to him here. They paused on the shaded walk while Chloe pulled the door closed. He caught her hand when she would have walked on.

"Let's not have dinner with your family tonight."

She looked up, startled. "What do you mean?"

"I mean, I'd like to have a little private time with my make-believe sweetheart, if that's all right with you." Again he had to suppress his built-in warning system. "There must be some restaurant where we can have a quiet dinner."

"I guess I can find one."

There was a question in her eyes. "We can talk business, if you like," he offered.

"Can we?" The dimple at the corner of her mouth made its appearance. "That would be a treat."

"I thought you'd like that." He took her hand. What he'd said was true enough, although he hadn't thought of it until then. They should talk business, just a little. It was past time for him to tell her his decision about Angel Isle.

But that wasn't why he wanted to go out alone with her, he knew perfectly well. He wanted to prolong those moments when they seemed able to see into each other's hearts. Dangerous or not, he wanted that.

They walked toward her grandmother's house, hands linked between them. He had to be out of his mind.

He didn't care.

"Wow." Daniel leaned against the door to Chloe's room, widening his eyes in exaggerated admiration. "Chloe's all dressed up, must be a special night."

David appeared next to him, his gaze softening as he looked at her. "Nice."

"Nice, indeed," Miranda scoffed, fluffing the skirt of the new yellow dress she'd insisted Chloe wear for her dinner with Luke. "Our Chloe is a beautiful woman. Can't help it if you two are too dumb to notice, heah."

The familiar Gullah word made Chloe smile in spite of the bad case of nerves she was having. All of them had known a smattering of Gullah, the language of the sea islands, since they'd started to talk. Hearing it in Miranda's soft voice made her feel a part of the endless island life again.

The twins went on down the stairs, and she heard their joking voices continue in Gullah through the hall and out to the porch. Luke would wonder what on earth they were speaking.

If she came home to stay, if she told Luke she wouldn't be returning to Chicago and her job, this would be her life again. Could she do that? Could she sever all ties to her Chicago existence, just like that?

She wasn't sure. But she was sure that she couldn't go back to the way things had been between them. She couldn't be Luke's faithful right hand and ignore the fact that she loved him.

"Luke's waiting for you, honey." Miranda gave her a little push toward the hall.

Luke was waiting. She tried to calm the tension that bounced along her nerves. She couldn't go on this way, pretending.

She'd tell him. Tonight she'd tell him that she was considering staying here when he went back. If things had changed between them, if he'd begun to care about her, if his kiss had meant anything, surely that would bring it out.

She started down the stairs, the soft silk swishing against her legs. Her stomach twisted, and she felt as if she were fifteen again, going down these same stairs to greet her first date.

She had to know. One way or the other, she had to know.

Luke, bending over the puzzle Sammy was working on, looked up at her step. His eyes met hers, and she nearly missed the next stair. That stunned expression in his deep blue eyes had to mean something, didn't it? The thought floated her down the rest of the flight.

He came to her, holding out his hand, something that might have been a question in his eyes.

"Ready?"

She nodded, suddenly having nothing to say. The thought of telling him she wasn't going back seemed impossible. Maybe it was unnecessary. He might say—

"I don't know why y'all are going someplace for dinner. Gramma is fixing chicken tonight. You oughta stay here with us."

Miranda, who'd followed Chloe down the stairs, smiled at her small son. "They want to be by themselves for a change."

"But they can—"

Miranda put her hand gently over his mouth. "Enough, sugar. 'Bye, you two." She gave them a knowing smile. "Y'all have fun now, you hear?"

Luke opened the door. "Your carriage awaits, m'lady."

Sure her cheeks were as red as Gran's tulips, Chloe went through the door.

Once they were in the car, it should have been better. At least they were away from her family, with their obvious expectation that something special would happen tonight. They probably imagined that Luke had an engagement ring hidden in the pocket of his navy slacks.

She knew better. Maybe that had been admiration in his eyes when she'd come down the steps; maybe he had enjoyed kissing her. But when it came to rings and wedding bells, Luke would marry with his eyes on the prize he wanted. That meant money and power, not a girl-next-door type with no prospects.

"Looks as if there are more people around town." Luke stopped at Caldwell Cove's only traffic light.

"The season's perking up as the weather gets warmer. Easter will really kick it off." He was probably thinking about the potential for a Dalton resort in the area. "Places like the Crab House, where we're going tonight, will extend their hours as things get busier."

Luke nodded, a frown creasing his forehead. Calculating the possibilities? She didn't know.

"Turn in here." She leaned forward, indicating the crushed-shell parking area of the Crab House. "Sorry, I didn't want you to miss the turn. What were you saying?"

He just shook his head, pulling into a space next to the dock. "This looks like the real thing."

"That it is." Chloe slid out, standing for a moment to drink in the scene. The fishing boats at the docks, their nets lifted, were old friends. "This is a working dock. When they tell you the seafood is fresh here, they mean it was swimming in the ocean a few hours ago."

Luke's hand closed around hers in a gesture that had begun to feel natural. "So what are we eating tonight?"

"Shrimp, oysters, crab, or the day's catch. And the she-crab soup is the best you're ever going to taste, so don't miss that." Chloe inhaled the salty, fishy aroma of the docks. "Come on, let's see what's on the menu."

They sat at a table overlooking the sound, and the familiar land-and-waterscape reminded Chloe that she had planned to tell Luke she intended to stay. But somehow the moments ticked by, and the words never quite came out.

"You were right." Luke leaned back in his chair after the soup course. "The she-crab soup was delectable. What makes it so good?"

"Low-country secrets," she said, teasing. "You don't want me to betray them, do you?"

He reached across the small table to put his hand over hers. "We're on the same team," he said. "That's not betraying, is it?"

She shook her head, smiling. Somehow she didn't think being on the same team meant quite as much to Luke as it did to her. "My mother's promised to give me her recipe as a wedding present."

"That's almost worth getting married for." He squeezed her fingers, then reached toward his pocket. "By the way, I have something for you."

He pulled out a small jeweler's box, setting it on the

table between them. She read the name of the Savannah jeweler on the lid, and her heart nearly stopped.

Don't be silly, she told herself fiercely. *It's not what the family imagines. You're not foolish enough to think that.*

She had to clear her throat so she could speak. "What is it?"

"Something that made me think of you." He pushed the box toward her with one finger. "Go ahead, open it."

She reached out slowly, trying not to think, not to imagine. She pressed the latch, and the lid flipped up. Inside, a gold dolphin attached to a chain as fine as a cobweb nestled on a bed of white satin. Her throat closed; she couldn't say a word.

"What's wrong? Don't you like it?"

She blinked rapidly to keep tears from spilling over. "It's beautiful," she said carefully. "You shouldn't have."

"I wanted to." He lifted it from the box, and it dangled from his fingers, glinting in the candlelight. "Let me fasten it for you."

She turned her back to him, closing her eyes when his fingers brushed the nape of her neck. The necklace was featherlight, and the dolphin seemed to warm where it touched her skin.

"Thank you," she whispered. "I love it."

She did love it. It wasn't Luke's fault that her heart yearned for something else.

She couldn't do this any longer. This evening had to come to a close now. "Maybe we should—"

"Look—"

She followed the direction of Luke's gaze, relieved that he wasn't looking at her. The sun had slipped lower, hiding behind the clouds that massed on the mainland horizon. Then, quite suddenly, the color began to change. Gray clouds tinged with lavender, then mauve, then pink, the colors streaking across the darkening sky until the whole horizon glowed.

"If you saw that in a painting, it would look artificial." Luke's voice was soft.

"God's handiwork," she said, her own words just as soft. She wished she knew whether that meant anything to him.

She longed to look at him, but instead watched the sound, a sheet of silver in the fading light. A fishing boat drew a diagonal line across the water, and a pair of pelicans bobbed and rocked in its wake.

"I see why you love it."

Luke stroked the back of her hand, and she seemed to feel that delicate touch with every cell of her being.

"A person could get lost here and never want to be found," he said.

She should tell him, she thought again.

Later, a little voice seemed to whisper in her ear. *Tell him later, because this precious moment will never come again.*

She was being a coward, but she didn't care. She'd enjoy this evening, and do her best to pretend it never had to end.

Chapter Twelve

They stepped out of the restaurant into what Luke was beginning to recognize as a Southern night, with the air so warm and moist it felt soft against your skin. He stopped in the parking lot for a moment, holding Chloe's hand as his eyes grew accustomed to the dark.

Across the sound, the mainland was a dark silhouette against a paler gray sky. Lights winked on, sparkling in clusters along the horizon.

"It looks like another world, doesn't it."

"Maybe it is." Chloe took a deep breath, as if to inhale the musky sweetness of the air. "Have you made a decision yet about going back?"

Going back—to that other world. The reluctance he felt astonished him. Before they went back—before they even considered it—he had to tell her his decision.

"Chloe, there's something I've been wanting to tell you."

She stiffened, her hand drawing out of his. "I have something to tell you, too. I—"

She stopped, looking beyond him. An instant later he heard the noise, too—running footsteps, heavy breathing, a muffled shout. He spun.

A single slim figure shot around the corner of the nearest building, closely followed by three or four more. Even in the half dark, he recognized the boy. It was Theo, and he was in trouble.

Instinct kicked in almost before conscious thought. "Stay here." He snapped the order to Chloe, then ran across the parking lot, shells crunching under his feet. The sound transmuted in his mind to another that fit the emotion better—to feet pounding on hard pavement, shouts echoing off brick walls and bouncing crazily in the confines of an alley.

He knew the feeling. He didn't need to see the hand grab Theo's T-shirt and pull him around, or the punch that bounced off the boy's shoulder as he dodged. He'd been there. He knew what would happen next, with four of them, all bigger and heavier and meaner than Theo was.

Well, not tonight. Theo didn't have to face this alone. Luke was there.

And so was Chloe. He came to a stop a foot from the

boys, assessing the situation. Chloe, breath coming quickly, stopped behind him. Of course she'd ignored his order. Chloe was too gutsy to hang back when someone was in trouble, and she'd go to the wall for her family.

Defuse this before it gets any worse, he ordered himself. His fists clenched, and he seemed to hear the survivor of a hundred street fights jeering in the back of his mind. At some level he was ready for a fight, and sixteen years of civilization threatened to vanish in an instant.

He put his hand on Theo's shoulder, moving next to him, letting his size register on the combatants. Slowly he looked them up and down, using the icy stare that had worked equally well whether cowing would-be brawlers in the boardroom or the back alley.

Three of the four retreated a step. The fourth, the one who'd hit Theo, stood his ground. He wore a look that said his old man owned the earth, and running shoes that had probably cost more than Theo's whole wardrobe.

Luke longed to wipe that cocky expression off the kid's face, but he shoved the urge down. Give everybody a chance to save face, and they might get out of this with no more damage.

He drew Theo a little closer. "Good to see you, Theo." He kept his tone casual. "You and your friends want to join us for coffee?"

Theo straightened, eyes never wavering from the face of the biggest kid. "I will. I reckon these guys are headed for home."

Luke lifted an eyebrow, inviting a response. "That right?"

My-daddy-owns-the-world sneered. "I 'reckon' this geechee better stay on his side of the island—isn't that right, boy?"

Luke's control slipped. This kid was everyone who'd ever looked down on him. The boy didn't know how close to the line he was treading.

Apparently mistaking his silence for cowardice, the kid shoved Theo's shoulder. "I said—"

Luke suddenly discovered his hand fisted in the kid's shirtfront. Rage flamed along his veins. He'd—

"Luke." Chloe's voice was soft but it called him to his senses. He saw the fear in the boy's eyes and held on a moment longer, making sure the kid knew his fear had been seen. Then he released him, smoothing the kid's shirt.

"You know," he said easily, "Theo's people have been here two hundred years or so. I guess that gives him the right to go anywhere he wants."

He let his gaze move from one to another of them. None of them met his eyes, and he knew it was over. "I don't think your parents especially want to bail you out tonight, do you?"

They took that for the dismissal it was. In a moment they'd faded back around the corner.

Time to assess damages. Theo had a bloody nose, and the look that met Luke's eyes was half ashamed, half defiant.

"Hope you didn't mind the interference," he said as casually as if he asked the boy about school. He heard Chloe's indrawn breath and hoped she wouldn't gush over the kid.

"Of course he doesn't." Her voice was tart, but her hand lingered against her brother's cheek. "Theo doesn't want his daddy to bail him out tonight, either, do you, pest?"

Theo managed a smile. "Guess not."

No, he didn't need to worry that his Chloe would put her foot wrong when it came to helping. He might have been surprised at his reaction to this little encounter, but he wasn't surprised at Chloe. She was true-blue loyal to people she cared about.

Something twisted in his gut. How many people would say that about him?

Chloe decided that her stomach wasn't going to disgrace her. If she let herself think about that moment when she realized Theo was in trouble—her stomach lurched again, and she blanked the picture out of her mind. It had been okay. Luke had been there.

"Well." She decided she could trust her voice. "Guess we'd best get you cleaned up before Momma gets a look at her baby boy."

"In here." Luke jerked his head toward the restaurant. "We could all use a cup of coffee right now."

As soon as they were inside, she saw the blood on Theo's T-shirt. Her stomach tightened all over again. Luke took her brother's arm and turned him toward the rest room.

"You order the coffee," he said.

Chloe battled down her resentment at his assumption of authority. She hadn't resented it when he'd jumped into Theo's battle, had she? She slid into the nearest booth and ordered coffee for three.

When the waitress had gone, she wrung a napkin between her fingers. If Luke hadn't been there, what would she have done? Well, she'd have helped Theo, of course. But she might have had to yell for help, involved other people, maybe even the police. She shuddered at the thought of the scene.

No, Luke was right. None of them wanted Daddy to bail them out tonight.

The coffee arrived, and she poured a cup for herself without waiting for the other two. Luke had taken control, all right. For a moment she'd actually thought he was going to hit that smart-mouth kid.

She stirred the coffee, starting a dark whirlpool that

seemed to match the one in her mind. What had she seen in Luke in those moments? Something wild, something dark, something completely at odds with the sophisticated, urban professional he was the rest of the time. She didn't know where that other person had come from, and she wasn't sure what to make of him.

The rest room door swung, and they came out. Theo's shirt was damp but clean. He shivered a little in the air-conditioning as he slid into the booth, and she shoved a coffee cup toward him.

"Have some. It'll make a new man of you."

The bench creaked as Luke sat next to her. "Some for me, please. I could stand to be a new man."

She glanced sideways at his face. His mouth was a straight, hard line, and some emotion she couldn't guess at darkened his blue eyes. Uncomfortable, she looked at his hands, instead. His strong fingers tore a napkin methodically into strips. He seemed to become aware of that, and he pressed his hands flat against the table.

"I guess I owe you one." Theo stared down at his coffee and grimaced. "Boy, is Daddy gonna say, 'I told you so.'"

"Your daddy doesn't seem like the kind of man to do that."

Luke's voice was calm; the streak of wildness she'd seen vanquished for the moment.

"How'd that get started, anyway?"

Theo shrugged, the movement of thin shoulders under the damp T-shirt bringing a lump to her throat. It seemed like yesterday that she'd been teaching him to ride a bike. Now he was nearly grown.

"It was a girl."

Luke's mouth quirked. "Theo, most of the trouble men end up in starts with the same words. 'It was a girl.'"

Chloe punched his arm, her fist bouncing on hard muscle. "That's right, blame it on Eve."

That brought a smile to Theo's troubled face. "Guess you're right, at that. Anyway, seemed like she liked me. Made them mad. They were waiting when I got off work." His jaw worked. "I should have fought them. Reckon I acted like a coward."

The misery in his voice put a loop around Chloe's heart. What could she say that would make it better? If only Miranda were here. Miranda always knew what to say when someone was hurting. Poor Theo was stuck with the wrong sister tonight.

"Yeah, right. That'd make your daddy proud." Luke's brisk words were like a dash of cold water. "He'd really appreciate your brawling in the street."

Well, it wasn't the dose of sympathy she'd been looking for, but it made Theo sit up a bit straighter.

"I guess that's so." Theo seemed to search Luke's face for answers. "But shouldn't a man defend himself?"

"Looked to me as if you were ready to fight if you didn't have a choice. And there were four of them," Luke reminded him. "There's a difference between being brave and being stupid. That's a line I crossed a time or two myself."

Theo seemed to process that and come to the same conclusion Chloe had. "You knew how to handle yourself out there."

Just what she'd been thinking. Luke had behaved like a man who'd been in that spot more than once.

Luke shrugged. "It didn't take much to scare them off, once they saw they didn't outnumber you."

"Four to two," Theo said.

Chloe ruffled his hair. "Four to three. I didn't grow up running with the twins without learning a thing or two, remember."

Theo grinned. "My sister, the bantam-weight."

"Just one thing bothers me." Luke had a question in his eyes.

"What?"

"What exactly is a geechee? Or is it so bad I shouldn't ask in polite company?"

Laughter bubbled up, dissipating the last of Chloe's tension. "Actually, we consider it a badge of honor. A geechee is anyone born and bred in the low country—roughly speaking, the coast from Georgetown down to the Ogeechee River in Georgia."

"Then, I guess I better get you two geechees home." The ugliness that had marred the evening disappeared entirely as Luke tossed a bill on the table and stood.

Chloe slid out of the booth, feeling his hand close on her elbow. Something, some trace of that other Luke she'd seen tonight, lingered in his touch.

Which was the real Luke? Was she ever going to know?

The inn slept behind her as Chloe stepped out onto the front porch a few hours later. They'd gotten Theo into the house without encountering anyone. Whether or not the boy decided to confide in Daddy was up to him now.

She should have fallen right to sleep from sheer exhaustion. Instead she'd tossed and turned, listening to Miranda's even breathing from the other bed. Finally she'd gotten up and slipped on jeans and a shirt. Maybe a breath of air would counteract the coffee she'd drunk.

The sweet, musky scent of the marshes filled her as she leaned against the porch railing. It always soothed her. It soothed her now. But the question still bubbled beneath the surface. What secrets did Luke hide? How did she reconcile the man she thought she knew with the glimpses he'd given her of his hidden self?

Something moved out on the dock, and a figure was silhouetted against the gray water beyond. Her heart recognized him, even in the dark. *Luke.*

She'd taken three steps off the porch before she'd made a conscious decision to go to him. Well, she had to thank him for what he'd done for Theo tonight, didn't she? But she knew she had another, deeper reason. She had to talk with Luke because she had to know what was going on inside him.

She felt Luke's gaze on her as she crossed the path and stepped onto the dock. The weathered boards echoed hollowly under her feet. He sat at the end, his back against a post.

"Hey." She dropped down next to him.

"Hey, yourself. How's Theo?" His baritone rumble seemed scarcely louder than the murmur of water against the dock.

"Sound asleep." She hesitated, not sure what else to say, her gaze tracing the line of moonlight on the water.

He followed the direction of her gaze. "Beautiful, isn't it. Almost looks like a path."

She smiled. "Gran used to tell us bedtime stories about fishermen who sailed up that path and spent the night throwing their cast nets and pulling in stars. Then we'd go to sleep and dream about it."

"You had a magical childhood, Chloe Elizabeth." His voice had roughened. "Plenty of people would envy you that."

She held her breath as she turned to meet his eyes. "Including you?"

Shush, shush, shush. Three waves caressed the dock before he answered.

"You want to hear my story, Chloe? You wouldn't like it."

The bitterness in his voice startled her, but she wouldn't let it scare her off. They'd come too far for that.

"I want to know whatever you're willing to tell me about yourself." She kept her gaze steady on him, knowing her heart was in her eyes.

He shrugged. "I gave myself away tonight. I knew it. I always knew the street kid was still there. I just didn't realize how close to the surface he was, until I saw those creeps chasing Theo. I wanted to smash someone."

His fists clenched as if he felt the urge again. She put her hand on his, feeling the tension that pounded through him. "You didn't."

"I could have." He grasped her wrists suddenly. "Do you really want to know who Luke Hunter is? You want to hear what happens to a kid who never knew a father, whose mother forgot he existed, who was on the streets by the time he was eight? It's not pretty."

His pain wrapped around her heart, hurting her, too. "Who took care of you?"

"Nobody." He spit out the word. "Foster homes for a while, each one worse than the last. I finally figured out that I could get lost on the streets and take care of myself. Live hard, die young—that was my motto."

She wanted to put her arms around him. She wanted to hold him the way she'd have held Theo when he was little and hurting. But his grip on her wrists held her off, and that had to be deliberate. Couldn't he let her in?

Oh, Lord, please. Help me to help him.

"What changed?"

Her soft question seemed to pull him back from whatever blackness he looked into. His grasp eased, as if he became aware that he might be hurting her.

"I met someone." He paused, then continued. "I walked into the Fresh Start Mission in search of a free meal."

Things fell into place in her mind. "It was like the Sonshine Center."

He nodded. "Figured I'd find some patsy I could milk for a few bucks. But the Rev was no patsy."

"The Rev?"

"That's what we called him. The Reverend Dr. Thomas Phillips. A Harvard degree, a stint as a military chaplain in Vietnam, and twenty years' worth of scraping kids off the street and pounding some sense into them. He took one look at me and decided he saw something worth saving." A muscle twitched in his jaw. "Can't imagine what."

She stroked his fingers, longing to soothe him and not sure how. "Intelligence. Tenacity. Integrity."

"Is that what you think you see?"

His voice was angry, but she heard the longing underneath the pain. She touched his cheek, her fingertips smoothing the tension away. "That's what I know I see. Whatever you came from, whatever wrong was done to you, that's who you are."

"Chloe, honey, I'm not sure you know what you're saying." His tone was half laughing, half despairing.

She paused for a heartbeat, hearing the soft splash of some night bird after a fish. "This place—since we came, I've begun to see who I am. Maybe that's the magic here. It makes you see who you are. It makes me know I'm not wrong about the man Luke Hunter is, no matter what he came from."

His hand covered hers, pressing her palm flat against his cheek. His skin warmed to her touch, connecting them at some level she couldn't comprehend.

"I hope you're right. Chloe, I only hope you're right."

He drew her hand against his lips, and she felt them move in a gentle kiss. Then he pulled her into his arms, and his lips found hers.

Her arms slid around him. They fit together perfectly, as if they were meant to be that way.

Home. She really had come home.

Chapter Thirteen

Why was God confronting him with his past now, when he was on the verge of achieving everything he'd always dreamed he wanted? Luke leaned against the porch railing Monday morning, unable to get the question out of his mind. First the Sonlight Center, then Theo's trouble, reminding him, refusing to let him hide who he was.

He hadn't hidden anything Saturday night when he'd told Chloe things he'd never told anyone, when he'd kissed her and tried to believe they had a future together. The feeling had gained momentum during the service in the tiny chapel on Sunday, continuing to build throughout the family gathering that apparently was a given for the Caldwell clan on Sunday afternoon.

He still didn't have an answer. He'd tried bargaining with God. Hadn't he played fair? Hadn't he sent a monthly check to the Rev to support his mission, even when he couldn't afford it? What more did God want from him?

A white gull swooped down to perch on the dock where he'd sat with Chloe on Saturday night. He'd expected a reaction from her when he told her his past. He hadn't expected warmth, affection, acceptance. *Love.*

His native caution shied away from that word. What did love mean to somebody like him? He'd never known the kind of love Chloe had experienced every moment of her life. How could he possibly hope to give her that?

One thing was certain, through all the doubts that clouded his mind. He had to tell Chloe what he'd decided about Angel Isle. He'd kept that quiet far too long, making excuses for why they were staying when he was actually researching siting the hotel on Angel Isle.

He heard the creak of the screen door and knew it was Chloe even before he turned. She wore her usual shorts and T-shirt, but she exuded a confidence that was new to her. It almost seemed she'd gained all the confidence he'd lost.

"Hey." Her eyes were lit with pleasure. "I have a surprise for you." She crossed the porch to link her arm with his.

"What surprise?" Maybe the surprise was that her most casual touch made him want to kiss her.

"The twins have to go to Savannah today, so I volunteered us to lead their kayak tour." She smiled up at him. "Since you're turning into such a pro with the kayak, I thought you wouldn't mind."

"I've only been out twice, remember? That hardly makes me a pro." Once he'd have thought the suggestion insane. The fact that now it sounded great only proved how far he'd fallen.

"All you have to do is paddle along with me. We're taking them into the salt marshes, anyway. The worst that can happen if someone topples out is that they'll get their feet muddy. Okay?"

"Okay." At some point during this excursion, they'd have the opportunity for a private talk. He'd tell her about his plans and draw her in. He'd make her understand that Angel Isle was the perfect spot for the new hotel, make her see how her family would benefit.

He tried to suppress his misgivings. She'd go along with him. They were a team, weren't they?

Somehow the opportunity for a private talk didn't come as easily as he'd expected. During the ride to the public dock where they were to meet their group, Chloe briefed him about the trip. And once they arrived, the small group of tourists totally occupied her.

He helped unload the kayaks from the truck and watched Chloe slip into her tour guide persona. She gave a quick orientation, handed out life jackets, assigned people to kayaks. He assessed the group. Two older couples, one father and teenage son, one single man with a paunch and a Hawaiian shirt.

Mr. Hawaiian Shirt was the only troublemaker. He didn't want to put on a life jacket.

"I'm sorry, Mr. Carey." Chloe's tone was perfectly polite and perfectly inflexible. "Life jackets are required. If you don't care to wear one, I'll happily refund your money."

Grumbling under his breath, the man yanked on the life jacket. Luke hid a grin when he had to pull it back off to let the straps out. This was going to be an interesting trip.

Chloe finally had them all into the boats and headed down the creek into the marshes.

"Nice guy," Luke commented softly, nodding toward the troublemaker as he matched his stroke to Chloe's.

She flashed him an understanding look over her shoulder. "There's always at least one in every trip— the hotshot businessman who thinks the rules don't apply to him."

"Ouch. That wouldn't include present company, would it?"

Her grin was mischievous. "What do you think?"

Before he could come up with a snappy response, she'd raised her voice so the whole group could hear.

"That's an osprey off to your left, fishing for his dinner. And coming up on the right, you can see several egrets. The salt marsh teems with food for all kinds of shorebirds."

"What about dolphins?" the teenager called out. "Your brochure said we'd see dolphins."

"There's a good chance of that." Chloe rested her paddle across the boat and pulled her ball cap down over her eyes. "They come into the marshes to feed, too."

They paddled past the watching egrets, elegant on their long legs. "You're going to have a disappointed kid if you don't produce dolphins," he said under his breath.

Chloe shrugged. "We can only show them what's here. Trouble is, people don't realize these are wild creatures, not house pets."

A turtle glided past, surprisingly agile in the water, and then a pair of herons made an appearance. The kayaks rounded a curve in the sea of marsh grass, and Chloe raised her hand to stop the procession.

"There," she said, and Luke heard the love in her voice. "Dolphins."

"Wow." The boy let his kayak drift closer to theirs. "What are they doing? Is something wrong with them?"

"It's called strand feeding. Don't get too close, and we'll be able to watch them. They actually throw themselves up on the bank to feed, then slide back into the water."

"Awesome."

Luke knew how the kid felt. Three dolphins threw

their bodies in shining arcs out of the water, then slid back in perfect rhythm. It was like watching a ballet.

"No closer, please," Chloe snapped, and Luke tore his gaze from the dolphins.

Predictably it was Carey, paddling toward the dolphins, then juggling his paddle to raise a camera.

"Gotta get a picture of this." Ignoring Chloe, he pushed closer, then lost his paddle with a splash.

Two of the dolphins slid back into the water and disappeared. The third dolphin, apparently startled into losing his rhythm, stranded, floundering helplessly in the mud.

"Get back." Chloe grabbed the paddle as it floated by and tossed it to the man.

"Hey, I paid my money. I've got a right to take a picture."

Luke planted his paddle against the offending kayak and gave it a fierce shove. "Back. Now."

The man swallowed, then let his kayak drift out into the center of the stream. Luke turned to Chloe. "What do we do?"

She watched the dolphin intently, then shook her head. "He's never going to get off there by himself. I'll have to help him." Before he could guess what she was about, she'd slid out of the kayak and was standing waist-deep in the water. "Stay there."

"Not likely." He slid out of the kayak, too, feeling his feet sink ankle-deep into the soft bottom. He shoved their kayak over to the boy. "Hold on to this for me. And don't let anyone get any closer."

The boy nodded, eyes wide.

Chloe moved gently toward the dolphin. Mimicking her movements, Luke closed in on the other side. "Tell me what to do," he whispered.

"We'll have to try and slide him back. He's not going to like being touched." Her eyes never left the dolphin as she eased in next to it.

She reached out slowly, obviously trying to avoid frightening the creature. The instant she touched it, the dolphin went into a frenzy of movement, struggling to get away from her.

Luke closed in on the other side, grabbing for a handhold on the slippery body. The only thing he got for his trouble was a face full of water. He wiped his eyes and looked at Chloe. "Now what?"

"Let me try." She leaned closer, crooning softly. The dolphin's dark, liquid eye seemed to watch her. "There, now, beautiful. We're not going to hurt you. We're just going to get you back into the water, back where you belong. It's all right."

Maybe the creature was too exhausted to fight any longer. Or maybe it heard the love in Chloe's voice. This time when she touched it, there was no struggle.

She slid the dolphin back an inch, then another. Luke had the sense that everyone watching held his breath.

She paused, then nodded to Luke. He took hold gingerly, feeling smooth skin throbbing with life.

"Now," Chloe whispered.

They pulled together. The dolphin slid, caught, then slid again into the water. For an instant it simply bobbed on the gentle current. Luke felt it tremble under his hands. Then, with a surge and a ripple that nearly knocked him off his feet, it was gone.

Chloe wiped water from her face. "We did it." Her voice choked a little on the words, and her eyes filled with tears. "We did it."

"You did it."

You're amazing. That was what he wanted to say, but he contented himself with brushing a strand of wet hair off her cheek. They stood waist-deep in the warm water, sharing their triumph, and he felt so close to Chloe that it terrified him.

In a haze of happiness, Chloe loaded the last of the kayaks and said goodbye to the tour group. All she could see was Luke's face as they had watched the dolphin swim free. Surely that had been love in his eyes when he looked at her.

Sunlight glinted on the water, and in the distance she saw the silver crescents of the dolphins working their way toward the sea. They were back where they belonged.

Did she and Luke belong here, together? Her heart

seemed to swell at the thought. A few days ago she wouldn't have dared dream of that. Now, anything seemed possible. If a new Dalton Resort did become a reality somewhere in the area, Luke might decide he'd had enough of the pressure cooker that was corporate headquarters. They might—

Luke rounded the truck, a dark shadow with the sun behind him.

She lifted her hand to shield her eyes. "So, what did you think of your first dolphin tour?"

"I hope they're not all that exciting." He nodded toward the departing cars. "Carey's still complaining that I ruined his picture. He's lucky I didn't ruin more than that."

"The customer is always right, remember? You should hear some of the stories the twins tell about the groups they've taken out. It would turn your hair gray."

He smiled, but it was almost mechanical, as if his mind worried away at something else. A chill seemed to settle on her, in spite of the heat of the day.

She tried to tell herself she was imagining things, but it didn't quite work. Something was wrong—she knew Luke too well to be mistaken about that. "Is something wrong?"

"I need to talk with you."

It was his office voice, the voice that gave orders and expected them to be obeyed. She felt herself tighten.

"You want to sign up to lead another tour?" She

adjusted the cord on the kayaks, keeping her voice light, trying to hold off whatever was coming.

He moved impatiently, then planted his hand against the truck, leaning close to her. "This is business."

She nodded, trying to assume her office self. But she seemed to have lost that person during the days they'd spent on the island.

"What is it?" Her voice didn't sound natural, even to herself.

"I've made a decision about the site I'm recommending."

He frowned, not looking at her, and that fact sent her tension level soaring. Whatever he'd decided, she wasn't going to like it.

Then his gaze fixed on her, as if to compel her agreement. "I've decided on Angel Isle."

Shock leached the sunlight from the day. "You can't be serious." This was a joke—it had to be.

Luke's frown deepened. "I'm always serious about business, Chloe. If I get the go-ahead from the office, I plan to make your father an offer for the tract of land from the cottage down to the end of the island. Angel Isle is the perfect site. I'm sure you've thought that yourself."

She could only shake her head, as if to shake off his words.

"No, I haven't. You can't." Maybe she should have seen it coming, but it had completely blindsided her.

"Can't?" He lifted his eyebrows in disbelief, probably because subordinates didn't say "can't" to Luke Hunter. "That's why I'm here, remember?"

"I know, I know." Her words tumbled over each other in her rush to make him understand. "But not Angel Isle. You've seen how much it means to us. To me."

That was the crux of it. That was why her heart hurt so much that she pressed her hand against her chest. Luke had to know what Angel Isle meant to her. Yet his decision made one thing very clear. His career was far more important to him than she could ever be.

"I don't understand you, Chloe." Every line of his body spoke of his determination. "Angel Isle is perfect for the new hotel. Your father will find Dalton's offer very appealing, and you can't tell me he doesn't need the money. This could mean a world of difference to your family financially."

Fresh pain clutched her heart. This really was the old Luke speaking, the one who valued money and status above everything. He couldn't see beyond that.

And what about Daddy? If Luke made the kind of offer he was talking about, would her father refuse? Or would he feel compelled to accept whether he wanted to or not, in order to secure his children's futures? None of them would want to sacrifice their right to Angel Isle, no matter how much money was involved. But Daddy might not see it that way.

She could tell her family the truth—that there was no relationship with Luke. That this was all a lie, and Luke had come here for business purposes only. She cringed away from the hurt and disappointment she'd see in their faces.

Please, let there be another way. Please, Lord.

"Luke, please." It was difficult to speak calmly about something so vital. "You have to understand what the island means to us. We can't let it go."

"You wouldn't lose the cottage, Chloe. We can negotiate a deal that leaves it."

"It wouldn't be the same."

His eyes darkened, and he looked at her as if from a great distance. "That's up to your father to decide, isn't it? You told me he owns it."

"Please," she said again, grasping for the words that would open his eyes.

The cleft in his chin seemed chiseled from stone. She put her hand on his arm, and it felt like iron. Why had she ever imagined he was softening toward her? Luke was moving into deal mode. She knew what that meant. If you didn't go along with him, you could expect to be flattened. But she had to try.

"There are plenty of beautiful spots that are much more suitable. I've shown you a dozen or more."

"Nothing as good as Angel Isle."

"But without a bridge, every guest would have to

be ferried across to the island. That's got to add to the difficulty."

"And to the appeal," he shot back. "People like the idea of getting away from everything to a deserted isle."

Her deserted isle. But that was a selfish way of looking at it. She had to concentrate instead on all the future generations of Caldwells who wouldn't have the island as a haven if this deal went through.

She tightened her grasp on his arm, looking into his eyes. "Just do this for me. Give me a few days to find a site that will work as well. Please."

She held her breath while Luke stared at her, frowning. The seconds ticked away, punctuated by the cry of a gull. It sounded as desolate as she felt.

Finally he nodded. "All right, Chloe. If it means that much to you, I'll take a little more time. But I don't understand."

He didn't understand. The dreams she'd harbored about their future dissolved like the ebbing tide spreading out on the sand. He didn't understand, and he never would. If she'd been looking for something to illustrate the differences between them, she couldn't have come up with anything clearer than this.

He'd been landed back in the real world with a painful *thump.* Luke snapped his cell phone closed and stalked to the window of his sunlit bedroom at the inn.

Two hours ago, he'd told Chloe he'd give her time to find another site for the hotel. Now he didn't have any time to give.

The sound of Dalton's voice had been enough to remind him where he belonged. And Dalton's message had been perfectly clear. He wasn't interested in waiting. He didn't want to consider other possibilities. Everything was a go on the Angel Isle site; wrap it up before the locals get wind of it and prices soar. The implication was clear. If Luke couldn't close this, he wasn't vice-presidential material.

Luke stared at the small boat nosing idly into the dock. A gull swooped down and perched on its rail, looking as if it welcomed the boat home.

Fantasy. Everything about this place had the air of a fantasy. It wasn't for him. His world was back in Chicago, at corporate headquarters. He belonged there, in a plush new corner office.

And Chloe? Where did she belong?

The question came, unbidden. Even back in Chicago, Chloe had been somehow a little different. She'd always seemed to belong somewhere else.

His jaw clenched. The thought reminded him uncomfortably of the Rev's favorite sermon topic. *Always remember that this world isn't really your home. God designed you to live forever with Him.*

He'd been thinking far too much about the Rev and

the mission since he'd been on the island. The mission had been its own little world, too. Maybe that was why.

Not my world, he told himself again. The future he'd envisioned all his life hinged on this deal, and he wouldn't let it slip away.

Determination hardened inside him. He'd find Chloe, he'd tell her what he had to do, and he'd wind up the deal. In a month, these days and nights on Caldwell Island would be just a memory.

He walked quickly out of the room and down the steps, fueled by determination. See Chloe, make her understand. Then he'd approach her father.

But Chloe was nowhere to be found. And when Luke stepped out onto the porch in search of her, Clayton Caldwell was coming up the steps, limping a little.

"Luke." Clayton greeted him with considerably less suspicion than he had that first day. "How did the kayak trip go? You lose any tourists?"

"No, we brought them all back. But there was one I wouldn't have minded losing."

Clayton smiled. "Guess there always is." His smile faded. "I've been wanting to thank you. My boy told me what happened Saturday night. I'm grateful to you."

"It was nothing." Luke tried to shrug it off. "Lucky I was there, or Chloe might have started a riot. I'm glad Theo told you about it. He's a good kid."

"Guess he's not such a kid as I thought. He went right

back to the club the next day, faced down those boys. Told me a man doesn't run away from trouble."

Luke's own words echoed back at him. "So he's okay?"

Clayton nodded. "Even got a date for Saturday night out of it." The lines in his face deepened, and Luke knew he was thinking about his own experience. "Guess maybe attitudes have changed a little, at least."

Clayton put his hand on Luke's shoulder, as he might with one of his own sons. "Anyway, I'm grateful to you," he said, with such gravity that he might be making a solemn oath.

Luke cleared his throat. "You know, there's something I've been wanting to talk to you about."

"No time like the present." Clayton leaned against the porch rail.

Chloe would think *any* other time better, but Chloe wasn't here. And he had to get this wound up before his goal slipped from his grasp.

"Chloe and I were talking about the land you own on Angel Isle. I'm interested in making a deal for a piece of it. I—"

Clayton shoved himself away from the railing, beaming. "Is that what's been on your mind? Boy, why didn't you tell me that before?"

The response startled him. "Chloe thought I should wait."

"No point in waiting, when a man knows what he wants."

"There'll have to be a survey. We'll look at the market value, of course."

Chloe's father thrust out his hand. "We'll do what's fair. We both know that. My hand is my bond."

Luke took his hand. Either he was dreaming, or this was the easiest negotiation he'd ever done. "I appreciate your confidence. Now, about the details—"

"Luke!"

He turned. Chloe stood in the doorway, eyes wide with shock and hurt.

Chapter Fourteen

"Luke." Chloe pressed her hand against the door frame. The worn wooden edge felt real. It was the only thing that did. "What's going on?"

Say something, she demanded silently. *Tell me that what I think is happening isn't. Tell me I'm wrong, and that you didn't just betray me.*

Her father smiled. "Luke and I came to an arrangement, sugar. He's buying a tract of land on Angel Isle." He glanced at Luke. "Am I talkin' out of turn? You didn't say it was meant to be a secret."

"No, it's not a secret." Luke's voice flattened, giving nothing away. "Chloe knows about it."

"I know that you promised me you'd wait." She had to fight to keep the pain from her voice, and she probably wasn't succeeding, because it throbbed along her veins and choked her throat. "You agreed to give me time to find an alternative site."

His face froze into his competitive mask—edgy, determined. "The situation has changed."

"What has changed?" She pushed herself away from the door and stalked toward them, trying to concentrate on her anger so she wouldn't feel the pain. "What could possibly justify breaking your word to me?"

His jaw was clenched so hard it looked as if it might break. "This is business, Chloe. You know that. Mr. Dalton called. He wants the deal completed at once. I didn't have the luxury of waiting for you to be ready."

That business arrogance of his—she'd seen it turned against other people. She'd never expected to see it turned against her.

"Dalton?" Her father looked from her to Luke. "Who's Dalton?"

"The head of Dalton Resorts," Chloe said before Luke could answer. "The company we work for."

"What's he got to do with Luke buying land so he can build a home for the two of you?"

She had thought she couldn't hurt any worse than she already did, but this stabbed her in the heart. Daddy thought Luke wanted a home with her. A *life* with her. That was why he'd agreed. This had happened because she'd lied to the people who mattered most in the world to her.

"You misunderstood." To do him justice, Luke

looked as appalled as she felt. "I wasn't making the offer for myself, Mr. Caldwell. I was making it for Dalton Resorts. We want to build a hotel on Angel Isle."

"A hotel," her father echoed. He frowned at her. "Chloe, does any of this make sense to you?"

"Daddy—" She went to him then, clutching his hands in hers, trying to convey her regret through her touch. "I'm sorry. This shouldn't have happened. None of this should have happened." Shame burned deep inside. *I'm sorry, I'm so sorry. Forgive me.*

"Chloe, you don't have to say anything." Luke frowned at her, and his message was clear. She didn't have to expose the charade she'd carried out.

But he was wrong. She did have to.

She took a deep breath, wondering how her heart could keep on beating when it hurt so much. "Daddy, this has all been a lie. Luke and I have never been involved with each other. We're not a couple."

Her father shook his head slowly, as if her words didn't make any sense. "Then, why did he come here?"

"I wanted to check out the area for a new Dalton Resort," Luke said, apparently determined not to let her speak for him. "I'm sorry about the confusion, but that's all I'm interested in."

All he was interested in. Chloe bit down hard on her lip and tried not to think about those words.

Her father didn't look at Luke, only at her. "Chloe? Child, why did you do this?"

There weren't any reasons good enough. "I'm sorry, Daddy." She blinked back hot tears. "Gran thought we were dating, and she invited him to her birthday. And he—"

"It was business," Luke said. "Just business. I asked Chloe to play along, to give me an excuse for being here."

He probably thought he was helping, but he wasn't. Her father didn't so much as glance at Luke. He just stared searchingly into her eyes, and she felt very small and very ashamed.

"I'm sorry," she whispered again. "I shouldn't have let it go this far."

"No." Her father's level gaze told her just how disappointed in her he was. "No, you shouldn't have."

She tried to wrap her mind around a way to make things right. "At least you don't have to go through with this. You don't have to sell."

He straightened. "I gave my hand, child, and I don't back down when I've given my hand." He looked at Luke then, and his expression was almost pitying. "You'll tell me when you have the papers ready."

Without waiting for an answer, he turned and disappeared into the house.

Luke tried not to let the relief he felt show on his face. For a moment he'd seen the whole deal dissolving, seen his future at Dalton dissolving right along with it. Dalton wouldn't easily have forgiven his spending this much time and coming back empty-handed.

The deal was safe, but Chloe still had to be placated. "Chloe, I'm sorry."

"You're not sorry." The face she turned on him was the face of a stranger. "Why should you be? You're getting what you want."

"I'm sorry for the way it happened. Sorry that it all came out that way. I certainly didn't plan that. But Dalton put pressure on me to wrap this up quickly."

"So you put pressure on my father."

He'd never known her golden-brown eyes could look so scornful. He beat down the little voice that said she had every right.

"I didn't pressure him. I just opened the subject, and he agreed before I had a chance to give him the details."

"He didn't understand." She threw the words at him. "Thanks to our playacting, he agreed to something he never would have otherwise."

"You don't know that. When he heard what Dalton is willing to pay, he'd have jumped at it, anyway." He would, of course he would. Anyone would.

"If you really believe that, let him off the hook." Her words challenged him. "Start all over again and make your offer."

She was asking the impossible. "Chloe, I can't do that, not now. You must realize that. Dalton wouldn't forgive me if I let the deal slip between my fingers at this point."

"And that's all that matters to you."

She was judging him again. He embraced anger. She had no right to judge him. She didn't. No one did.

"I'm doing what I was hired to do. If you don't understand that, maybe you don't belong at Dalton Resorts."

The instant the words were out of his mouth, he was appalled. He didn't want to lose Chloe. He didn't want to think about returning to Chicago without her.

But the alternative seemed to be losing his dream, and he couldn't do that, either. He couldn't give up the goal that had sustained him all these years.

Chloe went white but her gaze never wavered. "Maybe you're right about that. Maybe I don't belong there, any more than you belong here."

There didn't seem to be anything left to say.

"I'll pack my things." He moved past her to the door. "It will be better if I move to a hotel on the mainland."

She stepped aside, as if touching him might contaminate her. "Yes. That will be better."

He yanked open the screen door. "Please tell your father I'll call him to arrange a meeting with an attorney to sign the papers."

Something inside cried to him to say something else, to mend this with Chloe no matter what the cost. He slammed it down hard. He couldn't change now, not when he was on the verge of having everything he wanted.

Then, why did that seem so hollow?

By evening, her family's sympathy had become intolerable. Chloe huddled in a rocker on the porch, feet pulled up, arms wrapped around her knees. If she'd ever doubted their love, she couldn't doubt it now. The knowledge of her deception had rocked them. They had to be disappointed in her. But one and all, they'd rallied around.

Daniel had suggested taking Luke for a nice long boat ride and marooning him. David wanted to call an attorney. Miranda thought if they just explained how they felt, surely Luke would understand. Theo had been at first disbelieving, then furious. His idol had shown his feet of clay, and Theo wasn't going to find that easy to forgive.

The bottom line, though, was that Daddy wouldn't change his mind. Whatever it cost him, his path was clear. He'd given his word.

It was her fault. Chloe leaned her forehead on her knees. When she was six and had done something wrong, she'd curled up in a ball in the futile hope that she could just disappear. It hadn't worked then, and it didn't work now.

They were going to lose Angel Isle, and it was all her fault.

Daniel's truck pulled into the drive. A door slammed, and Gran marched toward her. The family had called in the big guns, she thought tiredly. But Gran was just someone else to whom she owed an apology.

"Gran, I'm sorry." She wouldn't have thought she had any tears left to shed, but they welled in her eyes. "I deceived you. I'm so sorry."

Gran just stood for a moment, hands folded on the front of her flower-print dress. "You are a pretty sorry sight, Chloe Elizabeth."

Chloe planted her feet on the floor and wiped her eyes with the back of her hand. "Yes, ma'am."

"As for deceiving me—" Gran sat down in the rocker next to her "—looks to me like the person you most deceived was yourself."

Gran had an uncanny knack for getting right to the thing you least wanted to talk about.

"I guess that's true," she admitted. "I cared about Luke. I kidded myself into believing he cared about me. But he doesn't. He just cares about getting where he's always wanted to be."

"That's him. What about you?"

The question jerked her head up. "What do you mean?"

"I mean *you*, Chloe Elizabeth Caldwell. Why are

you sitting here feeling sorry for yourself? Why aren't you doing something about this?"

It was like a cold wave in her face. For a moment she just stared at Gran, and then she managed a smile. "That's what I love about you, Gran. You get right to the point."

Gran sniffed. "No sense my reminding you I love you, is there? You already know that. What about this young man of yours? You love him?"

"I do." She took a shaky breath. "It seems like a pretty stupid move right now, but I do."

"Why?"

The abrupt question took her aback. "Well, I…" *I just do* wasn't a good enough answer. Gran wanted specifics. "Because he's not really like this. At least, I don't think he is, down inside. But he had a terrible life when he was young. He came up from nothing, and he had to fight for everything. He thinks getting this vice-presidency will prove he's arrived. That's been his goal for so long that he can't see past it."

Gran gave a short nod. "'Bout what I figured. He's lost, that's what."

"Lost?" It was a new idea, and she considered it. "I guess you could look at it that way." Although Luke certainly didn't think he was lost.

"It's the truth." Her expression softened. "Like you,

Chloe-girl. Our Chloe was lost for a while. But then Luke brought you back, and you started to see what God wants for you, didn't you?"

For a moment, she'd thought what God wanted for her was a life with Luke. But she understood what Gran meant. If she hadn't come back to the island with Luke, she might never have looked at what God's will for her life was. She might never have seen that just having a job and a salary wasn't enough. She had to contribute—had to be needed.

"I guess so, but Luke isn't like me. I'm not even sure what he believes. He had faith once, but it seems like it got buried under all his ambition."

"Lost," Gran said again with certainty. "He's lost, and you've got to rescue him."

"Me? Gran, he's not going to listen to me." *He doesn't care,* her heart cried.

"Chloe Elizabeth, you hear me now." Gran looked at her sternly. "If he were drowning out there in the surf, you'd risk your life to save him, wouldn't you?"

Like the first Chloe. "Yes, but—"

"No 'buts' about it. That young man of yours is drowning, and he doesn't even know it—wanting things and success more than God's plans for him. It's up to you to straighten him out, you heah?"

There was only one answer Gran expected when she asked that. "Yes, ma'am. But it's not going to be easy."

"If it was easy, anybody could do it. It wouldn't take Chloe Elizabeth Caldwell."

Gran clasped her hand firmly, then stood up. "Now I got to talk to that son of mine. Make sure he's doing this because he thinks it's right, not just because he knows it's the opposite of what his brother would do."

Chloe just stared after her. That would never have occurred to her, but obviously Gran was considerably wiser. She knew more about people than Chloe would learn in a lifetime.

And Gran thought Chloe could do this thing.

Chloe forced herself to look at the possibility. How could she make Luke see he was wrong?

One thing was certain. She wouldn't make the mistake again of trying to create a plan without taking it to the Lord. She closed her eyes, seeking the quiet place in her soul that she would feel in the chapel or on Angel Isle. Listening.

A few minutes later she opened her eyes and found she was looking at the *Spyhop*, rocking gently at the dock. Angel Isle. The boat.

An idea began to form in her mind. *Is this it, Lord? Is this what I should be doing?*

A quiet sureness filled her soul. She knew what she had to do. She had to confront Luke with who he was, and she knew just where to do it.

Whether he'd listen to her or not—well, that was up to him. She knew what God expected her to do, and that was enough.

Chapter Fifteen

Luke stood at the public dock in Caldwell Cove the next day, wondering if anything could be more futile than this effort. Why had he come? His meeting in the local attorney's office to sign the preliminary agreements was set for less than three hours away. He wouldn't believe he'd actually pulled this off until he had the agreements in hand.

So why was he here?

He didn't have to search hard for the answer. He knew why. Chloe had called him, Chloe had wanted to see him. And even though he didn't think it would do any good, he had to see her again.

Chloe's face filled his mind, her green eyes dancing, her golden-brown hair curling against sun-kissed skin, her generous mouth smiling at him. He tried to push it away, to replace it with an image of the corner office that would soon be his. The task was more difficult than it should be.

All right, he could deal with this. He'd spent his life setting goals and letting nothing keep him from achieving them. He didn't intend to change now.

The only reason Chloe intruded on his plans was that he didn't like the breach between them. He cared about her, not just as his valued right hand but as…

What? His mind stalled on that. He knew how to think of Chloe as his assistant. He wasn't sure he knew how to relate to her as anything else. But things had changed since they'd come to the island, he couldn't deny that.

He wanted to mend things with her. That much was clear in his mind. Whether or not there could be anything else between them—he just didn't know.

He saw her face again—eyes filled with a sense of betrayal—and something clamped around his heart. Then he looked up and saw the *Spyhop* nosing into the dock with Chloe at the wheel.

She tossed the rope to him, and he caught it automatically. His mind seemed empty of the words he wanted to say. He just looked at her, noting the dark smudges under her eyes and the determined set to her soft mouth.

"Are you all right?" That wasn't what he'd intended to say, but his heart took over.

She shrugged, unsmiling. "I've been better." She gestured to the boat. "Hop in. Let's go for a ride."

"Can't we just talk here?" He glanced at his watch.

"You have plenty of time before your meeting." Her voice was edgy. "Get on board. I want to make one last trip to Angel Isle before your meeting."

"Chloe, I don't think that's a good idea. Look, let's go get a cup of coffee and talk."

She shook her head stubbornly. "Angel Isle." She met his gaze evenly. "I think you owe me that."

Angel Isle was the last place he wanted to go today. But there was a determination about Chloe that was new to her, as if she'd done some growing up overnight. She wasn't the team player, ready to go along with anything he wanted. If he wanted to talk to her, he'd have to do it her way.

"All right." He stepped lightly into the boat. "If it means that much to you."

She didn't answer—just backed away from the dock so quickly he nearly fell into his seat. He clutched the railing with one hand and watched as she turned her face into the wind and the nose of the boat into the channel.

She wasn't looking at him. Eyes narrowed, she stared straight ahead.

"Chloe, look, we have to talk."

She shook her head, gesturing toward her ears.

"Can't hear well enough here. Wait until we get to the island."

"We've talked before on the boat. Why not now?"

She swung the boat in a wide semicircle around the end of the island. "You're in a hurry to get to your meeting, remember?" She revved the motor. "So let's just get there."

They passed the yacht club dock, and he wondered if Theo was working today. With a pang, he realized the kid who'd looked at him with so much admiration the other night probably wouldn't speak to him now.

Then Chloe turned the boat into Dolphin Sound, accelerating so that they rocketed across the waves. He clung grimly to the rail and wondered if she was trying to make him seasick. No looking for dolphins today— all he could do was hang on.

Finally she eased in to the dock on Angel Isle, and he took a deep breath and waited for his stomach to catch up with him.

"Trying to make me remember I'm a landlubber?" he asked, climbing onto the dock and making the ropes fast. He wouldn't admit how much he wanted to feel firm ground under his feet.

Chloe scrambled up beside him. "Just wanted you to have a taste of what the sound will be like once there's a resort on Angel Isle—hotel launches rushing back and forth, pleasure boats crowding the water."

She pointed, and he saw the dolphins then, their crescent shapes moving through the waves. Funny, he almost felt he could identify them, the way Sammy had that first day.

"Say goodbye." Chloe's tone was grim. "I don't imagine they'll hang around once the sound becomes jammed."

He ought to be able to find something to say to that, but he couldn't. *It's not my fault.* That was what he wanted to say. "Look, we both know the hotel will bring prosperity. People will be glad we did it. The dolphins will adapt."

She just looked at him. Suddenly he was back waist-deep in the warm water of the marsh, looking at the triumph in Chloe's face as the dolphin shuddered between them and then took off for the sea.

He blinked, shaking his head, shaking away the image. But looking at Chloe today proved just as disturbing. The gold dolphin necklace he'd given her lay against her skin. For an instant his fingertips tingled, as if he were fastening the clasp against the delicate arch of her nape.

He took a step back from her, and the dock moved gently under his feet. "Let's take a walk," he said abruptly. Maybe he'd be able to think more clearly if he wasn't looking at her.

She nodded, and he followed her off the dock and

down to the stretch of beach. They fell into step with each other on the hard-packed sand. He frowned, trying to come up with the words that would make things right between them. It shouldn't be this difficult to make peace with Chloe. He'd handled far more costly negotiations than this, without this terrifying sense that the wrong word would ruin everything.

"They won't, you know." Chloe glanced out at the water.

"Who won't?"

"The dolphins. They won't adapt."

"Chloe—" He stopped, again gripped by that fear of saying the wrong thing. "You know you can't stop progress. It's going to come whether you want it or not."

Her glance flashed to him. "Not stop it, no. But progress doesn't have to take away our island."

"Look, I know you love it here." *I feel closer to God on Angel Isle than anyplace else on earth.* That gave him pause. "But are you sure you're not being a little selfish? Don't other people have the right to share the beauty?"

The shadow in her eyes told him the shot had hit home.

"The place as we know it won't exist in ten years if the hotel goes in. That's what you don't understand. Angel Isle is too fragile. Other places can stand up to it, but not Angel Isle."

He'd agreed to let her help him find an alternative

site, and then he'd gone back on his word. He'd had a good reason for that, hadn't he?

"Dalton didn't give me a choice." That sounded defensive even to him.

"You always have a choice, Luke. It just depends how big a price you're willing to pay."

They seemed to have cut through all the external arguments. It was as if they spoke to each other's hearts.

"You don't know what you're asking me." He stopped, swinging to face her.

She met his eyes. "I might be the one person who does know."

He knew, suddenly, what he was seeing in her eyes. Love. For him. It crashed over him like a wave, knocking him off his feet.

"Chloe." He took her hands, feeling her pulse beating rapidly against his fingers. "Chloe, I want—"

What did he want? What was he willing to give up to have her? Everything?

He drew her slowly toward him. This was bigger than ambition, bigger than the corner office. This was everything he'd ever wanted. "Chloe." He said her name again softly as she moved into his arms—

The sound ripped through the stillness. He spun.

The *Spyhop's* engine roared, and the boat shot away from the dock toward the open sound with Theo at the wheel.

The meeting—without the boat, he'd never make the meeting. Chloe had invited him here. Chloe had betrayed him.

Chloe stared blankly after the *Spyhop*. "Theo!" she shouted, even knowing how impossible it was for him to hear her. "What does that boy think he's doing?"

She swung to Luke, as if he might have an answer, and then she saw his face. He thought she had done this.

"Luke, I didn't." Tears stung her eyes. Why now, of all times? Surely she'd been getting through to Luke. He'd looked at her as if…as if he loved her.

He didn't look that way now.

"Congratulations, Chloe." His fists clenched. "That was a move worthy of Dalton himself."

"You can't believe I had anything to do with that. Theo's come up with some crazy plan on his own." Probably because Theo had been hurt to discover Luke wasn't the hero he'd thought.

"I'm afraid that's giving your little brother a bit too much credit." He looked at his watch, and his blue eyes darkened with fury. "Perfect timing. I miss the meeting, your father assumes I've backed out, and the deal is off."

"I didn't." She said it again, helpless against his anger. He'd never believe her.

"On the other hand, maybe not such terrific timing." His expression was wry. "Because I was about to give in. About to give up everything for you, because…I thought we were in love."

I thought we were in love. She did feel her heart break then, she was sure of it.

"What happened to that loyalty of yours, Chloe? It seems to be a pretty flexible commodity these days."

Anger welled up suddenly, and she welcomed it. If she held on to the anger, maybe she could withstand the pain for a bit.

"Loyalty? You're a fine one to talk about loyalty. About love." She had to fight a fresh wave of pain before she could go on. "Don't even talk about changing for me. You should be making this decision because it's right, not because of me."

She had lost him. No, that wasn't right. She couldn't lose what she'd never had. But she could still grieve for what might have been.

"What's right is doing the job I came here to do. The job you were supposed to help me do."

"What's right doesn't have anything to do with business." Her head throbbed with the need to make him see.

Oh, Lord, let me get through to him.

"You talked about Reverend Tom and what he meant to you. How he led you to the Lord. Do you actually remember any of that? Do you ever think about doing anything because it's God's will for your life, instead of what you want?"

He went pale. "Don't preach to me, Chloe. You don't have the right."

"I love you." The words she thought she'd never speak had a bitter taste. "I think that gives me the right." Before he could say anything, she swept on. "You asked me where my loyalty was. I can tell you that. It's to the man I've always thought you were, inside. But if you go through with this, you're not that man."

No use, it was no use. He wasn't hearing her. She spun on her heel.

"Where are you going?"

"Theo had to have come by boat." She flung the words over her shoulder at him. "I'm going to find it. If you expect to make that meeting, you'd better hurry."

Without waiting to see if he was following, she jogged down the sand. She had a pretty good idea where Theo would have beached his boat—same place he'd beached it when he'd run away. And if she concentrated on that and kept moving, maybe she could run away from the pain that threatened to overwhelm her.

Sure enough, Theo's boat was pulled up under a sweep of Spanish moss not more than twenty feet from the dock. She tugged it toward the water.

"We're going across the sound in that?"

"It's the only way." She resisted the impulse to imply

it wasn't safe. Her father had raised her to act honorably. She wouldn't disappoint him again. "Theo does it all the time."

"All right." Luke's jaw set. "Let's do it." He grabbed the boat and dragged it to the water.

Of course he'd do it. Chloe shoved them out into deep water. The word *can't* wasn't in Luke's vocabulary. He'd sacrifice anything for the rewards this deal would bring. Anything.

She saw the flash of a dolphin out in the sound, and closed her eyes for a second against her agony.

Gran had been wrong. She wasn't like the first Chloe. She didn't have the strength to save the man she loved.

Chapter Sixteen

He was doing what he had to do. Luke repeated the words to himself as the small boat chugged up to the dock in Caldwell Cove. *What he had to do.* Even Chloe must recognize that. She hadn't spoken to him all the way across the sound.

Just as well. He was furious at the thought of her betrayal. He should be used to that. It was business. But not Chloe. Chloe didn't do things like that.

She eased the boat into the dock, and he looped the rope around the piling and made it tight. Quickly he climbed out, brushing at the water stains on his slacks.

It wasn't the way he'd choose to appear at an important meeting, but it would have to do.

Do you ever think about what God wants you to do? Chloe's voice echoed in his mind, and he blocked it out.

He turned to her. "I assume you're going to the attorney's office, too. You may as well ride with me."

Her mouth pressed into a thin line, and she shook her head. "I'll walk."

A spurt of anger surprised him. "Don't be ridiculous. You've just spent two hours with me. Another five minutes isn't going to compromise you."

For an instant she just stared at him, and he couldn't read her usually expressive face. Then she jerked a nod and stalked to the car.

He followed, unable to reject the thought that swept through him. He cared about those five minutes. He cared because they could be the last ones he'd ever spend in her company. After today, he'd probably never see her again.

Against his will, he took a quick sideways glance at her as she slid into the seat next to him. *He'd never see her again.* It was like having a piece of himself cut away. Chloe knew him better than anyone else in his life.

And he knew *her* better. The thought stuck. He knew Chloe bone deep. He knew what she could do, and what she couldn't. And she couldn't have connived to strand him on Angel Isle so he'd miss the meeting. She couldn't. His certainty shocked him.

He was still grappling with it when he pulled up in front of the office of Caldwell Cove's only attorney.

Chloe jumped out as if she couldn't bear to be in his company any longer.

But he was out and around the car before she could reach the door. "Chloe, wait."

He grasped her arm, and it was like grasping a live wire. He felt the shock right to his heart. He released her as she swung toward him.

"What I said before—about you plotting with Theo to maroon me on the island." This was incredibly awkward to say with her looking at him as if he were an insect. "If you didn't, I'm sorry for what I said."

She just continued to stare at him, and he realized he'd been wrong about her look. She wasn't looking at him as if he were an insect. She was looking at him as if he had a repugnant and possibly contagious illness.

"It really doesn't matter now, does it." She turned and walked into the office.

He followed, feeling emptier than he had in a long time. She was right. It didn't matter.

Preston James was a fussy, probably inefficient elderly man who'd obviously known the Caldwell family forever. Luke was prepared to find him trouble to deal with, but the paperwork had been drawn up as he'd requested. Ten more minutes and this would all be over.

James gestured them to seats around a long mahogany table that looked as if it belonged in someone's dining room. Chloe, her parents, the twins and Miranda lined up in the chairs on one side. Luke took his place across from them, alone.

"Well, I guess we all know why we're here." James put documents in front of Luke and Clayton. "Take one more look at this, please." His comment seemed to be directed more at Clayton than at Luke.

Chloe's mother put her hand on her husband's. His children seemed to draw closer to him. They might not agree with what he was doing, but they were there to support him. They'd stand by him, no matter what happened.

The attorney put down a pen in front of Luke, and it clicked against the table, the only sound in the office. No, not the only sound. Luke could hear his own heart beating. A wave of panic swept over him, like a riptide pulling him to the bottom of the ocean.

When was the last time you asked God what He wanted from you?

Images flickered through his mind, so quickly he could barely identify them, as if he were drowning and his life was passing before his eyes—the Rev, beaming with pride when Luke's college scholarship came through; the day he'd received his MBA, with no one there to help him celebrate; his first office, barely bigger than a broom closet.

His pulse pounded in his ears. Was he having a heart

attack? He tried to focus on the document, but other pictures blocked it out. Chloe—hugging her grand-mother, frowning over her brother's misdeeds, saving the dolphin. Chloe, looking at him with all her generous heart in her gaze, saying she loved the man she thought he was, inside.

What do You want from me, God?

The question he'd avoided all his life thundered in his mind, ripped from his very soul.

What do You want from me?

He was vaguely aware of the lawyer saying something, vaguely realized the others were looking at him strangely.

"Are you ready to sign, Mr. Hunter?" The man held the pen out to him.

The answer he'd tried to escape pooled in his mind, crystal clear.

"No." He stood, scraping his chair back. He looked at Clayton. "The offer is withdrawn."

He turned and walked out.

Chloe stood on the dock alone, watching the sunset paint the sky with pink and purple. Alone. She'd strug-gled through the rest of this unbelievable day, trying to get her loving family to leave her alone.

After they'd finished wondering and exclaiming and praising God for the unexpected turn of events in the lawyer's office, the advice had begun. *Go after him,*

Chloe. That was the gist of it. *Go after him. He did the right thing, in the end, so go after him.*

She couldn't, not now. Her heart ached. Luke was fighting it out with Dalton, and more importantly with God. This part he had to do alone. The only thing she could do now was pray, and she'd been doing that with all her strength for the past hour.

You showed me the truth about myself, Lord. Please be with Luke. Show him the person he was meant to be.... And bring him back to me. I don't want this to be a selfish prayer, Lord. But bring him back to me.

She heard a step on the dock. When she turned, Luke was there.

For a moment he just stood, looking at her. She met his eyes, half afraid of what she might find there.

Relief swept through her. Peace. That was what she saw at last in his eyes. Peace.

"You came back." She couldn't seem to find any other words. "You came back."

He nodded, stepping closer. But not touching her. "I had some things to take care of." He grimaced. "With Dalton Resorts."

"What happened?" Dalton wouldn't have taken it well, she knew that. She knew exactly what Luke had risked by his actions—the vice-presidency, the future he'd planned for himself.

"Let's just say I'm not in the running for vice-president any longer."

"I'm sorry."

"I'm not." He shrugged. "Funny, I never thought I'd say that, but I'm not. Anyway, I finally talked Dalton into considering another site in the area. I'll be staying long enough to find it. Then—well, I've had a lot of thinking to do today about where my life goes next. You know, don't you?"

"Wrestling with God. That's what Gran calls it. Wrestling with God."

"Exactly." His face looked relaxed, almost younger. "I'd managed to avoid that all my life, and all of a sudden, thanks to you, I couldn't anymore."

The last bit of fear she'd been holding onto vanished. Whatever happened between them, Luke had found his way back to his Father. "Not me," she said. "You did this on your own."

"Only because you made me face it. 'Have you asked what God wants of your life?' That's what you said. That's what wouldn't let me go."

Gran had said Chloe would have to rescue him, and Chloe had thought she couldn't—known she couldn't in her own strength. But she hadn't done it alone.

"If I said the right words, it was because God gave them to me."

Luke reached out then, touching her cheek gently. "I

know. God made a lot of things clear to me, once I started listening—" His voice broke suddenly, and he cleared his throat. "I looked at your father, willing to sacrifice something he loved for the sake of honor. And I knew that's the kind of man God wants me to be."

Her heart was so full she couldn't speak, and tears filled her eyes. She let them spill over onto her cheeks, and Luke wiped them away, his fingertips warm on her skin.

"That's the man I've always seen, inside," she whispered. "An honorable man. The man I love."

Luke spread his hands wide, empty. "This is all I have to offer, Chloe. Just myself, and an uncertain future. Will you have me?"

She stepped into his outstretched arms and felt them close around her.

"That's all I ever wanted," she said, heart overflowing with love and gratitude. "Just you."

Epilogue

Two months later

"Come away from that door, Chloe Elizabeth Caldwell. Do you want the groom to see you before the ceremony?"

Gran closed the door into the sanctuary, but not before Chloe had seen St. Andrew's filled to capacity with family and friends. They'd cheerfully overflowed to the groom's side, taking the place of the family Luke didn't have.

Even Cousin Matt was there, all the way from Indonesia this time. The faintest shadow clouded her happiness. Something was wrong with Matt. She'd sensed it, and so had Gran. Something aside from the wedding had brought him home.

Keep him in Your hands, Lord. Let him find what he seeks here on Caldwell Island.

"It's all right, Gran." Chloe squeezed her grandmother's hand. "Theo's keeping Luke safely out of sight." Theo, having been struck dumb by Luke asking him to be the best man, had recovered to a determination to be the best best man anyone had ever seen.

Miranda, her long skirt flowing about her, knelt to adjust the folds of cream silk around Chloe's ankles, and her mother fastened the last button on the long sleeves of the dress she'd worn for her own wedding.

"Perfect," she said, smiling through a sheen of tears. "Just perfect."

Perfect, Chloe echoed silently. How could it not be perfect, when she was marrying the only man she'd ever love, the man God had chosen for her.

The door opened, and Sammy popped his head in. "The Rev says they're ready when you are."

Miranda frowned at him, ready to correct him for using Luke's nickname for Reverend Tom, but Chloe shook her head. Reverend Tom had become part of the family in the few days since he'd arrived to assist with the ceremony. Chloe had been prepared to love him on sight, and she had.

It was thanks to his wise counsel that Luke had taken a job with the Sonlight Center, once the new Dalton hotel had been sited on the land they bought from Uncle Jeff, next to the yacht club. Dalton was happy, Caldwell Cove was happy with its new source of income, and Luke had found a job that would let him pay back a little of what had been done for him.

And, as if to round out her happiness, they were living back in Caldwell Cove, where she could use her skills at the inn and be a volunteer at the center. They were both doing things that mattered. They'd both come home.

"There." Gran opened the box she held and lifted out the creamy lace veil—the one Caldwell brides had worn since the first Chloe. It fluttered over Chloe's hair, light as an angel's wing. "Now you're ready."

She pushed the door open. Daniel stood ready to escort their mother, and David offered his arm to Gran with a gallant bow. Miranda started Sammy down the aisle with his precious cargo of wedding rings, then blew a kiss to Chloe as she took her place.

Her father held out his arm. "Ready, Chloe-girl?"

She slipped her hand into the crook of his arm, feeling his strength. She let her gaze drift across the small sanctuary, treasuring every inch of it. Even the bracket where the dolphin had stood was filled with the arrangement of beach roses and baby's breath that Miranda had put there.

Finally she looked at Luke. His eyes met hers, and

she could see his love for her shining across the length of the church.

Thankfulness filled her soul. She squeezed her father's arm. "I'm ready," she said.

* * * * *

Dear Reader,

I'm so glad you decided to pick up this book. I've been longing to return to the Carolina coast that I love, so I'm especially happy to be writing the stories of the Caldwell kin—an extended family whose members learn the truth of the Scripture passages Gran Caldwell chose for each of them when they were baptized. I love stories about big families, and I hope you do, too.

Chloe Caldwell, the heroine of *Hunter's Bride,* has let Gran believe she's dating her boss, corporate executive Luke Hunter. Her charade explodes in her face when Gran invites Luke to Caldwell Cove for her eightieth birthday celebration. To her horror, Luke announces he'll attend as the beau Gran believes him to be. Luke and Chloe are convinced that their romance is just an act, but there are surprises in store for them when Chloe's loving, interfering family decides she should be the next Caldwell bride.

I'd love to hear from you and send you a signed bookplate or bookmark. Please write to me: Marta Perry, c/o Steeple Hill Books, 233 Broadway, Suite 1001, New York, NY 10279. Or visit me on the Web at www.martaperry.com.

Marta Perry

A MOTHER'S WISH

And we know that in all things,
God works for the good of those who love Him,
who have been called according to His purpose.
—*Romans* 8:28

This book is dedicated to my daughter Susan
and her husband, David, with love and thanks.

And, as always, to Brian.

Chapter One

If he had to go into exile for the next six months, he couldn't pick a better place than this. Matt Caldwell paused outside the office of the *Caldwell Cove Gazette* and took a deep breath, inhaling a mixture of sea, salt and the rich musky aroma of the marshes. Home—Caldwell Island, South Carolina. He'd know that distinctive smell in an instant no matter where he was on the globe. Quiet, peaceful…

Pop, pop, pop. A sharp sound broke the drowsy June silence. Matt's stomach lurched. He ducked in the response that had become second nature in the last few years, adrenaline pumping, fists clenching. He had to get everyone to cover.

Fragmented images shot through his mind. He smelled the acrid smoke of explosions, felt the bone-jarring crash, heard the cries of children.

It took seconds to remind himself he was in Caldwell Cove, not on a bomb-ridden Indonesian street, seconds more to identify the sound. Some kid must be playing with caps in the lane beside the newspaper office.

A few quick strides took him around the corner of the weathered gray building. Sure enough, that's what it was. The gut-wrenching fear subsided, to be replaced by anger. Those boys were way too young to be playing with caps.

"What are you doing?"

His sharp question brought two young faces looking up at him. Their faces wore identically startled expressions. Almost identical, he realized. They had to be brothers, both towheads with round faces and big blue eyes. The older one couldn't be more than six or seven. Definitely too young to be smashing a strip of caps with a stone. He was surprised kids could even get their hands on those things now.

"We weren't doing anything." The speaker clasped his hands behind his back. His little brother nodded in agreement, blue eyes round with surprise. "Honest."

Matt frowned at the word. "Honest" was the last thing the kid was being. "You were playing with caps. Don't you know that's dangerous?"

The older boy tried a smile. "We were careful. We didn't get hurt."

"Yet." It wasn't any of his business, but these two

might injure themselves. He couldn't just walk away. "Where's your mother?"

When they didn't answer, he planted his hands on his hips and glared, waiting. "Well?"

"I'm their mother."

The woman flew around the corner as she spoke. She grabbed the boys and pulled them against her. Matt looked into eyes the same shade of blue as the kids', sparkling with indignation. Her softly rounded face and curling brown hair reminded him of a Renaissance portrait, but her expression spoke more of a mother tiger, ready to protect her young.

"Why were you shouting at my sons?" She threw the words at him.

"I wasn't shouting."

"I heard you." Her indignation sparked his own.

"Maybe you'd shout, too, if you were paying attention to your own kids." As he said it he knew he was going too far, but the emotions of the past months still rode him, erasing normal politeness. "Or don't you care what they're up to?"

The woman's mouth tightened, and she looked as if she reviewed several things she might say before responding. "I can't imagine what concern my child-rearing is to you."

"It isn't. But I have to care when I see kids in danger." He forced away the images that still haunted his dreams—of crying children huddled into makeshift bomb shelters or lying still on crowded hospital beds. "Your little angels were playing with caps."

"Caps?" That stopped her dead. She looked into her kids' faces with a hand on each one's shoulder. "Ethan? Jeffrey? Is that right?"

He waited for the quick denial again, but it didn't come. Apparently they had more trouble fibbing to her than to a stranger. The younger one looked down; the older flushed and nodded.

"We didn't get hurt, Mommy."

"Ethan, that's not the point. You know better, both of you. Where did you get caps?"

The kid looked as if he searched for an appropriate answer and didn't find it. Finally he shrugged. "We found them. In that old shed back there." He pointed toward the rear of the building, where a tumbledown shed leaned against the next building.

"I told you…" The woman stopped, and Matt saw the pink in her cheeks deepen. She probably didn't want to be having this discussion in front of him. "Go to your room, both of you. Right now. We'll talk about this in a bit."

The boys scampered around the building, and the woman looked as if she'd like to do the same. But she turned to face him, her color still high.

"I'm sorry." The words were stiff, making it clear

she hadn't forgiven his sharp words. "I appreciate your concern."

He shrugged. "It's nothing." He wanted to walk away and get on with his own affairs, but the awkward moment seemed to demand something more. He was back in Caldwell Cove now, where everyone knew everyone else, usually for a generation or two.

"I'm Matt Caldwell, by the way."

"Matt…" Her eyes widened with what might have been surprise but looked like shock. "I should have recognized you."

He started to make the polite response he always did when someone gushed that they'd seen him on television, reporting from one trouble spot or another. But she didn't give him the chance.

"I'm Sarah Reed."

Sarah Reed. Now he was the one left speechless with surprise. The woman he'd basically accused of being a careless mother was his new partner at the *Caldwell Cove Gazette.*

Sarah took a deep breath, then another, searching for some measure of calm. She'd known Matthew Caldwell was coming home to the island where his large extended family still lived. She'd known, too, that he'd undoubtedly want to discuss the investment he'd made in the *Gazette* over a year earlier, before her husband's death.

She hadn't expected to be taken by surprise like this, however. When she'd imagined their first meeting, she'd been in the office, neatly dressed in the blue suit she almost never wore, coolly prepared to discuss the fact that, since her husband's death, she was now his partner.

She certainly hadn't expected to get into a wrangle with the man before she even knew who he was. Her cheeks grew warm, and she smoothed her hands down the denim skirt that was far too casual for a first meeting with a business partner.

To do him justice, Matthew Caldwell looked just as appalled as she felt. And he managed to recover first.

"Mrs. Reed." He held out his hand, something a little rueful showing in the hint of a smile that touched his firm mouth. "I'm sure this isn't how either of us wanted to begin."

If he was prepared to be gracious, it was the least she could do, as well. She met his grip, and his hand enveloped hers, firm and strong. A faint shiver of awareness went through her at his touch, and she brushed it away.

"Perhaps we should start over," she said. "Welcome back to Caldwell Cove, Mr. Caldwell."

He grimaced. "In view of our partnership, maybe we'd better dispense with the formality. Sarah." He said her name cautiously.

She'd have preferred to hang on to some measure of

distance between them, but she could hardly say so. "Fine." She took a step back, gesturing toward the building. "Why don't we continue our conversation in the office?" Maybe there she'd be able to regain her composure and get this encounter back to the way she'd imagined it. But she suspected that was a lost cause already.

She stole a glance at Matt as he walked beside her to the front of the building. She should have recognized him the instant she saw him. Maybe she had, at some level, though she hadn't identified that jolt of familiarity when she'd looked into his eyes.

She'd known of Matt Caldwell first as her friend Miranda's cousin, which was reason enough to watch for his face on the evening news broadcasts from around the globe. Then her husband had accepted Matt's investment in the paper, and she'd had more reason to be interested.

But this Matt Caldwell looked different from the tall, composed figure she'd seen standing with a microphone in front of a bombed-out building or a refugee camp. It was the same strong face, the planes of it looking as if they had been chiseled from stone, the same dark hair brushed ruthlessly back from a broad forehead.

He had the look of the Caldwells she knew already, but he had none of their casual, relaxed manner. He was dressed with a touch more formality than most men on the island, wearing chinos, not jeans, and a white shirt open to reveal a strong, tanned neck.

The lines in his face were deeper than she'd noticed on her TV screen, and the fan of wrinkles at the corners of his chocolate-brown eyes spoke of tension. Even his hand, braced against the door as he opened it for her, looked taut, as if he might fly into action at any moment.

And he wasn't half a world away. He was here, in Caldwell Cove, disrupting her peace and interfering with her children.

The bell she'd put on the door jingled, and his hand jerked involuntarily. She frowned. What was going on with the man? He'd overreacted with her boys, no matter how wrong they'd been, and now the slightest sound seemed to affect him. Then she remembered all those danger spots she'd seen him report from and realized she knew the answer.

"Hi, Mommy." Andi looked up from the computer, and her little face grew solemn at the sight of a stranger. At eight, Andi took being the oldest very seriously, especially since her daddy's death.

Amy, at eighteen months, felt no such restraint. She banged a plastic hammer on the rail of her play yard. "Up, Mama! Up!"

"In a minute, sweetheart." She glanced at Matt and intercepted a frown. He'd probably never envisioned the newspaper office populated by a round-faced toddler clutching the rail of a play yard, nor a pigtailed little girl peering at him from behind the computer monitor.

Well, he'd just have to accept it. She couldn't afford to hire a baby-sitter every minute of the day, so the children had to be where she could watch them.

A tinge of guilt touched her. She hadn't been watching the boys closely enough. If she had, that quarrel with Matt would never have taken place. She should have realized that tumbledown shed behind the building would attract them sooner or later.

"Well." She forced a smile. "Here's the office. Is it the way you remember it?" Miranda had told her Matt had worked at the paper as a teenager, and she'd assumed that was why he'd decided to invest in it. A sentimental whim, probably—a connection to his home when he was halfway around the world.

He turned slowly, assessing the sunlit room, its worn wooden counter and elderly wall clock contrasting with the modern computers. "The computers are new. Harvey Gaylord wouldn't even have an electric type-writer in the place. He insisted on using his old upright."

"We put the computers in when we bought the paper from him." Behind the casual conversation her mind worked busily. What did he want?

It was natural enough for him to check on his invest-ment, she assured herself. And if he had a complaint about the return he was getting on that investment—

well, surely he'd realize that no one got rich running a small-town weekly. They were lucky to be able to pay the bills some months.

She ought to bring the subject up herself, instead of worrying about it, but she couldn't quite do that.

"Did you...I guess you wanted to see the operation for yourself." It was as close as she could come to asking him outright why he was there.

"What?" He glanced up from his study of her computer, dark eyes frowning.

Wariness shivered along her nerves. There was something, some emotion she didn't understand, suppressed under his iron control.

Please, Lord. The prayer was almost involuntary. *Don't let him tell me he wants to pull out his investment. We couldn't survive that.*

"Your arrangements with my husband," she said, trying for a casualness she didn't feel. "I know they were made long-distance, through your attorney. You probably want to see the operation for yourself, while you're here on the island." She tried to manage a smile, knowing that the charm that had come so easily to Peter was totally missing from her makeup.

"Not exactly." He transferred the frown to her, and she sensed that he was searching for words to tell her something.

"Then what, exactly?" She was probably being too

blunt, but she couldn't seem to help it. The newspaper was too important to her family to beat around the bush. "If you have bad news for me, I'd rather you just came out with it."

His face tightened, if that were possible, and he braced one hand against the counter. "I don't know whether you'll consider it bad news or not. The fact is, I'm here because I intend to help run the paper."

She could only stare at him. "Run the paper." She repeated the words, hearing the disbelief in her voice.

Apparently he heard it, too, because the lines in his forehead deepened as he gave a curt nod. "That's right. Run the paper. I own half of this operation, and I want to help run it."

"But…" Her mind spun. She could almost hear Peter's voice in her mind, that day last spring when he'd told her he'd accepted an investment offer from Matt Caldwell. This would be an easy solution to all their money problems, he'd said. Caldwell would be half a world away, not here, bothering them, and the money would bail them out of a tight crunch.

Now Peter's solution didn't look so easy. Their silent partner didn't intend to be silent any longer.

Matt moved impatiently, drawing her gaze back to his determined face. "Is that a problem for you?"

She took a breath, trying to ignore how off balance the man made her feel. More to the point, trying to find a tactful way of telling him she neither wanted nor needed his help. "Not a problem, exactly." Her too-expressive face was probably telling him exactly the opposite. "But it wasn't part of my understanding of what our agreement involved."

"Our agreement gives me a half share in the paper. That means I have an equal say in how it's run." He said it uncompromisingly.

Well, why wouldn't he sound sure of himself? He'd known what he intended, after all. She was the one left unprepared by this sudden attack on her peaceful life.

She tried to summon up defenses. "But why? You have a successful broadcasting career. Why would you want to give that up to run the *Caldwell Cove Gazette?*"

His face looked closed, his brown eyes shuttered, denying her any glimpse of his feelings. "Let's say I'm ready for a break, and running the *Gazette* will give me that."

There was more to his decision than that; she could sense it. But he certainly wasn't going to confide in her. She sought desperately for another argument, any argument that might stave off this unwelcome development.

"I'm afraid you'll be bored to tears within the next month."

His smile had nothing of humor about it. "Let me worry about that."

"There's not really enough work for two. We have a couple of part-timers who help out when we need them, but otherwise, I can handle it myself." She could only hope she didn't sound desperate.

"You worked with your husband. How is it any different to work with me?"

There were so many answers to that question that she couldn't decide which one to pick. A chill touched her. She'd seen Matt Caldwell's type before—arrogant, determined, sure he was right and the rest of the world wrong. What might he do if he were running the paper? But he'd decided on this course, and he wouldn't be easily dissuaded.

"Mommy?"

She blinked, turning to Andi. She'd forgotten her daughter was there, watching them with the level, serious stare that was too old for her eight years.

"Mommy, what's wrong? What does he want?" Andi trained that solemn look on Matt.

"Nothing's wrong, honey." Nothing, except that the precarious balance she'd attained since Peter's death was seriously disrupted. Nothing, except that Matt Caldwell proposed to interfere in the running of the paper that was the livelihood for her little brood.

She looked from Andi to Amy, chewing on the rail of the play yard, thought of the two boys in their bedroom, hopefully reflecting on their misdeeds. She was all they had. She had to provide for them. If Matt presented a threat to her ability to do that, she had to find a way to defeat him.

She forced herself to meet his gaze. "This isn't a good time to discuss our business." She gestured toward the children. "Could we get together later?"

He looked ready to argue, but then he glanced at Andi and gave a reluctant nod. "When?"

No, he wasn't a man who would give up easily. "We live in the apartment behind the office. Can you come by about seven? That will give me time to get the children settled."

"Seven it is." He made the words sound like an ulti-matum. Then he turned and walked quickly out of the office without saying goodbye, the bell jingling as he closed the door.

Sarah let out a breath she hadn't realized she'd been holding. That didn't do any good. She couldn't relax, not yet. Matt's energy and determination still seemed to bounce from the office walls, rattling her as much as his presence had.

"Mama! Mama, up!"

She had to push herself to walk to the play yard, lift Amy, cradle her close. The baby wrapped chubby arms fervently around her neck, and then planted a wet kiss on her cheek.

Andi followed her. "What did that man want, Mommy?"

Persistence was one of Andi's strongest qualities. A good quality, but right now she could do with a little less of it. She needed time—time to think through that encounter with Matthew Caldwell, time to analyze what it would mean to them if he did what he intended.

"Nothing, sweetheart. Everything's okay."

Sarah drew in a breath. Everything's okay. She'd like to hear someone say that to her sometimes, when she struggled with the responsibility of raising four children and running a business. No one did. If Peter were here…

But dealing with trouble had never been Peter's strong suit. Peter had been laughter, charm, quicksilver. If he were here, he'd dismiss her worries with a laugh.

She closed her eyes briefly.

Father, you've helped me through everything else. Please help me handle this.

She held her daughter closer, drawing comfort from the warm, wiggling bundle of energy. She couldn't react with Peter's laughing charm, even if she wanted to. She had four children who depended on her for everything. Running the paper by herself might not be easy, but she'd proved she could make a living at it. She wasn't ready to risk that on Matt Caldwell's whim.

Her pulse gave an erratic jump as she pictured Matt, leaning toward her with tension in every inch of his body. He was tall, like the Caldwell men she knew on the island, but there the similarity ended. He was dark where they were fair, closed where they were open, driven and intense where they were casual and welcoming. How did he fit into the sprawling Caldwell clan?

She remembered something Miranda Caldwell had said once, the words dropping into her mind. *Matt's a crusader, out to set the world right. Always has been, always will be. He never gives up.*

He never gives up. The words repeated themselves uncomfortably in her mind. If she were going to best a man like Matthew Caldwell, she'd need some ammunition. And she only had until seven o'clock to find it.

Chapter Two

She couldn't win this battle. Three hours later Sarah sat at the kitchen table, staring at the contract Peter had signed with Matt Caldwell. There was no way out. Matt owned fifty percent of the paper, and he had just as much right to run it as she did.

Peter, why did I let you talk me into this?

She leaned her head in her hands, trying to think of something, anything. She hadn't wanted to take Matt's money to begin with, but Peter had been so optimistic, so sure this would solve their problems.

It was futile to hope Matt Caldwell would disappear back to Egypt, or Indonesia, or wherever his recent travels had taken him. He was here. It didn't take much insight to see that a man like him—driven, intense, competitive—wouldn't just give up and go away. She had to find a way of dealing with him.

The doorbell rang. She glanced at the clock, and her heart seemed to stop. She had to find a way of dealing with him *now*.

Sarah stole a quick glance through the small window at the top of the door just to be sure, then took a deep breath. It was Matt Caldwell, all right. He carried a manila folder and wore an expression of suppressed impatience. He looked ready to take over as editor in the next ten minutes.

She rubbed her palms down her skirt, then grasped the knob. She could handle this.

Please. She sent up a fervent, wordless prayer and opened the door.

Matt gestured with the folder by way of greeting. "I have my copy of the contract."

"Please, come in."

His quick stride brought him into her living room, and Sarah had to fight an instinctive desire to push him right back out again. He was too big, too overpowering—he filled up the room with his masculine presence, and everything about him seemed alien and disturbing.

Well, alien or not, she'd have to find a way to deal with him. He swung toward her, sending her stress level soaring. The children, she reminded herself. She would fight anyone to protect her children's security.

"You've done a nice job with this place."

His opening words, when they came, were so mundane that she blinked.

"Thank you. We had to do a lot to make it livable."

She glanced around, wondering how her home looked through his eyes. Shabby, probably. He wouldn't see the love she'd put into this place.

She'd been so delighted to have a home of her own, after years of following her army-officer father from one post to another. No amount of work to make the apartment livable had seemed too much. She had scrubbed the wide pine planks of the floors, added in-expensive rag rugs and bright pillows to the bedrooms. This had become the kind of home she'd always longed for—permanent, filled with love and laughter and prayer.

Matt would only see how cheap it all looked in comparison to the Caldwell mansion.

He glanced around again, as if assessing the value of the furniture or noting the titles of the books on her shelves. "I suspect Harvey Gaylord didn't think much about interior decoration." Matt's face softened when he spoke of the paper's former owner. "As long as he had his books and his pipe, he was satisfied."

"Did you know him well?" This sounded like a casual conversation with a neighbor. It wasn't. It was a fencing match with the man who had the power to change her life.

"As well as anyone did. I worked for him all through high school."

"I suppose that's how you got into journalism. He was your mentor."

He smiled at the term. "The bug bit me then, not that Harvey ever let me actually write anything. I was a gofer, nothing more."

"Still, he must have been proud of your success when he turned on the television and saw you reporting from China or Taiwan or Indonesia."

Some emotion crossed his face at her casual words, so quickly, she almost couldn't identify it. Then she recognized it. Pain—pain so intense it wrenched her heart. What did rich, successful Matt Caldwell have to agonize over?

"I suppose so." His voice turned colorless, the betraying expression wiped from his face as if it had never been.

But she'd seen it, and that emotion changed the pattern between them in a way she didn't understand.

He took a breath, as if mentally changing gears. "I wanted to say again how sorry I am about your husband's death."

"Thank you." He'd sent flowers, she remembered, after Peter's accident. He'd undoubtedly heard about it from his family.

The Caldwells knew what everyone else on the

island knew, that Peter Reed had skidded into a culvert on a flooded road coming back from Charleston. They didn't know what she'd found out later—that he'd never taken out the insurance he'd said he would, that his death had left his wife and children with nothing to support them but the newspaper.

"I realize you hadn't anticipated my wanting to help run the paper." Matt seemed to be picking his way carefully through the words. "Maybe I should have written to you about it."

"Maybe you should have." At least then she'd have been prepared.

Matt's face tightened, the sun lines deepening around his eyes. "That wouldn't have changed anything."

No, it wouldn't. She couldn't change the past. She'd have to find a way to cope.

She tried to block out her awareness of Matt. He stood too close to her, and his intensity seemed to reach across the inches between them. She knew what he was waiting for. He wanted her to admit that he had the right to do this.

He moved impatiently. "I assume you've looked over your copy of the contract."

"Yes, of course."

He lifted an eyebrow. "And?"

She didn't have a choice. "And I agree. If you want to help run the paper…" The words seemed to stick in her throat. What would it be like, working with Matt every day? Being forced to get his approval every step of the way?

She forced herself to go on. "I guess we're partners."

"I don't think I'll ever understand females."

Matt watched his niece run across the lawn at Gran's house toward the picnic table. A moment ago she'd been grumbling at the thought of the Sunday picnic at her great-grandmother's. Now she couldn't wait to find her cousin.

Adam, Matt's brother, smiled. "As far as I can tell, Jennifer is nine going on twenty. Nobody can understand that, especially a father." For an instant a shadow crossed Adam's face, and Matt knew he was thinking about his late wife.

The shadow disappeared as quickly as it had come. "Or did you mean your new partner?"

Matt shrugged. "Her, too, I guess. I was ready to get busy at the paper on Friday, but Sarah insisted we wait until Monday."

He'd wanted to get started. Maybe then he'd be able to erase the sense that this enforced time away from his career branded him a failure.

"Sarah's a good friend of Miranda," Adam said. "Go easy. You don't want to start another family feud."

Adam didn't say the obvious—that the Caldwell

family already had to deal with a feud between their father and their uncle. Even now, their father was at one end of the crowd gathered on Gran's lawn, and Uncle Clayton was at the other.

Jefferson Caldwell, with his mane of white hair and expensively tailored clothes, looked like what he was: a successful businessman. And Uncle Clayton—well, Uncle Clayton was an island fisherman at heart.

Matt shifted restlessly, not liking the reminder of the difference between his father and the rest of the clan. "You think I could skip the picnic? I'm not feeling very sociable."

Adam grinned. "Only if you want to take on Gran."

Naomi Caldwell marched toward them, still as erect at eighty as most people half her age.

"'Bout time you got here, Matthew."

Matt bent to kiss her cheek, inhaling the scent of lily of the valley that surrounded her. "Yes, ma'am."

Adam kissed her other cheek. "What about me?"

Gran swatted him affectionately. "You go help your cousins put up another table, heah?"

"We'll need more than one." Adam headed off.

"Adam's right." Matt glanced at the throng gathered under the trees. "Looks like you invited half the town."

"Folks want to welcome you home." Gran fixed him with a challenging stare. "You tell me, Matthew James Caldwell. Why weren't you in church this morning?"

"Still a little jet-lagged, Gran." He had a feeling that excuse wouldn't work with her.

"Nonsense. You should have been to worship."

His muscles tightened. *You should have been to worship.* That's how Gran would see it, of course. If he told her that the endless parade of tragedies he'd witnessed had soured his soul, had made him rail at God for allowing them, she'd probably have the same answer. *You should have been to worship.* Naomi Caldwell hadn't found anything in her life that wasn't made better by turning to God.

She hasn't seen what you have, a voice whispered in his ear. *She doesn't understand.*

He couldn't hurt her by arguing with her about it. He gave her a quick hug. "Next week. I promise."

She patted his cheek. "Whatever brought you home, God can help."

Before he could react, she'd turned away. "I'd best see about that crab boil. You go visit with folks."

"Yes, ma'am." The crowd shifted, and he saw the one person he hadn't expected to find at his grandmother's house. "You invited Sarah Reed."

"'Course I did. She's your new partner." Gran gave him a searching look. "Something wrong with that?"

"No, Gran, nothing wrong with that."

In fact, everything was right with that. Getting better acquainted with Sarah was just what he needed. He watched her, realizing he liked looking at the smooth grace of her movements. Her hair was loose on her shoulders, tumbling in curls touched gold by the sun.

Sarah turned from saying something to Andi, and he could sense the exact moment she spotted him. Her expressive face went still, and her hand froze in mid-gesture.

He might want to get to know her, but he suspected Sarah had entirely different feelings about that.

Sarah's breath caught at the sight of Matt's tall, lean figure. She'd known she'd see him at the picnic, of course. She just hadn't known that it would jangle her nerves so badly. He looked very tall, smiling down at his tiny grandmother. Then he looked across the lawn, and their eyes met. For an instant it was as if no one else was there.

She bent to set Amy on the grass, letting the movement hide her face for a moment. She couldn't panic at the sight of the man, for pity's sake. And she couldn't run away, any more than she could have skipped the picnic.

Amy toddled a few steps, then plopped down and started pulling grass by the handful. Sarah caught the baby's hand. "No eating grass, sweetheart."

Miranda ran to give her a hug. "You made it." Miranda, the single mother of a son about Andi's age, had become a good friend.

"I wouldn't miss it."

They joined a group of women arranging food on the long picnic table. And what food—mounds of creamy potato salad, bowls heaped with chilled shrimp, crocks of steaming chowder. The Caldwells certainly knew how to throw a picnic.

By the time the crowd had worked its way through eight kinds of pie and several gallons of coffee, Sarah had begun to relax. She'd be able to go home soon, and she'd managed to avoid saying more than hello to Matt. She rose from her lawn chair to look for the children, turned around and nearly walked into him.

She stumbled, and he clasped her hand to steady her. The warmth from his grip seemed to flow up her arm.

Nerves, she chided herself.

"Sarah. I've been hoping to talk with you." The polished voice she'd heard on television had slipped into something slower and warmer, as if he'd put his professional voice away and donned instead his comfortable, sea island tone.

"I should check on the children," she said quickly, drawing her hand away from his.

"They're fine. And we need to talk." He smiled as he said it. Anyone watching them would see only a friendly conversation. But she felt the strength that emanated from him, demanding she agree.

"The children…" she began.

"Gran's just starting to tell stories. You don't want to deny your youngsters the chance to hear a real island storyteller."

She couldn't argue with that. Her three older ones had joined the cluster of children around Naomi Caldwell, and Amy slept peacefully on a blanket with several other babies.

Matt nudged her arm. "Have a look at Gran's flowers with me."

She didn't want to go anywhere with him. She was too aware of him next to her, too conscious of his aura of coiled strength. All of Caldwell Island didn't seem big enough to get away from him.

"Fine." She summoned up a smile. "Show me your grandmother's flowers."

They strolled across the grass, toward the flower border against the white fence that separated Matt's grandmother's yard from the churchyard beyond.

Matt nodded toward the white frame cottage. "Did you know Gran's house is one of the oldest on the island? She's lived here next to the church since she married my grandfather."

Sarah couldn't help contrasting that with her own family; no one had stayed in one place for more than a year or two. But Matt didn't need to know that. "Your family has deep roots here."

"The deepest." He nodded toward the circle of

children around his grandmother. "She's telling the family legend now, about the first Caldwell—a ship-wrecked sailor who was saved by an island girl." His face softened as he watched the storytelling. "She's been telling it as long as I can remember, and it never changes. 'He took one look at her and knew he'd love her forever.' That's what she always says."

His words struck a chord, vibrating into her heart. Was that how love was supposed to be? If so, maybe some people were born incapable of it.

She shook the thought off, watching the group clustered around Matt's grandmother. Everyone, not just the children, was intent on the story—their story. It was part of them, and they were part of it. She hadn't felt like such an outsider since she'd come to the island.

"Is the story true?" She glanced at Matt, and he shrugged.

"Their names are in the chapel registry, and they're buried in the graveyard. The wooden dolphin he carved for her stood in the sanctuary for years. And Caldwells have been here ever since."

They'd been here ever since. The words echoed in Sarah's mind. Matt Caldwell belonged here—

But he'd chosen to go away.

The thought stuck in her head, and she was almost afraid to look at it too closely. He'd gone away. He'd built a name for himself out in the wide world. Maybe

Matt Caldwell was as much a wanderer as that ship-wrecked-sailor ancestor of his must have been.

She glanced up at him, wondering. Was that really the face of a man who'd settle down in a backwater town to run a weekly paper, where the most exciting story in the last month had been the theft of a shrimp net?

No. She knew a wanderer when she saw one. After all, most of her life had been spent with a father who moved from one army base to the next with as little concern as most people would spend on changing a shirt.

Maybe she didn't have to battle Matt over who would control the paper. She could just wait him out. Sooner or later, probably in weeks, not months, he'd tire of this quiet life, and he'd be on his way. If she saw him again, it would be on her television screen.

That should make her happy. It did make her happy. She assured herself of that fact. Matt would go away, and she could go back to life as it had been before he'd walked through her door.

Chapter Three

Sarah glanced again at the children. Miranda's father had brought out a fiddle, and her brother David was leading the children in a song. Apparently the Caldwells were good at devising their own entertainment.

She and Matt stood near the flower beds that overflowed the border along the fence.

"Your grandmother must have a green thumb." Anyone watching them would think they had nothing more on their minds than the flowers.

"Gran's good at a lot of things. Flowers, needlework, quilting…and like I said, she's a born storyteller."

"Maybe that's where your journalistic talents originated."

Her comment seemed to take him by surprise, and the corners of his eyes crinkled with amusement. "I'm not sure that would please Gran. She doesn't like the places my career has taken me."

"You're here now. That must make her happy." She held her breath, waiting for him to admit he probably wouldn't be here long.

The amusement wiped from his face. "Yes." His mouth clamped shut on the word, chilling her. Obviously he didn't intend to confide in her.

She sought for something else to keep the conversation going. "You mentioned the dolphin in the chapel. I've never seen it."

"It disappeared one summer night, years ago." The lines deepened in his face, as if he mourned the loss of that symbol.

"No one knows what happened to it?"

"No."

"Sounds like the sort of story a reporter might have tried to investigate in his younger days."

He frowned, as if he hadn't considered that. "I suppose I might have, but I never did. I guess I looked farther from home for my stories."

"Maybe you were born to be a wanderer." She held her breath, wondering what he'd say to that.

"Maybe so." Again she had the sense that this wasn't something he'd talk about with her.

Their steps had taken them around the corner of the house. Matt gestured to the flower beds that ran along the sheltered side of the building. "Gran's roses. Nobody on the island has any to compare."

"They're beautiful." Sarah touched a pale yellow rose with an apricot center, inhaling its rich perfume. "What's her secret?"

"No one knows."

His hand encircled hers, touching the rose. She felt a jolt that traveled up her arm, warming her skin. Her breath caught, and she snatched her hand away, feeling as if her cheeks were on fire.

That hadn't happened. It hadn't. She couldn't possibly be attracted to anyone. That part of her life had ended with her husband's death. She had her children, and that was enough of a life for her.

And if she were going to be attracted to someone, it certainly couldn't be Matt Caldwell, of all people.

Sarah Reed had to be the most frustrating woman he'd ever met. Matt rode along the beach early Monday morning. He'd expected to be at the office first thing, but Sarah had said that since she always worked late getting the paper out on Friday, she didn't start until ten on Mondays.

So he'd decided on an early-morning ride, hoping the horse's pounding hooves and the sea breeze in his face would clear his mind and let him approach the situation with Sarah rationally.

That didn't seem to be working. Instead of hard beige sand and blue water, he saw Sarah's face when they'd stood talking by the roses. One minute they'd been communicating, and he'd begun to believe they'd find a way of working together that would satisfy both of them. The next minute she'd turned away, gathered her kids together and left.

The pounding of Eagle's hooves echoed the pounding in his head. Nothing about his return was going as smoothly as he'd anticipated.

He'd managed to forget, when he was far away, how much the breach between his father and the rest of the family bothered him. And he'd managed to ignore the fact that taking up his partnership at the paper was bound to bring on a new set of problems. Of course, if he'd had a choice, he wouldn't have come back.

But he hadn't had a choice. *You'll take a leave of absence,* his boss had said. *Six months at least. That's the best I can do. When you're over this and ready to come back, I'll find a place for you if I can. Meanwhile, try to forget.*

The trouble was, he couldn't forget. Every time he closed his eyes, he saw himself running toward the mission station. He heard the blast, saw the walls collapsing inward, felt the concussion throw him to the ground. He'd struggled to his feet, knowing he had to help get the children out, knowing James was in there someplace.

James had been. They'd found him under a collapsed wall.

How could You let that happen, God? How? James was serving You, and You let him die.

He yanked the reins, and Eagle tossed his head in protest. "Sorry, boy." He patted the horse's neck. "Sorry."

He'd nearly broken down on the air. That was the unforgivable thing, as far as the network was concerned. He couldn't go back, not until he knew that wouldn't happen again.

Matt slowed the horse to a gentle jog. Running the newspaper would help him get himself together. It would prove to him that he was himself again—the detached journalist who didn't let personal feelings get in the way of a story. So that meant he and Sarah had to find a way of working together that satisfied both of them.

And he'd have a chance to talk to her about it, sooner than either of them had expected, probably. A small group walked along the edge of the surf ahead of him, and the morning sunlight picked out gold highlights in Sarah's light brown hair. Sarah and her kids.

Good. They could start over and have a simple, businesslike conversation. There was absolutely no reason for the unexpected wave of pleasure he felt at the sight of her.

He slowed Eagle to a walk as they approached. Sarah

looked up, shielding her eyes against the sun with her hand. He couldn't see her expression.

"Sarah." He stopped and slid from Eagle's back. "Hi, kids."

"Is he yours?" Andi's eyes were huge. "Is that horse yours?"

He had to smile at her excitement. "Yes, he's mine. I don't get much chance to ride him anymore, but he's mine."

The child took a step closer, and he realized she was quivering with excitement. "What's his name?"

"Eagle. Because he can run like the wind when he wants to." He caught a sudden movement from the corner of his eye and saw Ethan dart toward Eagle's haunches. He shot his hand out to grab the boy's shirt. "Don't do that!"

He sensed Sarah's instant flare of resentment at his tone and felt an answering irritation. He was only trying to keep her kid safe. But Ethan looked scared, and he patted the boy's shoulder.

"You don't want to run up to the horse's hindquarters when he doesn't see you." He ruffled the boy's hair. "He might think you're a horsefly and kick at you."

"I'm lots bigger than a horsefly." Skepticism filled the kid's eyes.

"Well, you still don't want to startle him." Matt took out the bag of carrots he'd stuffed in his jacket pocket.

"If you do just what I say, I'll let the three of you feed him a treat."

"Me first." Ethan jumped up and down.

Matt smiled at Andi. "I think Andi's first, if she wants to be."

She nodded, apparently speechless, and held out her hand.

"Keep your hand flat and let him eat the carrot," he cautioned. "You don't want him to mistake your finger for something to eat." He half expected Sarah to object, but when he looked at her, she was smiling, almost as if she approved of him.

Andi stood very straight, holding her palm out. Joy filled her small face as Eagle's lips moved against her hand. "It tickles," she breathed. "I think he likes me."

"I think he does," Matt said gently.

He looked over the child's head at Sarah. Her smile lingered, and she had a dimple in her cheek in the same place Andi did. She looked gentle. Vulnerable.

Something twisted inside him. That was what came of having a family. It made you vulnerable, put demands on you to keep them safe in an unsafe world.

He wouldn't put himself in that position—he'd figured that out somewhere in the middle of reporting an endless stream of tragedy. He wouldn't take on the responsibility of a wife or kids.

But in a way, he'd let himself in for a share of responsibility for Sarah and her little family. He didn't like the idea, but he couldn't escape it. Somehow he and Sarah had to make this work.

Sarah watched Matt. When she'd seen him riding toward them, her first instinct had been to hurry the kids up the path. Somehow she'd been caught, mesmerized by his effortless control of the huge animal. It was as if he and the horse were one.

Now he was so easily making one of Andi's dreams come true. She should say something, thank him for this....

Amy, clutching her mother's skirt for balance, toddled a few wobbly steps carrying her sand pail. She sat down abruptly on a well-padded bottom and emptied the sand over Matt's polished boots.

Would she ever have an encounter with this man when something embarrassing didn't happen? She bent to scoop the baby up, but Matt reached her first.

"Hey, little girl." His smile looked strained, but his voice was gentle as he handed her back the bucket. "Why don't you dig some more?"

"So she can empty it on you?"

Matt rose, shaking the sand from his boots. "No problem," he said easily.

"Can I give the horse a carrot now? Please?" Ethan tugged at Matt's sleeve.

Jeffrey hovered a step behind his brother. "Me, too. Me, too."

Sarah put her hands on Jeffrey's shoulders. "That's his favorite phrase, I'm afraid."

"I had a big brother, too, you know." Matt shook carrots out of the bag for each boy. "I probably said that a lot."

He smoothed Ethan's hand out. "Remember what I told Andi. Keep your palm flat."

"I remember." Ethan smiled up at him with a sudden display of trust that startled Sarah. "So he doesn't eat my finger. I'm not scared."

"Good. You shouldn't be scared of Eagle, just cautious. He wouldn't want to hurt you, but he's a big animal."

She didn't seem to be needed in this activity. Sarah sat down on the sand next to Amy, watching as Matt let her kids feed and pet the horse. He probably hadn't been around children much—he seemed to talk to them as if they were small adults—but his gentleness surprised her. *Gentle* wasn't a term she'd necessarily associate with the hard-driving reporter she knew he must be.

Finally Matt led the animal a few feet away and dropped the reins on the ground. "Eagle is ground-tied." His firm gaze touched each of the children. "He won't go anywhere unless someone startles him, so you need to stay away."

The three of them nodded soberly.

"Why don't you see if you can find any shells to add to our collection?" Sarah suggested. She'd feel more confident they'd obey if they were occupied.

The children scattered toward the edge of the water. Matt crossed to her, standing like a dark shadow between her and the sun. Then he dropped to the sand next to her.

"That was nice of you. I'm afraid Andi is horse-mad," Sarah said.

"I figured that out." His gaze was on the children, and his smile lingered.

Talking about Andi was certainly easier than discussing their business relationship. "She reads every horse book she can find, even the ones I think are too hard for her. You've just made her day."

"My niece, Jennifer, is the same."

She nodded. "Jennifer's in the same Sunday school class as Andi. She's such a pretty child."

Humor flickered in his eyes. "My brother's planning to have a nervous breakdown when she hits her teen years."

"Is that why you decided to come back? I mean, because of your family?" She was getting dangerously personal, but if she were ever to understand what made him tick, she'd have to.

"In part." His expression closed abruptly, as if he had

no intention of letting her in. "Gran thinks Caldwells always come back to Caldwell Island. She says they can't ignore their roots. I'm not sure I buy that."

Since she'd never had any roots, she could hardly offer an opinion. It was what she hoped to find for her children in Caldwell Cove.

"Don't you find it a little dull here after what you've experienced?"

She'd thought his expression couldn't get any tauter, but it hardened to an unreadable mask.

"I found I needed to get out of the conflict zone."

Why? She knew she couldn't ask outright.

"So you're giving up network television for a small-town weekly?"

"For the present." He didn't look as if the thought gave him much pleasure. "If you're thinking I'll take off again tomorrow and leave you in the lurch, I don't intend to."

"I see." So much for her idea that he'd quickly tire of this and go away. But he might not know himself as well as he thought he did.

"Look, Sarah." Matt spoke slowly, watching the children scamper along the waves. "I know we didn't get off to a good start. I know this has been an unpleasant surprise to you. Can't we find some way of working together without clashing?"

At least he seemed more conciliatory about the

whole situation. "What did you have in mind?" she asked cautiously.

He lifted an eyebrow, as if wondering how she'd react. "Suppose I become the publisher, and you continue as editor."

"Meaning you make all the decisions? I don't think so." If she gave in to him that much, she'd never have a say in where the *Gazette* went. She had too much of herself invested in the paper to agree to that.

"Well, what would satisfy you?" He looked as if, for once, he were really willing to listen to an answer.

It would satisfy me if you went back to your hotshot television job and let me run the paper.

No, she couldn't say that. But really, in spite of his protestations, how long was Matt likely to enjoy the quiet life in Caldwell Cove? He might think it was what he wanted now, but he'd soon be longing for the excitement he'd lived on for years.

If she could just hold on long enough, he'd go away. Things could go back to the way they'd been, and she wouldn't have Matt Caldwell messing up her life.

She took a deep breath. "Copublishers, coeditors."

She expected an argument. She didn't get it.

"Done," he said firmly, and held out his hand.

She blinked, hardly believing he'd agree without more argument. "Done," she agreed, her voice shaking a little on the word.

His fingers wrapped firmly around hers, and their warmth seemed to travel across her skin. Her gaze met his, almost involuntarily.

Matt's dark eyes seemed to grow even darker, and her breath caught. She couldn't breathe, let alone speak. It was as if they really looked at each other for the first time, without the lens of disagreement clouding their vision. Looked. Liked what they saw.

Oh, no. This couldn't be. She fought down a wave of panic. It was bad enough to be forced into an unwilling partnership with this man. Letting herself be attracted to him—worse, letting him know she was attracted to him—that was more than difficult.

It was just plain crazy.

Chapter Four

The bell over the office door rang for what seemed the hundredth time later that day, and Matt's jaw ached from gritting his teeth. That had to be the most annoying sound in the world.

Elton Hastings ambled to the counter, shoving his ball cap back on his balding head. He smiled at Sarah. "Hey, Miz Reed."

Matt lowered his gaze to his computer. He didn't have to watch or listen to know what happened next. He'd already seen it a dozen times or more since they'd arrived at the office from the beach.

Sarah would embark on an extended conversation, as she did with everyone who walked through the door. It didn't seem to matter whether they wanted to place an ad, complain about a story or stop a subscription—they'd end up telling Sarah Reed their life story.

He peered cautiously around the computer monitor. Sarah leaned forward, her brown hair swinging against her shoulder as she listened with apparently rapt attention to Elton recount his gallbladder woes. He'd known the pace of a small-town weekly would be different, but this was ridiculous.

It was past time the *Caldwell Cove Gazette* became a professional operation. He'd decided that the moment he walked into the office, and he hadn't changed his mind.

But he'd agreed that he and Sarah would be coeditors and copublishers. Looking back on that conversation, he wasn't sure why he'd agreed so easily. If he'd pushed, he might have been able to secure a stronger position for himself. In a similar situation, his father would have negotiated a better deal—he felt sure of that. He also felt sure that he didn't want to follow his father's example when it came to running a business.

He'd have to talk this over with Sarah. They were partners—she'd realize that meant a little give and take. He'd explain to her how much more efficiently the office would run if she didn't waste time chatting with every person who came in the door.

She said something that made Elton laugh, the sound almost rusty, as if the old man hadn't laughed in a while. Matt studied her face from behind the shield of his monitor. There was strength in the line of her jaw, balanced by the vulnerability of her mouth and the soft warmth that seemed to radiate from her face. Everything about her shouted that here was a woman both capable and willing to take care of others.

Everyone responded to Sarah's warmth, even a crusty old coot like Elton. Nothing wrong with that, except that this was a place of business, not a church social. Warmth and chatter were inappropriate here, along with the tinkling bell and the plate of homemade cookies on the counter.

One of those cookies had mysteriously migrated to his desk. He took a bite, tasting oatmeal, chocolate and peanut butter. Giving out homemade cookies was definitely not what he expected in a newspaper office. Still, as long as he'd started the cookie, he might as well finish it.

Elton finally sauntered out the door, standing a bit taller than he had when he'd come in. Matt frowned at the tinkling bell, then turned to Sarah.

She lifted an eyebrow. "What's wrong?"

"What makes you think something's wrong?"

The eyebrow arched a little higher. "Well, it might be the way you stared at me the whole time I talked to a customer."

"Was that what he was, a customer?" He feigned surprise. "The way he confided in you, I thought he was a long-lost cousin."

She swung her swivel chair around so that she faced

him more fully. "You don't want me to be pleasant to the people who come in?" She made it a question.

"I think this operation could be a little more professional, that's all." It was probably inappropriate to take her to task for unprofessional behavior when he had chocolate smeared on one hand from the cookie he'd polished off. He wiped his hand. "This is a business."

He expected her to flare up at that—to remind him that she'd been running the paper without his help for some time. Instead, she tipped her head to one side, as if considering.

"What exactly did you have in mind?"

You could stop being so appealing. No, that wasn't what he meant. He'd mention the cookies, but eating one himself had undercut that argument.

"Listening to people's life stories. You didn't need to spend the last fifteen minutes hearing about Elton's gallbladder, did you?"

The corner of her mouth twitched. "It wasn't the most scintillating conversation I've ever had. But maybe Elton needed to talk."

"Then let him get a friend. Or a dog." He shoved out of his chair, too restless to sit still any longer. "And another thing—that bell."

She sent a startled glance toward the door. "What about the bell?"

"It makes this sound like a candy shop instead of a

newspaper office." Two steps took him to the counter. He leaned against it, looking down into blue eyes that held a spark of amusement instead of the anger he half expected.

"You wouldn't say that if you were back in the copy room and nearly missed a paying customer because you didn't hear her."

"That would only happen if you were alone. You have a partner now, remember?"

Her wide eyes narrowed. "I'm finding it impossible to forget."

"It's not that bad, is it?" He realized he was leaning toward her, just as he'd seen Elton do, and he stiffened. He wasn't going to get drawn in by a pair of big blue eyes and a vulnerable mouth. "I think with a little effort, we can bring the *Gazette* into the twenty-first century."

She got up suddenly, the movement bringing her even closer. He caught a whiff of some light, flowery scent, and for a moment he was in a meadow instead of an office.

"Fine. You stay here and bring the paper into the twenty-first century by taking the bell off the door. I have a story to cover."

"Story? What story?"

She slung the strap of the camera bag over her shoulder. "Elton mentioned that Minnie Walters is celebrating her hundredth birthday today. That's worth a picture, don't you think?"

"It's not a step toward world peace." She probably wanted him to admit that her conversation with Elton had been worthwhile, and he wasn't about to do that.

"No, and we're not the *New York Times*. Our readers want to know when their neighbor hits the century mark." She turned toward the door, then swung back, holding out the camera. "Of course if you'd like to do it…"

"No, thanks." Clearly it would take more than one conversation to win this battle with Sarah. "You go ahead. I'm sure you'll get more out of Minnie than I would."

Her smile flashed, and it was like a burst of sunshine on a chilly day. "I don't know about that. She might be thrilled to have a man come calling."

"Not this man," he said firmly. "In our division of responsibilities, little old ladies who hit their hundredth birthdays are definitely your department."

Sarah's laughter mingled with the tinkle of the bell as she went out the door.

Well. The office seemed oddly empty without her. He wasn't sure who'd won that round, but at least she'd agreed he could remove the bell.

Fifteen minutes later he'd taken down the bell and begun leafing through a file of story ideas. The door from Sarah's apartment swung open, and her children surged through. The teenage baby-sitter he'd met earlier followed them, carrying the baby on her hip.

"Tammy has to go," Andi announced importantly. "Where's our mommy?"

"Go where?" He turned to the teenager, hoping he didn't sound panic-stricken. "Their mother had to go out. They can't stay here."

"I'm awfully sorry, Mr. Caldwell." She dumped the baby unceremoniously into his unwilling arms. "But my mama called, and she needs me to go home 'cause she has to work late."

"But the kids…"

She was already at the door. "They'll be fine 'til Miz Reed gets back. Just watch out for the baby— she's teething."

Watch out for the baby? She made the kid sound like a ticking bomb. "I can't. You'll have to stay."

He was talking to a closed door. He'd been left alone with Sarah's kids.

This was definitely not the way he'd planned to run this office. He looked at the tot in his arms, and she stared back at him, round blue eyes full of innocence.

He sat, balancing her on his knee, and turned to the other three. They looked a bit more doubtful about the situation than the baby did.

What on earth did he know about watching kids? How could Sarah let him get stuck like this?

"Well." He cleared his throat. He'd interviewed the leaders of angry mobs, questioned arrogant tyrants. He could surely talk to little kids. Just treat them as if they were responsible adults, and they'd respond that way. "Your mother will be back soon. Maybe you can amuse yourselves until she gets back."

"What can we do?" Andi asked.

"I want to play with the computer," Ethan said.

Jeffrey's face clouded up, and he looked as if tears were imminent. "I want Mommy."

Matt glanced at the baby, to discover that she was chewing on the strap of his wristwatch. When he tried to disengage her teeth, she started to wail.

Sarah, where are you?

Sarah hurried down the street toward the office, the camera bag bouncing against her hip. She'd been longer than she'd intended, but the elderly woman had been so thrilled with the whole idea of being in the paper that Sarah hadn't had the heart to cut the interview short. Besides, Minnie's tales of Caldwell Island in the early years of the century, before there'd even been a bridge to the mainland, were just what the *Caldwell Cove Gazette* readers loved.

Matt probably wouldn't agree. His determined face formed in her mind's eye, dark eyes serious, chiseled mouth firm. Her pulse gave an erratic little flutter. Maybe she needed another lecture to herself.

Matt clearly intended to keep their relationship businesslike. She must, too. He'd stay detached; she'd stay detached. She'd wait him out, and before long he'd grow tired of Caldwell Cove and the *Gazette* and take his disturbing self right out of her life.

She pushed the office door open. The first thing she noticed was that the bell was missing. The second was her children, busy enveloping Matt's desk in a sheet of newsprint.

"What—what's going on here?"

Matt straightened. He held Amy in one arm, and she was chewing on a plastic tape dispenser. "What does it look like? We're building a fort."

She was almost afraid to ask why. "But where's Tammy?"

"Gone. Something about her mother having to work late." His look was accusing. Clearly he thought she should have anticipated that and made other arrangements. Well, he was right. She should have.

Matt shifted Amy to his other arm, and the side of the fort he'd been holding collapsed, leading to a muffled shriek from Andi.

"You have to hold it." Andi peeked out from under the desk. "Or I can't stick the tape on right."

"Never mind that." Sarah hustled to the desk, hauling children out from beneath it. "You shouldn't be in here bothering Mr. Caldwell."

"We weren't bothering him," Andi protested.

"He was watching us," Ethan said.

Watching them. Their first day of working together and already she owed him a major apology.

"He doesn't need to watch you now. I'm home." She headed the three of them toward the door. "Andi, you take your brothers to the kitchen and get their snack. I'll be back to check on you in a few minutes."

"But, Mommy…"

"No buts." She marched them to the door. "Go on, now."

When they'd gone, she turned to apologize, only to realize that Matt still held the baby.

"I'm sorry." She scooped Amy into her arms, sure her cheeks must be fiery. "This shouldn't have happened. I don't know how to apologize."

Relieved of the baby, he brushed his sleeves back into place. "We seem to have survived," he said dryly. "But I hope this isn't going to become a habit."

"Of course not." Apparently he couldn't accept her apology without lecturing.

"You need adequate child care if you're going to run the paper."

She suppressed the urge to tell him she'd been running the paper and her family quite nicely without advice from him. "I have adequate child care. I just should have talked to Tammy about what to do if she had to leave."

She plopped Amy into the play yard, removing the tape dispenser and substituting a squeaky toy before the baby could cry at being deprived of it.

"Bait and switch," Matt said.

She blinked. "What?"

He nodded toward the toy Amy had just stuffed into her mouth, and she grinned at him around it. "I tried to take the tape dispenser away, but she wouldn't give it up. You did a nice move substituting that toy." He lifted an eyebrow. "Come to think of it, that's what you did with me."

"I don't know what you mean." She was probably blushing again.

"I think you know perfectly well." He frowned, the momentary ease between them gone.

She recognized the reason for the frown. Matt had a passion for truth. She'd only known him for a couple of days, but she'd already seen glimpses of that quality. Here was a man who didn't recognize the polite little fictions most people accepted just to get through the day.

Well, she did. Sometimes perfect truth was unnecessary, even hurtful, whether Matt realized it or not. "When did I pull a bait-and-switch on you?"

"When you gave in on the bell to distract me from other things."

Other things, like cutting down on the time she

spent talking to people. She took a breath, trying to phrase her concern in a way he'd understand. Trying not to sound annoyed.

"Maybe that's true. If it is, I'm sorry. I just don't know how to change the way I relate to people. And I'm not sure I'm ready to try."

She expected him to take up that challenge. Instead, he studied her for a long moment. His determined gaze almost seemed to touch her skin.

"Fair enough," he said, surprising her. "We can fight about it if we have to. Just don't try to manipulate me, even if you think it's for my own good."

She lifted an eyebrow. "Nothing but honesty?"

"Nothing but."

For some reason she thought of Peter, with his smiling charm, telling people what they wanted to hear. Matt Caldwell would certainly never be guilty of that. He was far more likely to tell you bluntly the last thing you wanted to hear.

She put the thought away for later consideration. "All right. I promise I won't try to manipulate you, even if you need it. Satisfied?"

The slightest hint of a smile quirked the corner of his mouth. "For the moment."

He retreated to his desk, and she sank down in her chair. Her heart pounded as if she'd been running a race. Maybe she had. If so, she'd probably lost.

The image brought Saint Paul's words to mind. "Casting aside all that hinders me, I run the race that is set before me." That passage never failed to spark her determination.

I know the race I have to run, Father. I have to love and protect and provide for the children You've given me. Please show me the way through any obstacles caused by this partnership with Matt.

Slowly her heartbeat returned to normal. She could do this. No matter how difficult, she'd find a way to make this partnership work, because her children's future depended upon it.

For the next hour she and Matt worked in the same room, the quiet only disrupted by the two trips she made back to the apartment to solve disputes among the children. Amy fell asleep in her play yard. Slowly Sarah began to relax. This wasn't so bad, was it?

"Hey, Sarah. You're looking lovely today. What happened to your bell?"

Jason Sanders stood gazing at the doorframe, as if searching for the missing bell.

"We decided to take it down." She carefully avoided looking at Matt, although surely he wouldn't object to her chatting with Sanders. The man owned the only real-estate agency on the island, and he was a big advertiser. "What can I do for you?"

"I really just stopped in to welcome Matt back

home." He advanced on Matt, hand outstretched. "It's great to have the famous correspondent back among us."

Matt stood, facing him, and she thought she'd never seen two men so opposite. Jason was the original glad-hander: quick with a smile, a handshake, a compliment. It was only after she'd known him for a while that she'd realized how facile that smile was, how trite the compliment. He seemed to have a stock of them that he rotated routinely.

As for Matt—nothing facile or charming about him, that was for sure. She studied him while the men exchanged small talk. He was always guarded, but he seemed even more so with Sanders. He stood stiffly, fists planted on his desk, expression shielded.

What did Matt have against Sanders? When the man finally waved his way back out the door, spreading a few more compliments along the way, she suspected she was about to find out.

Matt swung toward her, his stare inimical. "What was he doing here?"

"You heard him. He came to welcome you home."

He snorted. "The day Jason Sanders welcomes me anywhere is the day it snows in July."

"I take it you don't like him." That appeared to be putting it mildly. "But it must be years since you've had anything to do with him."

"Sanders was always a bully. I don't suppose his nature has changed all that much, even though he's got a better facade now."

She blinked. He'd put his finger on exactly what bothered her most about Sanders—the sense that underneath his charming manner lurked someone who always got what he wanted, no matter what it did to others.

"He's a big advertiser," she pointed out.

Matt closed the gap that separated them, planted his fists on her desk and leaned toward her. "Is that all that counts?"

Her pulse jumped. He was too close—so close she could count the fine lines at the corners of his eyes, almost feel the pulse that beat at his temple, almost touch the corded muscles of his forearms.

"N-no. Of course not." She took a steadying breath and tried to pretend he was someone else—old Elton Hastings, for example.

"Well, then, why do we have to put up with him?"

Pretending Matt was a bald seventy-year-old didn't seem to be working.

"We put up with him because our job is producing a newspaper," she said as evenly as she could manage. "It's not our job to pass judgment on our readers or our advertisers. Not unless we're running a tabloid instead of a newspaper."

She saw that hit home.

"Are you saying I'm letting my personal feelings get in the way of my professionalism?" His reluctant smile was even more disturbing than his glare had been.

Speaking of personal feelings, her own seemed to be running amok. "You told me to tell you the truth."

He winced. "Touché. That'll teach me." He squeezed her shoulder, his hand firm and warm. "Thanks, partner."

The warmth from his hand traveled all the way to her throat, trapping her voice. She swallowed. "Anytime."

Anytime now would be the time to get over this, she lectured herself. Like now, for instance.

Unfortunately, she suspected it would take more than a lecture to neutralize the effect Matt Caldwell had on her.

Chapter Five

He didn't have any excuse for being at Sarah's apartment a few nights later. Matt paused outside the back entrance to the newspaper building, the one that led to Sarah's home, not the office. What exactly was he doing here?

He shifted the folder he was carrying. Of course he had a reason to be here—a business reason. He'd compiled a list of suggestions he wanted to talk to Sarah about, and the endless interruptions during the day made that impossible. It had nothing whatsoever to do with wanting to see her again.

Repeating that to himself, he knocked on the door. He frowned, then knocked again. Noises from inside assured him someone was home.

He glimpsed movement through the small pane at the top of the door, and finally the door swung open. Sarah stood there, her sky-blue shirt speckled with darker spots of water. Her brown hair, also damp, curled wildly around her face.

Amy, wrapped in a towel, was equally wet. At the sight of him, she babbled something incomprehensible and lunged for him.

Sarah caught her in midlunge with the ease of long practice. "No, Amy, no. He doesn't want to hold you. You're as wet and slippery as a dolphin."

"And as pretty." Relax, he told himself. Relax. He smiled at the baby, getting an enchanting grin in return. "I'm sorry. I guess I've come at a bad time."

Sarah blew a soft brown curl out of her face. "I've never figured out how getting a baby clean can make Mommy such a mess. But, no, it's not any worse than any other time. What can I do for you?" Her tone made it clear office hours were over.

"Sorry," he repeated, feeling irrationally annoyed that he was getting off on the wrong foot with her. Again. "I thought we might be able to talk about some ideas I have for the *Gazette*. I forgot you'd be busy with the children. I can come back later."

"It's bedtime," she pointed out, probably thinking any idiot would know that. "But if you care to wait, we can talk once I get the children settled."

He suspected only courtesy had compelled that offer, but decided he'd take it at face value. It might be the only way he'd achieve his objective.

"That's fine." He stepped into the small living room. "I'll wait."

He thought Sarah suppressed a sigh as she closed the door. She nodded toward the sofa.

"Make yourself comfortable." Before he could sit down, she'd whisked out of sight, trailing the pink bath towel.

Matt turned toward the sofa. Three pairs of blue eyes surveyed him. Andi was curled up in a shabby armchair with a book. The two boys had blocks and toy cars spread across the carpet. They all looked at him.

Loosen up, his brother's voice echoed in his mind. Adam had been amused when he'd told him about being left with Sarah's kids one afternoon. *They're little kids, not the enemy. Just relax with them.*

He'd try, because this seemed the only route to the discussion he wanted to have with Sarah. He squatted down on the rug next to Ethan.

"Building a racetrack?"

The boy nodded. "It's going to be the longest one ever. Want to help?"

He tossed his folder onto the coffee table and sat on the floor. The carpet felt thin beneath him. "Hand me a couple of blocks."

Their track led across the floor, under the side table, around the armchair. Ethan kept up a constant stream of chatter, most of it telling Jeffrey what to do.

Matt had to smile. His memory provided a picture of himself and Adam at about the same age, relating in the same way. Adam had always acted the big brother.

Andi looked up from her book now and then to watch them, and from somewhere in the back he could hear Sarah singing to the baby. This should have felt uncomfortable, but it didn't. Maybe he was getting the hang of relating to kids.

"Look out, here comes my race car." Ethan grabbed a car and sent it speeding along the track. It hit an unevenly placed block and flew off, crashing.

Matt picked up the car. "Went off track that time. Why don't you give it another try?"

"It hit a culvert," Ethan said firmly. "It's wrecked too bad to try again."

Almost before he had a chance to think it odd that Ethan knew the word *culvert,* Andi slammed her book down. "Don't say that!" she shouted. "Don't you say that!"

"Will if I want to!" Ethan shouted back.

The peaceful little playtime had disintegrated before his eyes. So much for his idea that he could relate to Sarah's children—not that he wanted to anyway. But he could hardly keep a safe distance when he was right in the middle of the battle.

"Hey, take it easy. It's okay." He touched Andi's arm, but she jerked away from him.

The tears streaking down her cheeks shocked him. Then he realized what was going on. It wasn't okay. The cars, the wreck, the culvert—that was how their father died. It hit Matt like a fist in the stomach.

He wanted nothing so much as to get up and walk right out the door. This wasn't his concern. It was Sarah's problem. It was everything he'd come home to avoid.

But no matter how he justified it, he couldn't get up and walk away.

"I'm sorry," he said quietly, holding out his hand to Andi. "Ethan didn't mean it."

He looked at Ethan. For a moment the boy stared back rebelliously, but then he nodded. "I didn't mean it, Andi-pandy. I'm sorry."

Andi scrubbed the tears from her face with both hands. "Daddy's in heaven now," she said with a little quaver in her voice. She looked at Matt. "Did you know that?"

He suppressed the doubts that haunted his dreams. This wasn't the place to let them out. "Yes." His stomach twisted. "I'm sure he is."

"Time to put the racetrack away, boys." Sarah stood in the doorway. Her voice sounded calm, but he could tell by the strain around her eyes that she'd heard some of the conversation.

Perhaps cowed by their sister's tears, the two boys made no argument. Matt slid into a chair and tried to be inconspicuous while they hustled around, throwing cars and blocks into a plastic bin. In a few minutes the room had been cleared of toys.

"Good job." Sarah managed a smile for her kids. "I'll just be another few minutes," she informed Matt. She didn't even try to smile at him. She shepherded the children toward their rooms, leaving him alone to try and regain control of whatever was left of his mission.

The minutes ticked by. He heard soft voices from the bedrooms, realized Sarah was hearing their prayers. The gentle murmur was oddly soothing, as was the shabby room. It had a warmth that the Caldwell mansion had never achieved.

By the time he heard Sarah's step in the hall, he knew he had to address the situation with the kids before he could possibly bring up business.

"I'm sorry," he said before she could speak. "I don't know if that was my fault or not, but I'm sorry."

Sarah shook her head, sinking down into the chair Andi had vacated. "It wasn't your fault. The children come out with something about Peter's death every once in a while, usually when I'm least expecting it."

"That must be hard." He leaned toward her, wanting to say something soothing, but not knowing what it could be.

She nodded, resting her head against the chair, lids flickering closed. For the first time he noted the smudged violet shadows under her eyes, saw the lines of tiredness that she usually concealed.

She'd lost her husband less than a year ago, he reminded himself. She was raising four children all alone, and as far as he could tell, she didn't have any family to help or support her. He thought briefly of his own sprawling clan. Whether he wanted them to be or not, they were always there.

Sarah opened her eyes, straightening as if that momentary lapse had been a failure. "We do all right," she said with a firmness that had to be assumed.

"I'd forgotten."

Her blue gaze darted to his face. "Forgotten what?"

"That tragedy and loss aren't confined to war zones." His mouth twisted. "They even happen here in Caldwell Cove."

The words were out before he realized how they'd sound. For a moment he thought he'd hurt her. Then she nodded slowly.

"True enough." She got up. "I think we could both use a cup of coffee before we talk business."

He started to protest that he didn't need any coffee, then realized she probably needed an excuse to have a moment alone. The way she hurried toward the kitchen and swung the door shut behind her confirmed that.

He took a deep breath, trying to relax taut muscles. How exactly had this happened? He'd come here tonight to talk business with Sarah. Instead he'd seen deeper into her heart than he had any right to. And he'd exposed more of himself than he'd ever intended.

Sarah leaned against the kitchen counter, staring absently at the coffeepot, seeing only Matt's tense face and the battle in his dark eyes over that flare-up of emotion with Andi. Something was wrong with him. She didn't know how she knew it, but she did. Something had happened to put the strain in his eyes.

Something on the job? She ran up against a blank wall of ignorance. She'd never really thought about how they did their jobs, those people she saw on the news every night. Had Matt run into some problem out there in his other life that had carved those deep lines in his face, that had put up the barricades that screamed *Don't touch me?*

Her hands felt cold as she mechanically filled the pot with water and put coffee into the filter. Something— what had he said? *Tragedy and loss.* Had he lost someone he cared about? Was that what had brought him home?

She didn't want to know. She didn't have a right to know. But he was hurting, and she couldn't just ignore that.

Show me what to do, Lord. Is this a burden I'm supposed to pick up?

One thing was clear. Knowing why he'd come back could help her understand how long he intended to stay. From a purely selfish point of view, she wanted to know that.

I'm sorry, Lord. I don't mean to be selfish. I just can't help thinking about how Matt's actions affect my children's future. It's not wrong to worry about that, is it?

She didn't have an answer by the time the coffee was ready. She arranged cups on a wooden tray, straightened her shoulders and went back to the living room.

Matt sat on the sofa where she'd left him. The folder he'd carried in with him lay, apparently forgotten, on the side table.

"Cream or sugar?" she asked as she placed the tray on the coffee table.

"Black, please."

The routine of pouring out the coffee and handing it to him soothed her. She glanced at his face, still brooding, and knew she had to try and understand what drove this enigmatic partner of hers.

She stared down at her own cup, as if it might hold an answer. Maybe there was no way to do this but to dive right in.

"Was that why you came back?" She suspected she didn't need to explain. His words probably still hovered in his mind as they did in hers. "Because you'd seen too much tragedy?"

His long fingers curved around the cup, as if seeking

heat in spite of the warm summer evening. "That was part of it." His guarded tone warned her off.

"I suppose…" She felt her way carefully. "I suppose correspondents in dangerous places have to be like doctors. They have to stay detached in order to do their jobs."

He clutched the cup so tightly she thought it would shatter. "That's what's supposed to happen. Sometimes it doesn't work that way. When you're in the middle of a fight, innocent bystanders can get hurt."

Her gaze flew to his face. "Were you injured?"

"Not physically." A muscle twitched in his jaw, the only sign of the iron control he must be exercising. "Let's say I lost my detachment for a while. I started to burn out."

"So you decided to come home." To heal? That was what she suspected, but she thought he'd reject the idea. She also suspected he wasn't telling her all of it. Why should he? They were virtual strangers, linked together by circumstance.

"I decided—we decided, my boss and I—that I needed a break. I took a leave of absence."

"A leave of absence? That means you intend to go back. You didn't tell me that."

He set the cup down with a little clatter, and his eyes met hers. "No, I didn't tell you. I guess I should have."

"I thought you meant to stay for good." She grappled to get her mind around this new idea. He'd never intended to stay at the *Gazette* for the long haul. Knowing that to begin with could have saved her some agonizing. "What happened to partners telling each other the truth?"

That might have been a shade of embarrassment in his expression. "All right, you've got me. Maybe I'm a little too used to answering only to myself. I should have been up-front about my plans."

Yes, you should have. "Why don't you start now? How long is this leave of absence of yours supposed to last?"

"Six months." He said it as if it were something to cling to. "Six months of peace and quiet. Then I go back."

"What if you're not ready in six months?"

Anger flared for an instant. "I'll be ready. I'll go back."

Her own anger sparked. "So working at the *Gazette* was just something to amuse you while you're on leave."

"I'm not looking for amusement," he snapped. He shook his hand then, held up his hand as if to stop whatever she might say to that. "I'm sorry. I realize this doesn't make much sense to you."

"Explain it to me. You walk into our lives and turn them upside down, and then you tell me it's just temporary? You're right, it doesn't make much sense to me."

Whatever had been conciliatory in his expression fled. "I own a half share in the paper, remember? If I want to help run it for six days or six weeks or six months, I can."

She felt suddenly tired. He was right. He could do whatever he wanted, and she couldn't stop him.

"Sarah, this doesn't have to be a problem. Being a part of running the paper will let me keep my hand in my profession while I'm off. What would you expect me to do? Help my grandmother prune her roses for six months?"

Her mouth curved in a reluctant smile. "No, somehow I don't see you as the rose-pruning type."

His face relaxed a fraction. "You must see that this was the obvious solution for me. And it can be a break for you, too."

"What do you mean? I can't take six months off."

"No. But you could take a few hours a day off, with my help. You can't tell me you wouldn't welcome that."

"You mean I can work twelve-hour days, instead of fourteen?" She said it lightly, but somehow it didn't come out that way. If she ever admitted how tired she was, she might collapse and never get up again.

"Something like that." His gaze searched her face. "We share the work for six months, right? We both gain. At the end of that time, when I go back, we can look for some extra help for you."

She wanted to protest that they couldn't afford extra help, but maybe that was an argument better saved for another day. She'd wanted to know what brought Matt home, wanted to know how long he'd stay. Now she had both of those answers. It should make her happy.

It did make her happy, she assured herself. She had to put up with Matt's interference at the paper for six months, and then he'd be gone. She could go back to handling things the way she wanted to. Surely she could deal with anything for six months.

"Well, I guess that's settled, then."

"I guess it is." Matt glanced around, as if he were searching for something he'd forgotten. Maybe he just wanted something to get them away from the dangerously personal ground they'd been treading.

He reached for the folder he'd brought with him.

"Your plan of action?" She raised an eyebrow.

"Suggestions," he said firmly. "Ideas I have for the paper." He held it out to her. "Take a look and tell me what you think."

She took the folder gingerly.

"It won't bite." His mouth curved in a smile.

Won't it? She opened the manila cover with a sense of inevitability. Whatever Matt proposed, it meant change, and none of the changes she'd endured recently had been pleasant.

She read through the pages, schooling her face to impassivity. She hadn't quite finished when Matt put his hand impatiently on hers, making her pulse jump.

"Well, what do you think?"

"You have some interesting ideas," she said carefully. "But I'm not convinced some of these will work for *Gazette* readers."

"Why not?" He shot the question at her.

She suspected the brief interlude of peace between them was over. "You have to realize people want different things from a small-town paper than they do from a television news program."

He was already shaking his head. "Oh, I know you have to do the local stuff. People expect that. But there's no reason why the *Gazette* can't cover more important issues, as well. After all, things that happen at the state and national level affect all of us."

"But, Matt…"

His hands clasped both of her wrists, sending their warmth straight to her heart. For the first time, she saw his face as it must have looked before stress and tragedy had left their mark on him—alive with passion and enthusiasm. "There are stories waiting to be told here in Caldwell Cove, Sarah. Let's take a crack at telling them, all right?"

She knew he wasn't really asking for her permission. He'd found the road he wanted to travel, and no one would deter him, least of all her.

She swallowed hard, trying to slow the race of her pulses. Matt would only be in her life for the next six months. But in six months, he could do irreparable damage to the newspaper.

And if she weren't careful to guard against it, he could also do irreparable damage to her heart.

Chapter Six

"How are you surviving with your new partner?"

The question fit so exactly into Sarah's thoughts that it startled her. She turned to smile at Miranda Caldwell, letting a tidal wave of Sunday school children scurry past them to the tables in the churchyard. The church coffee hour had been moved out under the trees on this beautiful June Sabbath.

"Fine, I think." She suppressed all the worries she couldn't express to anyone, and especially not to Matt's cousin. "Maybe you should ask him that question."

Miranda's smile broadened. "I did. And he said, 'Fine, I think,' just like you did, sugar. Seems the two of you think alike."

Sarah's gaze rested on Matt's tall figure as he stood beneath a tree, balancing a coffee cup and talking to his brother. "I don't think I'd say that, exactly."

"Then what?" Miranda nudged her arm, her green eyes alight with mischief. "You can tell me. We're family, Matt and I."

And that was just why she couldn't. Did Matt's family recognize the strain implicit in the stiffness of his shoulders? Did they see the despair she sometimes glimpsed in his eyes? Or was she imagining the whole thing?

She had to respond to Miranda in some way. "Let's just say Matt takes more of a world view toward a small-town paper than I do."

"Crusading, is he?"

Sarah thought of the stories Matt had proposed over the course of the last week. "Yes, I guess you could say that. He has good ideas. Just maybe not sensible for us to tackle."

"That's Matthew. He's always been a crusader." Miranda smiled in reminiscence. "I remember when we were kids. He was always the one who took on the schoolyard bully. Never to defend himself—always to defend somebody smaller or weaker. That's our Matt."

She hadn't viewed Matt that way, but it fit. "The *Gazette* isn't exactly the schoolyard." And Jason Sanders, even now handshaking his way around the coffee hour, wasn't the bully Matt apparently remembered.

"Maybe you need to tell him that," Miranda said. She nodded. "Seems like you're about to have the chance."

Sarah looked up to see Matt bearing down on them,

moving with the determined stride that said he had important things to do.

"See you later," Miranda murmured, and slipped away before Sarah could suggest that she stay.

It wasn't that she needed a barrier against her new partner. It was just that Matt was sure to ask what she thought of the article he'd written about Jason Sanders's acquisition of small parcels of land from some elderly island natives. And if she told him what she thought, it would lead to a quarrel she didn't want to have, at least not on Sunday morning.

"Good morning, Sarah. Nice service, wasn't it?"

"Very nice." Did he really think that? He hadn't been in church the previous Sunday, and she thought she'd detected an extra measure of tension when her gaze had strayed toward him during the service. Maybe he'd been looking at the empty bracket where the Caldwell dolphin had once stood. Caldwells must be reminded of the story and the missing dolphin each time they went into St. Andrews.

"Gran got after me for sleeping in last Sunday." Matt seemed to be reading her mind. "She doesn't accept excuses for missing worship."

"If you're looking for sympathy, you've come to the wrong person," she said firmly. "I have four kids to get ready, and I still managed to get everyone here for Sunday school."

His face relaxed in a smile, and he held up both hands as if to fend her off. "Okay, I surrender. No sympathy here." He glanced toward the group of children playing tag under the trees, while three teenagers corralled the nursery toddlers on a blanket. "At least you get a break once you bring them here."

"The nursery helpers are good with the children. I just wish I could find someone reliable to watch them during the week when I'm working. Tammy's good with them, but she's not available often enough."

That was a constant concern, and she hadn't been able to take seriously Matt's contention that she could take time off now that he was working with her. Getting the paper out provided more than enough work for both of them. Matt was a fast learner, but he came in knowing little of the everyday mechanics of getting the paper out.

So far, Matt hadn't complained about her children playing hide-and-seek under his desk, but she suspected that was just a matter of time.

"Speaking of work, what did you think of the article I asked you to read?"

It had taken even less time than she'd expected for him to bring up the prickly subject.

"I thought it was interesting. Well written."

His eyes narrowed. "That means you didn't like it."

"I didn't say that. It just raised some concerns in my

mind, that's all." Such as whether they'd lose their biggest advertiser if Matt printed that story.

"I went over the piece with a microscope," he said stiffly. "I can assure you there's nothing in it but the truth. He's been pressuring people to sell who don't know the potential value of their property."

"But it's the truth told as bluntly as possible." They were at war again, this time at a church coffee hour, of all places. "You could have softened it. But maybe you didn't want to. Maybe you were fighting the schoolyard bully again."

"You've been talking to Miranda." His gaze shot sparks, but his voice was soft.

She met his look defiantly. "How can you be sure you're not letting your history with him affect your decision?"

"I don't know, Sarah. How can you be sure you're not letting his advertising dollars affect yours?"

Anger stiffened her spine. "Advertising is what keeps a weekly paper alive. I have to be concerned about that. You don't."

He looked surprised by the direct attack. "What do you mean? I'm just as interested in the paper's success as you are."

The worries she'd bottled up all week seemed to be spilling out in a most inappropriate place. "You can't be," she said flatly. "To you, the paper is just something to keep you busy for the next six months, until you go back to your real life."

"I care about the *Gazette.* Maybe you think I'm not committed—"

"Committed? Tell me something, Matt. Where's your passport?"

It didn't take the betraying movement of his hand toward his jacket pocket to tell her what she'd already guessed. He wouldn't put that passport away, because it was a lifeline to the world he wanted.

"This is just a temporary aberration in your life. But for me, for my family—"

"Miz Reed?"

She blinked, so intent on making Matt see that for an instant she couldn't refocus. Then she saw the girl leading Jeffrey by the hand.

She was on her knees next to him immediately. "Sweetheart, what is it?" She brushed fine blond hair back from his flushed face. "Don't you feel okay?"

He shook his head, leaning against her. "My head hurts, Mommy. And my tummy doesn't feel too good."

She picked him up, straightening. "We'll go home right away." She glanced at Matt, but he was looking at Jeffrey.

"That's too bad, buddy." He put his hand on Jeffrey's forehead.

It was the simplest gesture, one she'd made herself more times than she could count. But the sight of the man's strong hand, gentle on her son's head, made her heart clench.

She pushed the feeling away. She'd analyze it later. "I'd better round up the other kids."

"Let me." Matt frowned. "Better yet, let me bring the older kids home later. They're happy playing for now. That way you can get the little ones settled."

"I can't impose—"

"It's not an imposition." His smile wiped away all trace of their quarrel. He took Jeffrey from her. "I'll carry him to the car while you get the baby and settle the other two."

She should be annoyed at his assumption of responsibility. She'd been handling her family on her own for quite some time. But it felt so tempting to let Matt bear a little of the burden, just for now.

She shouldn't give in to that feeling. Matt would be gone soon. She shouldn't let him become so entangled with her family. But she couldn't seem to help it.

"Here we are, kids." Matt pulled up at Sarah's door. He'd been relieved to finally leave the church with them. He'd found it hard, as long as he was at St. Andrews, to keep his eyes from straying toward the stained-glass window of Jesus blessing the children. He didn't want to look at it, but for some reason it tugged at him.

He opened the car door for Andi and Ethan, wondering if he could just dump them and make his escape. Unfortunately, being back on the island seemed to reactivate all the Southern manners that had been drilled into him since birth. The answer was no, he couldn't. He had to go in and speak to Sarah, at least.

He would have knocked, but Andi already had the door open when he reached it. He was surprised to see Sarah apparently ready to go out.

"What's going on?"

She looked harried. "I can't get Jeffrey's fever down. I'm going to run him over to the clinic." She managed a distracted smile. "Thanks for your help. Andi and Ethan, let's get in the car."

"But, Mommy—"

"No arguments, please." She had Jeffrey in one arm and Amy in the other. "Just bring my bag, Andi."

"I'll watch them." The words were out of his mouth before he realized it, and part of him stood back and watched, appalled, as he reached out to take the baby from her.

"I can manage." Sarah clutched Amy.

She was clearly just as reluctant to let him as he was to do it. Somehow that made him more determined.

"Don't be silly." He pried the baby out of her arms. "You need to concentrate on taking care of Jeffrey."

An image of the children he hadn't been able to help

flickered through his mind, and he buried it. He wouldn't let Sarah's kids remind him of that.

"If you're sure—"

"I'm sure." He pushed her gently toward the car. "We'll be fine until you get back. If there's anything I need to know about the baby, Andi will tell me."

Jeffrey gave a little sob and burrowed his head into Sarah's neck. She stroked his hair gently.

"It's all right, sweetheart. The doctor will make you better." Her gaze met Matt's. "Thank you," she said softly.

The door closed behind her. Amy wailed and lunged toward it. With a convulsive movement, Matt caught her before she lunged right out of his arms. His heart pounding erratically, he set her down. She'd be safer on the floor. If she got hurt while he was watching her… The images came again, and this time it took more effort to oust them.

Amy wailed for another moment, then grasped the chair and pulled herself up to stand, holding on, wobbling a little. Apparently her storm was over.

He looked at Andi and Ethan. "You have to tell me, guys. What are we supposed to do now?"

"Watch television," Ethan began. "And then—"

"We change out of our church clothes first," Andi said firmly. "Then we have peanut-butter-and-jelly sandwiches, and we play quietly while Amy takes a nap."

Looked as if Andi was the one to count on. "Okay, let's do that." This shouldn't be too difficult. Anyone could make peanut-butter-and-jelly sandwiches and put a baby down for a nap.

An hour later he decided he'd been overly optimistic. The sandwiches had gone fine, although Andi pointed out that Mommy always cut them in triangles, not rectangles. And Andi and Ethan were, indeed, playing relatively quietly. But Amy didn't want to take a nap.

Frustrated and helpless at her wails, he lifted her back out of the crib and sat down in the cushioned rocker next to it. He could picture Sarah in the sunny nursery, rocking and singing.

"Come on, little girl." He patted Amy's back, and her cries reverberated in his head. "Give me a break."

He tried to think. What would Miz Becky, the Gullah woman who'd raised him and Adam after their mother died, have done in a situation like this?

A fragment of memory slipped through his mind. He seemed to feel warm, comforting arms rocking him back and forth while a rich Southern voice sang.

He may as well give it a try. Nothing else seemed to work. He rocked. "'Hush, little baby, don't say a word—'"

What came next? He couldn't remember, but then it came back to him. He hummed the bits he didn't remember, rocking in time to the song. Amy's wails diminished, then ceased. It became a game, trying to remember the verses, hearing Miz Becky's voice in his mind. It seemed to comfort him as much as it did the child.

By the time he'd remembered all the words to all the verses, Amy was asleep on his shoulder. He watched her, feeling a kind of wonderment. She was so relaxed and trusting, deep into slumber. He could see the fine tracing of blue veins under rose-petal skin, the soft crescents formed by her eyelashes against her cheeks.

He expected the moment to be shattered by his nightmare images of wounded, hungry children, but it wasn't. He could only feel…what? He sought for the word. *Blessed,* that was it. He could only feel blessed to share this peace.

Andi tiptoed into the room, clutching a book, and inspected the sleeping baby. "You can put her in the crib now," she whispered. "She's asleep."

"I know." He smiled. "I'm afraid she'll wake up if I move."

"Just hold her close against you." Andi adjusted his hands. "And then put her right down. That's what Mommy does."

"If it's good enough for Mommy, I guess it's good enough for me." *Please don't let me wake her.*

It was only after he'd put the baby safely into the crib

that he realized that was the first time he'd prayed without anger for a long time.

He and Andi tiptoed back out of the nursery. "Thanks, Andi. You were a big help." He noticed the cover of her book. "That looks like a good horse story."

She nodded. "I wanted to ask you something." She opened the book to the place she'd been holding with one small finger. "See what it says here? About using a pick to clean the horse's foot?" Her blue eyes were anxious. "Doesn't that hurt the horse?"

"Not at all." He put his hand on her shoulder, surprised by the fragility of her small bones. "The horse doesn't have feeling in that part of his hoof. But if a stone got caught under there and he walked on it, that would hurt."

He could almost see her process that. "It's like my fingernails," she said.

"Exactly." He felt an irrational pride at her swift intelligence. "Maybe you can come over to my house one day, and I'll show you how to do it."

Andi's breath caught, and she clutched the book against her chest. She looked as if he'd promised her the moon. "Could I really?"

He was probably offering something he'd later regret, but at the moment it seemed worth it. "Sure." He squeezed her shoulder. "We'll do that."

She skipped out to the living room, probably to tell

Ethan about the promised treat. He followed more slowly, wondering at himself. He wasn't going to get involved with Sarah and her kids—wasn't that what he'd told himself? He didn't seem able to keep that promise, and he wasn't quite sure why.

By the time Matt heard Sarah at the door, he'd finished a rough draft of his editorial and played three games of Chutes and Ladders with Andi and Ethan.

"How's Jeffrey?" Matt got up to close the door for her as she carried him in.

"Feeling better, I think. The doctor says it's a virus that's going around. I just hope everyone doesn't catch it."

He couldn't help but notice the tired shadows under Sarah's eyes as she stroked Jeffrey's silky hair, and he felt a surprising, unwelcome wave of protectiveness. He wanted to wipe her exhausted look away, but he couldn't.

"Do you want me to carry him to bed?"

"I'll just let him rest on the sofa for now." She lowered the child to the corner of the sofa and tucked an afghan around him. "Okay?"

Jeffrey nodded, his eyes drifting shut.

She turned to Andi and Ethan. "Why don't you go outside and play for a bit, okay? I'll call you when Jeffrey wakes up."

When they'd gone, she smiled at the game board

spread out on the coffee table. "I hope they weren't boring you to tears with that game."

"Actually, I learned quite a lot this afternoon." He started to put the pieces back in the box, but found he was watching Sarah instead. "I learned the rules of Chutes and Ladders, I learned I really do remember all the verses to 'Hush, Little Baby' and I learned that Andi is the most responsible little girl I've ever met."

"Too responsible, I'm afraid."

Sarah sat and leaned back in a chair, brushing a strand of hair away from her face. He could almost feel the silkiness of it against his own fingers.

"Was she always that way?" He didn't want to bring up her husband's death, but he wondered.

"She was a caretaker from the moment she was born, I think."

"Like her mother."

She looked at him with faint surprise. "Is that how you see me?"

"Definitely." He might not understand everything about Sarah, but that he knew. "You're like Miranda—always taking care of everyone."

She smiled. "Whether they want it or not." Faint worry lines showed between her brows. "Andi's been worse since her daddy died. I wish I could convince her she can just be a little girl."

He thought of his niece. Jennifer was nearly a year

older than Andi, but in some ways she seemed younger—certainly more carefree. Well, why wouldn't she? She'd lost her mother, but she had family who'd take care of her no matter what.

"Too bad I can't give you a little of my excess family."

Sarah looked startled for a moment, and then she seemed to follow his train of thought. "I guess my children are a little lacking in that department. No cousins, no aunts and uncles…"

"No grandparents?" He ventured the question.

Sorrow touched her face. "I'm afraid they just have me."

"I'm sorry."

She nodded in recognition of his sympathy, then seemed to turn away from it. "What about Ethan? Did you learn anything about him this afternoon?"

He thought he detected wariness in the question. "I learned he doesn't like to lose at Chutes and Ladders." He wasn't about to say that he'd caught the child in a clumsy attempt to cheat.

"Yes." The shadow in her eyes told him she understood what he didn't say. "Ethan does like to win. Well, most children are like that at his age. He's just very competitive." Defensiveness threaded her voice.

"He has a lot of charm." He put the lid on the box. "Reminds me of your husband."

Her mouth tightened. "Peter was always charming." She said it as if he'd implied an insult.

"Nothing wrong with that." What was going on behind those big blue eyes? Was there something about Peter Reed he should know?

"No, there's not." She stood up abruptly and held out her hand. "Thank you, Matt. I appreciate your help today. It was very kind of you."

Apparently he was expected to leave. Well, that was what he wanted, wasn't it?

He took her hand, feeling the warmth that seemed to flow from her every touch. "It was a pleasure," he said formally. "I like your kids, Sarah." To his surprise, he realized it was true.

And something else was true, something he wasn't about to say. He liked Sarah Reed, too. Maybe a little bit too much.

Chapter Seven

"Looks pretty good, doesn't it?" Matt unfolded the fresh issue of the *Gazette* on Friday morning, feeling a ridiculous surge of pride. He leaned against Sarah's desk, willing her to agree with him that the first issue he'd had much input on had turned out well.

Sarah nodded. "Not bad for a small-town weekly. And there's your name on the masthead."

"So it is." He couldn't seem to prevent a smile.

She tilted back in her swivel chair. The blue shirt she wore made her eyes even bluer. "Come on now. You've been featured on the television news. You're not going to tell me the *Caldwell Cove Gazette* holds a candle to that."

"Well, I have to confess it's the first time I've covered the important story of the garden club's annual awards night."

"Not big enough?" Her voice was gently teasing.

"It's important to people in Caldwell Cove. They want to know who won the award for the best roses. Oh, let me see." She pretended to consult the story. "That happens to be your grandmother."

"I told you no one could grow better roses than Gran." The smile lingered on his mouth. A couple of things surprised him about this day. One was the pride he felt in his first issue of the paper. The other was the pleasure his new relationship with Sarah engendered.

He looked cautiously at that. Things had changed between them during the last week. It wasn't just the fact that he'd helped on Sunday when she'd needed it.

They'd grown closer to each other. He hadn't intended that, but it had happened.

You're just getting used to having her around, he told himself. That's all. There's nothing more to it than that.

Used to having her around, used to having the kids around. He glanced over at Amy, contentedly chewing on a teething ring in her play yard. The little imp had been steadily working her way into his heart, and he couldn't seem to prevent it.

The other kids were back in the apartment, watched by yet another in the string of teenage baby-sitters Sarah had to rely on. Jeffrey seemed to have recovered from his bug. Matt could hear his voice raised in protest about something.

Sarah was reading through the front page, frowning a little. Looking for errors, he supposed. He'd learned, getting this issue of the *Gazette* out, that she was a perfectionist.

He'd learned a few other things, too. His gaze traced the soft line of her cheek, her straight nose, her stubborn chin. In just over a week he'd discovered Sarah's particular combination of strength and nurturing.

The warmth that made her reach out to every person who came through the door no longer seemed annoying, as it had that first day. It was as much a part of her as her attention to detail and her swift intelligence.

If he were honest with himself, he'd admit that he couldn't ignore the attraction he felt for her. He'd sensed it the day they met, and being around her every day had made it grow stronger. He didn't intend to act on it, of course. That would be unthinkable.

Except that he was thinking about it, especially at moments like this, when he stood close enough to smell the light, flowery scent she wore, close enough to see the smallest change in her expression.

As if in response to his thought, her expression did change. A slight frown creased her brows, and he knew she was reading the story he'd done on Jason Sanders.

"You still don't like it, do you?" He didn't need to explain what he meant. She'd know.

"It's not a question of like." She seemed to pick the

words out carefully. "You did a good job of reporting the story."

Her caution annoyed him. Or maybe he was more annoyed at the fact that she questioned his judgment.

"You still think I made a mistake in running it."

"I'm just worried about repercussions." She shook her head, forcing a smile. "Forget it. I worry too much. I'd better start setting up the ads for next week's issue."

She turned to her desk, as if dismissing the question. The trouble was, he knew she hadn't dismissed it, not entirely.

She'd gone along with his decision to run the story. That was the important thing. There was no point in beating the subject to death.

Returning to his desk, he opened the file of projected feature stories. Maybe he ought to take on something a bit less controversial for next week's issue.

He was mulling over the possibilities when the phone rang. He heard Sarah's cheerful answer, then heard the way the happiness drained from her voice.

He swung to look at her. She pressed the receiver to her ear, and a wave of brown hair flowed over it.

"I'm sorry to hear that." Her tone was carefully contained. "Is there anything I can do to change your mind about this decision?"

She paused, listening. He found he was listening, too, as if he could hear the voice on the other end of the line.

"No, I'm afraid we can't. I'm sorry you feel that way about it."

Sarah winced, as if the caller had slammed the phone down in her ear. She returned the receiver gently to the cradle.

"What is it?" He was afraid he knew.

"Jason Sanders." She looked at him, her face expressionless. "He's just withdrawn all his advertising from the *Gazette*."

He stood. What was there to say? "You warned me this might happen."

She grimaced. "Oddly enough, I'm not taking too much pleasure in being right."

"Look, Sarah, this isn't so bad. We can do without Sanders's advertising. It won't make or break us."

Sarah pushed her hair back from her forehead, as if it had gotten heavy. "Maybe not," she said noncommittally.

"Running the story was the right thing to do. We can't pick and choose our stories based on our advertisers." He hated the fact that he sounded defensive. "We're going to be all right. You'll see. We'll pick up more readers."

"Readers don't pay the bills. Subscribers and advertisers do. That's the reality of a weekly paper."

"Then we'll get more advertisers." Was he trying to convince her or himself?

"I hope so." She pressed her hands flat against the

desk, as if to ground herself. "Whether we do or not—" Her expression seemed to harden. "I agreed to this partnership. I'll take the consequences."

He wanted to argue, wanted to protest that he was right in this. He didn't doubt that. He was right.

Unfortunately he wasn't the one with the most to lose from this decision. Sarah was.

She was beginning to read Matt too well. Sarah bent over the folder of community calendar events, but her gaze was on Matt. He'd been quiet since that morning's call, but she could almost sense what he was thinking.

He felt regret, she was sure of that—regret that he'd caused problems for her by his actions. But he didn't regret writing the story. It wasn't in him to turn back from doing what he thought was right.

She suppressed a sigh. That might be a very admirable quality, but it wasn't an easy one to live with.

Not that she ever anticipated doing such a thing, she assured herself hurriedly. But she had to work closely with him, and the result was the same.

She studied Matt's face, straight dark brows drawn down over his eyes as he worked. He gripped a pencil with his right hand, turning it over and over in his fingers.

She had to push down the warmth that resulted every time she looked at him too closely. She had some regrets of her own over this situation. She regretted the loss of the comradeship she'd begun to feel with him since Sunday. But she certainly wasn't foolish enough to think there ever could be anything else.

Amy began to fuss, shaking the rail of the play yard. Sarah started to get up, but Matt beat her to it.

"I'll get her." He jerked a nod toward the folder he'd been looking through. "I'm not making much progress anyway."

He lifted the baby, holding her close against his cheek for a moment, and Sarah's heart lurched. Did Matt even realize how much he'd bonded with Amy since Sunday? And if he did, would it make a difference?

She already knew the answer to that question. Nothing would turn him back from doing what he thought was right. She could only hope he wouldn't find any other advertisers to antagonize.

"She's really close to walking." He bent over, putting her down on her feet, holding Amy's tiny hands in his large ones, and she toddled a few proud steps.

"Amy's a little later at that than the others were." She'd much rather talk with him about Amy than about business. "I think it's because she's always been such a placid baby. She didn't feel the need to get going as soon as they did. Andi in particular." She smiled reminiscently. "She was only ten months when she took her first step. I remember Peter said—" She stopped abruptly.

"What did he say?" Matt prompted.

She didn't talk much about Peter, but this was a happy memory. "He thought she'd end up being a track star because she moved so fast."

"Maybe she will. Caldwell Cove High could certainly use one."

"Maybe." If they were still here when Andi was ready for high school. If the paper survived, so that she could afford to stay here. If—too many ifs.

I want to stay, Lord. I want to put down roots here for my children. Please show me the way to make that happen.

Was that a selfish prayer? She should probably be asking God to show her the right path, instead of being so sure she already knew it. But surely He wouldn't have given her such a strong need to make her home here unless it was in His plan.

Matt chuckled. Amy had let go with one hand and stood wobbling, trying to reach out to the rung of his chair with the other.

"Take it easy, little girl. I don't think you're quite ready for that yet." His voice was gentle, his face as relaxed as Sarah had ever seen it.

If he ever looked at her that way— Sarah stopped that thought before it could go any further. She wasn't looking for romance, and certainly not with a man whose idea of settling down was six months in one place. She had the children, and that was all she could handle in her life just now.

A wail sounded from the apartment, followed by the sound of Wendy, the new sitter, calling her name.

"I'm sorry." She sent Matt an apologetic look as she started for the door. "Do you mind keeping an eye on Amy for a moment?"

"We're fine." He waved her off.

She scurried back to the apartment and settled a quarrel that a competent sitter should have been able to handle on her own. If she could only find someone really reliable to watch the children, this would be so much easier. Matt must be bothered by the constant intrusion of her family life into work, even though he didn't say anything about it.

She was on her way to the office when she heard a thump, followed by a cry from Amy and a muffled exclamation from Matt. She raced back through the door, heart pounding.

Matt clutched Amy against him, and blood dotted his shirt. His face was so white she thought him the injured one, but then she saw the cut on the baby's lip.

"She's hurt." He sounded almost frantic. "We've got to get her to the doctor."

She reached him then, taking the baby in her arms, automatically searching for other injuries as she soothed her. "Hush, sweetheart, hush. Let Mommy see." She grabbed a clean diaper and pressed it against Amy's quivering lip as she sank down into the chair. "It's okay."

"It's my fault. I should have been watching her more closely." Matt pulled out his keys. "I'll drive you to the clinic."

"I don't think that's necessary." She cradled Amy against her. The piercing wails turned into muted sobs. "It's not a deep cut."

"But the blood—" He sounded so shaken that she looked up at him. His face was still white, his eyes filled with grief and remorse.

"Facial cuts bleed." She tried to sound matter-of-fact. "Believe me, I've rushed to the doctor more times than I care to count. This isn't bad. Look, it's nearly stopped already." She stroked Amy's cheek. "She bit it with one of those new teeth of hers. It happens."

"It was my fault," he said again.

Why was he overreacting to this? "Matt, it wasn't anybody's fault. Babies fall. She'd have fallen if I'd been watching her." She smiled, reaching out to him with one hand. "Honestly, you didn't do anything wrong."

Matt shook his head, his mouth tight. Then, before she could say anything else, he turned away. In a moment he'd gone, and she was left staring at the closed door, wondering what on earth had just happened.

She searched Amy's little face. "You okay, darling?"

Amy responded with a smile and a babble of baby talk. Sarah hugged her close.

"Sure you are." She frowned at the door. "But Matt's not."

She didn't know why, but the small incident with Amy had upset him way out of proportion to the cause. She'd thought she was beginning to know him, but maybe she was wrong. Maybe she didn't understand him at all.

He'd let himself be responsible, and a child had gotten hurt. Matt stared at his reflection in the baroque mirror that graced the center hallway of the Caldwell mansion. Guilt seemed to look back at him.

The nightmares he'd hoped were gone would be back tonight. He could be sure of that.

The doorbell chimed, interrupting his thoughts. He glanced at the grandfather clock against the wall. Nearly nine. They weren't expecting anyone tonight, as far as he knew.

He pulled the door open. Sarah stood there.

For a moment he just looked at her, caught by the way the fanlight put gold highlights in her hair. Then reality hit.

"What's wrong? Is it Amy? Was it worse than you thought?" A dozen frightening possibilities chased each other through his mind.

"Amy's fine." Sarah reached toward him with that warm reassurance he'd seen her extend to the children. "Matt, she's okay, really. Just a bit of a fat lip to show for her tumble." She shook her head. "It probably won't be the last one, unfortunately."

Relief flooded him. "Then what?" He realized how brusque that sounded. "Please, come in. I'm just surprised to see you."

She stepped into the hallway, her sandals clicking on the black-and-white-tile floor. She'd traded the slacks she'd worn earlier for a skirt of some soft material that moved when she did. She looked around with frank curiosity.

"So this is how the other half lives."

He grimaced. "Just a tad ostentatious, isn't it?"

Before she could make what would have to be an awkward reply to that, Jennifer came bouncing down the steps.

"Hey, Miz Sarah. Is Andi with you?"

"Andi's home getting ready for bed." Sarah smiled at his niece.

Jennifer pouted. "I wish you'd brought her with you. We could have played. I want to show her my new dollhouse."

"I'm sure she'd like that," Sarah said gently. "Another time."

An idea tickled his mind, and he put it away to be

considered later. "Mrs. Reed and I have to talk, Jenny-girl. I'll see you later."

When Jenny looked mutinous at being dismissed, he took Sarah's arm. "Let's go out to the veranda. It'll be quiet there."

She nodded, letting him guide her through the door. She probably thought he didn't want her in his home. That couldn't be further from the truth.

The reality was that nothing about the mansion felt like home to him any longer, if it ever had. And he had no desire to discuss business with Sarah while they chanced being interrupted by his father.

Business must have brought her here, since Amy was all right. His father already thought him crazy to have bought into such a poor investment as the *Caldwell Cove Gazette.* He'd undoubtedly have some caustic advice about holding on to advertisers, if he knew about Jason Sanders.

They walked to the end of the veranda and sat in the wicker swing, piled high with cushions, that had always been his favorite spot for thinking. Sarah's skirt draped over the print pillows as she settled.

Her gaze seemed to trace the length of the veranda, and he wondered what she thought of it all. Did she see the showplace his father wanted it to be?

"Jenny's a sweet child." Her comment, when it came, surprised him. "It was nice of her to invite Andi over."

"She's quite a little person. I feel as if I've just finally gotten to know her."

"Maybe you were never here long enough." Sarah tilted her head to look at him, and moonlight touched her face, turning it silver.

"Maybe not." Maybe he shouldn't be here now. He didn't seem to belong after all this time. "Jenny really warms up this cold house." He gestured toward the Tara-like mansion that loomed over them.

"Cold?"

He couldn't see her eyes clearly in the moonlight, but he could hear the caring in her voice. He shrugged.

"Sounds like I'm whining, doesn't it? But this house has always been more showplace than home. After our mother died, the only really comfortable spot was the kitchen. Miz Becky always made sure we had plenty of loving."

"Who was Miz Becky?" Her voice was so soft it prompted the feelings he'd often thought but seldom expressed.

"Is, not was. Miz Becky takes care of us all. She raised four kids of her own, then took on the two motherless Caldwell boys. I'm not sure what we'd have done without her." He took a deep breath, clenching his fist on his knee. "Okay, enough small talk. You can let me have it."

A frown wrinkled her brow. "What do you mean?"

"You must be unhappy to go to the trouble of hiring a sitter so you could come here tonight. I figure that means you want to speak your mind about the paper without anyone around to overhear. I caused you enough trouble today. The least I can do is take the heat."

She shook her head, her hair moving like silk. "That's not why I'm here."

He resisted the impulse to touch her. "Why then?"

"Because I'm worried about you." The caring in her voice seemed to cross the inches between them and wrap around his heart. "You really overreacted to Amy's little mishap today." She put her hand on his. "Please, Matt. Tell me. What happened to you?"

Chapter Eight

Sarah held her breath, waiting for Matt's anger to spike, waiting for him to tell her to mind her own business. Or, worse, waiting for him to laugh at her presumption.

He didn't seem to be laughing. A shaft of moonlight cast his face in light and shadow—all bone and muscle without daytime's color to soften the effect. It was a study in determination, a warrior's face.

"I don't know what you mean." He said the words stiffly, without any emphasis at all. "If that's why you've come, I'm afraid you've wasted a perfectly good baby-sitter."

She wouldn't be put off. She'd spent too much energy arguing with God about coming at all, and she'd lost.

"I don't think so." She chose her words carefully,

trying to find the ones that would unlock the riddle that was Matthew Caldwell. "I saw your face this morning when Amy was hurt."

He shrugged, but the attempt at casualness wasn't convincing. "I'm sure there are plenty of men who get queasy when they see a baby bleeding."

"Matt, that wasn't queasiness. Believe me, I've seen enough sick kids to know the difference."

"Fine, have it your way. Whatever you think you saw in me—"

He started to get up, and the swing lurched beneath her. In a moment he'd be gone.

"Grief," she said. "Overwhelming grief and remorse, just because the baby fell."

He turned toward her, the swing's chains creaking in protest at the abrupt movement. Now the anger she'd been expecting flared in his face. "All right, have it your way. I overreacted. That's all. I overreacted."

"Because of something that happened to you while you were overseas." She didn't know why she was so sure. She simply knew.

Matt's face hardened to a bleak mask. "What happened is none of your business."

At least he'd admitted that there was something. "Matt, it doesn't help to keep things bottled up inside. You need to talk about it."

His hands moved, as if pushing that away. "Trust me,

Sarah. If I felt the need to unburden myself to someone, I have plenty of family to choose from."

Yes, he did. She had none, except the kids, so she couldn't understand what that was like.

"I know you do. Have you talked to any of them?"

"No." He bit off the word.

Please, Lord. You put this burden on my heart for him. You made me see I had to come here tonight. Please show me the words that will help him.

"Matt—" She couldn't tell him she'd begun to care. She didn't want to admit that even to herself. "I realize we haven't known each other very long. But we're partners. If something affects you, it affects me."

"Does it?" He almost sounded as if he wanted to believe that.

"Yes." She spoke firmly. He'd never know that she had feelings for him, but that didn't matter. What mattered was that he was hurting, and she wanted to help. "Please. Tell me what's going on with you."

"You won't like hearing it, Sarah. You might not be strong enough to hear it."

She sensed the longing beneath his bitterness. He wanted someone to listen and to care. He couldn't ask, but he wanted that. She reached out to clasp both his hands in hers.

"Tell me." The words came out a little breathlessly, but not because she was afraid he'd turn back now. She could feel the current running between them through their clasped hands. They were linked in a way she didn't quite understand, as if they'd known each other a long time ago and had just come together again.

Hearing what was burdening his heart would bring them even closer, and that closeness would eventually bring her more hurt. But Matt needed her right now, probably more than he realized. She couldn't let him down.

"I haven't talked to anyone about this since I got home."

She could hear something rustle out in the marsh beyond the veranda, but Matt's need kept her attention pinned to him.

"They haven't asked?" She gripped his hands more tightly, as if she could send comfort through them. Hadn't his family seen the pain in his eyes?

He shrugged. "I think my grandmother knows something's wrong. That's why she keeps reminding me of my verse."

"Your verse?"

His mouth twisted in what might have been an attempt at a smile. "It's another one of those Caldwell family traditions, like the dolphin. We all have a Bible verse we were given when we were baptized. Gran picked them for each of her grandchildren, the way her mother and grandmother did before her."

"A family tradition." It sounded like a good, comforting thing, like the swing rocking gently under them. "What is your verse?"

"Romans 8, 28." He stopped there, as if he didn't want to say the words.

But she knew them. "'And we know that in all things, God works for the good of those who love Him, who have been called according to His purpose.'"

"That's the one."

"It's a good promise to live by," she said softly.

"That's what James used to say." His voice roughened.

He looked down at their clasped hands, and the lines in his face seemed to deepen, as if she saw him growing older right in front of her.

"James?"

"James Whitman. He ran a mission station in Indonesia. I'd known him in college, so I looked him up when I was sent there to report on the Timorese situation."

Scattered memories flickered through her mind—images of bombed streets, frightened civilians, gangs of soldiers and militia. "That was a dangerous place to be."

"James used to laugh about that. It had been so quiet since he'd arrived it was almost boring, he said. Then the political situation changed, and nothing was quiet anymore." He shook his head. "That didn't stop him. He went right on doing his job, running his school, feeding anyone who came to his door in need, even if they turned around and robbed him."

"He sounds like a good person."

"He was."

Matt's grip tightened on her hands until it was painful, but she didn't pull away. She couldn't.

"I wanted to do a story on him, to showcase the good he was doing in the middle of chaos. He said no, but I kept after him. Finally he agreed. He should have kicked me out the first time I mentioned it."

"It didn't go well?" This had to be worse than a botched story.

"Actually the interview went very well. James was articulate, the kids were photogenic, everyone at the network was pleased."

A night bird cried somewhere out in the marsh, and Matt jerked as if it had been a shot. She tried to soothe him with the firm clasp of her hands.

"What went wrong?"

He grimaced, as if in pain. "Unfortunately it hadn't occurred to us that the terrorists watched television, too. The night after my report aired, I heard a rumor they planned to attack the mission station. I tried to get there to warn James and the others. I was running toward the gate when the bomb went off."

She made an inarticulate sound of grief. His hands jerked spasmodically. He might want to stop, but he wouldn't be able to now.

"We found James and a co-worker in the rubble.

Dead." The words rolled out inexorably. "Seven of the children were seriously injured. We had to dig them out. I can still hear them crying."

Her throat was so tight it seemed impossible to speak, but she had to. "Matt, it wasn't your fault. It was a terrible thing, but it wasn't your fault."

"Tell that to the people who died." His mouth twisted bitterly.

"You couldn't have known. James must have been more familiar with the situation than you were, and he didn't suspect that would happen."

"That doesn't make me any less guilty." He sounded as if he were passing judgment on himself.

"The people at the network didn't blame you, did they?"

"Blame me? No. I'm sure they regretted the bombing, but it certainly made quite a story for my next broadcast." His bitterness ran so bone-deep that she didn't know how it ever could be relieved.

"They didn't expect you to—"

"Report my friend's death?" His tone mocked her. "Of course they expected it."

Her heart seemed to be crying. "How could you possibly do that?"

"Not very well. I nearly broke down on the air. Funny, but that's the one thing they couldn't forgive. That's why I'm in exile. Not because I did an interview that led to a good man's death, but because I nearly broke down on the air."

Sarah felt as if she hadn't breathed in a long time. She took a breath, steadying herself. "So you decided to take a leave of absence to get over it."

"I didn't decide. My bosses decided. 'Get a grip on yourself, Caldwell. You're no good to us like this. Go back to your island until you learn to cope out here in the real world.'"

She struggled to get her mind around that. She'd assumed that this leave of absence was his idea. Now it turned out it hadn't been. He was here under protest, trying to put himself back together.

"So you'll go back, once you've come to terms with this. Your job will be waiting for you."

She tried to sound reassuring. He'd go back. Odd, that his presence could have come to mean so much to her in such a short period of time.

"That's my life. Ugly as it can be, it's my life. I want it back." His voice roughened. "When I get it back, believe me, there won't be a repeat performance. I won't ever let myself get that close to anyone again."

Matt couldn't believe those words had come out of his mouth. Shock rippled through him. How could he be saying these things to anyone, especially to Sarah?

He'd told her things he hadn't told anyone else. Not even his brother knew the whole story behind his return. And he'd just spilled it all to a woman he'd only known a couple of weeks.

"Matt—" Sarah's voice was troubled. "You can't live detached. No one can."

"I can try." He wanted to pull his hands free of hers, wanted to cut this short and walk away.

But he couldn't. Talking to Sarah, feeling her caring, had begun to melt something that had been frozen inside him. Like thawing cold hands, it hurt, but he knew it was doing him good.

"Is that really what you want for yourself?" She shifted a little, and the swing moved beneath them as she turned toward him more fully.

He wanted to say something light, something that set them at a safe distance. But Sarah was looking at him with her generous caring heart shining in her eyes, and he couldn't do that.

"Want?" He should let go of her hands. He should get up and walk away. "I don't know that *want* is the right word. It's what I *need* to survive out there." He jerked his head toward the mainland. She'd know he meant everything out there, beyond Caldwell Island.

"Maybe you don't belong out there any longer." Her voice was so soft, he leaned closer to hear it. "Maybe your life is meant to be here."

"No. My life is waiting for me." He tried to sound sure of that. He *was* sure of that.

But the moonlight tangled in Sarah's hair, etching it with silver, and the soft lowcountry night closed around them, cradling them in its warmth. Warm—almost as warm as Sarah, leaning toward him, longing to make him better.

"Sarah Reed." He touched her hair, feeling the springy curls wind around his fingers. "Sympathy her specialty, given to anyone and everyone, regardless of whether they deserve it or not."

"It's not a question of deserving."

"No?" He said it softly, prolonging the moment.

Her eyes, soft in the moonlight, met his. Her lips parted, as if she were about to say something, and then she seemed to forget whatever it was. He heard the soft sound of her breath, felt her hand tremble under his.

"Sarah." Her name was gentle on his lips, as gentle as she was, with her combination of softness and strength. She'd gotten under his guard in a way he'd never expected anyone would, ever again.

"Matt, I—"

He touched her cheek, smooth and sweet as the skin of a fresh peach. Stroked the line of her jaw. Cupped her chin in his hand and tilted her face toward his. Found her mouth with his.

Longing surfaced within him. He drew her closer,

feeling her respond as if she, too, had been waiting for this moment. As if this kiss had been predetermined from the first time they saw each other.

Maybe it had. He held her close. Maybe it had.

Sarah drew back, too soon, with a small sound that might have been protest. He trailed a line of gentle kisses across her cheek. Sarah was everything he needed now—warmth, caring, peace. This might be a mistake, but he couldn't let her go.

"We shouldn't." Sarah breathed the words. Her hand moved against his chest to push him away, but then she clutched his shirt instead, feeling the steady beat of his heart beneath the smooth cotton.

"I know, I know." He held her close within the protective circle of his arm. He took a deep breath, as if he'd been without oxygen for too long. "This isn't a good idea."

"We're partners." She sought for all the rational arguments she knew were there, somewhere, if only she could find them.

"We have a business relationship." She thought there might be a thread of amusement under his agreement, but she didn't know if it was at her or himself. "We shouldn't mix that up with something personal."

"No, we shouldn't." She straightened her spine, pulling free of the comfort of his strong arm around her.

She didn't need to lean on anyone, she reminded herself. Certainly not Matt Caldwell.

"I'll be leaving soon." He said it with certainty. He moved, withdrawing his arm, putting another inch or two between them. "You know I can't deny I'm attracted to you, Sarah. But it would be a mistake to start something that has to end. Especially where your children are concerned."

The children. She fixed her mind on them, trying to ignore the way her heart continued to flutter at Matt's nearness.

"We agree, then. It would be too hard on the children to let them think—well, think there was something between us that's not going to be."

There, she'd put things in perspective. Matt would understand that. Now she just had to convince her own heart, which was showing a surprisingly rebellious streak at the idea.

"We're partners," Matt said again. "Friends."

She nodded. "Friends. That's all. Just friends."

He clasped her hand briefly, then released it. "You helped me tonight, Sarah. I didn't know how much I needed to talk about James until you forced me into it."

She tried to smile. "You make it sound as if I used a baseball bat."

"No. Just a persistence and determination that would do credit to a reporter on the trail of a hot story."

She sensed his relief that they had moved into less emotional territory. She wanted to stay there, too. It was safer. But something nagged at her, something that had to be said.

"Matt, if we are friends, will you let me give you some friendly advice?"

He nodded, but she thought he stiffened.

"When Peter died, I was angry with God." She picked the words carefully. "I thought He had let me down, leaving me alone with four kids to raise."

Matt didn't respond. Maybe he knew where she was going and didn't want to hear it. But he had to. She had to say it, because no one else would. He hadn't opened up to anyone else, so this was her responsibility.

"Eventually I realized God hadn't gone anywhere. He was right there with me, helping me every step of the way." Her voice choked in spite of her effort to keep it calm. "I wouldn't have made it without Him."

Matt nodded stiffly. "I'm glad for you, Sarah. But I—"

"You're angry with God," she said quickly, before he could finish. "You think God let you down. Let your friend down."

He swung on her then. "Didn't He? How else would you explain it? Or do you have some nice little platitude that will make the pain go away?"

His words hit her like stones, and she tried not to

flinch. "No platitudes," she said softly. "Just my own experience. God was big enough to handle my anger and grief and bring me through to the other side. He's big enough to handle yours, too."

Matt got up, setting the swing rocking. He stood looking down at her, as remote as a stranger.

"I appreciate what you're trying to do, Sarah. But I'm going to have to handle this my own way."

"Are you handling it?"

"Yes." He bit off the word. "I'm handling it fine on my own."

He wasn't, but he wouldn't admit that, not yet.

"I guess there's nothing else to say but good-night, then."

Something seemed to soften his stern expression. "I didn't mean—" He stopped, shook his head. "Thank you, Sarah. I'll walk you to your car."

Their heels clicked as they walked the length of the veranda. Matt held the car door for her, then stood for a moment looking at her. He was going to say—

"Good night, Sarah." He turned away.

He didn't want God's help, didn't want her help. She started the car, and shells spun under her wheels as she pulled through the white pillars that marked the gate.

Well, Matt might not want her help, but he needed it. She'd have to go on trying. Despite whatever they felt or didn't feel for each other, she couldn't let him wall his soul off and not try to help him.

And if she succeeded? She tried to look at that steadily as she drove down the narrow street. If she helped Matt heal, she knew what would happen then. He'd go away, taking her heart with him.

Chapter Nine

He didn't know why he was so nervous about this. Matt glanced across the office at Sarah a few days later, wondering at himself. He had a simple suggestion to make, one that Sarah should welcome. So why was he acting like a teenager about to ask a girl on a first date?

The kiss, that's why, the small voice of truth murmured in his heart. You kissed her, and you haven't figured out how to deal with that.

He had dealt with it, he argued. They both had. They'd agreed that anything other than friendship between them would be a mistake. They both knew that, and they'd go on from there.

He watched the tiny lines that formed between Sarah's brows as she looked over something on her desk. That attention to detail was part of her. She brought the need to do things right to everything she touched, including her kids. Maybe that was why he hesitated to approach her on this.

No perfect words appeared in his mind. He'd better just do it.

"Sarah." He approached her desk. She glanced up and a soft brown curl caressed her cheek, momentarily distracting him.

"Is something wrong?"

"No, nothing. In fact, I have an idea that might be very helpful." He marshaled his arguments in his mind. "How would you feel about your kids spending afternoons at the house with Jenny and her baby-sitter?"

"The house?" She looked blank.

"My house. My brother thinks it's a great idea."

Distress crossed her face. "You're bothered by having the children around. I know this isn't a conventional way to run an office, but—"

"No, that's not it at all." He should have realized she'd jump to that conclusion. "You must know by now that I like your kids."

As soon as he said the words he realized how true they were. He hadn't intended this to happen—it certainly wasn't part of the detachment he'd been cultivating. But her children had worked their way into his heart when he wasn't looking.

"Then why are you trying to get rid of them?" Sarah

pushed her chair back, her face guarded, as if preparing for a fight.

"Look, I think we could deal with two problems at the same time here. Jenny needs playmates—there are no young families close enough to the house to make that easy. And you need a few hours a day when you're free to concentrate on the paper, instead of always wondering if the current baby-sitter is up to par."

"There's nothing wrong with my baby-sitters." She was quickly defensive. "They may be young, but—"

"But all the older kids have other summer jobs. I know. I remember what it's like." He sat on the edge of her desk, trying a smile, hoping to relax the conversation. "Every teenager on the island who wants to work can find a summer job, and baby-sitting comes at the bottom of the list."

Sarah didn't relax. "Even if that's true, I don't expect you to come to my rescue. Providing childcare is not one of your partnership responsibilities."

He lifted an eyebrow. "Are you always this prickly when someone wants to do something for you?"

"I don't like to take charity." Her clear blue eyes clouded. "I remember—" She stopped.

"You remember what?" He leaned forward, suddenly wanting to know what brought that distress to the surface. "This isn't charity, but never mind that for now. What do you remember?"

He saw the struggle in her face. She wanted to tell him; she didn't want to tell him. "Come on, Sarah. I've leveled with you. Don't I deserve the same?"

Her smile flickered briefly. "It's nothing very important."

"Then there's no reason not to tell me why that's such a hot button for you."

She shrugged. "Have it your way. My father was career army. He was posted all over the world, and since my mother died when I was a baby, I went with him."

"I didn't know that." Maybe that explained why Caldwell Cove was so important to her. She wanted a stable home for her own kids.

"I wasn't much older than Andi when we lived in Germany." She frowned. "I don't know why money was so tight, but it was. I had to have uniforms for the school there, but Dad couldn't afford them. So the headmistress called me in, and they had this big box of cast-off uniforms. The teacher went rooting through them, trying to find something that would fit. Nothing did, and Dad certainly didn't know how to alter anything." She looked down, as if seeing a too-big school uniform. "I went through that whole school year looking like a ragamuffin." She grimaced. "Silly, I know. But it made me a little touchy where accepting charity is concerned."

She'd ended on a light note, but his throat was ridiculously tight. He kept seeing the little girl she'd been, with blond pigtails like Andi's, feeling hurt and ashamed that she wasn't like the other kids.

"As I said, this isn't charity." He tried to keep his tone brisk. "At least, not for you. We want to provide a job for Miz Becky's niece, so she can earn next year's college tuition. She keeps insisting watching Jenny isn't enough work."

She smiled. "And you think watching my crew would be enough to justify hazard pay."

He smiled back, relieved that they seemed to have moved out of emotional territory. "Something like that. You can consider it helping a deserving young woman get her education. So, will you do it?"

Sarah held his gaze for a long moment, as if probing his intent. Finally she gave a hesitant nod. "I guess we can try it for a day or two."

"Fine." He got up quickly, before she could change her mind. "We'll start this afternoon."

She looked startled. "Wouldn't it be better to wait until a few days? We should give Jenny's sitter a chance to prepare."

"Wanda's ready now. And Jenny can't wait to have them there to play. We'll run them over around one. You mentioned your sitter has to leave then, so this will work out perfectly. All right?" He could feel the resistance in her.

"We'll try it," she said again. "If it's too much for the sitter—"

"It won't be," he said, inordinately pleased that he'd pulled this off. Sarah would accept his help. She'd undoubtedly give him an argument about who paid Wanda, but he'd deal with that when it happened.

The important thing was that he could help her and, in a way, make the paper run more smoothly. He silenced the little voice whispering in his mind that this was another giant step into each other's lives.

How had she let herself be talked into this? Sarah got out of the van, looking nervously up at the pillared veranda as she took Amy out of the car seat. She couldn't feel at home in a place like this. Her kids didn't belong here. What if they broke something?

"We're ready." Matt shooed the kids toward the veranda. "Let's go find Wanda and Jenny."

At least the children didn't seem to sense her nervousness. Andi skipped along at Matt's side, perfectly confident, while the boys peppered him with questions.

Sarah tried not to let her gaze slip sideways to the swing where they'd sat Wednesday night. Where they'd kissed.

Matt held the door open, and the kids scurried inside. He gestured for her to enter.

She should have stuck with her initial no. Working

with Matt every day was bad enough. Having her children in his house was worse.

There was only one solution—she'd have to find some reasonable excuse to get out of this. Clutching Amy, she crossed the threshold into the Caldwell mansion.

She stood in the wide center hallway, getting her bearings, noticing things she'd been too preoccupied to see on Wednesday night. To her right was the formal dining room, with its crystal chandelier and mahogany table and chairs carved in the rice design that was typical of the sea islands. To the left, a ceiling fan circled lazily above elegant Queen Anne furniture placed on what seemed an acre of Oriental carpet.

Ahead of her a circular staircase soared upward, looking as if Scarlett O'Hara would descend at any moment. But that wasn't Scarlett coming toward her down the steps. It was Matt's father.

Jefferson Caldwell approached with cool assurance, holding out his hand. "Ms. Reed. Welcome to Twin Oaks."

"Thank you." She shook hands, trying to assess her impressions as Caldwell turned to his son with a question. *Distinguished*—that was probably the word. That leonine mane of white hair, those piercing eyes— Jefferson Caldwell looked like a man who was used to getting what he wanted.

She glanced from him to Matt, wondering. Coolness

tainted the air between them. She couldn't help but see it.

Was this because of Matt's partnership in the newspaper? If his father disapproved of that, she could hardly imagine that he'd want her children cluttering up his house.

Jefferson turned to her, looking as if his mind had already moved past her to something more important. "Miz Becky is waiting for you in the kitchen, and I expect the others are there, too. Y'all go on back. Make yourselves at home."

"Thank you." She relaxed marginally. At least Caldwell Sr. didn't seem actively opposed to their presence. But if he had been, that would have given her the perfect excuse to call this whole thing off.

"This way." Matt shepherded them through a swinging door at the end of the hallway, his step quickening.

Suddenly they were in a different world—one with linoleum underfoot, geraniums blossoming on the windowsills and a ginger cat weaving around the legs of the woman who turned to greet them.

"'Bout time you were getting back here with them, boy." Miz Becky buffeted Matt with an affectionate blow to his shoulder, but her eyes were on the children. "Y'all are welcome in my kitchen, y'heah? Andi, Ethan, Jeffrey." She greeted each of them with a gentle touch to head or cheek. "And this little darlin' is Amy."

She scooped the baby from Sarah's arms, murmuring to her softly in Gullah, the language of sea island natives. Sarah could only look on in amazement as Miz Becky charmed her children.

Matt had said she'd taken care of him and Adam after raising her own children, so Miz Becky had to be sixty, at least. But she was as proudly erect as any queen, and the glossy black hair that wrapped around her head in a kind of coronet showed not a trace of gray.

This part of the house looked different, smelled different, felt different. Where the front was all cool elegance, Miz Becky's kitchen felt warmly loving.

The biggest change was in Matt. The tension she'd sensed when he was with his father had disappeared entirely. He teased the children gently in Gullah as he helped Miz Becky carry a pitcher of lemonade and platter of molasses cookies to the back porch.

Sarah followed, wondering. What kind of home was it, when the son of the house felt more at home in the kitchen with the housekeeper?

"This is my niece, Wanda."

The tall young woman who'd been playing a game with Jenny at the porch table rose to shake her hand. "It's nice to meet you, Ms. Reed." She smiled. "And the children. Andi, Ethan, Jeffrey." Like her aunt, Wanda called them by name, but her language didn't have as much of the slurred Gullah accent. "I see Aunt Becky has already laid claim to the baby. I'll be lucky ever to get my hands on her."

"But—" Sarah looked at the woman who cradled Amy against her cheek. "I don't want to impose on you. I'm sure you already have plenty to do running a big house like this."

"Sugar, you couldn't make me happier if you tried." She rocked Amy gently, and the baby's eyes started to close. "I've been longin' for another baby to love around here, and it started to look like that wouldn't happen."

Matt held up his hands in defense. "Hey, I've brought you Amy. You can't ask for more."

His quick words jolted her heart. No one could ask for more from Matt. She'd known that since their talk Wednesday night. His experiences had convinced him the only safe life was a detached one, and that undoubtedly extended to having a family of his own.

That was his decision. The twinge in her heart was totally uncalled for.

She still wasn't convinced that the Caldwell housekeeper should be watching her baby. Had anyone bothered to consult Jefferson Caldwell about that?

"Miz Becky, I'm just not sure—"

"Hush, child." She jerked her head toward the kitchen door. "Come in and see what we've fixed up for this little one."

Matt had joined the children and Wanda at the round

table on the porch and was pouring out lemonade. She followed Miz Becky into the cool kitchen and then to a small room that adjoined it.

Becky's gesture encompassed it. "This used to be a maid's room, but nobody lives in it anymore. Matt helped me get it ready."

Sunlight slanted through the window and lay in patches on the wide plank floor. The room had been turned into a nursery, with a crib, changing table and a box of baby toys.

"You've gone to so much trouble."

"No trouble." Miz Becky lowered Amy to the crib. The baby stirred, then slipped deeply into sleep, one hand curled against her cheek. "These things were our Jenny's when she was a baby. She was right excited to help us get them out for Amy. And Matt was the most at peace I've seen him since he got home." She smoothed one hand along the crib railing. "That boy needs a little peace. If he gets it from helping your young ones, that's not such a big thing to ask, is it?"

Sarah blinked back tears, thinking of Matt's face when he'd talked about the children he'd heard crying for help after the bombing that killed his friend. Maybe this could be a step in his healing.

"No," she said softly. "It's not a big thing to ask at all."

They walked back to the porch.

Wanda had the children lined up on the step while

she laid out the house rules for them with quiet authority. "Y'all listen when I call you, stay out of the front of the house and don't run through the flower beds or my daddy will get after you. He takes care of those flowers, and he's right proud of them. All right?"

Sarah half expected Andi to argue or Ethan to try and wheedle his way out of the rules, but all three nodded solemnly.

"That's fine, then." Wanda flashed them a wide smile. "Let's have a game."

The children followed her onto the lawn, and Matt rose, moving to her side. "See?" he said. "Plenty of room for them to play safely. That's the stable, beyond the garages, with the vegetable garden beyond that."

"And that?" She pointed to the raw skeleton of a building rising behind the outbuildings.

Matt grimaced. "My father's latest project. He's putting up a few new houses on the lane behind the estate."

"Don't you like the idea of neighbors that close?" Or was it something about his father's business that bothered him?

He shrugged. "Doesn't matter to me." Implicit in it was that he'd soon be gone. "Well, Sarah?" He gave her a challenging look. "You find any flaws in our arrangements for the kids that would let you back out?"

He shouldn't be able to read her that easily. She felt a twinge of panic. How had she let him get so far into her life?

"No flaws." She managed a smile. She could be gracious about this, after all.

"Then let's get back to work."

He took her arm as he spoke, his hand warm against her skin, and her pulse jumped. Work—just the two of them in the office. Before, the children had always been nearby, forming a buffer by their presence. Now she and Matt were really going to be alone together.

"The worship is ended. Let the service begin." Pastor Wells held up his hands in benediction, and the organ burst out in joyful music.

Sarah stood still in the pew for a moment, letting the peace she'd been seeking for the last several days seep into her. St. Andrew's Chapel—its minister and its people—had been a blessing to her since the day she arrived on the island. She loved it—loved the tiny wooden sanctuary that felt almost like a boat inside, loved the ancient stained-glass windows, loved Pastor Wells's sermons, always so filled with joy.

A fragment of guilt touched her. She had to admit that she hadn't listened as closely as she should have to the day's message. Matt had been seated three rows ahead of her. She'd forced herself not to look, but even when she'd had her gaze fixed on the pulpit, awareness of him hovered at the edge of her mind.

Stop it, she lectured herself sternly. She saw more than enough of Matt all week. They probably both needed a break from each other on Sunday, especially now that the children spent afternoons at the mansion. Hopefully by the time she picked the children up from the nursery and the junior church, he'd be gone.

When she emerged into the churchyard a few minutes later, people still clustered under the trees, chatting. Before she could head toward the car, Jason Sanders broke away from a nearby group and approached her. Tension skittered along her nerves. She hadn't talked to Sanders since the day he'd withdrawn his advertising.

"Good morning, Jason." She hoped he wasn't planning to be difficult.

"Sarah, good to see you." He beamed as if she were a long-lost relative. "How's everything at the paper?"

The children, apparently considering this a reprieve from going home, scurried off to chase each other around the sprawling branches of a live oak.

"Just fine." She shifted Amy to the other arm. Sanders had to know his actions had put a dent in their budget, but she wasn't about to admit that.

He lifted an eyebrow, some of the joviality leaving his face. "Can't be easy for you, breaking in a new partner. Especially someone like Matt Caldwell."

She felt her smile freeze on her face. "Matt's doing fine."

"Still, can't be like working with Peter." He sighed. "Terrible loss. I always liked Peter. It'd be a shame to see the paper change from his vision for it."

Her lips felt stiff, but she managed to make them move. "Nothing has changed about the *Gazette*." She glanced past him, seeing Matt approach. "Perhaps you'd like to talk with Matt about it."

"Think I'll skip that pleasure." He turned to move off, then glanced back at her. "I'd like to resume my advertising, Sarah. I surely would."

"I hope you'll think about it."

He nodded, then was gone before Matt reached her.

"What did he want?" Suspicion colored Matt's voice as he glared after Sanders.

"I'm not sure." What had been the point of that little exchange? She didn't know, but she knew it made her uneasy.

Matt shook his head, as if dismissing Sanders. "Pastor Wells has something he'd like to talk with us about."

Amy, hearing Matt's voice, made a lunge toward him. He caught her as if he'd been doing that all her life and carried her as they walked to the minister. "Tell Sarah what you were just telling me. She'll be interested."

Was that his way of palming something off on her that he didn't want to do?

Pastor Wells tickled Amy's cheek. "I was asking Matt if he realized the two-hundredth birthday of the church is coming up this year." He looked lovingly toward the frame building. "It's hard to believe, isn't it?"

"I hadn't realized. You must be planning a celebration." Somehow she had the feeling they were going to be asked to do something.

"Yes, of course. And part of that celebration should be a recognition of the role St. Andrews has played in the island's history."

She nodded cautiously, hoping that didn't mean he wanted her to write that history.

"So I thought the *Gazette* would run a series of articles." He beamed, as if he were giving them a present. "I have boxes of historic material, and I know people would want to read about it."

"I'm sure you're right, Pastor. That's exactly the sort of thing our readers love." She glanced at Matt, daring him to argue. Certainly it wasn't the sort of article he loved.

But Matt nodded. "Great idea. Let me know when the material is ready, and I'll stop by to pick it up."

"Wonderful." Pastor Wells clapped his hands together, beaming. "I'll have it ready in a day or two."

Someone else called his name then, and he moved off, still smiling.

"Admit it, Sarah." Matt lowered his voice, standing close enough that none of the other parishioners gathered on the lawn could hear. "You thought I was going to turn the poor man down."

Once again he seemed to be looking into her mind. "I was afraid you might not find the church's birthday celebration hard-hitting enough."

"Even I know St. Andrews's bicentennial is important," he said. "Besides, how involved can it be? You'll look though the material, find some way to present it so it's not as dry as dust—"

"Hold it right there. How did this suddenly get to be my job?"

"Human-interest stuff is more your forte than mine."

"But this is your church, your town. You grew up here." She thought of the Caldwell legend and the missing dolphin that still meant so much to all of them. "You know all the old stories. I'd say that makes it yours."

A smile tugged at his lips. "Okay, ours then. We'll work on it together. Agreed?"

"Agreed."

His smile faded as he glanced across the churchyard. "I have another story I want to pursue, as well. Something that will be more hard-hitting."

She followed the direction of his gaze, and her heart sank. "You're tackling Jason Sanders again."

Matt's expression hardened. "I got a tip that there's something shady about a deal he has going at the far end of the island. I intend to look into it."

Reason told her that Sanders had already withdrawn his advertising. He couldn't do anything else to them. But a warning voice whispered in her mind that he wasn't a good enemy to make.

"Do you have to do this?" She knew before she asked the question what his answer would be.

"Of course. That's what a journalist does." He looked surprised that she could even ask. "If I could break an important story…" He let that trail off.

But she seemed to know what he was thinking. If Matt broke an important story, he'd be proving that he had himself together again. That he was ready to leave.

He'd be gone and she'd be left to pick up the pieces.

Chapter Ten

If only she'd found some way to stop him. Sarah shook her head as she drove toward the Caldwell mansion to pick up the children the next afternoon. That was wishful thinking, and she knew it.

Matt wouldn't be deterred from the expedition he'd made to the county courthouse in Beaufort in search of information about Sanders's real-estate deals. She hadn't bothered to try. He was one of the most single-minded people she'd ever met. In that respect he reminded her of her father.

Duty, honor, country had been her father's motto. Unfortunately his only daughter had come in a poor second to that.

She tried to rationalize away the sense of worry that had been hanging over her since the day before, when Matt had made it clear he wasn't finished with Jason

Sanders and his real-estate dealings. That concern wasn't caused only by her fear of making an influential enemy.

Matt was evading his own spiritual problems by concentrating on Sanders's possible misdeeds. She wasn't sure why she was so convinced of that, but she couldn't shake the feeling. Matt needed to heal. He needed to find peace, as Miz Becky had pointed out. He wouldn't do that by plunging headlong into a battle with someone he'd disliked since childhood.

She gripped the steering wheel.

Please, Lord. I'm not sure how to pray for Matt. I just know he has to turn to You, or he's never going to be at peace again. If I'm supposed to help him, please show me how to do it. I don't seem to be doing too well on my own.

She pulled between the twin pillars, shaded by century-old live oaks, that marked the circular drive of Twin Oaks, the Caldwell mansion. Matt's car pulled in just ahead of her. He'd gotten back from Beaufort then, with or without the information he'd gone after.

"Sarah." He got out and closed the door, waiting for her to catch up with him. "I thought you'd probably left the office by now, so I didn't bother to stop there."

"How did you make out at the courthouse?"

Matt lifted an eyebrow. "Are you sure you want to know?"

"I'll have to, won't I?" She looked up at him,

noting the lines of tension between his eyes. "If you're going to plunge the *Gazette* into controversy, I'd better know about it."

He leaned against the car, apparently preferring to have this conversation in the driveway, where no one could hear. "Controversy sells papers."

"Controversy also makes enemies." She'd learned that the hard way the first year they'd owned the paper. "A small-town paper can't afford to have too many of those if it's going to stay in business."

"That's a judgment call, isn't it?" He moved restlessly, his brow furrowed, and she could see that whatever peace he'd found a few days earlier had vanished now.

Guide me, Lord.

She could hear the children's voices from the back of the house, raised in play. All of her judgment of what to do had to be weighed in the balance of what was good for her children. That was what Matt didn't seem to understand.

"Why don't you tell me what you found out, and I'll tell you what I think?"

"No smoking gun, I'm afraid. But Sanders has been buying up a lot of small pieces of land down at the south end of the island, apparently for various private individuals."

"That doesn't sound so dire."

He frowned, drumming his fingers on the roof of the car. The sound played on her nerves. "Could be private home buyers, I suppose, but it seems odd that all his dealings lately have been in the same area."

"Odd, but not illegal." She suspected that logic wouldn't stop him.

"Worth looking into a little more deeply, I think." He straightened, the movement taking him closer to her, and his tension seemed to leap the distance to dance along her skin.

"Sarah, I promise you I won't run anything unless I have proof, not just suspicion, of wrongdoing. Is that good enough for you?"

"I suppose it will have to be."

He frowned at her for a moment, looking as if he wanted to say something more, but a clamor of voices from the back lawn made him swivel in that direction. "Maybe we'd better see what all the noise is about."

She walked up the path beside him, hurrying a little. If her children were in trouble—

They rounded the corner of the house, and Sarah's heart sank. The picture in front of them was regrettably self-explanatory.

The gardener, Wanda's father, stood on one side of a trampled flower bed, ball cap pushed back on his gray hair, hands on his hips. Opposite him stood her two sons. Jeffrey's small face was a picture of guilt, while

Ethan tried on a smile that was an echo of his father's. It didn't seem to be working on the gardener.

"Jeb, what's going on?" The sound of Matt's voice had the gardener turning to him.

"These two young rascals rampaged right through the marigold seedlings I just planted, that's what."

"It wasn't us," Ethan said quickly. "Honest, Mommy. It wasn't us."

Ethan turned the smile on her, and an image formed in her mind. Peter had worn that same winsome smile when he was about to spin a story about why he hadn't paid a bill or was overdrawn at the bank.

No. She rejected the image, overwhelmed with guilt. Peter was beyond his faults. She shouldn't think such things about him.

"Ethan…" she began.

"It was me." Andi scurried off the porch and ran to the gardener, tugging on his sleeve. "I'm sorry, Mr. Johnson. Really I am. I'll fix it."

The old man's face softened as he looked down at her. "I don't think so, missy."

"Those are Ethan and Jeffrey's footprints in the bed, Andi." Matt spoke before she could say anything else. His voice was a gentle, reassuring rumble. He knelt by the soft earth and pointed to the telltale sneaker prints.

This just kept getting worse.

"I'm sorry." Sarah hurried into speech. "I'm afraid

this was a bad idea. I shouldn't have agreed to it." She looked at the gardener, because she didn't want to look at Matt. "I hope you'll let me repair the damage before we leave." And they wouldn't be coming back.

"Sarah, that's not necessary." Matt stood and took a step toward her.

"I told you I didn't want to cause problems for your family. I think it best if we go back to the way things were."

"The boys—" he began.

"The boys are my responsibility."

Hers, and hers alone. No matter how tempting it was to share her burden, she never should have let Matt take on even a little piece of it.

Matt frowned, trying to understand the distress on Sarah's face. She looked so distraught that his heart twisted. He had to talk to her about this, had to try and understand what she was feeling. But maybe he'd better defuse the situation with Jeb and the kids first.

He knelt next to the boys so that he looked from one small face to the other. "Seems to me you forgot what Wanda told you about the flowers."

They looked back at him, their blue eyes almost identical. For a moment he feared they wouldn't respond. Then Jeffrey's face crumpled. "I'm sorry." His voice was so soft, Matt could hardly hear it, but it gave him a sense of triumph. That was the first time he could remember that Jeffrey hadn't relied on Ethan to talk for him.

"We forgot," Ethan said quickly. He clutched Jeffrey's hand. "We didn't mean to do it. We're sorry."

"Since you're sorry, you'll want to help Mr. Johnson replant the flowers, won't you?"

Ethan swallowed visibly, giving Jeb a quick sidelong glance, then nodded. "If he'll let us."

Matt looked up at Jeb, knowing he could rely on the old man who'd been a fixture at Twin Oaks for as long as he could remember. "What do you say?"

Jeb shrugged, his face solemn but a twinkle lurking in his eyes. "Guess I can use a little help, all right." He fixed a firm gaze on the boys. "You younguns come over here, and I'll show you what to do."

Matt rose, taking Sarah's arm. "There," he said softly. "All settled."

"I don't think—"

"Leave it, Sarah." He nudged her away from the flower bed and toward the porch. "They'll learn more planting flowers with Jeb than they will from a lecture." He smiled. "Believe me, I speak from personal experience. Come and sit down, and leave it alone."

He could feel the reluctance in her, but she let him lead her to the steps. The back porch had its own swing, an old wooden one that had hung in the same spot as long as he could remember. They sat down, and the chains creaked as he pushed the swing with one foot.

"Now," he said gently, "let's talk about this nonsense. You're not going to back out on our arrangement because of one little hitch, are you?"

"I think it would be best." She sounded stubborn, but there was something beyond stubbornness in her eyes, something that told him he'd have to push her for the truth.

"You remember the other day?" His hand brushed hers between them on the swing. "You told me I was overreacting when Amy got hurt."

That brought the ghost of a smile to her strained face. "You were."

"Well, now you are." He felt her start to protest and gripped her hand. It felt small and capable in his grip. "You are, Sarah. The boys were careless, that's all. They'll learn something. End of story."

She shook her head. "The children are my responsibility."

"Sure they are. I'm not trying to take that away. I just don't want you to throw away a good thing because of one little problem. That would be overreacting, Sarah. Wouldn't it?"

"Maybe." She sounded defensive, but at least she wasn't gathering up her kids and running for home. "I'm a single mother. That's natural enough."

So it was. All of Sarah's energy and devotion went to her kids, and that was the way it should be.

"You've been here nearly five years. That's long enough to have friends who are willing to help."

"Five years," she repeated. "Longer than I've been anywhere. Peter was always on the move, looking for the next opportunity. But I'm still the only one responsible for my kids. No one else."

He pushed the swing a time or two, wondering. "The other night I told you a lot more than I intended," he said, watching the boys chatter to Jeb, their guilt apparently forgotten, as he showed them how to set out the young plants. "Seems as if you could open up to me in return." He turned back to her, a challenge in his eyes.

She blinked. "I didn't mean to be rude. I just—" She stopped, took a breath. "No, I don't have any family. Peter and I were both only children. There's no one but me to take care of the children and provide for them. And since Peter didn't leave any insurance—"

"Wait a minute. Peter didn't leave any insurance?" He made it a question, hardly willing to believe he'd heard correctly.

She pulled her hand away from his, folding her arms defensively. "Well, naturally he never thought anything would happen to him."

"That's a poor excuse for leaving his family unprotected." Anger surged through him, and it showed in his voice.

It must have startled Sarah, too, because her gaze lifted, wounded and surprised, to his face. "I'm not sure that's any of your business."

The business—he latched on to that, confused at the rush of emotions her revelation had brought on. "He at least had mortgage insurance on the property. I remember seeing that when we signed the agreement."

She shook her head. "He canceled that. He said the premiums were too high."

"Too—"

Maybe he'd better not say anything else, because if he did he'd probably say something Sarah wouldn't forgive. Fortunately he heard Amy's waking-up cry.

Sarah got up quickly, obviously eager to end this conversation. "I'd better see to the baby." She whisked inside.

He shoved himself off the swing and took a couple of quick steps to the edge of the porch. The emotions that roiled inside him demanded action. A good long ride on the beach might help, but he could hardly go off at this point. Sarah would jump to the conclusion he was angry with her or the children.

"Look, Matt," Ethan called to him from the flower bed, waving a muddy trowel. "We planted almost a whole row. Jeb says they'll have flowers soon."

"Good job." He managed a smile. But watching the two boys working so diligently in reparation, Andi giggling with Jenny on the low branch of the live oak, little Amy, just waking in the room behind him, Matt couldn't believe their father had left them with no support, no safety net, nothing. How could any man do that?

He recognized the emotions that raced through him like blood through his veins. Anger. Jealousy. He was furious with Peter Reed for leaving his family unprotected. And he was jealous. How could Sarah have loved someone who'd been so unworthy of her? If she loved him—

He stopped that thought, shocked at it. Sarah didn't love him. He didn't want her to love him. He couldn't. He'd decided, in the midst of tragedy and horror, that he wouldn't take on the responsibility of a family. Nothing had happened to change that.

Besides, in a few months he'd be gone. His life lay out there, beyond the horizon. Sarah's lay here, where she was so determined to put down roots for her family. That was the way it should be.

He wouldn't let himself feel anything for Sarah. He couldn't.

Sarah pressed her cheek against the baby's soft hair, trying to suppress the dismay that filled her. How could she have done that? How could she have confided in

Matt that way? It wasn't any of his business what Peter had or hadn't done.

Her cheeks went hot with shame. She owed Peter her loyalty, and telling Matt something negative about him was a betrayal. She'd always been so careful to tell the children nothing but good things about their father. She didn't want them ever to know, ever to think—

Maybe it was best not to finish that thought. She went into the kitchen, carrying Amy. With any luck, the boys had finished their planting by now. She'd gather her children and go home before anything else happened.

And would they come back the next day? She hesitated, wondering if Matt still sat in the swing. She didn't want to discuss the question with him again. She'd have to think about it, preferably well away from his disturbing presence.

She reached the screen door and stopped. Matt wasn't on the swing any longer. He sat on the top step of the porch, and Andi sat next to him. She was looking up at him with a solemn expression on her face.

"…they're my little brothers. Shouldn't I take care of them?"

Sarah held her breath. Should she go out and interrupt this conversation? Or should she stay out of it? Andi was her daughter, one part of her mind argued. She should be the one Andi came to with questions.

But she hadn't. Andi had come to Matt with this one. It would be wrong to try and prevent him from answering it.

"Well, you love them, right?" Matt didn't have any hesitation about dealing with this.

Andi sat up very straight. "I love them. Even when they tease me or get into my stuff."

Matt brushed the fringe of bangs back from Andi's eyes, his big hand very gentle. "It must be hard to love them when they do things like that."

"I'm the oldest," Andi said, as if that were an irrefutable answer. "It's my job."

The lump in Sarah's throat would have kept her from speaking if she wanted to. Andi shouldn't have to feel so responsible. She was just a little girl herself.

"Sure it is." Matt's voice sounded gruff, as if he'd been affected by her daughter's answer, as well. "If you love somebody, then you want what's best for them, don't you?"

Andi nodded. "That's why I said I did it. So they wouldn't get in trouble." She leaned close to Matt, reaching up to tug his sleeve and bring him a little closer. "Ethan's afraid of Mr. Johnson," she whispered. "'Cause he has such a loud voice. But you can't tell. It's a secret."

Matt nodded solemnly. "I won't tell. But maybe it wouldn't be the best thing for Ethan if you took the blame." He pointed. "See? Ethan looks pretty happy, working with Mr. Johnson. I think he got over being afraid of him."

Andi looked as if she were puzzling over the moral dilemma. "Mommy says it's better to tell the truth. Do you think it's always better, even if it gets somebody you love in trouble?"

"Sugar, I think Mommy's right about this one. You can't cover up for people you love. It just makes things worse, for them and for you."

His words hit Sarah's heart like arrows. That was what she'd been doing with Peter. That was why she felt disloyal for letting it slip about the insurance. She'd been covering up for Peter, just as Andi tried to cover up for Ethan.

Oh, Lord, is that why she does it? Did Andi learn this from me?

The thought was a weight on her heart.

If I needed to learn this, maybe that's why You brought Matt into my life. So I'd see what was happening before it was too late.

"Mommy?"

Andi had glanced back, had seen her. Sarah struggled to compose her face as she stepped onto the porch. "Are you about ready to go, sweetie?"

Andi shook her head. "Matt says—"

"I heard." She tried to smile. "It sounds as if Matt was giving you good advice."

"Oh." Andi got up. "Well, I'll try to tell the truth all the time. But I'll bet Ethan isn't going to like it."

That surprised a laugh from her. "I think he'll learn to deal with it. You go get your stuff together now, okay?"

Andi skipped down the steps. "I'm going to leave my paper dolls here 'cause Jenny and me want to play with them again tomorrow. Wanda said she'll show us how to make new clothes for them. Okay?"

Was she doing the right thing? She could only hope so. "Yes, that's okay."

Her daughter ran off. Matt stood, the movement bringing him closer to her. "Does that mean you'll let the kids come again?"

"Yes." She had to force herself to look up at him, and when she did she seemed to get lost in his eyes. "Thank you, Matt." Her voice was barely more than a whisper.

"For what?" He took a step closer, and her breath caught. Being this close to him wasn't safe, not even in the middle of the afternoon with the children playing on the lawn.

"For what you said to Andi." She struggled to find the words. "You helped her in a way I hadn't been able to. Maybe you helped me, too. I'm grateful."

He took her hand in his, putting his other hand on the baby. His clasp was warm and strong. Protective. It had been a long time since she'd felt that anyone was protecting her.

"You're helping me," he said softly. "It seems like the least I can do."

"I hope I am," she said. She tried to mean it. She tried not to let herself think of what her life would be like when he was gone.

She'd told herself that she had her children, and that was enough. But every day she spent with Matt, he became dearer to her. Maybe just being a mother wasn't going to be enough for her anymore.

Chapter Eleven

Matt balanced the box of church history materials on one knee as he fumbled with the key to the newspaper office. The sun was just disappearing over the mainland, casting an orange glow that reflected from the windows of the closed office. Sarah would probably be tucking the children into bed about now, and he didn't want to disturb her.

The door opened, and he lugged the box Pastor Wells had given him inside and set it on the worn wooden counter. He was tempted to put it on Sarah's desk, but he had yet to convince her that this was one story she should handle.

He frowned down at the box. If he told her—

"Who's there?" Sarah's voice came sharply through the closed door to her apartment.

"It's Matt." He should have realized she'd hear him and might be alarmed. "Don't call the cops."

The door swung open, and Sarah stood there, barefoot, in jeans and a soft T-shirt. The light from the apartment turned her tumble of brown curls into a halo surrounding her face.

"You're lucky I didn't call them first." She stepped into the office and stopped, seeming to realize she didn't have shoes on. Then she shrugged and crossed to the counter opposite him. "I didn't know you planned to work late."

"I don't." He put a hand on the box. "I just wanted to drop this off. It's the materials Pastor Wells offered us."

"Great." She pulled at the box lid, blue eyes lit with excitement as if it contained buried treasure. He resisted the impulse to touch her cheek and helped her open the box instead.

Her enthusiasm didn't move him, he assured himself. He was just pleased, because that made it more likely she'd relieve him of the project.

"Since you're so interested in the church story, I hoped—"

Sarah looked up at him, and for a moment he lost his train of thought. He gave himself a mental shake. When had just looking at her started giving him this need to touch her? It was irrational.

"You hoped?" she prompted.

Back to business, Matt. "I thought you might like to take on this story."

She smiled, and he saw the dimple that was just like her daughter's. "And why did you think that? I was under the impression we were doing it together."

"Well…" His father had told him once that anyone who started a proposal with that word was in a poor negotiating position. His father was probably right. "I'm putting in a lot of hours on the real-estate investigation."

"Which might or might not turn into a story."

"You have a blunt way of putting things, you know that?" He leaned on the box, bringing his face closer to hers. "Can't we just say the church story isn't my cup of tea?"

"We could if we had a staff to pick up slack when one of us didn't want to do something." She pretended to look around the office. "Let me see… Where are they? Oh, that's right. It's just the two of us."

If she didn't look so appealing in her jeans and bare feet, he might be able to come up with something stronger in the way of argument. "All right, Madame Editor. What will it take to get you to do this story?"

Her face sobered. "You tell me the real reason you don't want to be involved, and I might consider it."

"That is the real reason."

She just lifted an eyebrow.

"All right." He heard the edge in his voice and tried

to suppress it. He seemed to have become transparent where Sarah was concerned. "It would bring me too close to too many memories. I don't think the paper will benefit from having a cynic who's angry with God doing a story like this. Is that what you want to hear?"

"Matt…" Her face got that troubled look it wore when one of her kids had done something wrong. He understood what it meant. She was worried about him.

His throat tightened. "It's okay," he muttered. "Just don't push me on this one, all right?"

"All right." The frown lingered between her brows. "I'll do the story, on one condition."

"What's that?"

"You go with me to the interviews." She held up a hand to stop his protest. "You know as well as I do that we have to talk with some of the older church members if the articles are to have any life at all. They know you. They'll talk if you're there." She grimaced. "Nearly five years here, but I'm still a newcomer in their eyes. How long does it take to belong?"

"Couple generations," he said lightly, then wished he hadn't. Sarah, with her longing to establish her family here, didn't need to hear that. "Just kidding," he said quickly. "Okay, you have a deal. I'll go along on the interviews, but you're writing the articles. Agreed?" He held out his hand.

"Agreed." She put her hand in his, smiling. But as

his hand closed around hers, the smile faltered. Her eyes darkened.

Longing swept over him. He took a long breath, then lifted her hand to his lips. He kissed her wrist, feeling the rhythm of her pulse, knowing his own was beating just as fast.

"Sarah." He spoke her name, lips moving against her skin. It was a good thing the wooden counter stood between them, or he'd take her in his arms. For an instant he let himself visualize that, almost able to feel her softness against him. Then he shook his head. "You know this is driving me crazy."

"It—it's not doing me too much good, either." Her laugh trembled, and her lips looked very soft. "Maybe we should avoid tête-à-têtes in the future."

He dropped another kiss on the tender spot at the inside of her wrist, then let her go reluctantly. "A little hard, when we work together every day."

She took a step back. "That's business," she said. "We just have to remember that. It doesn't make sense for us to be anything more than partners. You'll be leaving, and—" She stopped, something shadowing her face. Regret, maybe?

"Yes. I'll be leaving." Surely he wasn't feeling regret, too, was he? Getting back to his real life was all he wanted. "But that doesn't mean we can't be friends, at least, as well as partners."

The office had grown dim with the setting of the sun. He reached out to switch on the desk lamp, wanting to see her face.

But she turned away, straightening, as if facing up to something. "Friends. Of course we're friends." She looked back at him, her smile a little stiff. "I'll say good-night. I need to check on the children."

He stopped her with a touch on her arm, suddenly unwilling to let her go. "One thing. My father reminded me that the kick-off reception for the new resort hotel that's being built is Friday night at the yacht club. He wants his sons there, since he sold the land for the hotel."

She nodded. Of course she'd know about the Dalton Resorts Hotel that would be going up soon near the yacht club. "I suppose we should cover the reception. The new hotel is the biggest event on the island in a long time. Since you're going, you can do that."

"We should both be there. As you said, it's the biggest thing to come along in years. I want you to go with me, as my guest."

She gave him a level look. "I'm not sure that's such a good idea. Didn't we just decide—"

"This is business." He didn't know why it was so important to him; he just knew he wanted Sarah by his side that night. "And I agreed to do the church interviews with you, remember?"

He could sense the mixed feelings in her—the caution she wore as an armor against him battled with her anticipation. How long had it been since Sarah had had an evening out without her kids? Longer ago than she could remember, probably.

"Business," she repeated. "I guess as long as it's business, it's okay."

"Strictly business." He clasped her hand once, quickly, then turned to go. "Good night, Sarah. I'll see you tomorrow."

He'd better get out now, before she changed her mind about going with him. Irrational as it was, he wanted one lovely evening with Sarah before their time together was over. One lovely evening to remember.

"Now you sit right down there and make yourself comfortable." Matt's grandmother led Sarah to a padded rocker, then perched, upright and bright-eyed as a sparrow, on a straight chair. "Matt says y'all want to talk to me about the church."

Sarah glanced toward Matt. He'd done his best to efface himself, it seemed to her, choosing the chair that was farthest in the corner and leaning back as if this interview were no business of his.

"Matt and I are interviewing longtime church members for a series of stories on the church's bicentennial," she said, stressing his name a little. His gaze flickered toward her with a slightly amused look, as if he caught the point but didn't intend to cooperate.

Well, whether Matt cooperated or not, he was here. If listening to the faith stories of people he cared about didn't reawaken his own spiritual side, she didn't know what would.

Is this the right thing, Lord? I want to help him turn to You, and this was the only thing I could think of that might help.

"Stories about the church?" Mrs. Caldwell's eyes lit with pleasure. "I 'spect you won't find anyone who knows more about it than I do. I've been going St. Andrews to worship for eighty years and counting. Now let me see…"

Sarah switched on the tape recorder and settled back to become lost in Naomi Caldwell's stories of when Caldwell Cove was young, life was harsh and all the islanders had to count on was faith and family.

Several stories later she glanced at Matt again. His gaze rested on his grandmother with a love that touched Sarah's heart. His face was relaxed, the tension and wariness gone from it.

"And then there's the dolphin," his grandmother said. "You've heard the story, a' course."

Sarah nodded. "Matt told me the legend—about the first Caldwell on the island and how he carved the dolphin for his bride as a symbol of their love. I'm sure we'll want to include that."

Some of the light went out of Naomi Caldwell's expression. "You'll have to tell about how it disappeared, too."

"There's no ending to that story." Matt spoke for the first time since he'd greeted his grandmother. "It's an unsolved mystery, forty years old."

"If we look into it for the article, something new might come to light," Sarah suggested.

"I'm not sure that's a good idea." Matt's voice had gone flat, and the guarded expression was back on his face.

"Might be, at that." His grandmother looked at Matt, and Sarah almost imagined a challenge in her gaze. "Caldwells are s'posed to be married under that dolphin. That's what's meant."

"That's just an old wives' tale, Gran," Matt said quickly. "You know that. Cousin Chloe and her Luke seem happy enough, even without the dolphin there for their wedding."

"Things won't be put right 'til the dolphin's back where he belongs," his grandmother said stubbornly. "Maybe God means for the dolphin to be found again now, if y'all start looking."

Matt's jaw clenched. He didn't argue, but it was clear he didn't agree.

Just what was going on here? Matt and his grandmother seemed somehow at odds over the dolphin. It was almost as if they knew or suspected something about its disappearance.

Whatever the problem was, it had brought the familiar tension back to Matt's face. Sarah tried not to feel disappointed.

Reaching Matt wouldn't be done in a day. She just had to remind herself that God was at work in him, whether Matt knew it or not.

This evening is business, Sarah told herself firmly. Business, nothing else. Unfortunately it was a little hard to convince herself of that with Matt's hand warm against her back as he guided her toward the yacht club entrance Friday night.

"I've lived here nearly five years, and this is my first time at the yacht club." She was probably babbling, but that was better than concentrating on the protective strength of his arm against her. "It's lovely."

White lights glittered from the long building, draping in graceful swags along the docks and reflecting in the dark water of the sound. She just hoped she didn't sound like an impressionable teenager on her first date.

"I don't exactly spend much time here myself." Matt took her hand as they went up the three steps to the porch that wrapped around the building. "My father does a lot of business here, though." He pulled open the door. "Well, thanks to him, it's our night to shine."

Piano music drifted on the air, mingling with the clink of glasses and the murmur of voices. The room was filled with the fragrance of expensive perfume, imported wine and old money.

Sarah smoothed her hand anxiously down the coral silk of the only dress in her closet that had been remotely suitable for a dressy event. It had looked fine in her bedroom, but it didn't look so appropriate next to the designer models that studded the floor.

She looked at Matt, and her breath caught again at the sight of him. He looked entirely too handsome in that expensively tailored dark suit, his white shirt contrasting with his rich tan. He looked as if he belonged here. She didn't, she reminded herself.

He smiled at her, chocolate eyes crinkling as if he read her mind. "Don't look so scared. They're just people."

"Not the kind of people I'm used to being around." She touched her dress. "And I'm more comfortable in jeans and sneakers."

He put his hand back on her waist, and she felt his warmth through the thin silk. "You look beautiful," he whispered against her ear. "Every man in this room is thinking that."

His breath stirred her hair, and she made a firm effort to slow the racing of her heart. Business, she reminded herself. She couldn't let herself give in to the feeling that Matt's attentiveness meant anything. This was business.

"Maybe we'd better circulate." She drew another

inch away from him. "We have to report on this event, remember?"

He lifted the camera he had slung over his shoulder. "How could I forget, when you made me bring this thing along?" He nodded toward the small dance floor and lifted his eyebrow in the way that made her stomach flutter. "Sure you wouldn't rather dance?"

"Business first," she said as firmly as she could, given the fact that butterflies seemed to have taken up residence under her rib cage.

"So after we get our story, you'll dance with me?" He smiled at his advantage, as pleased as one of the kids at a promised treat.

She took an answer from her parenting mode. "We'll see."

"Matt." His father appeared before Matt could argue the point. "Ms. Reed. Glad you could come." His gaze darted around the room while he spoke, as if he counted heads. "Everyone's here. Be sure you get a photo of the bigwigs from Dalton Resorts, now."

"I'll do that."

Did his father recognize the stiffness in Matt's reply? Apparently not, because he gave them an automatic smile and moved on to another group. She wished she understood—

"Hey, Matt, you're here. Hi, Sarah. Quite a splashy

do, isn't it?" The woman who hugged Matt had a glow about her that said here was someone who'd found everything she wanted in life. Chloe Caldwell Hunter, Miranda's sister, had recently married and settled on the island. Sarah didn't know her as well as she knew Miranda, but she liked her.

"Mr. Dalton wants to make a good first impression." Luke Hunter smiled, holding out his hand to Matt, then put his arm around his new bride. "Looks like he and your father outdid themselves. Half the island is here."

"I haven't seen Miranda or your parents." Sarah glanced around, hoping to spot Miranda's bronze hair somewhere in the crowd. "I'd like—" She stopped, suddenly aware of an awkward silence.

"No." Color brightened Chloe's cheeks. "They won't be here. I'm sure the only reason we were invited was that Luke used to work for Dalton."

Sarah bit her lip. She'd obviously put her foot in something. A sudden flare of anger in Matt's eyes matched Chloe's embarrassment. What had she said?

"I'm sorry, Chloe." Matt bit off the words.

Chloe shrugged. "Not your fault, sugar."

"Come on, woman." Luke swung his wife toward the dance floor. "Let's enjoy the music."

"I'm sorry." Sarah spoke as soon as they were out of earshot. She could feel the heat in her cheeks. "I said something wrong, but I don't know what." She hadn't been here ten minutes, and already she'd managed to make a mess of things.

"It's not your fault." Matt clipped off the words. "Let's go out on the terrace and get some air."

She followed the pressure of his hand across the polished floor and out the French doors to the terrace. The door swung shut behind them, cutting off the buzz of conversation and music. Matt crossed to the rail, as if he wanted to get a little farther from it.

"I'm sorry," she said again. She went to lean against the railing next to him, looking out over the salt marsh. Spartina grass waved in the soft breeze, like ripples on a golden ocean, and the moon was a crescent sliver.

"I forgot you wouldn't know." Matt's voice had lost its edge. "It's one of those things that everyone on the island knows but nobody talks about."

"Except an outsider like me." This was the sort of inadvertent error that made her think she'd never belong here.

Matt's arm pressed against hers where their elbows were propped on the railing, and she felt the strength of his shoulder against hers—a strong shoulder, one a woman could put her head on and feel protected. His hand closed over hers.

"You're not an outsider. You just didn't know about it. No big deal."

The grip of his hand encouraged her to ask. "Why wasn't Chloe's family invited?"

His face was very close, close enough that she could see the muscle twitching at his jaw. "That would be my father's doing. He didn't want Clayton here. If he had a choice, he wouldn't speak to his brother at all."

"But—" Her mind raced, trying to understand. "They were both at your grandmother's picnic. And you seem close to your cousins."

"My father and his brother both try to put a good front on it where Gran is concerned. Guess we have to be thankful their feud hasn't extended to the rest of the family."

"But why? What happened?"

He shrugged. "Nobody knows the whole story but them. Something happened when they were teenagers to drive a wedge between them. Besides which, they're as different as they can be. Uncle Clayton's content to be what Caldwells have always been and live the way Caldwells always have."

He stopped then, and she wanted to nudge him. "And your father?"

"My father—well, you've seen what he's like. Success means everything to him."

He almost spit out the last few words. Obviously he had an emotional stake in the whole thing.

"Brothers can be different without being enemies," she ventured.

"Not those two." His mouth twisted. "My father tends to use words like *shiftless* and *lazy* when it comes to his brother. And Uncle Clayton—" He stopped.

"What does your uncle say?" She murmured the words, wondering if he'd answer.

His grasp on her hand tightened painfully. "He says my father traded his honor for success."

"Is that what you think?" She couldn't believe she'd asked the question. He wouldn't answer. He'd tell her, politely of course, to mind her own business.

"He's my father." He ground out the words.

She put her other hand over his where it clasped hers, willing him not to close her out. "He's your father. But you're an adult. Sometimes it's hard to start looking at our parents with adult eyes."

"That sounds like the voice of experience speaking." He turned the comment back on her.

"I guess I had trouble with that one," she admitted. "For a long time I was angry with my father for putting the army first after my mother died. I felt as if I always came in second. I resented being dragged all over the world. If he loved me, why wouldn't he settle down and give me a home?"

"You still feel that way?"

She took a deep breath, inhaling the pungent aroma

of the marsh. "After I had children of my own, I looked at it a little differently. I think Dad just didn't know what to do with me after Mom died. He tried. It can't have been easy for him, either, but he thought it was right to keep me with him." She shook her head, knowing her voice sounded choked. "I just wish I'd come to that understanding before he died. He knew I loved him, but I'd like to have cleared the air with him."

He turned so that they faced each other, very close, their hands still clasped between them. "That's why belonging here in Caldwell Cove is so important to you, isn't it?"

"Building a stable home for my kids is the most important thing in the world to me. We need to belong here." She tried to smile. "But maybe you were right. It takes a couple of generations."

"No." He said it so quickly she knew he heard the fear in her voice. "I didn't mean that. Of course you belong here. So what if you don't know every little thing that's happened?"

"Seems to me your family feud is a pretty big thing." She looked up at him. She couldn't see him distinctly in the darkness, but that didn't really matter. His features were clear in her heart.

"Trivia," he said firmly. "You know the important stuff, and you're learning more every day. Don't you think people notice the love and care you put into every story, whether it's the charity drive or the middle school science fair? It shows, Sarah."

"I'd like to believe that." She could hear the longing in her voice.

"You can believe it." As if he didn't know how else to reassure her, he drew her into his arms. "You belong here," he whispered against her hair.

His cheek was warm against hers. She put her hands on his chest, feeling the steady beat of his heart. *You belong here,* he'd said. He'd meant she belonged in Caldwell Cove.

Unfortunately where she wanted to belong was in his arms…forever.

Chapter Twelve

What was she going to do with this information? Sarah sat at her desk several days later, staring with dismay and consternation at the notebook she'd unearthed from Pastor Wells's box of church history. How could she possibly tell Matt that his father had been suspected of the theft of the carved dolphin from the Caldwell Cove church?

She leafed through the pages of cramped handwriting by the then-pastor of St. Andrews. This appeared to be a kind of personal journal he'd made during his years on the island. Pastor Wells couldn't have known about it; he'd never have given so inflammatory a document to Matt knowingly.

The notebook had been stuffed inside a church register. It seemed far more likely Pastor Wells had just dumped everything he thought might be interesting into the box, never realizing the notebook existed.

Her eyes were drawn unwillingly back to the pertinent page. After expressing the grief and shock that accompanied the discovery that the carved dolphin was missing from the sanctuary, he added his conclusions.

Although I can prove nothing, I keep remembering the day I found the two Caldwell boys in the sanctuary with one of the summer visitors—Emily Brandeis. Someone had taken the dolphin down, and the girl held it. Jefferson was quick to say that she just wanted to see the dolphin, but now—

His notes cut off there, as if he'd been reluctant to put anything else into words. But what he'd said was enough to make his suspicions clear.

Her hands clenched the notebook. She could bury it back in the bottom of the box. Matt would never look. He'd made it clear he didn't want to be involved with the church story.

She seemed to see him, standing on the terrace in the moonlight, talking about his mixed feelings for his father. If she showed him this, it would simply cause more trouble between them. But did she have the right to hide it?

Please, show me what to do. I don't know what's right. Please.

"Sarah? Is something wrong?"

She jerked, pressing her hands down on the telltale

notebook pages, and looked up at Matt. "You startled me. I didn't hear you come in."

"Maybe we should put the bell back," he said. He crossed to her, lifting an eyebrow in inquiry. "What were you so intent on that you didn't hear the door open?"

"It's nothing." The evasion came out before she considered, and she was appalled at her instinctive wish to conceal it from him. Memories flashed through her mind—Matt telling her not to manipulate him, even for his own good; the things they'd told each other that night on the terrace; the way she'd felt when he'd held her protectively in his arms.

He leaned against the desk, regarding her with a serious expression. "You don't look as if it's nothing. Level with me, Sarah."

She'd asked God to show her what to do with this knowledge. Was He giving her an answer? She stared for a moment at the rain-swept street outside, then made up her mind.

Slowly she held out the notebook to him. "I found this stuffed in with the materials Pastor Wells sent over. I'm sure he didn't know it was there. I think you'd better look at it."

Watching his face as he read the journal was like watching flesh turn to stone. He went through it twice, then flipped slowly through the succeeding pages, obviously looking for more.

She'd already done that. She knew there was nothing else, except for the pastor's mournful conclusion that they'd probably never know the truth.

"I'm sorry," she said at last, when it seemed he'd never speak again. "I didn't want to show you, but—" She faltered then, unable to go on.

"You had to show me." He closed the notebook carefully, but his strong hands twitched as if he'd like to rip it into pieces. He looked at her, his face shuttered. "I suppose you think I should talk to my father about this."

She folded her hands in silent prayer. *Please.* "I'm not much of an expert on father/child relationships, am I? But, yes, I think you have to talk to him. Otherwise you'll just go on suspecting him, when maybe there's some explanation."

"Somehow I doubt that." He tossed the notebook on her desk. "Maybe the smartest thing to do is to bury that thing wherever it's been for the last forty years."

She looked at him, sensing the pain under the mask he wore. Did he really believe he could do that?

"Your grandmother wants you to find the truth."

His hands clenched. "I think my grandmother already knows, or at least suspects."

That could be the undercurrent she'd thought she noted when Matt and his grandmother talked about the dolphin. "What makes you think so?"

Every muscle in his body seemed to tense. And every

cell in her body seemed aware of that. For a long moment she thought he'd launch himself off her desk, stride out of the office, running away from the thing he didn't want to face. Finally he shook his head, as if telling himself that wasn't an option.

"I heard them once—my grandmother and grandfather. I was just a kid, playing cowboys and Indians in the garden, trying to creep up on them without letting them know I was there." His mouth twisted. "Worked better than I expected. They didn't hear me, but I heard them. They were talking about my father."

Her heart was breaking for him. "I'm sorry."

He shook off her sympathy with a brief shake of his head. "You never knew my grandfather. Even as a kid, I recognized what he was—a man of integrity, all the way through. Maybe he never had more than two dimes to rub together, but every person on the island respected him, like they do my uncle Clayton."

What could she say, when she feared he was right? "Did they say something about the dolphin?"

"My grandfather thought my father had been involved. Said he'd tried to talk to him, straight out, and my father denied it. Grandpa didn't believe him."

She saw the truth then, so clearly, and wondered if he'd ever admitted it to himself. "That's why you left, isn't it?"

He flinched as if she'd struck him, and she thought

he'd deny it. After a long moment he shook his head. "I don't know, Sarah. I wanted to make a name for myself out there. But how much of that had to do with my feelings about my father—I just don't know."

"You never talked to him about it, did you?"

He gave her a wry smile. "You're a good journalist, Sarah. You know all the right questions. No, I never talked to him about it, not even when I was a teenager and butted heads with him at every turn. I could never say that his values disappointed me."

She sent up another frantic silent prayer. *Please don't let me make a mistake.*

"Maybe it's time you resolved that."

Anger flashed briefly in his eyes. "Like you resolved things with your father?"

She looked back at him steadily. "I don't want you to wait until it's too late, like I did."

He stood, staring down at her, the anger fading slowly from his face. She sensed the instant in which he made a decision. He picked up the notebook.

"Maybe talking to him about this will be a step in that direction."

Her throat was so tight she could only nod. He was right. Confronting his father about the dolphin was a step to resolving his feelings about him.

It was probably also another step toward Matt being ready to leave Caldwell Cove for good.

* * *

Hours later, Sarah's head jerked up at the sound of the door. Her nerves were strung as fine as fishing line, waiting for Matt's return. But it wasn't Matt; it was his grandmother. She came in, shaking rain from her umbrella.

"Mrs. Caldwell." She hoped she didn't sound disappointed. "How nice to see you. I'm afraid Matt's not here right now."

"Don't reckon that matters." She marched, erect as a woman half her age, to the counter. "I found some old pictures of the church I thought maybe you could use, if you want them."

"That's wonderful." She took the rumpled, used envelope. A sheaf of faded, black-and-white photos spilled out onto the counter. "Pastor Wells gave us a box of things, but there weren't many photos in it." She cringed inwardly at the memory of what it had contained.

Mrs. Caldwell seemed to hear something she didn't say. "Where did you say Matt was?"

"He—he went back to the house. He wanted to talk to his father about something." She couldn't say any more, couldn't give Matt's secrets away, even to someone who loved him as much as his grandmother did.

"I see." Naomi Caldwell's wise old eyes probed, as if she looked right through Sarah's face and into her soul. "'Bout time that boy had things out with his father.

He keeps too much inside himself. And takes on too much responsibility, like he has to save the whole world. Always has been like that."

Sarah thought about the little boy who'd taken on the schoolyard bullies to defend the smaller children, about the man who couldn't compromise the truth, even when it hurt him.

"Maybe he has. That's not a bad thing. The world needs—" she hesitated, searching for the right word "—warriors."

Matt's grandmother nodded, as if something satisfied her. "Reckon you're right at that. Trouble is, sometimes he's so busy righting wrongs, he doesn't stop to see that God can even bring good out of terrible things."

"That's the verse you gave him, isn't it?

"And we know that in all things, God works for the good of those who love Him, who have been called according to His purpose."

"He told you that, did he?" His grandmother smiled. "Someday Matt will see the truth of that. I just hope—" She paused, looking at Sarah searchingly. "You know, that boy has a powerful lot of love dammed up inside him to give someone."

Sarah felt as if the wise old woman had just lifted a lid and looked into her heart. Oddly enough, it didn't hurt.

"It might take someone very special to help him

release that love." And I'm afraid it's not me, however much I might want that.

"Reckon that's in God's hands, if Matt will let it be."

"Yes," she said softly. It was in God's hands, not hers.

Mrs. Caldwell patted the pictures. "Well, guess that's all I came in for." She turned to go, then paused. "You know, ever since Matt was a boy, if he was upset about somethin', he'd be out riding that horse of his on the beach. I guess, if someone wanted to find him, that's where he'd be."

There didn't seem to be much left in Sarah's heart that Naomi Caldwell's wise old eyes hadn't seen. And someone did want to find him.

For the first time Matt could remember, this wasn't working. He slowed Eagle to a trot, patting the horse's damp mane. The rain had stopped, to be replaced by a gray fog that closed in around him, making him feel as isolated as if he were the only man left on earth.

Cantering along the hard-packed sand still made him feel as if he were flying, but it didn't erase his father's words from his mind. The beach didn't take him far enough away to do that.

Sarah's insight echoed in his heart. *Had* he gone away because of the clash between his father's values and his own? He'd had plenty of good reasons to leave

Caldwell Island, but he'd never admitted the one she'd seen.

Her clear view into his heart dismayed him. Made him want to run, just like talking to his father had made him want to run—to go back out into that other world and find other dragons to fight.

He glanced ahead, seeing a figure silhouetted dark against the mist, waiting where the path went up through the dunes toward the house. He didn't have to see any better to know who it was. Sarah waited for him.

He slowed Eagle to a walk, patting the horse's neck. Eagle snorted, as if asking to continue their run.

"No," he said aloud, as if the horse had asked. "I guess I can't avoid this."

Sarah put up her hand to hold back the tangle of brown locks that curled wildly from the damp air. She got up from the sea-whitened log she'd been sitting on. How had she known he'd be here? Maybe the bigger question was, how did she know so much about him?

In a few short weeks, Sarah had found her way into the inner recesses of his heart. Worse, she and her little family had made him start dreaming again of things he'd made up his mind he'd never have.

Couldn't he? a treacherous little voice asked inside his mind. Couldn't he have a life like a normal person?

The answer he pledged himself to sprang out quickly. He couldn't. He'd seen too much, done too much. He wasn't the innocent he'd been when he left Caldwell Cove, and he couldn't be that person again. Sarah and her kids didn't need an embittered cynic in their lives. They deserved better.

"Sarah." Eagle stopped automatically when they reached her, as if Matt's body language had already told him that this was a person they didn't pass by.

For a moment something in him resisted. He didn't want to talk to Sarah now—didn't want to talk to anyone. This was his problem, and he'd handle it his own way. But even before he'd finished the argument in his mind, he'd dismounted.

"I was worried about you." She reached up to pat Eagle's neck, but her eyes were on Matt. "You didn't come back."

"I needed to get it out of my system. Riding does that for me."

The worry in her face was diluted with a slight smile. "That's what your grandmother said. She came to the office."

"You didn't tell her—" Alarm ran along his nerves like a warning signal.

"No. I didn't tell her." She lifted her shoulders in a helpless shrug. "But I'm not sure I fooled her at all. She just seems to know things."

A few pointed memories flickered through his mind, almost making him smile. "Yes, she does, doesn't she?"

Sarah straightened, and he saw her throat work as she swallowed. "How did it go?"

How could he tell her? How could he not? She was the one who'd found it, after all.

She shook her head quickly. "Look, I'm sorry. I'm not asking you to confide in me."

"Aren't you?"

"No," she said firmly, in much the same way she responded to Amy's attempts to touch something hot. "But you have to talk to someone, Matt. What about your brother?"

You already know more about me than anyone else, maybe including Adam.

"I've never talked to Adam about my father. If I were guessing, I'd say he knows how I feel. But Adam—well, Adam's made his own separate peace with who Dad is."

That was true—he realized as he said it. No one ever doubted his brother's integrity, but Adam apparently didn't feel the need to confront their father over it.

A bitter taste filled his mouth, and he turned away so she wouldn't see what he felt. He stroked Eagle's strong neck, feeling the moisture on the silky skin from the gallop that hadn't taken him far enough away. Somewhere out in the mist a foghorn sounded, deep and lonely.

Sarah covered his hand with hers, stilling its restless movement. Hers was small but strong, just like the woman herself. Sarah was strong enough to bear his bitterness. It scared him how much he wanted to tell her, wanted to feel her sympathy, like salve on a wound.

"I talked to him." The words came out in a rush, as if they couldn't be spoken fast enough. "I showed him the notebook."

Her fingers curled around his. She was close enough that he could smell the faint flowery scent she wore, close enough that he could feel the intake of her breath. They stood inside a circle of fog that encompassed them, cutting them off from the rest of the world.

"He denied it, of course." His voice was flat. "Said the minister had it in for him, said none of it was true."

"You didn't believe him." Her voice was as soft as the mist that touched her hair with moisture.

"No." He hadn't believed his father. He'd seen the spurt of panic before the lie that came so easily. "I almost walked away, then." He wasn't proud of that.

"But you didn't."

"I pushed him. And finally he came out with the story."

She didn't say anything. Just waited. But he could feel her warmth surrounding him, diluting the bitterness that came with the memory of his father's words. He knew he was going to tell her.

"He and my uncle were teenagers that summer. There was a girl—a daughter of one of the summer visitors, the yacht club crowd. Usually they didn't mix with islanders, but he said Emily Brandeis was different. Emily wanted to be with them. And it sounds like both of them were in love with her."

"She wanted the dolphin." Sarah seemed to have the same ability to read between the lines that his grandmother did.

"He said she teased them about getting the dolphin figure for her, so she'd have a memento of their summer."

Eagle tossed his head, chasing the mist, his movement the only thing that stirred. Sarah was so still, she might have been carved from wood herself.

"He didn't say so, but I'd guess this Emily favored my uncle. So one night, when a group of young people were having a picnic out on Angel Isle, he slipped the dolphin out of the chapel. He says he just wanted to show it to her, I guess to impress her."

He stopped, reliving the anguish he'd felt at those words on his father's lips. Sarah's fingers tightened on his. He could feel the warmth flowing from her. It was like a balm, coming from her gentle spirit straight to his troubled soul.

"There was some trouble—he wasn't very specific about that part of it. The party was raided by a bunch of yacht club parents. In all the confusion, he lost sight of the dolphin." He shook his head. "I'm not sure whether I believe that or not. He says he went back the next day, after things calmed down, but the dolphin wasn't there. And when he went to ask Emily, she and her family had left the island. My father claims he never saw it again."

"Do you believe him?"

He shrugged. "I'm not sure what I believe. And even if I were, what would I do with it? I certainly can't tell my grandmother that her son was responsible. It would be different if I could get the dolphin back for her, but I can't."

Sarah reached up to touch his face then, turning it so he was looking at her. He didn't know what he expected to see in her face, but all he found there was caring and sympathy. "Maybe it's not too late. If we pursued this Emily, we might find something."

"That's assuming there's any truth to what my father said."

"Perhaps you should assume that, unless it's proved otherwise."

He managed a smile. "I hate to point this out, but that's the exact opposite of what any good investigative reporter would do."

"In this case, you're a son first, a reporter second." Her touch took any criticism out of her words. "I think we need to try at least."

He put his hand over hers, pressing her palm against his cheek, feeling her generous heart speaking to him. "What makes you such a wise woman, Sarah Reed?"

Warm color surged under her skin. "I'm not so wise.

But I do know you have to go on loving someone, even when he's disappointed you."

"Who are we talking about, Sarah?" he asked softly. "My father? Yours? Or Peter?"

He saw that hit home and knew she had been thinking, in some way, of her late husband.

"That doesn't matter," she said. "If someone you love does something wrong—well, love wouldn't be love if it stopped then." She gave him a ghost of a smile. "God doesn't stop loving me, even though I know how often I disappoint Him."

She was so serious, so intent on mending him. He didn't want to disappoint her.

He put a kiss on her palm, then closed her fingers around it and moved a careful inch away, so he wouldn't be tempted to do more. "All right," he said. "We'll assume the best and try to find out the truth. I just hope we're not disappointed."

A smile blossomed on her face, and he knew what he was really thinking. *I don't want to disappoint you, Sarah. I don't ever want to disappoint you.*

Chapter Thirteen

Sarah stared absently at her computer screen the next morning, trying to concentrate on the day's work and knowing she couldn't. She couldn't get Matt off her mind.

There couldn't be a future for them. They both knew that. Admitting their mutual attraction should make dealing with it easier, but somehow it hadn't.

Well, attracted or not, God had laid a burden on her heart. She had to help Matt heal, and one of the big pieces of that healing must be his relationship with his father. Until he'd managed that, he'd probably not be ready to resolve things with his Heavenly Father.

Finding out what had happened to Emily Brandeis and the church's dolphin carving might go a long way toward that, but that search was proving unexpectedly difficult. She frowned at the records she'd called up on the computer, trying to see them instead of the pain in Matt's eyes when he'd talked about his father.

She heard the door and glanced up to see Matt's tall figure silhouetted against the June sunshine. He stepped into the office, and she saw that he was smiling.

"You're looking pleased. Has something happened?"

He crossed the office to perch on the corner of her desk. "I found out something interesting."

Her mind leaped to her own search. "About Emily?"

For an instant he looked blank. "Emily? No. About Jason Sanders." He lifted an eyebrow. "Would it surprise you to learn that every person for whom Sanders negotiated a purchase down on the south end was a friend or relative of his?"

"Well." She paused to assimilate that. "That's not illegal."

"No, but it is odd." Matt's smile had an edge to it. This must be how he looked when he tracked down an important story. A chill touched her. He looked different from the Matt she'd grown to know.

"What are you going to do about it?"

"I have some feelers out for information. Someone knows what's going on. Something will come in," he said confidently. "If Sanders is up to something dishonest, everyone's going to read about it on the front page of the *Gazette*."

She knew what else he was thinking—that breaking

a big story would go a long way toward showing his bosses he was ready to go back to work. She tried to ignore the ball of lead in her stomach at the thought.

"Now, what's this about Emily?" Matt seemed to shift gears.

"Nothing, unfortunately." She flung out her hand toward the computer screen. "I thought it would be fairly easy to find out what happened to her when she left the island, and for a time it was. Did you know that her father wasn't quite the success people seemed to believe?"

He leaned closer, his attention caught. "All I know is what my father said, and that's not much. I certainly got the impression Emily was one of the yacht club crowd."

"Brandeis's business apparently crashed not long after their visit to the island that summer. But Emily married well—a Savannah society type. Unfortunately it didn't last. There was a divorce, then a remarriage. She was on the fringes of Savannah society for a while. Then—nothing." She smacked her hand on the desk in frustration. "She vanishes from public record."

He stood up abruptly, startling her. "Let's go to Savannah."

"What?" She looked up into smiling brown eyes and felt a betraying weakness flow through her. "When?"

"Now." He held out his hand.

"We can't just take off for Savannah." She scrambled

for a good reason why she couldn't go with him. Alone. For the day.

"Why not?" He caught her hand, drawing her to her feet. Seeing his investigation into Sanders bearing fruit seemed to have given him confidence. "The kids are fine at the house."

"If we go into Savannah, we probably won't be back at the time I usually pick them up. I can't leave them there."

"Why not?" he said again. "Wanda would be happy to watch them, and Jenny'd be delighted to have Andi stay for supper."

"It's an imposition." She let the pressure of his hand pull her a step closer, trying to find the will to resist the attraction.

His smile said he knew exactly what she was doing. "Come on, Sarah. I thought you wanted to help me solve this mystery for my grandmother."

I want to help solve it for you, she thought. "How do you know we'll find anything there? Emily could have left Savannah ages ago."

"Possibly," he conceded. "But I'm betting she didn't. If there's one thing I know about old-time Savannahians, it's that they tend to stay put. I believe Emily Brandeis wouldn't stray too far, if she had a choice."

She felt herself weakening. "I suppose it wouldn't hurt. I should call and talk with Wanda first."

"We'll do better than that." His fingers tightened compellingly on hers. "We'll stop by the house on our way off-island. Come on, Sarah. It'll do us good to chase down this shadow together."

Together. How many more things would they be likely to do together? Matt would leave. She had no doubts about that. Couldn't she have one more memory to savor when he was halfway around the world?

"All right." She picked up her bag, knowing she was rationalizing this. "We'll go." Because she wanted to be with him, even knowing there was no future in this. She just wanted to be with him while she could.

"Pretty depressing looking." Matt looked from the run-down boardinghouse in a seedy Savannah neighborhood to Sarah's face. It reflected just what he was thinking. Emily Brandeis's life had gone steadily downhill after that summer she spent on the island.

"This is a far cry from the mansion over on Bull Street, isn't it?" Sarah said.

He nodded. "One bad marriage after another, apparently. Funny. The way Dad described her, she was the kind of golden girl who had the world at her feet."

"Maybe that's how she seemed, to him," Sarah said gently. "He was young, and it sounds as if she was his first love."

Something tightened inside him. "She married for

money and position." Just as his father had. If it hadn't been for his wife's money, Jefferson Caldwell's life, and hence his sons' lives, might have been very different. Or would he have found another way to the success and status he craved? Maybe things would have turned out the same in any event.

Luckily Sarah couldn't know what he was thinking. She glanced again at the boardinghouse, and distress was evident in her eyes. "Aren't we going in? If she's there, she might be willing to talk."

He shouldn't have brought her. She was more affected than he'd guessed she would be by this old story. He hadn't really believed, when he'd suggested this little expedition, that they'd find anything useful. He might as well admit it. He'd just wanted to spend the time with her.

"We've come this far." He took Sarah's arm. "I guess we may as well go through with it."

They started up curving stairs whose wrought iron railing had probably been beautiful before years of neglect.

"You were right about one thing." Sarah stepped over a paper bag blown by the wind against the rail.

"What's that?" He lifted the knocker and let it fall.

"Savannahians don't go far from home."

"No." Somehow being right didn't give him much pleasure at the moment. "She might not be in the Bull Street mansion any longer, but she's still in the city."

"Yeah, what?" The woman who flung the door open wore a St. Patrick's Day celebration T-shirt that stretched over her ample frame and argued with the garish orange of her hair. "You want something?"

"We're looking for Emily Watson." He used the last married name they'd found for her. "I understand she lives here."

"You relatives?" She looked them up and down. "You don't look like you belong in this part of town. Always said she come from money, but I never saw none of it."

"No, we're—" What were they? He suspected she wouldn't be forthcoming to reporters unless there was something in it for her.

"Friends of the family," Sarah said. "May we see her?"

The woman let out a short burst of laughter. "Reckon you'll have to go to Bonaventure Cemetery if you want to do that. She died three months ago."

The depth of his disappointment shocked him. He hadn't realized until that moment how much he wanted to resolve this situation—to find the missing dolphin, to heal the family feud, to bring his father back into the Caldwell clan.

"I'm so sorry to hear that, Mrs.—?" Sarah's voice was soft, sympathetic. "You must have become friends while she lived here. I'm sure it was a loss."

He was almost equally surprised to see the woman assume the air of a mourner at Sarah's words.

"Mrs. Willie, Gina Willie. I guess you could say that. I was probably her only friend."

"She didn't have any family?" Sarah asked.

"Well, she had a daughter," the woman admitted grudgingly. "Lived up north someplace though. Didn't come here much, 'til her mama got sick."

"I suppose she took care of all the arrangements after her mother's death—disposing of her belongings and so forth?" Matt held his breath. Were they actually likely to find some trace of the dolphin at this late date?

"The daughter packed up what she wanted. Left some clothes for me to give away. Emily didn't have much."

"I don't suppose you ever saw a wooden figure of a dolphin, about so high." He measured with his hands.

"Somethin' valuable, was it?" The woman's eyes narrowed suspiciously.

"Just something that belonged to the family." His family. "Did her daughter take it?"

But she was already shaking her head. "Never saw nothing like that."

He thought of his grandmother, mourning the loss of the dolphin even as she kept the story alive for each generation. He wanted to make this better for her.

"Do you have the daughter's address?" he asked abruptly.

The woman took a step back, her suspicion flaring again. He could sense Sarah's tension, as if she wanted this just as much as he did.

"If you're family friends, guess you'd know that yourself." The woman snapped the door closed in their faces.

Frustrated, he lifted his fist, ready to hammer until she opened up again, but Sarah caught his arm.

"Better leave it, before she decides to call the police."

He glared at the closed door. "I don't like dead ends."

"At least we found out what happened to Emily. Now that we know the daughter exists, we can find her."

"I wanted to come home with answers."

"You did a good thing today, Matt." Her voice was warmly encouraging. "Don't beat yourself up because you couldn't solve a forty-year-old problem in a day."

He had to smile, because that was exactly what he was doing. He took her arm to pilot her back down the narrow stairs, enjoying the feel of her softness against him.

"How did you get to know me so well, Sarah?"

"Just a lucky guess." She seemed to try for lightness, but he heard the undertone of emotion in her voice. Worse, he knew that his own had grown husky when he asked the question.

What's going on with us, Sarah? This isn't supposed to happen.

But it was.

* * *

"Sure you didn't want dessert?" Matt looked down at her as they left the restaurant overlooking the harbor, and she suppressed the familiar flutter of her pulse at his nearness. "They make a Key lime pie that's out of this world."

Sarah shook her head firmly. "I'd burst if I ate another bite. The dinner was fantastic." Also very elegant. She'd protested that she wasn't dressed for a fancy restaurant, but Matt had insisted she looked fine and had whisked her inside anyway.

He'd probably wanted to remove the taste of sadness, for both of them. And it was sad. Lovely Emily, the golden girl, had ended up poor and alone, with all her bright promise gone.

Sarah glanced again at Matt's face as they crossed the cobblestone street along the waterfront. He steered her carefully around a clutch of tourists, intent on seeing every shop in the renovated cotton warehouses, and onto the brick plaza. The lampposts created circles of light in the gathering gloom.

He hadn't said much about their day's search—he'd talked Savannah history all through dinner. But the frown lines between his brows told her he still thought about it.

They stopped, leaning against the wall and looking out over the water. A white paddle-wheeler moved slowly past them, white lights outlining its wrought iron railings, a calliope playing. Through lighted windows, she could see dinner being served.

"Nice way to spend an evening."

"The *Georgia Queen*," he said. "Going for an evening dinner cruise."

Behind them, the bell in the old city hall chimed, then struck the hour. Nine o'clock.

"It's getting late," she said. "I should go home."

"The kids are fine." His arm pressed against hers where they leaned on the wall. "You can't rush away without enjoying the view." He pointed to the island across the sheet of silver water. "That's Hutchinson Island. The building is the convention center. Down that way is Tybee Island, where the elite of Savannah used to go to escape the summer heat."

She stirred, remembering. "If Emily's family had gone there instead of to Caldwell Island that summer, things might have been different."

"Funny, I was just thinking that." He frowned absently at a brown pelican that rocked on the current. "Still, you never know. Sometimes I think things would have turned out the same, no matter what happened."

"Sounds awfully fatalistic." She wondered if he was thinking about his father and the dolphin, or about his friend, dying far from home.

"I guess it does." Now it was his turn to move restlessly. "If I said that to Gran, she would remind me that all things work together for good."

She hesitated. Matt had just opened a door to her, quite unexpectedly, and she wanted to choose her words carefully.

"You can't leave out the rest of the verse. '…In all things, God works for the good of those who love Him, who have been called according to His purpose.'"

She felt him stiffen. "What difference does that make?"

Please, Lord, give me the right words. "I've come to believe it means that if we're trying to do God's will, He can bring good things out of even our mistakes."

His gaze searched her face, and she thought she read longing in it, instead of the cynicism she'd come to expect. "Is that coming from your own experience?"

A boat whistle came from out of the dark, sounding lonely. She owed him a truthful answer, even though it might be difficult. He put his hand over hers, and his touch gave her the strength to continue.

"What we learned about Emily today—it sounded as if she married for all the wrong reasons. I guess I related to that."

His fingers tightened on hers. "You didn't marry for money or position, Sarah."

She had to smile. "No, certainly not that. But I told you a little about what my life was like with my dad. The constant moving, never having a home of our own, really had an effect on me. I think, now, that when I fell in love with Peter, I was just longing for a home of my own." She shook her head. "That's not a good enough reason to get married."

"What was Peter looking for?" His voice was a low rumble that was somehow comforting.

She thought about the charming, irresponsible young man who'd captured her needy heart. "I think maybe Peter wanted someone to hold on to. Someone who'd be his anchor."

"People have married for worse reasons."

"I suppose so." She shook her head, realizing that for the first time she was looking honestly at her marriage, instead of trying to surround it with some sort of halo. "I'm trying to say that I might have imposed my dream on Peter. That maybe it never was his."

"The dream of a home and a family." There was something strained in the way he repeated the words.

"Yes. Maybe I pushed him to be someone he was never meant to be."

He laced his fingers through hers. The pressure of his palm against hers was surprisingly intimate. "Peter was a grown-up," he said. "Whatever happened, he made his own mistakes."

"If we made mistakes, if our marriage wasn't part of God's plan for our lives, He still brought good out of the consequences." She felt her way through, only realizing what she'd come to believe as she verbalized it. "Even if I was wrong, God was faithful. I have the children. They're worth anything."

"That's true for you. But I can't accept that the blowing up of that mission station led to anything good." His voice had turned harsh with pain.

Am I failing him, Lord? Give me the words.

"I know it's hard." She put her other hand over their clasped hands, trying to infuse him with her concern. "But we don't know what all the results of that act are. Maybe we never will." She was losing him, she knew it. "What would your friend say, if you could ask him?"

For a moment she thought he wouldn't answer. Then he let out a breath, and the corner of his mouth twitched. "He'd say, 'Quit trying to play God, Caldwell. You're not big enough.'"

"He sounds like someone special."

"He was that." His voice roughened on the words, but she thought some of the grief had left his tone, and she took comfort from that. He turned, so that he faced her with only their clasped hands between them. "What about Peter? Are you still making excuses for him?"

She'd intruded into his life, so it was only fair to answer him as honestly as she could. "I don't know. Maybe I have been."

"He took on responsibility knowingly. He had a duty to carry it through."

"Oddly enough, I don't want to be considered a duty." She tried to say it lightly, but it wasn't easy with his gaze probing into her inner heart.

He lifted his hand slowly and brushed his fingertips along her cheek. The look in his eyes made her breath catch, and she seemed to feel that touch through every single cell of her body.

"Loving you wouldn't be a duty," he said softly. He touched her chin, tilting her face up toward his, and she knew he was going to kiss her.

She shouldn't let this happen. The moment stretched out, frozen in time—the gentleness of Matt's touch, the way his eyes darkened as he looked at her, the treacherous weakness that swept through her.

She should step away. The slightest movement would bring this to an end. She knew Matt well enough to know he'd stop the instant she indicated his embrace wasn't welcome.

She lifted her face, swaying toward him, and his lips met hers.

His kiss was warm and filled with longing, need, desire. His arms went around her strongly, holding her close.

She should pull away. She didn't want to. She wanted to stay within the circle of Matt's embrace and imagine what it would be like to be loved by him, even though her heart knew that could never come true.

Chapter Fourteen

The memory of that kiss warmed Sarah all night and throughout the next morning. She glanced across the office at Matt's desk. His chair was empty, but she could visualize him so clearly, brow furrowed and dark eyes intent, searching for the elusive fact or the right word to make a story come alive.

Giving in to the urge, she crossed to his desk. She did need the events calendar he'd borrowed the day before, didn't she? She wasn't just being silly.

She let her hand rest on the back of his chair. The wood felt warm to the touch, as if he'd just gotten up.

Now, that was silly. Matt hadn't come in to the office at all. He'd just called to say he had something to do and would see her at the house in the afternoon.

Today was the day Andi had been anticipating all week—the day Matt had promised to let her ride one of the horses. If she'd slept at all last night, it had probably been to dream of galloping through the surf.

Not that Matt would let the children do any galloping, of course. He'd assured Sarah that this was perfectly safe, and she'd be there to make sure they were okay. Her fingers tightened on the chair.

To be honest, she was acting like a teenager in love, mooning over memories of the night before, rehearsing what she'd say when she saw him again. She ought to have more sense at her age.

But somehow, despite her best common sense, she couldn't help but cling to a faint flicker of hope. Maybe this could work out. Maybe…

Maybe she'd better get back to work. She opened the desk drawer and took out the events calendar, revealing something blue and shiny. Her heart lurched. Matt's passport, left handy in his desk drawer in case he wanted it. How foolish was she being, dreaming of family and forever with a man who'd leave again at a moment's notice?

The sound of the door opening came hard on that thought, and she couldn't help the irrational flutter of excitement that stirred her blood. But it wasn't Matt. It was Jason Sanders.

"Good morning, Jason." She smiled at him, shifting gears in an instant. Jason hadn't been in the newspaper office since he'd made the decision to withdraw his advertising. His presence had to be a good sign. Maybe he'd reconsidered.

"Sarah, good to see you." He made it sound as if she'd been avoiding him. He sent a glance toward Matt's desk. "Matt not working here anymore?"

"He's out today." She moved to the counter opposite Jason. "I can have him give you a call later, if you like."

He reached across to pat her hand. "That's all right. I'd much rather talk to a pretty woman."

She resisted the impulse to yank her hand away. The reinstatement of Jason's advertising would go a long way toward easing the paper's financial woes, and she'd do a better job of dealing with him than Matt would.

Of course, when Matt finished his investigation of Jason's real-estate dealings, they might be right back where they'd started. Well, one problem at a time. She fixed a smile on her face.

"How can I help you?"

"You know, Sarah, I've been giving a lot of thought to my decision to take my ads out of the *Gazette*. A lot of thought."

"I'm glad to hear that." She slid her hand from beneath his and reached for a pen. "Nothing would make me happier than to see your advertising back in the paper. After all, we're Caldwell Cove's only newspaper, and your business is certainly important to the local economy."

"Well, now, it would make me happy, too."

She sensed a reservation in his tone, and it lit up warning lights. Sanders sounded like a man about to offer a deal.

"Shall we reinstate your usual ad, then?"

He held up a manicured hand. "Not quite so easy as that, I'm afraid. Before I start paying the *Gazette* for advertising again, I'd want certain reassurances."

Her heart sank. Maybe it was a good thing Matt hadn't come into the office this morning. She could imagine his reaction to that. "Reassurances?"

Sanders leaned toward her, his eyebrows lifting. "Did you two really think I wouldn't get to hear about all the poking around Matt's been doing? Nosing into my business, checking on the property transfers at the county courthouse?"

Apparently someone at the courthouse had been reporting to Sanders. "Matt is a journalist. Naturally he—"

He slammed his hand down hard enough to make her jump. "That doesn't give him the right to interfere with my business. You make him stop, and you'll see my ads back in the *Gazette*." He smiled thinly. "Might even do a full-page once in a while."

There was only one answer to that suggestion. A man with Matt's integrity wouldn't change course for all the full-page ads in the world, and she wouldn't want him to.

"I'm afraid that's impossible. Matt makes the decisions about what stories he'll pursue. Maybe if you explained what you're doing—"

"I'm not about to explain anything to Matt Caldwell." His eyes narrowed. "And you'd better hope I don't have to talk to him, Sarah, or you'll be sorry."

A shiver ran along her spine at his tone. Something bad was coming; she could feel it. "I don't know what you mean."

"I mean I might have to tell Matt about the little arrangement I had with Peter." He leaned forward, invading her space. "You wouldn't want Matt to know your husband took money from me to keep certain matters out of the paper. Now, would you?"

"I—I don't…" Her mind grappled to come to terms with his words. She wanted to deny it, wanted to say that Peter couldn't possibly have done anything of the kind. The trouble was that, deep in her heart, she feared he could have.

Sanders took a step back, apparently satisfied with the effect of his words. "Think about it, Sarah. If you don't want Matt and everybody else in this town to know the kind of a man Peter Reed was, you convince Matt to back off."

He turned and left the office with an assured stride. The door slammed behind him.

The kind of man Peter Reed was. His words echoed in her mind. Sanders wasn't kidding. If she didn't stop Matt's investigation, Sanders would tell him. He'd tell everyone.

But she knew more than Jason Sanders ever could about Matt Caldwell. She knew the kind of man Matt was—a man of integrity, a man who'd never accept the deal Sanders offered and would never understand someone who did. But if he didn't—

She put her hand over her mouth and choked back a sob. If he didn't, the children would know what their father had done. The whole town would know, and things could never be the same. The fragile roots she'd begun to put down for her children would be irrevocably damaged.

She had to tell Matt the truth before Sanders did. But how could she? How could she bear the look on Matt's face when he learned this?

Matt ran the brush down Eagle's silky neck, then patted the horse's strong shoulder. He'd already decided that the boys would have their ride on Jenny's placid pony, but Andi was something different. He had to smile again thinking about the expression on her face when he'd said he'd let her take a ride on Eagle. She'd looked as if an indescribably beautiful gift was within her grasp.

Sarah had looked much the same the night before, when he'd held her in his arms on the Riverwalk. When he'd kissed her and wanted to keep her there forever.

No. Some rational part of his mind still resisted.

How could he even let such a thought in? Even if he were sure he loved her, even if she loved him, too much still stood between them.

His life wasn't here, in this quiet backwater. He belonged back in his busy, dangerous world, where there was no room for a man with a family. And there was no point in kidding himself that some kind of long-distance relationship between them would work. Sarah and her kids needed a real husband and father, someone who'd be part of their lives every single day.

That couldn't be him. A wave of something like panic went through him at the thought, and he leaned his forehead against Eagle's warm neck. He couldn't take responsibility for their safety and happiness. His stomach turned as once again he saw the walls of the mission station crumble, heard the children's terrified cries, inhaled the acrid smoke from the bomb.

The only safe life is a detached life. He repeated the words he'd drummed into his heart.

Once he'd been convinced he could live by them. Now, since he'd met Sarah, he wasn't sure that was possible. He straightened, looked out the open stable door and saw her coming.

"Sarah." Careful, he cautioned himself. Think this through. Don't jump into something that will hurt everyone. The problem was, he didn't want to be careful. He wanted to take her in his arms.

"Hello, Matt." She lingered in the doorway, the sunlight slanting behind her and outlining her figure with gold. Did he just imagine the constraint in her voice?

"The kids are out at the paddock with Wanda and Jenny's pony." He lifted saddle and pad together to Eagle's back. "We'll be ready to go as soon as I finish saddling Eagle."

She came closer. "He still looks awfully big to me. Are you sure it's a good idea to put Andi on his back?"

"He's as gentle as can be." He reached for her hand and felt her swift, instinctive movement away. "I just wanted to show you how to pat him."

His stomach churned. Was that her reaction to what had happened between them the night before? Maybe he didn't need to worry about what he was going to do. Maybe Sarah had already decided this was no good.

"Sorry." She seemed to struggle to produce a smile as she held out her hand.

He took it in his, then smoothed her palm down along the strong, smooth curve of Eagle's neck. His own hand cupped hers, and her sleeve brushed his arm. Awareness seemed to hum between them.

"He's beautiful," she said softly.

He's not the only thing that's beautiful here. He wanted to say the words, but they stuck in his throat. He couldn't say anything.

The moment stretched out. The only sound in the stable was the gentle shuffle of hooves against straw. Dust motes rose lazily in the shaft of sunlight from the door. Sarah was close enough that her hair brushed his chin, close enough that he could feel her breath. He fought back the impulse to press a kiss to the pulse that throbbed in her neck.

"About yesterday," he said abruptly, needing to put some space between them.

Her gaze jerked up to meet his, something startled and wary in it. "What about yesterday?"

"I wanted to thank you for going with me to Savannah. I'm not sure I'd have done it without you."

Sudden warmth banished the reserve in her manner. "Of course you would have. But I'm glad I could help." She hesitated, then seemed to decide it was safe to ask what she must be wondering. "Did you tell your father what we found out about Emily?"

"Yes." He turned back to the horse, pulling the girth snug. How much should he reveal to her? Maybe there was no point in trying to hide anything. Sarah had already seen deeper into his heart than anyone else ever had.

"I told him everything." The memory of those moments on the Riverwalk leaped into his mind. "About Emily, I mean."

She nodded, patting Eagle's neck while he slipped

the bridle into place. "It was such a sad story. I'm surprised he never made an effort to find out what had become of her."

"Too proud, I'd guess. Caldwells tend to be like that. But when I told him—" He hesitated, reliving the look he'd surprised in his father's eyes. "It was years ago. Puppy love, he'd called it. But when I told him what had become of his golden girl, I saw tears in his eyes."

"She was his first love," Sarah said softly. "You can't forget your first love."

"It wasn't just that." He wanted her to understand. "I've never seen that side of my father. I guess I didn't think it existed. I didn't think he could be moved by anything except business. Seeing him that way—" He swallowed hard, knowing he needed to tell her the rest of it. "You remember telling me once that you had to go on loving people, even when they disappointed you?"

She nodded, and he saw something that might almost have been hope in her eyes. "I remember."

"I guess I finally understand what that means." He shrugged, embarrassed at the way emotion had thickened his voice. "I think my father and I have started to come to terms with each other. Thanks to you."

"I didn't have much to do with it. You were ready. Maybe that's really why you came home."

He wanted to tell her that she'd changed him, but he

couldn't seem to find the words and wasn't sure he should say them if he did. "I don't suppose things will ever be the way they were before, when I was Jeffrey's age and thought my father was a hero. But it's better now. I feel…" He searched for the word. "Comfortable. I feel comfortable here now."

He wasn't sure what he wanted her to say to that, but she just nodded. "I'm glad." She clasped his hand briefly, then moved a step toward the door, into the patch of sunlight.

Something tightened inside him, making it impossible to speak. The words he'd said about his father echoed in his mind. Maybe it was true he'd never see his father as a hero again. But he couldn't help longing, no matter how foolish it was, that Sarah saw him that way.

She had to tell him. She couldn't. Sarah leaned against the paddock fence, watching Matt with her children. What was she going to do?

For a moment, when Matt had talked about loving his father in spite of his faults, she'd felt a spurt of hope. Maybe he was learning that sometimes love could break through his rigid expectations of people.

Things will never be the way they were before, he'd said, and the words had shattered that fledgling hope. When he knew the truth about what Peter had done—

well, he might be able to accept the fact that she hadn't known about it. But he wouldn't be able to forget. And if she asked him to compromise his beliefs, let Sanders off the hook to protect her family…

He wouldn't agree. He couldn't. And even if he did, things would never be the same between them.

Help me, Lord. Her fingers tightened on the rough wooden plank until it bit into her skin. *I don't know what to do. How can I be honest with Matt and still protect my children from knowing what Peter did? How can I?*

She took a breath, trying to clear her mind, trying to listen for God's guidance, but nothing came. Maybe that silence in itself was her answer. She couldn't.

"Mommy, look at me!" Ethan waved wildly as Matt led him past on the black-and-white pony.

Matt gently put Ethan's hand back on the reins. "You can't let go, or Dolly won't know what you want her to do. You're the rider, so you're the responsible one, okay?"

Ethan clutched the reins, nodding solemnly. "Okay. I'll remember."

The scene caught her heart in a painful grip. Ethan was so like Peter in his manner. He needed the example a strong, honest man could provide to show him what it meant to be a man.

There was Jeffrey, arms draped over the lowest rail

of the fence, waiting so patiently for it to be his turn. Jeffrey had blossomed under Matt's attention. He'd begun speaking for himself instead of letting Ethan talk for him. Jeffrey needed someone like Matt, too.

Why wasn't this meant to be, Lord? It seems so right.

She watched, not moving or speaking, while Matt took Jeffrey for his ride. Then, finally, it was Andi's turn. When Matt helped her little girl onto the big horse, tension gripped Sarah. It was so far to the ground. Surely that horse was too much for Andi.

But Matt was slow, confident, sure as he showed Andi how to hold the reins, how to cluck to the animal. Everything about him radiated competence. Andi was safe with him.

And as for Andi—when Jenny swung easily into the pony's saddle and the girls moved off at a walk side by side, Andi's face was suffused with so much joy that Sarah wanted to weep.

Matt's eyes never left the girls as he walked slowly across to lean on the fence next to her. "Looks like she was born to ride," he said.

She swallowed the lump in her throat. "You've just made all her dreams come true."

"Probably not all of them," he said. He propped his elbows behind him on the fence, the movement stretching his shirt across his chest. His forearm brushed hers, sending a wave of warmth up her arm.

Jeffrey trotted up next to her. "Can I have another turn, Matt? Please?"

"We might be able to do that." Matt reached through the fence to pick the boy up, swinging him into his arms and then setting him on the top rail of the fence. Jeffrey perched there, breathless and grinning at him.

Her throat tightened again. Jeffrey opened like a flower to the sun when Matt was around. Why hadn't she realized how much he needed a man's attention?

A father's attention. The words slipped into her mind and she had trouble ejecting them. Matt gave her glimpses of a different relationship—one where she didn't have to shoulder all the burdens. One where love and responsibility could be equally shared. But even if it weren't for the knowledge of Peter's misdeeds, weighing heavy on her heart, too many barriers existed to a serious relationship with Matt.

Matt would leave. That was the bottom line. He'd always intended to go back to his important job. And when he found out what an ethical dilemma his partnership with her had landed him in, he'd probably race to leave as soon as he could.

Matt nudged her with his elbow. "I want to talk with you about the real-estate investigation. Why don't I stop by after the kids are in bed?"

Panic surged through her. If they talked about his investigation of Sanders, she'd have to tell him. She should have told him already, but she couldn't. She hadn't figured out how.

"Tonight's not good for me." She hoped her voice didn't sound as strangled as it felt. "Maybe tomorrow morning would be better."

She felt Matt's gaze on her face, questioning, and kept her own focused firmly on the horses. If he asked what was so important she couldn't meet with him tonight, what would she say?

He shrugged finally. "Okay. Tomorrow morning."

She should feel relieved, but she didn't. She'd only bought a few more hours in which to find a way to tell him about Peter. A few hours in which to enjoy the relationship that was doomed to end once she told him the truth.

Chapter Fifteen

A mostly sleepless night spent in prayer had shown Sarah what she had to do, little though she might like it. She had to be honest with Matt. He was her partner, and he had a right to know what Peter had done and what Sanders demanded of them.

Matt would never agree to Sanders's terms. She knew that without even thinking about it.

She glanced around the small apartment that was so precious to her. She could hear the children's voices in the kitchen with the sitter, smell the potpourri she'd put in the Delft bowl on the mantel, see the love she'd poured into making this place a home. Once everyone in Caldwell Cove knew that her husband had traded the newspaper's integrity for money, what were the chances she could still call this home?

Please, Lord, let us find some way of making this work out. Let us find a resolution that—

She stopped, knowing what she wanted to pray. She wanted to ask that somehow she and Matt and the children could become a family.

She couldn't ask that. She couldn't even let herself dream it. Even if there were no problem with Sanders, a relationship between them had been doomed from the start. Matt's life was elsewhere. He hadn't deceived her about that. He'd never be content with this life, and she had to put her children's security first. There was no compromise that would make them both happy.

Enough. She forced herself to move toward the door into the office. Matt was there; she'd heard him arrive. She just had to stop agonizing about it and go in there and tell him.

Stomach churning, she opened the door and stepped through, feeling as if she walked knowingly into a nightmare.

"Good morning." Matt looked up from his computer, a slow smile lighting his face as his gaze rested on her. "I thought maybe you were sleeping in this morning."

"No, I just…I was running a little late." It was the smile that hurt, she decided. The smile blindsided her with how much she'd grown to care for him.

Not just care. She'd better be honest with herself about that. She loved him.

She hadn't seen it coming. She'd thought she was safely armored against loving again. The children were her life now, and she didn't need anything else. But she loved him.

She took a deep breath. That couldn't make a difference in what she had to do. She had to tell him. "Matt, there's something I need to—"

"Take a look at this first." He gestured to the computer screen. "I've found it."

"Found what?" She went to his desk, leaning over his chair so she could read what was on the screen. Her hand brushed against his shoulder, and she snatched it back as if she'd been burned.

"Found the smoking gun." Triumph laced Matt's voice. "I know what Sanders has been doing down at the end of the island. He's been buying up parcels of land under different names, so no one would get wise. And he's negotiating to sell the whole thing to a commercial cannery."

"But…" Her mind whirled with the implications of that. "An outfit like that tried to come in a few years ago, and people made such a fuss that the town council blocked it. Nobody wanted a commercial outfit here, ruining the atmosphere and taking all the fish—that was the only thing the summer people and the islanders ever agreed on in their lives. How could Sanders hope to get it through now?"

"At a guess, he's got someone from the town council in his pocket. If he keeps it quiet until the permits have been granted, there won't be much anyone can do."

She nodded slowly, thinking about her guess that Sanders had an informant at the county courthouse. That was certainly the way he operated. And if it were true—

"Do you have facts?" she asked abruptly. "Solid, verifiable evidence?"

Matt lifted an eyebrow. "Worried about being sued? Don't be. There's enough here to stop Sanders in his tracks without any fear of that."

The implacable determination in his face chilled her. His was the face of a crusader. He wouldn't stop until he'd put every last fact on the front page.

"Matt, I want to tell you something." She gripped the chair back, trying to find the words. "There's something you need to know."

The tone of her voice must have penetrated his focus. He shifted away from the computer to face her, and his hand covered hers. "What is it? What's wrong?"

She could hardly bear the concern in his face. She had to tell him—now.

The office door swung open. Jason Sanders stepped in, looking from one to the other of them. Then he smiled. "I hope I'm not interrupting anything."

The change in Matt vibrated through the air between

them. In an instant he went from tender and caring to ready to battle.

"Not at all." Matt's calm, businesslike tone didn't hide the intensity beneath from her. "What can we do for you?"

Nothing, she wanted to cry. Just leave, that's all, and let me deal with this in my own way.

Panic cut through her like a knife. Sanders had come for their capitulation. She'd run out of time to tell Matt. Now he'd learn the truth in the worst possible way.

Jason sauntered to the counter as if he owned the place. "Just thought you might have something to tell me today."

"Tell you?" Matt's level brows lifted. "About what?" He leaned back in his chair, assuming a casual air he couldn't really be feeling, not when his evidence against Sanders spread across the computer screen in front of him.

Sanders glanced from Matt to her and back again. "I see your partner didn't confide in you."

Her panic edged up a notch. "I haven't had time to talk with Matt about it yet. If you'd like to come back later—"

Matt swiveled his chair to look at her. "What's going on, Sarah? Talk to me about what?"

"Just a little deal I offered Sarah." Sanders's tone spoke of his confidence that he would get what he wanted.

"You always have a deal to offer, Jason. Trouble is,

they usually only benefit you. You haven't changed in twenty years." The contempt in Matt's voice seemed to dent Sanders's assurance, and Sarah saw the flare of anger in his eyes.

"Matt, I don't think—" She put her hand warningly on his shoulder.

"Still the white knight riding to the rescue, aren't you, Caldwell? You'll find it simple to rescue Sarah, actually. All you have to do is drop this little investigation of yours."

Matt's tension tightened his shoulders. "In exchange for what?"

The truth rolled toward Sarah like a boulder, flattening everything in its path.

"In exchange for my silence. Somehow I don't think Sarah wants the world to know that her late husband took payoffs to keep my business affairs out of the paper." Sanders smiled. "Actually, I don't suppose you want it to come out either. It would reflect rather badly on the *Gazette.* Might even tarnish that fine reputation of yours, since you're a part owner."

She wanted to close her eyes and shut out the look Matt gave her. But she couldn't.

"Sarah, is this true?"

She couldn't speak. She could only nod.

Matt looked at her steadily for a long moment. Then he turned away.

She wanted to cry out, to tell him she was sorry, to say she hadn't known. But what good would it do, even if she could find the words? Matt wouldn't give in to Sanders. She'd known that all along. Truth came first with Matt. He'd never deny that.

"Making that public will hurt you as much as it will us." Matt's voice was icy.

Sanders shrugged. "If you print what you know, the sweetest deal I ever had is gone. Seems like a wash to me. I may as well take you down with me."

Matt stood, planting his fists on the desk, so rigid he might have been a statue instead of a man. He'd reject Sanders's deal. And then he'd reject her. She'd lost whatever small chance their relationship had because she hadn't told him herself.

"All right. You have a deal." Matt's words dropped into the silence, sending ripples through the room.

His agreement echoed in her mind. She couldn't believe it. Why would Matt give in?

"I'm glad we understand each other." Sanders seemed to be enjoying this. "You wouldn't want people to lose respect for the hotshot television reporter, now would you?"

That wasn't why Matt had agreed. She knew that as clearly as if she could see right into his mind. Matt had given in, had compromised his most cherished beliefs, in order to protect her and her children.

She couldn't let him do it. Through the chaos in her thoughts, that one thing stood clear, shining like a beacon. She'd asked God to show her what was right, and God had done that in the clearest possible way. She couldn't let Matt be false to himself to help her. It would be the worst betrayal in the world.

"No." Her sharp tone had both men turning to face her. "We won't do it."

"Sarah—" Matt's tone was warning.

"What do you mean, you won't do it?" Sanders clearly didn't believe her.

"Just what I said." She walked to the counter, hanging on to her composure with both hands. "We don't agree to your terms. We won't keep silent."

Sanders looked as if she'd snatched away a promised treat. "I mean what I say. I'll make my dealings with your husband public. I won't have anything to lose."

But I do. Despair threatened to overwhelm her. The respect of the community, her children's view of their father, maybe even the home she'd tried to build here. And she'd already lost Matt.

Do the right thing. She clung to the thought. She looked steadily at Sanders. "The story will be on the front page of tomorrow's paper. Including your deal with Peter."

Fury darkened his face. For a moment she thought he'd threaten again. Then he spun and stalked out.

The slamming door seemed to break the strength

that held her upright. She sagged against the counter. It was over.

No, it wasn't over, not yet. Pain ripped through her. Her children, her home…and Matt. The pain of letting him down cut the deepest. She turned slowly to face him.

"Matt, I want to explain—" The look in his eyes seemed to choke off her voice.

"Why didn't you tell me?" He ground the words out.

"I didn't know until yesterday. You have to believe that."

He looked at her as if she were a stranger, and his square jaw was set in the way that denied compromise. "You knew about this yesterday, and you didn't trust me enough to tell me."

"I tried. I wanted to. I just couldn't. Matt, please try to understand—"

He shook his head. "I have to go." He strode quickly to the door. "Do what you want about tomorrow's issue, Sarah. It's up to you." He was out the door before she could speak.

He had to go. Her heart shattered into pieces. He'd left the island before when his father hadn't lived up to his ideals. She'd just given him the perfect reason to leave again.

"But, Mommy, why does it have to be in the paper? It would hurt Daddy's feelings." Andi looked small against her pillows. Sarah had found her still awake when she'd come wearily back into the apartment from the office after working late into the evening.

She stroked fine blond hair away from Andi's face. "Honey, I think Daddy would want us to tell the whole story now, even if it hurts." The two boys had accepted the short version she'd told them, not realizing that this story could have an effect on their lives. But Andi couldn't be content with that.

"People will talk about it. They might say mean things about Daddy." Andi's mouth trembled. "I don't want that to happen."

"I know," she said. "Neither do I."

The headache that clamped around her temples throbbed, and she massaged her neck wearily. She'd worked for hours to reset the front page. For a time, she'd half thought Matt might come back to do his story.

Finally she'd given up and done it for him, using his notes. Matt wouldn't be back—she had to face that. It brought a fresh wave of pain.

"Listen, Andi." She ought to be able to think of a way of explaining this that would satisfy her daughter. "If we don't put the story in the paper, then someone else will get away with doing something that's really wrong. We can't let that happen. That would be like helping that person do wrong."

Andi's forehead wrinkled. "You mean, it's like what Matt said when I tried to cover up for Ethan and Jeffrey? He said it would hurt them more if I took the blame than if they owned up to it."

Regret clutched her heart. "Yes, I guess it's like that. Matt was right." About so many things.

"When's Matt coming back?" Andi wiggled restlessly against the pillow. "I want to see him."

"I don't know when he's coming back, honey." Maybe never. She should try to prepare the children for that possibility, however much it might lacerate her already-wounded heart.

"You know, Matt has another job, being on television." She was improvising, trying to come up with something that wouldn't hurt too much. "He might have to go away to do that job, but then you could see him on television. Wouldn't that be fun?"

Andi shook her head stubbornly. "Not as much fun as having him here every day."

"No." A dozen pictures flickered through her mind—working at the desk next to Matt; listening to his grandmother's stories with him; trudging through Savannah on the trail of the truth; standing close in the circle of his arms while a boat whistle blew a lonely accompaniment. "It won't be as much fun. But Matt might have to go away."

Andi was still shaking her head. "No, Mommy, he won't go away. I know he won't. Know why?"

Sarah touched her cheek gently. "Tell me why, sweetheart."

"'Cause he said he'd take me and Jenny riding again, that's why. He promised us. And Matt wouldn't ever break a promise." She leaned back against the pillow, satisfied.

Pain was a vise around her heart. She'd not only let herself in for the hurt of losing Matt. She'd let the children in for it, too.

She stared out the window, watching the last rays of sunlight paint the sky. *Where are you, Matt? What are you feeling?*

She might not know where he was, but Someone did. *Father, forgive me. My silence hurt so many people. Please be with Matt now. Touch his heart and heal it. Amen.*

Chapter Sixteen

The sun was setting when Matt pushed open the door to the church. He let it swing slowly closed behind him, not sure why he was here. He slid into a back pew, avoiding a sidelong look at the stained-glass window of Jesus and the children.

After he'd left the office, he'd saddled Eagle and ridden the beach until he and the horse were both exhausted. Eagle had been content once he was back in his quiet stall with his feed bag. Matt found he wasn't so easily satisfied.

Finally he'd started throwing things into a suitcase. Leave, get on the road again, find a place where the action would blank everything else out of his mind. That was all he could think. He had to go back to being his old, detached self.

Then he'd driven past the chapel and stopped the car,

almost without intent. Here he was, trying to run away again. Maybe that had been excusable when he'd been eighteen and trying to escape his father's shadow. It wasn't excusable now.

He leaned forward, propping his wrists on the pew in front of him and leaning his head against his forearms. The silence in the chapel leached the tension from him, and for the first time in hours he was able to look past emotion and assess what had happened.

Sarah should have told you, something in his mind whispered righteously. *She owed you the truth.*

Truth. He'd never been able to take the elastic view of that some people did. But Sarah— She had to have been shaken and appalled when she'd found out what her late husband had done. Knowing Sarah, she'd probably felt guilty, too, that she hadn't somehow been able to prevent it.

He knew her now, knew her bone-deep, knew her warmth and her caring. When he'd been hurting over his father's actions, she'd reached out with unquestioning support.

Today she'd needed support, and he'd walked away. The realization shamed him.

You have to go on loving people, even when they disappoint you. She'd said that. It was the way she lived her life. He admired that, but he wasn't sure he could do it.

He could leave. He could get in the car, drive to Savannah and hop on a plane to anywhere in the world. If his bosses weren't ready to let him come back, he could look for a job elsewhere—any job that would let him observe, report and, above all, not get involved.

He rubbed his face with his hands. He'd tried that. He'd come back here determined to do it. But Sarah and her kids hadn't let him. Their faces crowded his mind— Andi, determined and responsible; Ethan, needing a man to look up to; Jeffrey, wanting encouragement to be himself; little Amy, the unknown quantity with the engaging smile.

And Sarah. How could he walk away from Sarah's boundless love? But how could he stay and make himself responsible for their happiness?

The familiar image of the bombed-out mission pressed on him like a weight, until it felt as if his heart would burst. *Why, God? Why did You let that happen? Why?*

He knew what some of his colleagues would say. That there was no God, that people were at the mercy of random fate. In a way, that might be a comfortable belief, because they didn't have to question. He didn't have that luxury.

Why? He jerked upright, forcing himself to look at the window he'd avoided. *How could You let Your children be hurt?*

The children clustered around Jesus, looking up at

him. The final rays of the setting sun struck the window, making the pictured face glow with a love so pure and intense that it seemed to pierce his heart, cutting clear through, letting the pain spurt out.

Sarah's words came back to him, echoing in the stillness as if she were there, speaking them. *God isn't to blame for the bad things. People are. But God can bring good out of them, if we let Him.*

His throat was tight with pain. Bad things, like the injured children, like his friend's death, like the guilt that had driven him home. He looked again at Jesus and the children, and the tears he'd tried so hard not to shed spilled over in a healing stream.

Sarah stared at the telephone on her desk the next morning. The paper had been out for two hours. Wasn't it time for reactions to start coming in? She'd expected the phone to be ringing off the hook with people canceling their subscriptions.

Not that she wanted that to happen. But anything would be better than this silence. Silence gave her too much time to think about Matt.

If she thought about him she couldn't avoid the pain. She pressed her fist to her chest. Why did this hurt so much? She'd known all along that nothing could come of their relationship. She should have been prepared. At the moment, that thought gave her no comfort.

Be with me, Lord. No matter what comes, let me feel Your presence.

The telephone rang. She took a deep breath, composed herself and picked it up. "*Caldwell Cove Gazette.* How may I help you?"

She'd prepared herself for canceled subscriptions. She hadn't been prepared for renewals. But in the next half hour, over a dozen people called to extend their subscriptions.

While she was still trying to figure that out, the door opened. Her heart clenched at the sight of the tall figure, but it wasn't Matt. Of course it wasn't Matt. Instead, his brother, Adam, came in with new copy for an ad for the boatyard.

He'd barely gone out when Tracy Milburn came in with an ad for the bakery, followed by Josh Tremain wanting to buy an ad for his tackle shop. By noon, she'd sold more ad space in one morning than she'd sold in the entire last month.

Somehow she wasn't surprised when Matt's grand-mother trotted into the office, holding an ad for the upcoming church rummage sale. Her throat tight, Sarah held up the sheaf of orders.

"Are you responsible for this, Mrs. Caldwell?"

Naomi Caldwell pulled herself to her five-foot height. "Me? Why would you think that?"

Sarah blinked back an errant tear that had no place

in a business office. "Seems as if everyone in Caldwell Cove wants to place an ad or renew a subscription today. I get the feeling someone might have put them up to it."

Mrs. Caldwell shrugged, a twinkle in her sharp blue eyes. "Folks here appreciate courage. I reckon they wanted to show you that. After all, you're one of us."

The tears did spill over, then. "My husband—"

"Nobody blames you for what your husband did," Matt's gran said tartly.

Sarah shook her head. "I know there must be some who think I had to have known about it."

"More fool they, then." Naomi Caldwell patted her hand firmly. "Folks who know you know different. The others don't matter. You just remember that and hold your head up high."

"I'll try." Sarah managed a watery smile.

"And don't you shed tears over that fool grandson of mine. That boy's starting to find himself. He's just still got a way to go." A shadow bisected the sunlight streaming through the door, and she glanced toward it. Her face softened. "Or maybe he's finally found his way home."

She bustled out, giving Matt a pat on his shoulder as she passed him in the doorway. She closed the door, and Matt stood there, motionless, for a long moment.

Sarah couldn't speak. She wanted to, but she couldn't. She could only look at him, knowing her love must show plainly in her face.

He moved toward her at last, holding up a copy of the paper. "I saw the front page. Looks good. You must have worked until midnight."

"Not quite that late." If he wanted to keep this exchange on business, she'd have to try, no matter how much it hurt.

He came around the counter, dropping the paper on it. "You used my byline."

"It was your story. I just wrote it up."

"I understand the town council has already called an emergency meeting. Somehow I think Jason Sanders isn't going to get his way this time."

It was no good—she couldn't try to pretend they were just coeditors, discussing a story that had gone well.

"Matt, I'm sorry. I should never have—"

"Don't, Sarah." He put his hand across her lips, his touch gentle. "I understand why it was hard to tell me. What happened wasn't your fault."

"I should have known," she managed to say, her lips moving against his palm. "And I should have told you as soon as I found out. That was my mistake."

He took her hands in both of his then, and his look was so intent that it seemed he saw right into her soul. "We both made mistakes. Maybe—" He smiled slightly. "Maybe we needed to, so that God could teach us something."

Her heart seemed to swell. If this painful time had

made Matt turn back to God, it would have been well worth it.

"What did you learn?" she asked softly, hardly daring to believe it.

"That truth isn't anything without love," he said readily. "That I can find God's hand moving, even in the midst of pain." His voice roughened. "You taught me that, Sarah. Without you, I'd never have healed."

"You're okay now." She tried to keep her voice steady, tried not to let her broken heart show. "You're ready to go back."

"I could go back. But that doesn't seem as important as it once did." He gestured toward the paper. "Seems as if I can find important stories to tell here." He gripped her hands tightly. "Seems as if I can find someone to force me back into life here. Wouldn't I be a fool to let that end?"

All of his honest, valiant heart showed in the look he gave her. The intimacy and power of it robbed her of any ability to speak.

"Well, Sarah?" His voice had grown husky. "Will you let me be a father to your children? Will you let me be your husband?"

She still couldn't speak. Could she? Did she really have it in herself to be the person who loved him and was loved in return?

A sense of freedom swept over her. The past was gone. This was a new world for both of them. She stepped into his arms and knew that, like him, she'd found home.

"Matt!" The door to the apartment swung open, and Andi ran in. "See, Mommy, I told you he would come back." She raced to him, the two boys scurrying after her.

Matt knelt, gathering them into a hug. Amy toddled proudly across the floor, testing her new skill, and he swept her up into his arms.

"Well, Sarah?" He looked at her, face alight with love and confidence. "You still haven't answered me."

"Yes." Her heart seemed to overflow with gratitude. "The answer is yes, for all of us." She blinked back tears of joy. She'd made mistakes, but God had been faithful. He'd given her a man of integrity, a man she and her children could love and trust for all their days.

Epilogue

"Can't I take the blindfold off yet?" Sarah gripped Matt's hand as he guided her up the steps.

He grinned, wondering where she thought they were. He hoped he'd covered his tracks well, but it was tough to fool Sarah.

"Not yet, Mrs. Caldwell." He tried to keep the excitement out of his voice and failed. "I have a surprise for you."

"I think two weeks in Hawaii for our honeymoon was enough of a surprise."

"Didn't you enjoy it?" He pressed his cheek against hers.

"I loved it." She reached up to caress the planes of his face, and he dropped a kiss on her fingertips. "But now I'm ready to be home."

"Right." They reached the porch, and he scooped Sarah off her feet and into his arms. "Your wish is granted." He took several steps forward, across the threshold, and set her on her feet.

"Matt, what's going on?"

He fumbled with the blindfold, and it fell away. "You're home."

Miz Becky, who'd been holding the children back, let them go, and they rushed, giggling, into her arms. She knelt, clutching them close. He suspected she didn't see anything else.

"See, Mommy, see?" Andi broke free first, hopping on one foot and then the other. "See? It's our new house. Isn't it beautiful?" She darted to the tall Gullah woman who stood smiling near the doorway. "Miz Becky helped us fix it all up, and I have my own room with horses on the wallpaper."

"Our house?"

Sarah turned slowly, and Matt realized he was holding his breath. He saw the moment she recognized where they were—in one of the new houses on the lane behind Twin Oaks. But it no longer stood empty. Sarah's furniture, supplemented with pieces from the big house, filled the living room, and her pictures were on the walls.

She was quiet for so long that uncertainty assailed him.

"If you don't like it—" he began.

"Like it?" she echoed. She looked at him, a smile trembling on her lips, tears filling her eyes, and he knew it was all right. "I don't just like it. I love it." Her arms went around his waist, and she leaned into him. "I love it," she repeated softly. "I love you."

Andi danced back to them. "The whole family helped, Mommy. All the aunts and uncles and cousins. And Gran. And Grandfather Jeff." Andi proudly enumerated all the relatives she'd inherited on her mother's marriage.

Their family. His family. He looked at his Sarah, surrounded by their children. "Are you sure you like it?"

"How could I not like it?" She leaned into his embrace. "It's our home."

"Home." He repeated the word.

He'd come back to Caldwell Island hoping to regain his detachment, thinking that was what he wanted. But instead God had given him what he needed—love and a home.

…in all things, God works for the good of those who love Him… His heart overflowed with thanksgiving. Gran's promise for him had finally come true.

* * * * *

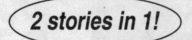

REQUEST YOUR FREE BOOKS!

2 FREE INSPIRATIONAL NOVELS
PLUS 2
FREE
MYSTERY GIFTS

Love Inspired®

YES! Please send me 2 FREE Love Inspired® novels and my 2 FREE mystery gifts (gifts are worth about $10). After receiving them, if I don't wish to receive any more books, I can return the shipping statement marked "cancel". If I don't cancel, I will receive 4 brand-new novels every month and be billed just $4.24 per book in the U.S. or $4.74 per book in Canada, plus 25¢ shipping and handling per book and applicable taxes, if any*. That's a savings of over 20% off the cover price! I understand that accepting the 2 free books and gifts places me under no obligation to buy anything. I can always return a shipment and cancel at any time. Even if I never buy another book, the two free books and gifts are mine to keep forever.

113 IDN ERXA   313 IDN ERWX

Name _____ (PLEASE PRINT) _____

Address _____ Apt. # _____

City _____ State/Prov. _____ Zip/Postal Code _____

Signature (if under 18, a parent or guardian must sign) _____

Order online at www.LoveInspiredBooks.com

Or mail to Steeple Hill Reader Service:

IN U.S.A.: P.O. Box 1867, Buffalo, NY 14240-1867
IN CANADA: P.O. Box 609, Fort Erie, Ontario L2A 5X3

Not valid to current subscribers of Love Inspired books.

Want to try two free books from another series?
Call 1-800-873-8635 or visit www.morefreebooks.com

* Terms and prices subject to change without notice. N.Y. residents add applicable sales tax. Canadian residents will be charged applicable provincial taxes and GST. Offer not valid in Quebec. This offer is limited to one order per household. All orders subject to approval. Credit or debit balances in a customer's account(s) may be offset by any other outstanding balance owed by or to the customer. Please allow 4 to 6 weeks for delivery. Offer available while quantities last.

Your Privacy: Steeple Hill Books is committed to protecting your privacy. Our Privacy Policy is available online at www.SteepleHill.com or upon request from the Reader Service. From time to time we make our lists of customers available to reputable third parties who may have a product or service of interest to you. If you would prefer we not share your name and address, please check here. ☐

LIREG08R

From *New York Times* bestselling author

JILL *Marie* LANDIS

One look in the mirror told Eyes-of-the-Sky she was
not a Comanche...yet she remembered no other life.
She watched the whites who had taken her in after her
"rescue," but questions remained: What am I? Who am I?

Jill Marie Landis weaves an unforgettable story about a
young woman adrift in two worlds, and her courageous
journey to discovery, belonging and love....

HOMECOMING

Available wherever paperback books are sold!